TOUCHED BY FIRE

Gwyneth Atlee

Zebra Books
Kensington Publishing Corp.

http://www.zebrabooks.com

*For Kayne, who showed me the path,
and Mike and Andrew, who never failed
to light its dark spots*

ZEBRA BOOKS are published by

Kensington Publishing Corp.
850 Third Avenue
New York, NY 10022

Zebra, the Z logo and Splendor Reg. U.S. Pat. & TM Off.

First Printing: June, 1999
10 9 8 7 6 5 4 3 2 1

Printed in the United States of America

ACKNOWLEDGMENTS

I am grateful to many people for their assistance with this book. First of all, thank you to those I spoke with at the Peshtigo Fire Museum and Peshtigo Library for their help in finding information.

Special thanks to Bobbi Sissel, Betty Joffrion, and Wanda Dionne for tirelessly reading and rereading the manuscript and for their incredible support.

I would also like to express my sincere appreciation to my agent, Meredith Bernstein, for her efforts. Tracy Bernstein, my editor, offered insightful suggestions that only served to strengthen.

Finally, I would like to acknowledge the incredible spirit of those caught up in the dreadful fires of 1871. The more I learn of their heroic struggles, the more I admire the human will to survive against all odds.

"We have felt, we still feel, the passion of life to its top. . . . In our youths, our hearts were touched with fire."

—Oliver Wendell Holmes

PROLOGUE

The hardest part was stealing the fresh blood. True, the shabby boardinghouse where Hannah Shelton now resided was just around the corner from the butcher's, and often the smell of death loomed large. Truer still, the old meat dealer was a drunkard, but even so he normally locked the slaughterhouse.

It took Hannah two weeks to find a night he'd been so drunk, he'd left it open. Two weeks more for the fabric of her dress to grow still thinner. Two weeks more to live on beans and half-stale bread. She'd been willing, even desperate, to find work, but none would have her. Shelton Creek's fine citizens wanted no part of the likes of her.

That wasn't true, she thought with a frown. There were some parts they wanted, at least the men in town.

Since she could not survive on that pittance the courts saw fit to leave her, Hannah thought it better if she died.

As she slipped out through the back shed with a half-bucket of fresh steer's blood, she sincerely hoped the townsfolk would suspect that Malcolm killed her.

After all, in many ways he had.

CHAPTER ONE

"Whole blamed place looks like nothing but a tinderbox."

"Gonna go up like a match head if we don't get some rain."

Hannah Lee Shelton ignored the deckhands' observations. She peered, instead, beyond them, off the bow and toward the Peshtigo dock. Would her future husband be there? Her gaze searched the small assemblage of loggers and farmers for a kind face, but nothing in the men's expressions eased her worry.

May God forgive my deceit, she prayed silently as she waited for the boatmen to tie off the steamer. Surely, if John Aldman guessed who—and what—she was, he would drown her in this very river rather than take her to home and hearth. There might be a shortage of women even now, in 1871, among the towering woods of northeastern Wisconsin, but still . . .

Hannah pushed back her shoulders and straightened her posture. She gathered the folds of her sensible gray skirt as if she were a princess and not a twenty-eight-year-old mail-order bride. If she were to survive here, she must first of all impress upon this strange man that despite the fact that she was bought and paid for, he would have to win her yet.

The moment she stepped onto the dock, a hairless, stooped man shuffled forward. Several teeth were missing, and he reeked of sweat.

Dear Lord, she thought, *is this what my treachery has earned?*

"Need a hand to carry your bags, ma'am?" he asked.

"I—I don't believe so. Thank you." Hannah thanked her God as well. She fished in her bag for a clean handkerchief, which she used to dab at her own perspiring forehead. For mid-September, the afternoon was warm, and the smell of wood smoke thickened the air. The drought that plagued her own Pennsylvania extended here, and a boatman had told her the woods were dotted with small wildfires.

Suddenly, she felt eyes on her, eyes that must be taking in her slender body, the thick brown hair, a few strands falling from an otherwise respectable upsweep, the fine features of her porcelain face. She imagined the shock of his appraisal, for she had never been called plain. Her reasons for entering into this abominable arrangement had been graver.

"You must be Mercy Wilder," a deep voice informed her.

She nodded at the alias, then turned toward an enormous man. Her heart leapt at the sight of him. He put her to mind of the buffalo she'd seen once in a traveling exhibition. Even through the plain tan fabric of his shirt, his muscles bulged and gathered. His dark brown hair curled near a simple band collar, and his hands looked powerful enough to mash fistfuls of walnuts. Still, for all his size, the giant's face was well formed.

After a moment's hesitation, she asked, "Are you—are you John Aldman, then?"

He shook his head, and the mane of dark waves gave off a fresh-washed smell. "I don't hold with paying any woman's passage sight unseen."

He followed his curt words with a sweeping gaze that seemed to measure her every curve. Frowning sourly, he added, "Though I suppose if looks are all he's after, my brother will be pleased with his good fortune."

How dare he ogle and insult her in such a manner? He might have been assessing a hog or a horse he intended to purchase! Hannah fumed silently and prayed that her fiancé had better manners.

After an awkward pause, he extended his right hand with obvious reluctance. "I'm Daniel Aldman, John's baby brother. John's had some trouble with his mare, so he sent me."

"Y-you—" Hannah stammered, "you're the *baby*?"

Daniel laughed, the roar of a grizzly. "Don't fret, Miss Wilder. My brother's no mountain. I brought the wagon for your baggage."

"There's very little," Hannah told him, for some reason embarrassed. Malcolm had robbed her not only of her name and reputation, but of her inheritance as well.

Once again she squirmed beneath the weight of Daniel's gaze. Maybe it was her imagination, but his frown looked suspicious.

"Don't suppose you'd be here if you had a pot to—" He interrupted himself with a quick shake of his head. "Never mind. That's just less for me to tote. You're to be put up in our aunt's house. Lucinda Pangburn—she's a widow-woman, and she dearly loves to entertain. But she's particular about her place. You keep your things neat?"

Hannah nodded. "I'm a good housekeeper, as I explained to Mr. Aldman in my letter."

"I suppose that you would say that. You quiet?"

"I engage in no boisterous behavior," she answered with all the dignity she could muster.

"Good," Daniel said. "Then you and Aunt Lucinda will get on just fine. But as for myself, I think it's too bad."

"Too bad? What's that?" Hannah asked.

"About the boisterous behavior. If you enjoyed that sort of thing, I might be tempted to distract you from my brother."

Hannah felt anger heat her face. "I will not tolerate these insults, Mr. Aldman. Surely you realize that Mr. Harlan's service excludes any—ah—disreputable young ladies."

Daniel grinned good-naturedly, as if he'd enjoyed provoking her reaction. "I'm just ribbing you, Miss Wilder. There, are these your bags?"

Daniel loaded her scant possessions and helped her into the wagon, a rather nice buckboard drawn by a handsome pair of chestnut-colored horses. Hooves and wooden wheels raised clouds of sawdust as he drove past a noisy sawmill and a large three-story building with a sign that marked it as a boardinghouse. A crowd of red-shirted rowdies laughed and drank in plain sight on the porch, even though it was the Sabbath. A trio of women, disgracefully dressed, laughed as loudly as the men.

"Found yourself another so soon?" called an apple-cheeked redhead. Hannah blushed at the names the woman's two friends shouted. She wasn't sure if they referred to Daniel or herself.

"Ho, Daniel! Come join us for a mug!" A man with a thick black mustache waved an arm to hail them. Another, a fellow with jagged front teeth, made a rude suggestion.

"Sorry, miss," Daniel apologized, but he was grinning. "The shanty boys come in from cutting timber only once a week. They don't see decent women much."

What sort of man would have such awful friends, she wondered. God help her if John Aldman kept the same company as his ill-mannered younger brother!

She glanced surreptitiously at his handsome face, but it gave away nothing. Perhaps he could have taken her by another route. Might he be testing her reaction to the vulgarities? Unsure, she ignored him as they drove through streets lined with a blacksmith's shop, a company store, and prim rows of wood frame houses.

A few houses past the righteous white face of the Congregational church, Daniel pulled the horses to a stop. "Despite what you must think of me, my aunt's a proper woman. She's promised to act as chaperone until you get to know my brother. She might act friendly, but she'll let him know what type you are, all right, and if he's wasted his money after all."

A pang of guilt tore through Hannah's breast. Of course John Aldman had wasted his money. He wanted a virtuous wife, a woman with whom he could raise a big farm family. If he only knew what she was, he'd turn her loose right then. She thought of those wild-looking girls lolling near the boardinghouse, and her stomach clenched. She hadn't been raised to end up like that. But besides this marriage, what else could she do?

She didn't know how to respond to Daniel, so she didn't try. He helped her out of the gig, his huge hand lingering on her arm an instant too long. Then, releasing her, he took up her three satchels as though their weight were a trifle. She followed him toward the two-story house and admired its neat, white painted angles. Along the walk, bright autumn chrysanthemums nodded in the dry breeze. Their vigor, amid the wilted town landscape, spoke of constant attention from some unseen hand.

A skinny child of about six burst out of the house and ran toward Daniel. "Papa!" she cried delightedly, and leapt into his arms.

"Amelia, there's a girl." He gave her wispy blond locks a tousle.

Hannah could barely believe that Daniel had a child. Could this mean the coarse brute was married too?

The child's sparkling blue eyes turned toward Hannah. "Will this be my new mama?"

The girl's question answered Hannah's. No doubt his wretched manners had driven off the mother.

Daniel gently put the child down. "Oh, no, Amelia, honey. Remember what we told you? This lady's here for Uncle John. Miss Mercy Wilder, may I present to you my daughter, Miss Amelia Lee Aldman?"

Amelia giggled at the mock seriousness of his introduction.

"We have the same middle name, Amelia. Mine's Lee too," said Hannah. At least she could be honest about that.

"Then that means we'll be friends," the child told her earnestly. "Let me show you your room. It's going to be right next to mine."

She took Hannah by the hand and would have led her into the house, except for the appearance of a pudgy woman with gray hair tucked into a neat bun.

"This must be Miss Mercy!" she cried with the voice of one who can barely hear her words. "Hope you don't mind if I call you that, young lady."

"Not at all," Hannah said. Perhaps if she heard it often enough, she would soon grow used to the false name. "You must be Mrs. Pangburn. It's so kind of you to allow me to stay here."

"Call me Aunt Lucinda, child. And kindness has nothing to do with it," the old woman told her. "I've been telling that nephew of mine to find himself a wife time out of mind. I feared I'd never live to see the day." Aunt Lucinda's dark gaze swept over her and judged her in a twinkling. "You're none too stout. You sure you're tough enough for farm life?"

Hannah smiled politely. "I'm stronger than you'd guess."

Lucinda nodded her approval. "If I weren't a Christian woman, I'd wager you're right."

Amelia darted around her aunt like a rambunctious puppy as Lucinda showed Hannah to a small room with an oak dresser and a narrow bed. The girl bounded ahead and jumped onto a beautiful blue and rose quilt that lay across the mattress.

"Off you go," Daniel told his daughter as he set Hannah's bags onto the bed.

"Go into your room now, child," the old woman scolded, "or our Miss Mercy will think we've raised a savage."

"Please," Hannah interrupted, "just call me Mercy. And, Amelia, come back later, and we'll have a nice visit."

"I'm gonna comb my Sally's hair, so I can introduce her too!" Amelia said with an excited grin. She raced off to her own room.

"Sally's her doll." Aunt Lucinda's voice dropped to a near whisper. "They're very close since we lost Amelia's mother three years back."

Hannah felt a twinge of guilt. That meant that Daniel's wife had died, not run away.

Daniel's voice was flat. "Amelia's been out shopping for a replacement. Wants to know if every woman she meets might be her new mama. She gets attached too fast."

"Particularly when the women come and go so quickly," Aunt Lucinda added reproachfully.

Hannah didn't want to intrude into this conversation. Instead, she became absorbed in a cross carved from dark wood that hung above the bed's headboard. Beside the dresser, she noticed a washstand containing a pitcher already filled with water.

"I thought you might want to wash up and rest a spell," Lucinda said.

It sounded like a fine idea, but Hannah answered, "As soon as I've unpacked. I'd hate to meet Mr. Aldman in a wrinkled dress."

Daniel cleared his throat. "John won't come today, Miss Wilder. Usually, I tend the sick stock, but that mare of his is something precious. He won't leave her with the colic."

Hannah nodded, half relieved. Although she was slightly insulted to be ignored in favor of a horse, she needed time to feel comfortable in her new surroundings, time to think about the enormous risks of this arrangement. The letters she'd received from her prospective husband had been stiff and formal, revealing little more than the prosperity of his farm, the long hours that he worked, and his desire for a "woman of good character" with whom to share his life. He was thirty-two and didn't object that she was only four years younger. In that respect, at least, she had been honest.

"Will you be seeing your brother, then, Mr. Aldman?" she asked Daniel quietly.

"Sure. We live in the same house."

"I see," Hannah said. "Then please give him my regards, and tell him I hope his mare is better. When my father was still living, I spent many an hour one cold night walking his best stallion. It was all we could do to keep the horse from rolling and twisting his gut."

Daniel nodded gravely. "I'm glad you understand why he can't come. You can't leave a colicked horse a minute, or he'll roll for sure. Did you save your father's stallion?"

"I'm afraid not, despite everything we did."

"Sometimes even our best efforts aren't enough," Aunt Lucinda said as she brushed some unseen lint off the quilt. "Oh, dear, Daniel, you tracked in those dead leaves. Let me get a broom."

Hannah spared the withered foliage outside the window a brief glance. "There was talk on the steamer about the drought and all the brushfires. Surely, your farm is in no danger?''

"There's always rain this time of year," he told her. "Then we'll all be safe. Until then, the men have formed committees. I come into town and join a brigade from the woodenware mill whenever John can spare me. We take care of any fires that get too close to Peshtigo. I wouldn't worry. Someone's always keeping watch."

Reassured, Hannah put aside her concern. But another nagged her even more insistently. She hesitated for a moment, unsure of how bold she might be. Then she took a deep breath and plunged ahead. "What will you tell your brother about me?"

Again he turned his dark eyes to survey her in a way that sent a cold thrill up her spine. "I'm going to tell him you're too beautiful," he answered. "And that I wonder why you've *really* come."

CHAPTER TWO

Malcolm Shelton glowered across Jeb Fulton's desk.

"What do you mean, you can't make me the loan? The old Lee farm is mine, and I still own the horses. I assure you, these setbacks are only temporary." He puffed on his pipe like a freight train.

"May I be frank, Captain Shelton?" the portly banker asked. Perspiration dotted his bald pate.

Shelton nodded, glad at least that Jeb still called him by his former rank. His war wound and his veteran's status sold a lot of horseflesh in these parts.

"It is the—ah—rather indelicate matter of the—er—former Mrs. Shelton's disappearance. When a gentleman deals in the horse and carriage trade, his good name is of paramount importance—"

"That inquiry proved nothing!" Malcolm thundered. He slammed a clenched fist on the banker's desk. "We don't even know that Hannah's dead! And if we did, perhaps one of her lovers slew her. We all know what kind of company she kept."

"Nevertheless, until some final determination can be made, I am afraid—"

Malcolm limped out of the office and slammed Jeb's door so hard, three other customers and a teller glanced up sharply. He glared at them with such fierceness, they quickly averted their eyes. Perhaps they feared him now, he thought as he left the building.

They should. He was an angry man. Someone had stolen his good name. Either the man who had killed Hannah, or the woman herself in some pathetic bid to gain revenge. Whichever way, he had to find her, to locate her real killer or drag her back and prove she was alive.

And if he did the latter, thought Malcolm as he whipped his team of horses to a gallop, he'd show his former spouse the proper way to have a woman killed.

CHAPTER THREE

Hannah awakened in the darkness to a familiar scent. Standing, she crept toward the open window and peered outside. Thousands of stars twinkled brilliantly despite the thin veil of wood smoke that hung between the earth and sky. The pungent odor made her restless, even though at home in Pennsylvania, the smell had always made her sleep more easily. There, it reminded her of warmth and safety, of her family hearth. But here, with all the deathly dryness, she felt like a woman made from kindling. One careless spark, and she'd ignite.

Might that spark be the one in Daniel's eye? She'd seen the look before, in men who'd coveted her when she was Malcolm's. And especially afterward. After what he'd done to her, they imagined her some wanton creature who would thrill to base suggestions. All the men in her hometown had thought it, and the women of good standing suddenly feared they might be seen exchanging pleasantries with her. A former friend. A former sister in town life.

She felt sick to think of it. All those self-righteous women, proudly flaunting myriad children. All those conversations, stopped abruptly the moment she set foot in church.

She wondered grimly, had any of them prayed for her, or had they merely spent their worship hour gossiping about what they supposed to be her failings?

Despite the evening warmth, she shivered and tried to imagine what John Aldman might be like. She found herself hoping he resembled his brother, Daniel, with his dark eyes and the wavy hair that smelled so fresh. Despite his rudeness, she had felt an unfamiliar stirring deep inside when she recalled his huge hand as it lingered on her arm.

Then she wondered, what kind of father could he be to little Amelia? How could he have sent her off to live in town? If Hannah had ever had a child, she could imagine no catastrophe great enough to drive her from it. If she'd ever had a child . . .

She shook her head to clear it of unwelcome memories and instead remembered Daniel's words. *I'm going to tell him you're too beautiful. And that I wonder why you've really come.* She recalled, too, the coarse young woman who'd called out after him from the boardinghouse. Any man who kept such company would be best avoided. But how could she avoid him if he lived in the same house as John?

The thick, predawn gray sky barely brightened with the rising sun. Instead, clouds reflected the orange glow of distant brushfires. Aunt Lucinda entertained Hannah cheerfully throughout the morning and reassured her the men had already fended off the worst this year. Lucinda was certain the low clouds boded rain.

"And besides, a young lady in your position has more important things to think on. You'll be meeting John today." Lucinda smeared pale butter on a fresh-baked roll.

"Please, tell me what he's like."

"My uncle John's a wonder. You just ask anybody," Amelia said enthusiastically. A sprinkling of flour frosted her nose from when she'd helped the women with their baking. "He's bringing me a kitten as soon as she's old enough to leave her mama. She's a fluffy calico. I'm going to name her Spice."

"That sounds lovely." Hannah had had a big yellow tabby once that she called Queen, back when she'd had a home. She wondered bitterly if Malcolm had shot the cat or simply given her away. He'd always hated inconveniences.

"Why don't you water the flowers along the walkway, Amelia, while Mercy and I talk?" Lucinda smiled after her grand-niece as the child went outside.

"To answer your question, John is wonderful. Responsible and sober. And you should see him with Amelia. He'll make a fine husband and father."

Inwardly, Hannah winced. She sipped her tea to hide it. "His letters were convincing, I'll admit. But still, a woman likes to know a few . . . personal details."

"His farm is everything to John. He's worked so hard since he inherited it eight years ago. I suppose that's why he wrote to your—ah—agency. He wouldn't make time for a proper courtship, and, of course, there aren't many young women hereabouts. Busy as John is, they're all snapped up before he ever meets them." The old woman reached for yet another roll. "It's too bad Daniel's not so steady."

"Really?" Despite herself, Hannah felt her interest quicken.

Lucinda laughed. "If I don't have a care, you'll pull tales from me like spinning. What about you, dear Mercy? You can't convince me this arrangement was your only prospect."

There it was. The question Hannah had long dreaded. Now she'd have to tell another bald-faced lie.

"I tended my father during a very long illness, up until his death." Her father had actually died suddenly, after a kick from one of his horses. She plunged ahead, afraid that if she paused, she'd blurt out the truth and damn herself here too. "After he was buried, I learned he had debts. And during the years I stayed with him, all my suitors had looked elsewhere or been lost in the war. I found myself without options, until a friend introduced me to Mr. Harlan and his service."

Aunt Lucinda nodded gravely. "There's no disgrace in doing your duty to your father, and the War Between the States ruined many a girl's prospects. But we mustn't sit here gabbing. John and Daniel will be here this afternoon, and there's still so much to do."

By the time the men arrived, Hannah had spent much of the day assisting Lucinda with the cooking. Pumpkin pie, fresh bread, and roast ham filled the hot kitchen with their sweet aromas.

Daniel was first through the door. "Aunt Lucinda, you've outdone yourself again. And there's Miss Wilder, pretty as I told you, John."

John came in, looking so unlike his brother, Hannah would never have imagined them to be related. Although he towered like a pine, he was lean in contrast to his brother's bullish musculature. His red-brown hair was neatly trimmed and parted crown to nape. A thick mustache made his mouth appear to droop. He corrected the illusion of a frown by offering a handsome, even smile.

Toward her he extended a long-fingered, callused hand. "I thought my brother had exaggerated my good fortune. As the apostle said so well, 'The woman is the glory of man.' I am *very* pleased to finally meet you, Miss Wilder."

"He might not be much on boisterous behavior, but the man's got a chunk of Scripture for every occasion," Daniel grumbled.

Ignoring Daniel's too-familiar wink, Hannah fixed her

gaze on John and groped for words. "Pleased to make your acquaintance, Mr. Aldman. Has your mare recovered?"

"She has. I'm very glad. She's a fine animal, and I'm very much attached."

"It's good to hear you appreciate good horses. My father brought me up to do the same." Hannah decided with relief that John Aldman was indeed the man his aunt described.

John did nothing during the evening but confirm her first impression. During the meal he spoke of his harvests and his plans for future crops. "But I'm especially interested in raising draft horses to supply the logging companies. They might not be as showy as my mare, but I admire their strength. Could you learn to appreciate workhorses too, Miss Mercy?" He favored her with a good-natured smile.

She nodded, pleased that he already wished to consider her opinion. "In my experience, they're a sight easier to manage than the highbred stock."

"And a sight more expensive to feed," Daniel offered as he spooned a second helping of potatoes onto his plate.

"All you big brutes are," John added, gesturing toward his younger brother.

Daniel laughed and tossed a roll at John's head.

Hannah bit back her own laughter. Daniel was like a troublesome boy in a schoolhouse, vexing, but difficult to ignore. John, on the other hand, would have been the young man always ready with his lessons, the one who would have carried her books home. He would have been the boy her parents wanted for her, even as her gaze roamed back to catch the miscreant's grin.

Playing the stern schoolmarm, Lucinda leapt to her feet. "I'll have none of that, you boys! Imagine, there'll be crumbs aplenty."

The "boys" apologized, but John smiled at Hannah while Daniel threw a wink her way. Amelia giggled with delight and sang, "Papa wants a whipping!" A warning glance from the old woman shushed her as well.

The rest of the dinner continued pleasantly enough. John peppered the conversation with enough polite inquiries to include Hannah in the conversation. Although Daniel seemed content to let his brother do the talking, his eyes occasionally sought out hers. When their gazes met, his lingered for a beat too long.

After the meal Hannah helped Lucinda clear the table.

"That was wonderful," Hannah said. "Here, let me help you with these plates."

"Fiddlesticks!" said Lucinda. "John will skin me alive if I keep you from him one more minute. I'll get Daniel to help as penance for throwing good food at the table. Now, get yourself out there on that porch. Anyone could see you need a breath of air."

Hannah hurried outside, and, sure enough, John joined her almost instantly. As she turned to look at him, her stomach fluttered. She felt just like a schoolgirl before elocution practice. A shiver of fear rippled through her. She had immersed herself so completely into this part she had chosen to play. Was her true self disappearing beneath the level of her lies? Already, they had become so real that she felt herself blushing like a maiden at the way he gazed at her.

"You're so much more than I had hoped for," John told her sincerely. "I've prayed for a good woman to be a helpmeet and a mother to my sons."

Hannah felt herself emerging from that sea of her deceit. She hoped he wouldn't notice the way she'd stiffened at those words.

Apparently, he didn't. "I never dreamed she would be beautiful and intelligent as well," he continued. Then he chuckled. "And modest too. You're blushing, I believe."

The color in her cheeks had nothing whatever to do with the compliments. Hannah looked down, hoping to

preserve the image of Christian humility. "I'm pleased as
well," she managed to say. "A woman in this situation fears
. . . so many possibilities. I'm glad to see you're as pleasant
as your letters."

"I don't want you to be afraid, Mercy." Cautiously, he
took her hand. His were roughened by farmwork, yet he
held hers as if he were cradling a paper rose. "Take some
time to get to know Peshtigo, to get to know me. This
marriage doesn't have to be tomorrow. I've waited this
long for you. I'm willing to wait a little more."

She squeezed his hand. "You're very kind, John Aldman.
And I am very glad to know you."

That night Hannah lay awake and tried to picture John
Aldman's handsome profile, his deep brown eyes, his
strong, straight nose, the auburn hair so thick and neatly
combed. She smiled and realized she had landed on her
feet. He might not be from an old, affluent family. He
might not be a man of letters, but he was all she could
have hoped for. More than she deserved.

So why was it, when her own eyelids slid lower, that she
found herself dreaming of his brother's not-quite-proper
gaze? Why was it she couldn't stop remembering the feeling of his huge hand as it lingered on her arm?

Late the following afternoon, John came, driving an
elegant gray mare. Hannah looked up from where she'd
been sweeping the front walk for Lucinda. John waved and
stepped down from the gig.

Leaning the broom against the house, Hannah walked
to meet him.

"This must be your prize. Absolutely gorgeous," she
said, letting her gaze roam over the animal's well-formed,
dappled limbs. "I see she's made an excellent recovery."

John's handsome face lit up. "That she has. I took Aunt Lucinda's gig to fix the seat. I thought I'd return it, and see you, of course."

Stepping even closer, Hannah ran her palm across the horse's silken neck. The animal turned to look at her, tiny ears pricked forward. "She has a lovely face. Those eyes are so full of life."

He laughed in reply. "Oh, she's lively enough all right. You should try her under saddle."

"Could I?" Hannah turned toward John, excited as Amelia.

"I meant only that when *I* ride her, she's a handful. Surely, you wouldn't wish to climb aboard."

"No, I don't suppose I would." Disappointed, Hannah stepped back from the mare. Ladies didn't ride, her mother always told her, particularly not astride. But as an only child, her father had indulged her by teaching her the art. Whenever she thought of riding, she remembered him. When she thought about Malcolm living on her father's horse farm, riding her father's stallion, Honor, she had to fight back unexpected tears.

Luckily, John didn't notice. He had turned to lead the horse toward the small stable, where Lucinda's gelding nickered a welcome. The mare laid back her ears.

"Faith isn't much on socializing," John said. "She's as shy as I am."

He pulled his saddle out of the gig before he began to unbuckle Faith's harness. The mare stamped impatiently and continued to lay back her ears in the direction of the other horse.

"You don't seem so shy," Hannah commented. "You're here again, aren't you?"

John shrugged and flashed a self-effacing smile. "Around you, I don't feel that way. Maybe I should, but something about you makes me feel . . . I don't know, at peace. I'm not usually like that. I make it a point to come into town at least once a week to see my aunt and Amelia and get to the church service. Other than that, I work. I get my satisfaction from having a house with a fresh coat of paint, from seeing young things grow, from harvesting my crops, and from studying the Bible. Daniel and I make a pretty decent team.''

Hannah listened even more intently, feeling slightly guilty that John's brother fascinated her. How could a man with such wretched manners hold even a moment's interest, with a man like John around?

"He can build most anything," John said, "and he's good at doctoring. He was a surgeon's assistant for a while in the war. And the best part is he eats the food I put in front of him without complaining. I'm no Lucinda in the kitchen, I can tell you. Daniel and I get along all right, if I keep my peace about his Saturday carousing. That's something he took up a few years back, but it's not for me. I have my life just about the way I want it. Some might find it a lonely life, but it suits me.''

Hannah wondered, could it suit her too? She'd had friends in Shelton Creek, or at least relationships with those she'd thought were friends. Thinking of the pain they'd caused her, she decided she would be better off without them. With a decent man like John, she could certainly survive.

In time, she might even convince herself that she was happy.

John came into town several more times that week. Hannah saw nothing more of Daniel, who was strangely absent from Saturday's family dinner. No one mentioned the reason, and it would be unthinkable of her to ask. She suspected he was gadding about with his rowdy friends and some of the unsavory young women she had seen. Gradually, the unpleasantness of their first encounter faded from her memory. She had John to think of now.

As she grew to know him, she came to respect his deep faith and his dreams about the future. He was ambitious, but very unlike Malcolm. His desires for a prosperous farm and a decent family weren't tainted by a wounded family pride. His wants weren't steeped in selfishness or a feeling of entitlement.

Guilt faded slightly as Hannah began to believe she would survive. Peshtigo, despite the drought, looked like a promising young mill town. John's farm, she soon saw, was quite a pleasant place, with a house built of real planks instead of logs. His cattle, hogs, and horses looked fit and well tended. Most important, John and Aunt Lucinda accepted her as if she were a long-lost friend.

"We must introduce you to Uncle Phineas soon," John said. "If you pass that old curmudgeon's inspection, you'll be family no matter what I have to say."

"Oh, don't you tease like that," Lucinda scolded. "Uncle Phineas's not a villain. He's just set in his ways, like a lot of old farmers. He's living near Marinette, so we'll see him by and by. And if I were you, young John, I'd keep an eye on Mercy. A pretty thing like her might change Phineas's mind about the joys of bachelorhood."

Whenever she thought of Lucinda's wink, Hannah grinned. It would all be fine, then, she decided as she adjusted to her new name, Mercy. Perhaps she'd gotten that second chance in answer to her prayers. Soon she found herself smiling more frequently, even laughing sometimes.

After a few days in Peshtigo, she barely even noticed the smoke on the horizon.

CHAPTER FOUR

Daniel Aldman wished he had more whiskey. Or apple brandy, or even ginger beer. Come Sunday morning, he always wanted something extra, to buy some sort of cease-fire for the cannon in his head.

Vicksburg. It sounded like the mortar guns at Vicksburg once again. The shooting that went on and on, reminding him of all the limbs and lives lost to it.

But the war was over six years now, and the banging meant only another hangover from another weekend spree. Stepping over an unconscious fellow reveler, he picked his way clumsily to the tavern door.

"Next time I'm in from the woods, I do the buyin'," slurred a half-drunk shanty boy.

"That'll be the day my upstanding brother joins us." Daniel grinned.

"Where'd that pretty French girl go?" the young logger asked. He tried to sit up, but the effort made him hold his head in both hands.

"Off to spend the money she lifted from your wallet. I

told you, those kind make decent drinking partners, and they're fine for a few laughs. But they're no good for more. They only look like the real thing."

"What do you know about nice women?" The young man slurred.

Daniel ran a hand through his dark waves to straighten them. "I was married to one once. And after you've known real love, you won't settle for some cheap replacement."

He stumbled over one last celebrant as he made his way into the smoke-dimmed morning light.

Though wildfires continued to plague the surrounding counties, people went about their daily lives. Aunt Lucinda decided to shepherd Hannah and Amelia to the morning service at the church.

"I love it when you brush my hair, Miss Mercy," said Amelia as she smiled in the looking glass. Then she whispered loudly, "Sometimes, Aunt Lucinda pulls the tangles."

"My mother used to call them rats," Hannah said. "She thought rats sneaked in and tied the knots at night."

"Aunt Lucinda would never let any old rats inside her house," the child said emphatically. She grinned first to her doll, and then at Hannah. "That's because she couldn't teach them to wipe their feet when they came in."

Hannah smiled and shook her head. "We'd better hurry, or we'll miss the service."

The three of them walked along the pathway, their progress noted by the nodding yellow mums. Amelia loosed her grip on their hands and picked one for each woman.

"Honestly, child," complained Lucinda loudly, "I don't plant them for you to—" She paused as Amelia's face grew somber, then continued. "Oh, they'll only dry up anyway with all this drought, or get nipped by the next frost. Thank you, Amelia, for sharing them with us."

Hannah tickled the girl's nose with the bloom until she sneezed. Then, laughing, Amelia looked up and saw a man on horseback in the street.

"Papa!" she cried. "Come to church with us!"

Dozing in the saddle, Daniel rode past at a trot.

"Oh, dear, he's getting just as deaf as this old woman," said Lucinda lightly, but she cast a troubled glance at Hannah. It was obvious her nephew had been drunk.

Hannah's opinion of Daniel plummeted. What a selfish man he was to ignore his family for the bottle!

Intent on distracting the child, she stooped and picked a showy golden blossom from the walkway. "Come here, Amelia. Let's tuck this in your hair."

Amelia looked after her father for a moment longer before turning back to Hannah.

Following the service, Lucinda introduced "Mercy" to some of the women of her church, respectable women of a type Hannah knew well.

"Miss Wilder is the daughter of a great friend of my husband's family," Lucinda told the women. When the service was over and the two of them were sharing tea, she explained. "There's no need for everyone in town to know the particulars of your arrangement with my nephew."

Hannah was grateful. She'd had enough of gossip to last a lifetime.

But even here it wasn't long in finding her. The following morning, as she walked toward the general store to buy some baking powder Lucinda needed for a cake, she was surprised to see the same round-cheeked adventuress who had called out to Daniel only minutes after her arrival. Hannah avoided eye contact and moved as far away as the sidewalk allowed, but the woman laughed raucously.

"You! I know what you are! Just another strumpet, so don't act so prim and proper. You ask me, there ain't a whisker's worth o' difference between a gal who'll keep the shanty boys happy and some 'lady' who'd come to marry a man she never met!'' The smell of whiskey on her breath was strong. "Leastways, if I don't like the fellow, I'm not stuck with him so long.''

Hannah's heart sank at the woman's loud voice and the old men staring from the store's front porch. It would be all over town now, just because of Daniel! She was sure of that. John would never have spoken to this—this wild creature. He would never have exposed her to ridicule!

If Daniel was going to carouse with ruffians, that was his affair, but his loose talk would ruin her good name.

The redhead staggered toward the old men, her hand out. Once refused, she whirled around and stormed down the street, swearing loudly to herself. Hannah, too disturbed to think, stood rooted to the sidewalk.

One of the old men left his bench and approached her. His face was rugged and reddened by years of wind and sun. He removed a worn hat from his gray head with his left hand, for his right was shorn off just below the elbow joint.

"Don't pay Rosalind no mind, miss. She ain't never been right since her babe died.''

Hannah looked up sharply. The old man's eyes were liquid.

"She never was a bad girl, but she always fell in with the wrong lads. Her mother and I . . . we tried. Please, forgive her. She don't talk sense when she's been at the drink.'' His eyes were beseeching as an old hound's.

"I'm sure you did your best. I—I'm so sorry,'' Hannah stammered. What else could she say? He had probably spent half his life apologizing for a daughter who appeared beyond redemption. Hannah wondered if there was anyone alive who would do the same for her.

The old man nodded, then consoled himself with a sip from his friend's flask.

Awkwardly, Hannah excused herself and completed her errand before returning to Lucinda's. They would all be going to the farm that evening for a dinner with John. She hoped fervently that Daniel would be there too, and that she would have the opportunity for a word alone with him. A drunken woman's accusations might well be ignored if Hannah could put a stop to Daniel's mischief. It was yet possible her name might be preserved.

To pull her gig, Aunt Lucinda kept a fat black gelding well past his prime. That afternoon the women loaded Amelia and a fresh cake and began the hour's drive out to the farm.

"Here, Mercy." The old woman handed her the reins. "Why don't you take these? You're so much better with Old Blessing than I am."

Despite her apprehension, Hannah managed a half-smile. "I can't imagine Old Blessing has cut any shines in a dozen years."

"That's 'cause he's too fat," piped in Amelia.

"Just because a person's a bit broad through the hind-quarters doesn't mean she—I mean *he*—can't still raise Cain on occasion," Lucinda proclaimed loudly. Her back stiffened the way it always did when she was vexed.

"You said 'person.' I thought Old Blessing was a *horse*," the girl answered with a grin.

"What's true of a person is often as true for a beast," the old woman said.

Hannah felt a sharp poke from Amelia's elbow, which she wisely ignored. She was too anxious about her imagined confrontation with Daniel to take part in baiting a likable, if sensitive, old woman.

After another ten minutes of dust, bumps, and hoof-beats, Amelia fell asleep, clutching her doll and leaning against Hannah.

"Perhaps now," Lucinda said quietly, "you can tell me what's been on your mind all day."

Hannah felt the blood drain from her face. "Not a thing."

"Pshaw. Ever since you went out for baking powder, you've been out of sorts. What happened?"

"Nothing at all." She would settle this with Daniel, not snivel over gossip to Lucinda.

"Come now," the old woman prompted, more insistently this time.

"Perhaps I'm missing home." That sounded reasonable enough, thought Hannah, even though she no longer had a home to miss.

Before Lucinda could say another word, Blessing stopped abruptly, his ears pricked and his head held high. Both women turned their attention to the horse. Beyond him, the trees looked indistinct and hazy, but it was impossible to tell from what direction the smoke came.

"Do you smell it?" Hannah asked, and sniffed again. "It's too close."

"All I smell these days is smoke," said Aunt Lucinda. "I clean ash off the mantel twice a day if I even crack the windows."

"This is stronger though." Hannah strained her ears, listening for the telltale crackle of flame through the dry leaves. Hearing nothing but light wind through the treetops, she gave the reins a tentative flick to gently urge the animal forward. The brushfire could be anywhere—behind, ahead, or to either side. Or it could be in all those spots at once, she thought with a light shudder.

Hannah shoved fear's dark head beneath the surface. Lucinda and Amelia needed someone sensible to drive them, so she refused to allow herself the luxury of panic. They weren't far from the farm now, so she decided to keep driving.

"It's all right, Blessing. No need to catch the jitters."

Strength and assurance flowed through Hannah's voice and down the narrow leather reins. After a moment's hesitation, the gelding broke into an easy trot.

"He trusts you," Lucinda told her. She patted Hannah's hand. "So do I."

Lucinda's earlier questions were forgotten. Instead, both women considered the towering trees that rose along their pathways, trees whose very dryness seemed to cry for flame.

Amelia woke in time to throw herself into her father's arms. After a quick kiss, she announced, "I'm going to find my kitten."

"I saw her playing back behind the barn." Daniel smiled after her as she ran in that direction, her flaxen pigtails bouncing against her back.

At least he was sober enough to notice his daughter today, thought Hannah.

The huge man helped each woman down from the gig.

"There was a lot of smoke across the road about a mile from here," Hannah told him. Despite her anger with him, her hand felt good enfolded inside his.

He released it with no sign of hesitation. "There's a lot of smoke everywhere today," he said, looking off to the horizon. "Probably nothing but the usual small hot spots, but I can't say I like the way that wind is picking up. Nothing like a breeze to fan up sparks."

"Mercy talked Old Blessing through it," Aunt Lucinda added. "I was mighty glad to have her along. Do you think we'll be all right here, Daniel?"

He nodded. "We've cleared a lot of acreage, and this house and barn sit smack-dab in the middle. We're safer here than anywhere that I can think of."

"You always know just what to say to an old woman," Lucinda told him. "Let me take this cake into the house and help John with the dinner."

"I'll give Daniel a hand here with the horse," said Hannah.

"You needn't do that," Daniel said as he unhitched the animal. He led the gelding toward the barn. "With a good rest and some hay, he'll soon forget his fright. Besides, I imagine you're just wild to go in and listen to John quote some more Scripture."

Hannah followed him inside. "Scripture's a sight more wholesome than the gossip *you've* been quoting. I'd like to speak to you a moment on the subject."

She paused, and Daniel faced her, his brows raised in surprise—or scorn. Behind him, several horses nickered greetings, their heads hanging out of neat box stalls. Two cows lowed a reminder that it was nearly time for milking.

After a deep breath, Hannah continued. "This morning I was accosted by your young lady friend. I believe her name is Rosalind."

His laughter was edged in mockery. "I wouldn't call Rosalind my friend, and there's few would bother calling her a lady."

"Yes, well, whatever you might *call* a woman of that sort, you needn't whisper gossip about me."

Daniel looked away from her and began unbuckling Old Blessing's harness. His fingers moved about the task with brisk efficiency.

Finally, he glared at her. "You think this two-bit mail-order romance you have with my brother is worth the time to spread around? Miss Wilder, I've got better things to do."

"Such as drink so much whiskey, you can't even recognize your little girl on Sunday mornings?"

"I don't see what business it would be of yours if I got blind drunk *every* day."

She put one hand on a hip and strode closer to him. "It's my business when you're out spreading secrets."

"So you're worried about secrets, are you?" Daniel

shook his head in clear disgust. "I'd wager you've got more than a few. I can't say I'm surprised about it either. I warned John a woman as fine-looking as you would likely be a basketful of trouble."

Hannah's pulse roared in her ears. He was just trying to rile her. He didn't know about her past. He couldn't. "Don't be ridiculous," she plunged ahead. "It's just that I don't want my arrangement with your brother fodder for the gossips of this town."

Daniel hung the harness, then retrieved a brush. His strokes, as he began to use it on the gelding, were quick enough to raise a cloud of horsehair, which hung like anger in the air around them.

"If you really think I told Rosalind, you don't know me very well. No matter what I think of his wife-buying venture, I wouldn't do anything to embarrass John."

"If you didn't tell her, who did?" Hannah demanded. "I refuse to believe John has had anything to do with that woman."

"You've got him sized up, all right. He wouldn't be caught dead around the boardinghouse. Some of his church friends might see him."

"You could learn a great deal from your brother. Starting with how to redeem your character. Church would be a fine place to begin. You could take Amelia," Hannah told him. She knew she should stop then, but Daniel's guess about her secrets had honed her words, leaving each one swift and sharp. "Perhaps the minister would preach a sermon on the topic of gossip, or the wages of sin, or how to pray to ask forgiveness."

Daniel threw down the brush. The straw near her feet erupted in a puff of dust and chaff. "I know damned well how to pray, Miss Wilder. You think I didn't try it when the doctor came to bleed my Mary? You think I didn't promise everything, say the fiercest prayers I knew? You think I didn't offer up my life if God would save her?"

He shook his head, his jaw clenched so ferociously, it was a wonder his teeth weren't pulverized. When he spoke again, his voice seethed with old resentment. "John calls Him the Good Lord, and so did I at one time. After the war ended, I sort of figured Mary was my reward for coming home. But then God took her away from me. Damned fever took her anyway."

"You still have a fine daughter." The words sounded flat and useless, even to Hannah. His wife, a woman he had loved, had died. Despite Daniel's rudeness, despite even his gossip, she hadn't meant to reopen that old wound.

"That I do." He nodded. "And you think I'm heartless not to have Amelia here with me. Well, the truth is, Aunt Lucinda likes living in town, and I want my girl to go to school. I won't leave her here alone all day while John and I work this farm."

"Or all night while you spread tales?"

Daniel glowered at her. "I didn't tell Rosalind. I admit I've got my faults, but I'm no skulking gossip. Maybe you'd better scold the telegraph operator on his morals, or his delivery boy."

"Telegraph?"

Daniel nodded. "Something came for John today from your Mr. Harlan. My brother's been out of sorts ever since."

Hannah's knees loosened, and she barely kept herself from crashing to the dirt floor of the barn. Heart pounding, she managed to form words. "What—what did the telegram say?"

Daniel shrugged and stared at her intently. "John wouldn't tell me, but from the looks of you, I'd say you know already."

Her hands were shaking, and suddenly, she didn't know quite what to do with them. Had Malcolm found her here? Had anyone?

Unexpectedly, Daniel laid his hand on her arm. The

flesh felt warm on her cool skin. "Maybe you should tell me, one sinner to another. Could be there's something I can do to help."

She shook her head without speaking. If she tried to say a word, the tears would flow. She'd borne so much, but just then she didn't know if she could stand to let him see her weeping.

"This past week," Daniel told her, "I've kept my eye on you, done some thinking on the reasons a woman like you might put yourself in this kind of situation. My brother likes you, Mercy, likes you a great deal. And why shouldn't he? You're smart, levelheaded, and prettier than store-bought lace. But everything I saw told me you must be running from some sort of past. Everything I see now tells me I was right."

Hannah stared at him through prisms created by the teardrops in her eyes. Just as that moisture had softened his features, her reaction had somehow softened his words.

"Could be I'm a man with secrets of my own," he told her, his voice low and calming, just as one would speak to a spooked horse. "Could be I've had troubles enough to help you deal with yours. We're a lot alike, more alike than you'd admit."

How she longed to throw herself into his arms, to tell him everything so he could make it right! But, of course, that was impossible. If John had somehow learned who she was, she was already well past saving. Her lies had earned her that.

"You're kind to offer," she managed to say weakly, "but I don't require any help."

He reached for her and pulled her close, then cupped her cheek in that big, warm hand. The fingertips felt callused against the smooth skin of her face. *Move away*, she warned herself, but she did nothing even as he leaned closer. Even as he sought her mouth for a long kiss.

Every fiber of Hannah responded to his touch. She felt

all the tightness of her body beginning to dissolve. She wanted nothing more than to explore, for hours, to her heart's desire, the deep want he'd awakened. She'd thought that part of her had died with Malcolm's accusations, and something in her revelled it had not.

Coming to her senses, she pulled herself away. "John's your *brother*," she accused. "I'm to marry him." She had to remind herself as well as Daniel of the reality of her relationship with John.

Daniel opened his mouth as if to explain, then hesitated. Confusion, guilt, and want all etched themselves in his expression. Finally, his features hardened into hostility. "That fact didn't keep you from kissing back, now, did it?"

"Your brother is a kind and decent man." She couldn't be disloyal, no matter what she feared. No matter what the telegram had said, or how her body ached for one more kiss. She could still taste Daniel and feel the firm muscles of his chest against her. She'd almost sell her soul for one more touch.

But not quite. Malcolm had already driven home the price of human want, at least the price a woman paid. Even the hint of scandal could ruin her forever—if she wasn't lost already. What on God's green earth was wrong with her? Her body had betrayed her desire to a man more familiar with harlots than decent women.

He looked about to argue, when a cry from outside interrupted their conversation. "Papa! I see fire!"

He ran outside and shouted, "In the house, Amelia! Go get John. It's coming this way, from the look."

Hannah ran, pulling the child along behind her and fearing the fire even more than her own demons. "John! John, come out!" she cried.

When he threw open the door, she caught the scent of chicken roasting above the more acrid smell of smoke.

Amelia rushed inside and flung herself into Aunt Lucinda's waiting arms.

"Daniel says the fire's coming!" shouted Hannah.

Without a word, John sprinted for the barn. When Hannah turned to follow him, she saw the flame at last, a glowing eddy of fire lapping at the brush piled near the edge of the west pasture.

"I'll get the plow!" John shouted in the direction of his brother. Hannah understood at once that he meant to put a break between the burning litter and the dried grasses of the cleared land around the house and barn. But John never had the chance to put his plan in action.

Flame tasted the loose bark of a towering dead elm. Hannah heard a hiss, and the tree exploded into flame.

That quickly, the nearest section of the dried tree crowns caught fire. Hannah cried out, but her scream vanished inside the whoosh of rising, heated air. Blazing leaves rained from the sky as the wind whipped them in their direction. And in the direction of the hay-filled wooden barn.

CHAPTER FIVE

In the space of a breath, the first burning leaves sailed into the open hayloft door. As if it had been steeped in kerosene, the hay exploded into flame.

"Dear God, the animals!" Hannah cried, neither knowing nor caring if anyone could hear her. She rushed into the wooden structure and quickly found Old Blessing.

"Let's not get breachy, darling." She forced the panic from her voice and patted his sleek neck soothingly. If she alarmed him, he might well refuse her lead. Blessing's eyes rolled and his nostrils flared at the crackling of the hay, the flickering orange light, and the smoke rolling downward from the rafters. He threw back his head and began to rise on his rear legs when Hannah spoke again.

"Poor Blessing. It's all right." With forced calmness she took him by the halter and began walking toward the door. The old gelding followed her this time.

John's prized mare squealed in protest as he tried to lead her out. Once outside, Hannah was relieved to see John follow and turn the animal loose. She did the same with Blessing and went back inside to help get out the remaining horses and the cows that had come in for milking.

The smoke roiled inside, far thicker than it had been just seconds before. Painfully, she drew thick air into her lungs and choked. Doubling over, she wiped her burning eyes, then managed to continue. She could see almost nothing, but frantic neighs and bellows led her toward the animals. Something grabbed her upper arm, and Daniel's voice boomed in her ear. "Get out of here! Don't want you burned up too!"

She'd go, Hannah decided, but she might as well take one more poor beast with her. She felt her way to one of the pair of chestnut horses and began to lead him toward the door.

Inside the barn, Hannah never saw John's gray mare wheel around and race toward what the animal thought of as a place of safety.

A shrill whinny gave Hannah only a fraction of a second's warning before the mare hurtled through the smoke-charged darkness and slammed her to the floor. Then another darkness, even thicker, overwhelmed her, and, at least to Hannah, the terrible cacophony grew still.

"I swear to you, Daniel, I should have left her there to burn." The voice was John's, harsh as Hannah had never heard it before.

"But you didn't. You brought her back out anyway." Daniel's voice, but somehow, she couldn't open her eyes to see him. He continued. "And well you should have. She was saving our own horses."

"Of course she was. They'd be hers if we'd married."

Hannah wanted to defend herself against the accusation in his tone, but she could not. Surely a cow had fallen across her chest. Her lungs felt ragged inside, and she suppressed a fit of coughing.

"She ran into a burning barn, twice, and brought out horses. And if your fool mare hadn't run her down rushing back to her own stall, Mercy would have gone back in for more. I don't know what the telegram says, but I'll say this: She's brave."

"Her name's not Mercy Wilder. It's Hannah. Hannah Shelton. The message was a warning about her from that Harlan fellow." John's voice crackled and sputtered, not unlike the barn had as it burned.

"Shelton?" Daniel's voice registered surprise and disappointment. "What else did it say? She some sort of swindler?"

"I don't know," John answered. "That's the worst part. I got only half a message. The telegraph wire's burned through, but it was a warning, Daniel. All I know is she's bad business."

"Too pretty," Daniel murmured. "I told you that right off. So what will you do now?"

"Soon as she gets better, I aim to put her on the boat that brought her. She may be a criminal, for all I know. She's at the very least a liar." Bitterness suffused John's voice, and Hannah felt tears coming to her eyes. Finding out had hurt him, and she added his pain to her substantial list of sins.

"I'm sorry, John," Daniel said. "I know I warned you, but I never wanted this to happen."

"A barn, my best horse, and my future wife—all gone. Right now I envy Job."

"At least the house is safe, and the brushfire burned itself out."

"We'll build a bigger barn once the rains come," John said.

"And you'll buy a better horse someday."

"I wonder if I'll ever find a woman I like half as much."

Sympathy rumbled deep in Daniel's throat. "I admit, I sort of fancied her myself."

"False Jezebel, may she rot in hell," John swore.

Hannah heard the door close as they left the room. The tears that squeezed out from her lowered eyelids choked her. She tried to suppress the sound, but her lungs and throat were both insistent. In a few minutes Aunt Lucinda came in with some water.

"Poor thing. Drink up, Mercy. You should have never gone inside that barn."

Hannah felt relief that no one had told Lucinda, at least not yet. The old woman washed her face with a warm cloth. Welcome as it was, this treatment wouldn't last, she knew. They would tell their aunt soon, and Lucinda would hate her just as Daniel and John must.

Maybe John had been right, she decided. It would have been best if he'd left her lying on the floor inside the burning barn. Even for her it would have been a kinder ending, for she had no hope now.

The thought brought fresh tears. That and the stench of smoke from her own hair provoked another round of coughing.

"It's all right, dear," Lucinda said, misunderstanding. "The barn can be rebuilt, and as for that blamed mare, someday John will have another just as fine. No other animals were killed, thanks in part to your help. Now, don't you try to talk. You've got a big knot on your head and a dose of that bad air. You just stay quiet; there's someone here to see you."

Hannah's heart thundered in her chest. What now? But it was only little Amelia, who ran in carrying her kitten. The girl hopped up on the bed and placed the calico fur ball beside Hannah on the quilt.

"I was scared when I saw your eyes closed. I thought you might be gone, like Mama." Amelia's voice rose fervent as a prayer. "Do you feel better now?"

Hannah nodded miserably. Her loss would be another heartache to this child, who had already lost so much. Amelia leaned against her, arms outstretched. The kitten's warm, sandpaper tongue began to lick her hand.

She hugged Amelia fiercely and wondered what lie they would tell her. The truth, that she'd deceived them, would of course be confined to the adults. Hannah hoped they'd choose a gentle tale, one that wouldn't hurt too badly.

"Now let's give her some peace and quiet," Lucinda told the girl.

As the pair left, Hannah knew that there was no one who could offer her what the old woman had suggested. All the quiet in the whole world would never buy her peace.

CHAPTER SIX

In the morning Lucinda brought her ham and pancakes on a tray, but the old woman's eyes had grown cold, her manner stiff, suspicious. Though normally garrulous, Lucinda didn't speak a single word. It was very clear the men had told her of Hannah's deception. Amelia didn't come at all, and Hannah suspected the child would no longer be allowed to see her. In some way, that loss was the most painful.

It was just as well Lucinda wouldn't speak, thought Hannah, for whatever could she say to soothe the hurt in those aged eyes? While alone, Hannah attempted the Lord's Prayer, but even that small comfort was denied her, for yesterday's thick smoke had left her throat so tight, she couldn't speak.

She chewed stubbornly on cold pancake and frowned at the bitter taste of ash. The ham, too, spoke of the old woman's ire, for it was dry and tough. Still, Hannah choked down every bite with warm tea and fresh milk. She had to, for she couldn't guess when she would eat again. She expected to be put out of the farmhouse and forced to walk through smoking coals all the way to town.

As she finished her tea, Daniel came into the room and dropped into a straight-backed chair beside the bed. Though the sun was still low in the sky, his work must have begun already. He was streaked with ash, as if he'd been digging through the rubble of the barn. His brown eyes, once so full of longing, were hard and distant now.

"John says your real name's Hannah Shelton. That's what you were hiding, wasn't it?"

She said nothing, and in doing so answered him completely.

"We don't take to liars here. We're sending you back home soon as you can manage. In spite of what you did, you got hurt helping us yesterday, and we're obliged. But I won't have you laid up here in my family's house. You hurt my brother and my aunt. Hell, you even hurt my little girl. So as soon as I can get a wagon through, I'm going to find another place for you to stay."

This felt terrible, thought Hannah, even worse in some ways than when Malcolm had made his accusations. At least when that had happened, she'd known she'd done no wrong. Now guilt combined with pain to create a slurry of self-hatred, the worst she'd ever known. "I'm—so sorry." The hoarse words triggered another round of coughing.

When she finished, Daniel stood. "If you weren't a woman, I'd beat you to a pulp." The door slammed in his wake, and once more she was left alone.

Hannah clenched her teeth. He hadn't even asked why she had done this. None of them had. Did it even occur to them that a woman could be driven to such desperation?

She spent the day resting uneasily in a house she'd never live in. In her troubled dreams, the ghostly gray horse barreled past her, desperate to face an unknown danger in its familiar stall. Again and again the animal exploded into flame, her shrill whinnies changing into human screams. Hannah woke up shivering beneath a layer of cool sweat.

She still smelled the ash outside, and when she raised the window shade, she saw a plume of smoke in the distance. Would all Wisconsin burn before the autumn rains fell this year? She almost felt relief that she would soon be leaving. Then she wondered where she would go next.

Could there be someplace where it wouldn't matter what she called herself? Or could there be a place where men so hungered for a woman that even the stigma of divorce meant nothing?

Hot tears coursed down Hannah's face. She wouldn't even want a man who wouldn't care about those things.

Once again she racked her brain to come up with some other way to earn her living. She knew how to work, and she knew horses. She could read and write and figure numbers well enough. Surely, there must be something she could do besides what coarser men suggested. Surely there must be some way to survive.

John and Daniel's wagon had burned, but they managed to pull Lucinda's gig out of the flames. The following morning, Daniel harnessed Chance, one of his team of chestnut geldings, and braced himself to go to Mercy's room.

Hannah, he corrected himself. The illusion calling itself Mercy died inside the barn.

The barn. He remembered how he'd kissed her there, how the heat built up inside him, as if his heart might burn right through his chest. No wonder the place caught fire, he thought with a sad chuckle. He hadn't realized how much he'd missed that spark of something real. And it was real. He was sure of it, for Hannah felt it too. Her body had loosened, and no matter what she said, he'd seen regret shimmer in her blue eyes. Then she pulled away and reminded them both of John.

Did she think he was the one with money? After all, their mother left the farm to John. As well she should have. John had been running it responsibly ever since their father died, when both boys were in their teens. John hadn't been so eager to run away to fight some far-off war. Daniel was besieging Vicksburg the night his mother died. He wondered, even then, if she'd forgiven him for leaving.

Returning to the present, he kissed Amelia and his aunt good-bye. "I'm going to drive *her* back to town, see if I can stow her with some friends."

Amelia wouldn't meet his gaze. Instead, she tightly squeezed her doll. She'd cried for hours when he'd told her Mercy and Uncle John had decided not to marry and how each thought it best if they did not remain in the same house. Even his promise that Amelia and Aunt Lucinda could stay there for the week had failed to comfort the child.

"Don't forget to pick up a few things at my house. And be careful," Lucinda said, her voice warning that she feared Hannah's deceit even more than fire.

"I'll be sure to, and I'll make certain the woods are safe for when you two go back home." He turned to the stairwell.

"Papa!" Amelia's voice sparkled behind him. When he turned, she continued. "I know! *You* can marry Mercy! Then she could be my mama, not my aunt!"

God, how he hated to snuff out her joy. He bent down and took her in his arms. "I know you love Mercy, and I know she loves you too. But sometimes things aren't right. She has people back home, family, and they miss her very much."

"But I'll miss her too. Won't you?" Her tears wet Daniel's cheek as he squeezed her close.

"Of course. Now go help Aunt Lucinda for a while.

Mercy's sad, and she might not want you to see her cry."
Lying to his daughter was almost as bad as dashing her
hopes, but how could he tell her the truth about Hannah
Shelton?

Lucinda took the child's hand and lectured her as they
walked toward the kitchen. "You be sure to stay away from
that hot rubble. Goodness knows what kind of filth you
would track in! Come now, we'll fix some of your favorite
apple dumplings."

Daniel trudged up the stairs and rapped on Hannah's
door. She let him in, and he could see that Lucinda must
have laundered her blue dress. Even so, a soot stain made
an ugly smudge across her chest. Thinking of her paltry
bags and wardrobe, he considered buying her a new dress.
Quickly, he dismissed the ridiculous notion. After all, her
passage and the cost of Harlan's "introduction" had
already set John back far more than that dress. Just because
she was a woman, that didn't excuse her deceit one bit.

"Just a moment," Hannah told him, her voice hoarse
with emotion. In one deft motion she wound up dark waves
that fell to her waist, then pinned them into a neat roll.
That simple task put Daniel to mind of his Mary, though
her hair had been fine and honey-blond.

A prolonged round of coughing left Hannah red-faced,
but she didn't let it stop her. With dignity, she preceded
him down the stairs, her posture stiff and arrogant as a
Philadelphia debutante. Positively shameless. Daniel shook
his head, amazed at her gumption. The woman wouldn't
hang her head if she'd just robbed the bank in Green Bay.

John was checking Chance's harness when they went
outside. Though he hadn't faced Hannah since the fire, he
didn't shrink away. Instead, he quoted Scripture. " 'Even as
I have seen, they that plow iniquity, and sow wickedness,
reap the same. By the blast of God they perish, and by the
breath of His nostrils are they consumed.' "

She hesitated before she reached out with one hand.

"John, I know you'll never have me, but I beg you to forgive me. I—I didn't know what else to do."

He slapped her hard enough to knock her down. His auburn hair flapping with each word, he shouted yet another Bible verse. " 'And I find more bitter than death the woman whose heart is snares and nets, and her hands as bands: whoso pleaseth God shall escape from her; but the sinner shall be taken by her.' "

Daniel grasped his brother's raised arm, shocked that he would strike a woman. Even when they were children, John had never engaged in fisticuffs. And before today the harshest words Daniel had ever heard him speak had been to berate a French farmer who beat his wife black and blue.

"She's not worth this, John," he warned. "You'll only be mad at yourself if you go on. Think on all that church teaching you're so fond of."

"And do what? Turn the other cheek? Let her plead with her demon's tongue and then forgive her lies?"

Daniel stepped between his brother and Hannah, who sat stock-still in the dust. "Go on in, John. Let me handle this the way we planned last night. You're not yourself this morning. I don't blame you, but I won't let you do this to yourself. When a man goes against what he believes, there's pure hell to pay later."

Daniel thought about the face of his last rebel and his own bloody bayonet. But John didn't know that story, and he'd be damned if he'd share the secret just to make a point.

Besides, what he said did the trick. John whirled and stomped back toward the house. The door banged so hard, Daniel wondered if he'd have to rehang it.

Daniel offered Hannah a hand, but she refused it. Though her left cheek was fiery red and swelling, she neither cried nor complained. He couldn't decide if bravery or sheer arrogance safeguarded her composure. She stood and brushed her skirts, apparently trying to hide the quick swipe she gave her eyes.

"I could get you a wet towel," he offered.

She shook her head. "No. I want to leave. That's all."

He didn't help her climb into the gig. She might act like a lady, but he couldn't forget how she'd hurt John, or the dampness on his own cheek from his daughter's tears.

As they began, she asked quietly, "How's Old Blessing?"

"He's fine. Thought he could use the rest though. He's twenty years old if he's a day."

After that they again fell silent as the gig bumped over half-burned branches. At one point they had to get out so Daniel could ease the emptied two-wheeled cart over a fallen tree. Hannah, right beside him, put her shoulder against the gig and pushed.

"You're still sick. You don't have to do that," he said as the wheels bumped forward.

"It's not my way to stand around like some fluff-headed ornament. I'm no stranger to hard work." Behind her, blackened trees stood leafless, like charred sentries.

"So what happened?" Unable to restrain the impulse, he faced her. "You're bright, you're beautiful. What on earth would make you—oh, never mind. I don't even want to hear whatever yarn you'll spin."

"That's right, Daniel Aldman." She began to cough, then fought her way back through the spasm. "You don't want to know. You'd rather judge me harshly, the way people judge you if they don't understand you're really grieving for your wife."

"Get back in the gig," he ordered roughly. "You don't know anything about me."

"I know you've suffered a great loss, as have I. You disguise it with drink and rowdy friends, so much so, you ignore your daughter half the time. Maybe you should face your heartache and move on. After all, the world respects a widower."

"I don't need anyone's respect, and I don't need advice from some woman who lies to earn her way. Shut your mouth and get in like I told you, before I leave you here."

Hannah climbed back into the gig without assistance. Within a half hour they worked their way through the burned stretch of wood. For the rest of the long ride she didn't say a word. Once back at Aunt Lucinda's, she packed her few bags quickly and met him at the door.

He started ahead of her, carrying the satchel he'd put together for his aunt and daughter and leaving her to handle her own bags.

"Wait," she said abruptly.

He turned to see her gazing toward the wilted chrysanthemums along the walkway.

"I'd like to water them." Hannah put down her bags and went to the backyard pump without waiting for his answer. It took her twenty minutes to complete the task.

"This won't buy you one thing," Daniel told her.

She faced him squarely. "It's obvious, Mr. Aldman, you know even less about me than you think."

The agent at the ticket office shook his head. "They won't bring in the boats because the smoke's too thick. It's so bad out on the bay, they're navigating just by compass, and the river's even worse. No more steamers till the rains come or the winds pick up and clear the smoke."

"If the winds pick up, God help us," Daniel answered. "It will only fan the flames."

She had met the man before, though Hannah hadn't known his name. The father of the tart-mouthed Rosalind, he had wanted her forgiveness when his daughter slandered her. And here she was, proving Rosalind's words. Hannah felt flame in her cheeks, and she could not lift her gaze from the spit-stained boards of the man's front porch.

"Hank, this is Miss Hannah Shelton. She's proved herself a fraud and a liar, and we don't intend to keep her at the house. I'd put her on a boat today if they were running. What I want to know is, would you and your missus keep her at your place till then? I know you take in a few boarders time to time. We'll pay in cash until she can be gone."

"Could always use the money, I suppose. And Faye won't mind a bit. We'll put her back in Rosalind's old room."

"Just watch her close," said Daniel. "I'd hate to have her rob you blind."

That was enough! She'd been cursed and assaulted, and she imagined she deserved both, but she was no thief! She curled her hands into tight fists and glared at Daniel. "I've never stolen a crust in all my life, you sanctimonious drunkard! And I'm tired of you speaking about me as though I'm not even here. I *am* here and I'm—"

She never finished because she took to coughing so hard that she couldn't catch her breath.

The old man laughed. "Yep, sounds like our Rosalind all over. Don't worry, Daniel. We'll take good care of her."

CHAPTER SEVEN

Hank Barlow's withered wife, Faye, did all she could to supplement his meager pension from the mill. She took in a few boarders when the opportunity arose, but their unpainted wooden house was too small and shabby to attract much notice. With his right arm cut off by a saw, Hank spent far too many hours sitting on front porches and gabbing with other idle men, but Faye was rarely still. Her days were often spent in mending or laundering single loggers' and millworkers' clothes, or in baking simple meat pies for saloons.

"There's more to do around here than sit and feel sorry for yourself," she chastised Hannah when she saw her staring blankly from the one chair in the plain gray room. "I see enough o' that in my old man and that Ros'lind to choke on, so here. Do something, I say."

She thrust a pile of shirts at Hannah, along with a needle and coarse thread. Numbly, Hannah took them and began to sew, replacing buttons, mending tears, sometimes

restitching seams. Her hands, at first, were clumsy, but as
the hours passed, they remembered their old skill.

Mrs. Barlow didn't mention money, and Hannah never
asked. She was too grateful for the work, for the simple
satisfaction of completing needed tasks. The silver needle
darted in and out through coarse brown wool and faded
cottons, mesmerizing, numbing, reminding her of other
stitches in a white dress long ago.

> "There I stand on Buttermilk Hill,
> Who can blame me cry my fill,
> And every tear could turn a mill,
> Johnny has gone for a soldier.
>
> "Sell my spinning, sell my wheel,
> Buy my love a sword of steel,
> So it in battle he may wield,
> Johnny has gone for a soldier."

Hearing her own voice, sweet and somber, Hannah
paused, the needle frozen like a stinger at midstrike. She
had nearly forgotten that old tune, those verses she had
sung so many times with such feeling, long ago. Fears
rushed back with every word, and images now ten years
dead and gone. The sight of Robert's back as he proudly
marched away, the desperation in her voice as she begged
God for his survival. That year, her eighteenth, she had
learned what love was, and two later, she had found that
God could turn a deaf ear to even the most heartfelt pleas.
Twenty-year-old Robert died near Gettysburg, not of rebel
bullets nor of cannonfire. He had died of typhus in his
camp.

The last verse of the old song came to her.

> "I'll dye my dress all over red,
> And o'er the world I'll beg my bread,

So all my friends may think me dead.
Oh, Johnny has gone for a soldier.''

A tear broke like a wave across the gleaming needle. Hannah wondered, after eight years, did she weep for her first love or for herself?

In the aftermath she'd married Malcolm quickly. He had returned from the war alive. With his dashing captain's uniform, he cut a handsome figure. His genteel manners swept her off her feet. The two of them shared a love of horses, and together they planned the business that would make them prosperous. In a month's time they were married. Hannah wore the white dress her sweet Robert had never lived to see.

She remembered her father, leaning forward to kiss her on the cheek. ''I only wish your mother had lived to see this day.''

Thank God she had not, thought Hannah now, for that day had been her ruination. That day, and that white dress, had led her inexorably to where—and what—she had become.

A divorcée and an accused adulteress. A liar and a fraud. Her mother's early death of apoplexy had spared her the disgrace the Barstows knew. Hannah wondered if her father had died in time as well, or if he'd somehow guessed the hell that Malcolm's lies would set ablaze.

Daniel nearly stopped off at the saloon for a quick drink, except that's what *she* would have expected. Calling *him* a sanctimonious drunkard, after what she'd done! If that didn't take some brass.

All the way home he fumed, imagining the words he should have told her. He might enjoy a spree now and again, but at least folks knew his real name. And he looked after his little girl just fine. Didn't he see to it she was cared for?

Smoke wafted through the interwoven trunks of saplings and across a dried-up bog. Amelia wouldn't go to school this week, not until he felt sure it was safe. The dryness of the air, the crumbling fallen leaves, and the eerie smoke-thick sky made him uneasy. What if everyone was wrong? What if this fall's rain came too late? He pushed aside his uneasy questions like a bad dream.

Or like an unpleasant memory from his past.

CHAPTER EIGHT

Plumes of dark smoke billowed across the water, and Malcolm could see distant firelight.

"Damnation!" he swore. That cowardly ship's captain would never take him to Marinette. If he could even get that close, he would buy a horse and ride to Peshtigo. Then he'd have the heartless bitch he had once married. And she would return with him, even if he had to drag her by her hair.

He thought about that hair, rich brown with its auburn highlights in the summer. He thought about the way it had felt slipping through his fingers long ago. She'd been so beautiful at twenty, so brokenhearted when he'd come bearing the news that her fiancé died at war. He'd been injured too; luckily, his wounded leg had not needed amputation. That bullet had kept him nearby in their hometown, but it had not staked him for the business he felt sure he deserved.

Hannah's father financed him when they became engaged, and with the old man's death not long after they married, his only daughter inherited his farm. He and Hannah continued raising horses, and he'd been glad to learn she knew her way around a barn.

It went so well for many years, but children never came. At first he tried not to think about it, but every prying question had needled him. As his own late father often insisted, a man needed sons, or else why bother to amass a fortune? Though his business thrived, he grew dissatisfied.

Malcolm Shelton, with his dark eyes and coal-black hair and beard, still had certain charms. For a while, a long string of women eased his melancholy, until Marcelia bore his bastard. Then he knew for certain the fault lay in Hannah. He took to staying more often with Marcelia, eagerly marking his son's progress, hoping his wife would offer him this joy.

She did not, and all his blame did nothing to make her womb receptive. She railed against his anger and finally turned hard.

"Divorce her," said his best friend, Jacob. "Put her aside and marry Marcelia if she makes you happy, or some other young girl if she doesn't." But how could he get rid of his wife and still keep his business? If he lost her family's land, he would lose everything.

His plan was simple. Foolproof. No one would take a woman's word.

No one had. He'd paid Tom Saunders to look shamefaced when accused of sleeping with his Hannah. He'd even struck the man in public, on the street. After that the word spread quickly. The beautiful Mrs. Shelton had committed the most grievous sin. When he divorced her, the ladies from her Bible study class—Hannah's own friends—delivered casseroles and other, far less Christian, offers. The judge gave her nothing but the scantiest support.

She'd stayed quiet for a long while, too humiliated to fight back. No one would listen to her protestations. No one dared anger her wealthy former husband by giving her a job. Finally, after he left Marcelia and married rich old Morgan's daughter, she had done this awful thing to wreck him.

Hannah Shelton faked her death—and turned the pack of gossips against *him*.

CHAPTER NINE

"Here's the ticket," Daniel told her. "It'll be good when-ever they start running boats again."

She had bruised where John had struck her, but she looked no less proud. It didn't matter she was sitting amid a pile of mending in a shabby rented room. It wouldn't matter if she were mucking out a filthy stall. He would always remember her as beautiful and proud.

She reached for the ticket. "Thank you for bringing this. I wish you would tell John something. I want to pay him back for all the money he spent on my behalf. I don't know when, but I *will* pay him, if ever I can find some sort of job."

"Looks like you can sew, at least," he told her. Not that it would matter. She would never pay John back. Then he remembered how she'd watered Aunt Lucinda's wilting flowers. He remembered the way she'd hugged his little girl. Maybe there was something to her after all, something more than her appearance. Maybe there was substance to justify the way his arms ached to hold her once again, the way he longed to taste the sweetness of her kiss.

"It's a hard thing to make a living at, with no man to fall back on."

"I imagine you could find someone. Just be sure to tell him your real name." He couldn't imagine why he was advising her as if she were some sort of friend. What difference could it make what became of her? One stolen kiss meant nothing, less than nothing, in her case.

Hannah's needle never stopped, but her battered face looked peaceful as she spoke. "No man would marry Hannah Shelton. I've given up that thought."

"You talk like your life's over. It's too soon to give up."

Her blue eyes looked so sad as she glanced up. "I might say the same to you."

On impulse, he knelt beside her bed and laid his hand atop her knee. "Tell me, Hannah. You have to tell me why you lied."

"You said before it didn't matter."

"It matters to me now." He felt like an idiot, kneeling there beside this woman, but he couldn't help himself. With her, he could never force himself to stop, even when he certainly knew better.

She shrugged, as if nothing could touch her anymore. "Don't fall in love with a lost woman, Daniel Aldman. I can never give a man a child, and because of that, my husband divorced me. But just because I was barren, he saw no need to part with my inheritance. So that faithless philanderer accused *me*, he called *me* an adulteress. That was the day Hannah Shelton really died."

He stared at her, shocked by the emptiness of her voice almost as much as by the revelation of her past. This must be the truth, he thought, for there was nothing she could gain with such a lie. Though he knew he shouldn't, he wrapped his arms around her.

"I'm so sorry," he told her.

"Let go of me, or I shall jab you with this needle," Hannah told him. "I don't want your pity, and I remind you, I am not one of your loose women, even if I am divorced."

He pulled away from her slowly, unwilling to let the moment pass. "Don't get so high and mighty with me, Hannah. I'm not trying what you think."

"Oh? Then I suppose that whole scene in the barn was just well-wishing and that your hand has not crept up my thigh."

He jerked it away from her. "I've never met another woman like you."

"No, I don't suppose Peshtigo has many divorcées, and I'm sure the harlots fall all over you. Please leave now. I believe I've already thanked you for delivering the ticket. I'll leave this town as soon as possible."

Defeated, Daniel stomped out of the house, his big feet raising dust along the porch.

"Damned proud, stubborn woman!" he muttered to himself.

"Just like my Rosalind used to be," Hank said from his perch on a warped split-log bench. "Just don't let her suffer too long, or all that pride'll dry up. And when it blows away, you'll have nothing left at all."

Hannah sat frozen, still savoring the feel of Daniel's powerful arms around her. She didn't want to move, or even breathe, lest the memory begin to fade. How long would it be before anyone held her close again? Why must she be so tempted? Couldn't she accept her lot and give up hope?

Although she had never been unfaithful, she had often, in those declining years of her marriage, longed to have someone hold her. Someone to offer sympathy. Someone to offer love.

Had Daniel offered that, for at least a moment? Or had he merely wanted the same thing as the noble gentlemen of Hannah's town?

"Come now," one had whispered. "It's not as if you're some young virgin."

She shuddered at the memory of Malcolm's best friend, Jacob, a deacon in their church. His hands, much smaller than Daniel Aldman's, but more active, were all over her at once. She slapped him and ran back to her room, his cries of "Evil temptress!" still ringing in her ears.

That was when she'd roused herself and formed a plan to leave. If she'd remained, she would be unable to stop the men who thought she was fair game.

So why hadn't she just left? Why had she decided she had to have it all, a new, unsullied name, a chance at happiness, or even love?

She should have never gone to Pittsburgh. She should have never lied about her past. Despite all that had been done to hurt her, it didn't excuse her from lashing out and hurting others in return.

An image of Amelia surfaced in her mind, a gold chrysanthemum forever tucked behind one ear. Amelia, who loved her great-aunt, her doll, and her new kitten, still needed most a mother in her life.

Could she have filled that void somehow? Could she have been a mother after all?

Faye Barlow came in without knocking, her face partly hidden by another load of mending.

"We could do all right together," she said, her voice muffled by the clothes. "Why don't you stay here?"

"Oh, I don't think the Aldmans would like that," Hannah replied.

"What difference does that make to you? Besides, that Daniel fancies you hisself." Faye tucked a battered silver cross and its tarnished chain inside her dress.

"What gives you such a ludicrous idea?" Hannah snapped.

"He's been working on the fire brigade, but he's managed to come by and check on you more than once this week."

"Maybe he's afraid I'll charge his brother with assault," Hannah suggested.

"Would you?" Faye sat beside her in the chair and pulled a threaded needle from her apron.

Hannah sighed. "Of course not. Not after what I did."

Faye shook her head and raised a hand, palm outward. "I don't want to know. You're a big help here, and to this old woman, that's what really matters. And you've got a good head on your shoulders, since you don't run after the men. 'Course, if they figured you were here, they'd prob'ly be hammerin' my doors down. Even so, I wish you would stay. You have anywhere particular picked out to go?"

Hannah shook her head. "Just somewhere. Somewhere new. I'll have to see how far I can get on that ticket Mr. Aldman brought me. But I appreciate your offer. It wouldn't be right for me to stay."

Faye shrugged. "Suit yourself. But you come back here anytime."

Both women looked up sharply at the sound of something breaking.

"What the blazes?" Faye put down her sewing, and Hannah followed her into the small kitchen.

Rosalind was unceremoniously dumping out the contents of Faye's flour crock. The top had fallen to the floor and shattered.

"Unless you're bakin' me a cake, young lady, you get out of there right now!" the thin woman scolded.

Her daughter kept pawing through the flour, stirring up pale clouds. "Where'd you put the money, Ma? I know you used to hide it here." Her voice shook with desperation.

Faye grasped one of her hands. "I told you, I won't give you anymore. You'd just use it for drink."

"It ain't for that. I'm hungry," Rosalind whined. She dusted her hands on a worn black skirt that showed far too much ankle.

"Then I'll feed you," said Faye. She turned to take rolls out of the bread box, which she placed on the table along with the butter and a pot of jam.

Hannah stooped to pick up some of the larger shards of crockery.

Rosalind looked sour, but she smeared butter on a roll before her gray eyes lit on Hannah. "Hmmph. How the mighty have fallen!" The sour look turned to a smirk.

A puff of flour rose as Hannah slapped her hand onto the table. "Did Daniel tell you, then?" She found herself hoping Rosalind would deny it. She didn't want him under the influence of this fallen creature.

"Dan Aldman? Hardly. He might buy a lady a drink now and again, but he's no talker."

"Then how did you know?"

Faye ignored the two of them and started sweeping up the broken crockery and flour.

Rosalind smoothed her red hair with the smug expression of a cat washing its paws. "Let's just say not many telegrams arrive here that I'm unaware of. Is it really true you came to Peshtigo using a false name?"

"I expect you understand there are times a woman does what she must to survive." Why was she explaining to this prostitute at all?

"That's how it is sometimes. Ma and Pa here, they don't realize that." Rosalind bit into a roll and chewed with all the manners of a cow. "I told you, we're not so different after all."

"I think we are," Hannah told her. "I haven't given up. Not yet."

Rosalind used her fingers to swipe at the crumbs on her round cheeks. "That's simple foolishness. You're a woman, ain't you? There's nothing you can do. Nothing anybody can except give up and let life have at you like a drunken logger. You drink yourself into the right attitude, you might even like it some."

Rosalind winked crudely, and Hannah spun on her heel and stalked off to her room. She might have been forced into making some hard choices, but she wasn't about to stand and be insulted by a two-bit adventuress who'd steal from her own mother.

Still fuming, she settled on the bed. Taking up her needle, she stabbed at a torn shirt from the mending pile. With each stitch, she struck at Rosalind's advice: . . . *give up and let life have at you like a drunken logger.* Hannah swore that she would never sink so low. Until she lay cold in her grave, she would *never* give up fighting. Somehow, she'd repair the damage her ex-husband's lies had done.

CHAPTER TEN

By three o'clock Hannah's eyes burned from the combination of the close work and the ashes on the wind. After hours of mending, her fingers, too, rebelled, cramping so badly, she had to rest. She decided to take a stretch on the front porch and try to find a breath of fresher air.

"Mercy!" shouted a high-pitched voice from the empty lot across the street.

Before Hannah could react, Amelia began running toward her, her blond hair flying. Tucked beneath Amelia's arm, her doll flapped wildly. Despite the awkwardness, Hannah couldn't help herself. She grinned widely and scooped the little girl into her arms.

"I came to say good-bye," Amelia panted into her upswept hair. "Papa said I shouldn't, but I knew you'd want me to."

Hannah kissed her cheek. "I am always glad to see you. How is Spice?"

"Uncle John let me take her home. He said a little kitten

would be safer here in town. Why don't you come back to Aunt Lucinda's? You can wait there for your boat."

Hannah took Amelia by the hand, and the two of them sat on Hank's bench on the front porch.

"I've had a disagreement with your family." Hannah took a deep breath and hoped she might choose the right words. "It would be best if we don't see each other anymore."

"But why? Why would they be mad at you?" Amelia squeezed her hand.

"I made a terrible mistake, Amelia. I told them a lie."

The child nodded gravely. "I did that once too. Aunt Lucinda sent me to my room. They didn't even tell me where you were."

"Then how did you find me?" Hannah asked.

"My friend Camille lives next door. Not much gets by her. When she told me a pretty lady with brown hair was staying here, I thought it might be you. So I waited a long time to see if I was right. You won't tell Aunt Lucinda I came, will you?"

"Of course not, if you promise you won't come back. I'll be leaving in a day or two, and you don't have permission. As much as I love seeing you, your family wouldn't like you to come here."

Amelia slipped into her arms again. "I wish you'd stay, Mercy. Why can't you just tell them you're sorry? They'll forget about that fib in a day or two. They forgot all about the one I told."

Dear Lord, it would break her heart to leave this child. Hannah squeezed her tightly, realizing this would be her last good-bye.

"Oh, Amelia. I *am* sorry, but someday you'll understand," she explained. "Some lies hurt so badly, you remember all your life."

* * *

Daniel sat beside the bar with his first drink of the evening, a pungent ginger beer. From his stool he saw the stranger enter, a dark-haired man with a neatly trimmed black beard. He started talking to a shanty boy called Petey. The man looked too well turned out for this crowd, with his gray suit and an authoritative voice, though Daniel couldn't make out what he was saying. He would have dismissed the stranger as a traveling businessman, but Petey pointed a finger across the bar toward him.

The stranger limped in his direction and stood beside the bar. "Good evening, Mr. Aldman. I wonder if I might have a word with you."

Daniel shrugged. "We're not buying more equipment for the farm right now. Be a waste to lose it in one of these brushfires. Other than that, you're more than welcome to sit down."

He did, and Daniel noticed streaks of gray at the man's temples. The women probably thought he looked distinguished, and his smug look said he knew it too.

"My name is Malcolm Shelton," he began, "*Captain* Malcolm Shelton, and I'm looking for a lady."

"Ain't we all?" the bartender interrupted. "But around here, we usually just settle for a strumpet. I know a likely prospect if you're lookin' for an introduction."

Malcolm ordered whiskey and ignored the other offer. When the bartender moved away, the bearded man continued. "I hear you met a woman calling herself Mercy Wilder."

Daniel sipped his beer. His heart was pounding in his chest. The man called himself Shelton. Did that mean this was Hannah's former husband? What would he want with her?

"I know of her," he admitted. Shelton doubtless knew that much already. "Why are you looking for her?"

"I intend to take her home, where she belongs." When Malcolm leaned forward to slap a coin onto the bar, his jacket flapped open, revealing a revolver strapped around his waist. The bartender left a glass of amber liquid in place of the coin. As soon as he receded, Shelton continued speaking. "I understand some money changed hands with a gentleman by the name of Harlan. You would, of course, be compensated for your loss."

"Let's suppose the lady didn't want to go with you," said Daniel. He already hated this man—the way he threw around his former rank, the way he threw around his money. "Let's suppose she said you had no claim to her."

"She's a divorced woman," Malcolm hissed, "a convicted adulteress! Do you really want another man's refuse?"

Daniel felt his fists clench. He was well known here, well liked. He always paid his bills. If he mashed Malcolm Shelton into sawdust, no one would bat an eye. He'd enjoy it, he believed. He'd never hit an officer before. He wouldn't likely get the chance though, not if Shelton managed to get out that Colt.

Even so, he stood, knocking his chair to the floor, and every man and the few women there turned to stare at him. Daniel Aldman never fought. His size alone prevented even drunken shanty boys from issuing a challenge.

"I have no idea where Mercy Wilder might have gone, Shelton," he told the smaller man. Out of the corner of his eye he saw Rosalind slip in beside the stranger.

Her voice was slick and wheedling. "Did I hear you say your name was Shelton? Funny, I believe I have a friend called by that name. How about you buy me a few drinks and we'll discuss it?"

* * *

Without finishing his beer, Daniel left the saloon.

"What'd he do to rile you?" Petey asked him.

Another red-shirted logger added, "You just give the word and we'll give him something to remember us by."

"Leave him be, boys. He's not worth scabbing your knuckles." Neither did he want one of his friends to be shot, but Daniel knew they wouldn't listen to that reason.

He ignored their invitations to have a mug and talk it over. A week ago he might have done that, and one mug would have become six. But not now, not when Hannah had taken over all his thoughts.

Though it was after ten o'clock, he pounded on the Barlows' door. Hank answered, a drink in his own hand. "Faye's asleep, but come inside. I'd be glad to have some comp'ny for a smile."

"I don't need a drink," Daniel told him as he stepped inside. "I need to see Miss Shelton. I need to see her now."

Hank laughed loudly. "I said you were sweet on her. But won't John holler loud enough to wake snakes when he hears?"

"Just see he doesn't hear it from you."

"He won't. She's asleep, most likely. Want me to go rap on her door?"

Daniel brushed past the old man and found her room, then pounded until the door opened a crack.

"I need to see you, Hannah."

"You have liquor on your breath." She sounded groggy, but no less rigid than before.

"Let me in. I won't attack you."

She opened the door a little more, enough for him to see her hair was tangled. "What? What's happened, Daniel? Are the fires coming close?"

"Could be, but it's something else." He lowered his voice. "I met Malcolm tonight."

She pulled him inside the room and shut the door to the sound of Hank's sniggers.

She turned up the lamp, and in its light he could see her fingers shaking. "My God! How has he found me?"

"I don't know that, but he said he wants to take you back. Right now he's waving money under Rosalind's nose."

"Dear Lord." She collapsed onto the bed and put her head into her hands. "Then he'll be here any minute. He'll surely kill me now!"

"Why? Why would he do that? You said he divorced you and stole your inheritance. What possible reason could he have to come here, with all the danger from the fires? Hannah, tell the truth. What did you take from him?"

When she looked up, the lamplight glistened off a tear trail on her cheek. "My life. I simply took my life."

"What kind of idiotic talk is that? You're no more dead than I am."

"That's not what people think. You see, I didn't want to risk that anyone would interfere with the new future I had planned. They'd made it impossible to live in Shelton Creek. The only chance I had at making money—" She shook her head. "I couldn't be a Rosalind. From the way they treated me, one would think they would be happy if I'd disappear. But it wouldn't be enough. There'd still be gossip, and it might have followed me to Pittsburgh. I couldn't take that chance."

The chair creaked under Daniel's weight as he sat down. "So you made people think you'd died? But how?"

Tears still leaked out beneath her lowered eyelids. "I broke in a window, and I splattered blood I'd taken from a butcher. I remember"—her voice hitched, but she suppressed a sob—"I remember hoping they would think Malcolm had killed me. He took *everything* from me. He even stole my father's farm!"

"God help you," Daniel whispered.

She shook her head. "Rosalind was right. I'm no better than she is. Or perhaps I'm worse. I tried to ruin Malcolm. My heart burned with hate. My soul will burn, too, for all the sins I've committed."

He reached out for her hand. "I was in Vicksburg, Hannah. We besieged that city for six weeks. When it ended, we could see— Those people ate their horses. Some ate their dogs, even. Men and women, even little children, dug into those hills like prairie dogs. Folks do what they have to to survive."

He could almost hear the mortar guns blasting away at those poor people. After it was over, he'd helped amputate so many limbs. He recalled a boy, about Amelia's age. They'd taken both his legs. But those people had been content to be alive, no matter what the cost. "Malcolm and that town besieged you too, the way I figure. So you did something desperate to survive. Like eating horse, it wasn't pretty, but you made it, and that's all that matters now. You can't let your ex-husband take you back. If you wrecked his name, he had to have it coming. Hell, *I* only just met him, and I'd already like to fix his flint."

"Of course I don't want to go with Malcolm. I came this far to escape him. But Rosalind will surely tell him where I'm staying."

"You're right, and he's carrying a gun. That's why you'll have to be gone by the time he gets here. Put your things together quick. I'm going to get you to that steamer. I'll borrow my aunt's gig and drive you all the way into Marinette, and you can catch it there."

This time she reached out and took his hand. "But it's so late, and there might be fires nearby. Oh, Daniel, why ever would you risk your life for me?"

He shrugged. "Maybe because I understand the things you've done. I've done some pretty wretched things myself."

She leapt up and started stuffing things into her bags. "And that makes a fellow sinner your responsibility?"

He chuckled darkly. "Maybe I just like your kind of boisterous behavior."

He stepped out of her room and warned her through the doorway, "You'd better hurry with that packing. We might not have much time."

Hank was still there, waiting.

"You two sneaking off?" the old man asked. "Lord bless you, then!"

Sensing that any explanation would be useless, Daniel closed the door and nodded. He waited in the kitchen while she dressed. Within minutes she was ready, and they said a quick good-bye to Hank. But it wasn't quick enough.

Malcolm stood waiting next to Daniel's horse. Hannah screamed when she caught sight of her former husband, who stood with his gun drawn.

"I see you know the slut better than you say," the bearded man said. "Hannah, I must commend you. I never gave you credit for such nerve. You cannot imagine the difficulties you have caused me."

"I'd like to," Hannah told him, her heart hammering in fear, "but I doubt it could compare to the pain you brought me."

Daniel interceded. "Sounds about like you got what was coming, Shelton. Just cut your losses now and call it even."

"So you can take pleasure from my former wife?" Malcolm laughed. "You don't even know she's barren. Take her, and you'll never know the joy a son can bring."

"Men marry more than wombs. They marry women. Pity you didn't understand that," Daniel said. "Near as I can tell, you drove a fine one to do some awful things. A man like you doesn't deserve a woman like Hannah."

"He's quite taken with you, darling," Malcolm sneered. "We'll see if he still wants you when I'm through with you.

You're coming home. I need to prove you're still alive and the only crime committed was one against my name.''

"I won't go anywhere with you! You're a lying thief!'' Hannah shouted.

Malcolm cocked the pistol and pointed it toward Daniel. "I need you alive, but I don't need your lover. In fact, I think he might try to interfere. You know how I detest inconveniences.''

She darted in front of the revolver. "No! Don't shoot him! I swear I'll go with you!''

"You must promise, Hannah, that you'll be a good girl. No crying, no scenes on the way back. As for my part, I'll release you once my name is cleared. You might even persuade me to drop any charges. You may be barren, but you still have other charms.''

Daniel started to protest, but Hannah interrupted. "No. Don't try anything. Malcolm means it when he says he'll kill you.''

"Not if I kill him first,'' Daniel muttered, but perversely, an image flickered through his mind like summer lightning. That bloody bayonet. The final rebel he had killed.

Hannah backed away and joined her former husband, who hoisted her onto Daniel's horse.

"You don't mind if she borrows him, do you?'' Malcolm asked. "We'll turn him loose after a bit, to give you long enough to consider what might happen if you follow. The horse will find his way back home.''

He led Chance toward where the gray he'd bought was tied and waiting, and the two of them rode off into the night.

In the distance, fires glowed, and smoke dimmed the starshine. Even the waning moon's light was diminished by the distant infernos nearly surrounding Peshtigo.

"I'll be damned if I burn for you," said Malcolm. "Fortunately, I've already attended to our lodgings."

They rode down side streets Hannah had never seen before, then stopped. With his Colt, Malcolm gestured for her to dismount. When she did, he slid off his horse, then swatted Chance on the backside. The horse's hoofbeats receded quickly.

Hauling Hannah by the wrist, he took her toward a dilapidated stable. Near its door, a boy dozed by a lantern.

"Not a word, or I'll make the gossip back home all too true." His whiskers brushed her ear and made her flinch. More loudly, he spoke to wake the boy. "Cool him down before you put him in a stall tonight."

The lad roused himself to catch a coin and then took the gray's reins. "You can trust me, sir. Thank you."

"Remember, you haven't seen a thing tonight. I'd be aggravated if we were disturbed." Malcolm's voice flowed sweet as sorghum, as if he'd planned only one of his seamy rendezvous.

"I take your meaning, sir. Don't worry. Ma has a strict rule. No jealous beaus allowed. They never pay when they break in the doors."

Malcolm urged her into a tiny cottage behind the stable. Once inside, he turned up the lamp. She looked around and shuddered. A rickety washstand stood in one corner, and beside it a poorly finished dresser peeled. A bed took up most of the remaining room.

Her former husband latched the door, then turned to gaze at Hannah intently. Her stomach roiled with nausea as she guessed the meaning of his stare.

He took one step toward her. "It's time for our reunion, Hannah. Now come and show me what I've missed."

She backed away, her legs bumping against a soiled mattress. "Don't you have a wife now?"

"She's not here, and I want you. You're far more beautiful than Melissa, and I remember well your passion. Come, and I'll be sure to keep you out of prison. Otherwise, I'm certain I could persuade my good friend, Judge Clarke, to make an example of you for your fraud."

"Just like you persuaded him to take everything from me?" Hannah shook her head. "No. I told you I'd go back, but I'd rather go to jail than bed you."

He slipped off his coat and laid down the revolver. She edged closer to the door.

He grabbed her arm and flung her to the bed. "You misunderstand. I'm not *asking* anything."

She couldn't let him do this! Of all the wrongs she'd suffered, she knew this she could not bear. Maybe if she could keep him talking, she could somehow get away.

"You threw aside your mistress too. What about that precious son she gave you? Did you leave him as well?" she asked.

He looked insulted. "Of course, Gerald will be well provided for. But I couldn't very well marry Marcelia. The woman was a mistress. Totally unacceptable."

"Your standards are so different for yourself." She glanced once toward the gun; then he leapt on her.

She tried to scream, but he clapped his hand across her mouth. Crushing his body against hers, he spoke into her ear. "Your struggles only make you more entertaining. I've imagined for so long what it would be like to take you this way. See how proud you are now, Hannah! Through everything, you've held your head up, but I swear, I *will* break you. Next time you try to put on airs, I want you to remember what I'm doing!"

He grabbed the neckline of her dress and tore it to her waist. When she fought, he slapped her hard until she lay still, dazed with terror. He pulled out a pocketknife and cut through her underclothing, then pulled back the pieces to expose her chest.

"No, Malcolm," she groaned. "You mustn't. Please, no—"

He silenced her protests with slobbering kisses. She thought she would vomit as he explored her mouth and then her ear with his questing tongue. All the while, his hands squeezed her breasts and pinched her nipples, far too hard for any lover's touch. Tears ran down her face to mingle with the moisture from his mouth. He began to pull her skirt up, then abruptly stopped to rip off his shoes and pants.

The pants around his ankles, Hannah saw her chance. Leaping from the bed, she grabbed the Colt revolver and landed on her knees. He jerked forward awkwardly, then stopped, seeing the gun's barrel was leveled at his chest.

"Get out!" she commanded as she stood. "Leave the shoes and trousers, and get out of here before I shoot."

"Hannah . . . surely, you can't mean to turn me out like this. Please, I'm sorry if I was a little rough."

"If you don't leave, I will shoot you. A man who would do this to a woman surely deserves to die."

"You don't even know how to use a gun." He waddled toward her, the pants hindering his movement.

The revolver clicked as she cocked it. "I wouldn't be so sure. You never did give me credit for the things my father taught me. Now, take the jacket and get out!"

A shout from outside distracted both of them a moment before a kick smashed open the door. Daniel Aldman and a pair of his lumberjack friends stood there with clubs made of old wood.

Taking in the situation, Petey laughed. "Daniel, it don't look like she needs our help after all."

With one hand Hannah pulled together the tattered remnants of the top part of her dress.

Daniel's eyes narrowed. "It looks like this man needs a lesson on how to treat a lady."

Malcolm stammered. "She—she seduced me! The woman's nothing but a slut."

Daniel punched him so hard, he flew backward onto

the floor. Malcolm grabbed his nose, and blood oozed between his fingers.

"Now, do what I said and leave here," Hannah told him. "But leave the shoes and trousers."

"Hannah, I—" Malcolm began to say. Dark rivulets dripped down his hand.

"I believe I have three witnesses who would offer testimony if this gun were to accidentally discharge."

The loggers nodded and Daniel grinned, amused.

"Make sure he leaves town," Daniel told his two friends.

"I'm not through with you!" Malcolm swore, but he did as Hannah bade him. The shanty boys followed, hooting catcalls and humiliating taunts.

Daniel closed the door and turned to Hannah. "I'm sorry it took so long to find you. Did he—"

She shook her head. "He tried, but as you see, I took his gun."

He took the Colt away from Hannah and set it down, then went to the washstand. There, he wet a small towel and brought it back to wash her face.

The two of them sat on the bed, where she trembled while he cleaned her. She flinched as the cloth touched her swollen cheekbone.

"He hit you, didn't he?"

She nodded.

"I should have beaten him to hell while I had the chance," Daniel said.

"Why?" she asked. "Why do that for me? I'm nothing to you, Daniel, nothing but a woman who tried to trick your brother."

"Oh, you're something to me," he said quietly.

"What am I?" she asked.

"I think you just might be my second chance." He bent his head to kiss her softly and thanked a God he'd long ignored when she began to kiss him back.

CHAPTER ELEVEN

Daniel held her and gently pulled her close. Their kiss continued, warm and sweet, and gradually, he felt her quaking cease, as if their contact were drawing out the poison of Malcolm's attack.

Finally, he pressed his lips lightly to her forehead. She leaned her cheek against his shoulder.

"I want to go back to the Barlows. Please take me to my room there," Hannah whispered.

He nodded, then pulled a threadbare blanket from the bed and helped her drape it over her shoulders. "I want you to stay in Peshtigo."

She smiled, but her blue eyes brimmed with tears. "I'm beginning to believe I misjudged you when we met. But there's no future for us, Daniel. Think about your family's feelings."

"Amelia loves you. That could be enough."

Hannah shook her head and rose. He tried to take her arm to help her, but she pulled away. "You can't base love on pity. That would never work. You think of me as something fragile to protect."

He laughed loudly. "After watching you point that revolver? Why, I've known loggers, drunkards, and notorious brawlers who would cross the street if they saw you coming down the sidewalk! I don't pity you. I admire you, Hannah Shelton, and if you'd let me get to know you better, I think that admiration could grow into something more."

"Please, just take me back. I don't have the strength to talk about this tonight."

Reluctantly, he nodded. "Don't answer now. Just think about it while you rest."

"I promise that I will," she said.

He picked up the Colt and walked her to the stable, where the boy was holding Chance. Daniel clapped him on the back.

"Thanks, Sid, and don't worry about the door. I'll be back to fix it later, like I told you." Then, to Hannah, he explained. "I was damned lucky to find my horse milling around in the street before some rowdy found it in his heart to give him a new home. Here, let me help you up."

For the second time that night, Hannah mounted the tall chestnut. Instead of adding his weight, Daniel led her through the streets.

When they reached the house, he roused the Barlows and explained to them that while they'd been walking, a hooligan had tried to assault Hannah in the street. Faye, with more kindness than Daniel had ever imagined she possessed, led Hannah away to bed.

"More to it, ain't there?" Hank asked. "I heard a commotion right after you went out. When I peeked past the curtain, I saw a stranger with a gun. By the time I could think of what t'do, he'd took her, and off you run."

"So what did you do then?" asked Daniel.

"Hell, I had another drink. What use is a one-armed man against that sorta scoundrel?"

Daniel grimaced, thinking of a dozen things he could have done to help. If he'd had a few more drinks before he had met Malcolm, would he have been as useless? Hank Barlow surely wouldn't keep Hannah from harm if her ex-husband returned.

"He might come back for her. You better let me sleep here too. I took his gun, and if he tries to get in, I intend to plug him right between the eyes." Daniel tried not to think of what that might cost him, of the nightmares he still had of the last man he had killed. He'd gotten a gut full of bloodshed, and, like now, the cause had seemed right at the time.

"I'll scrounge you up a blanket and a pillow. You sure you won't have a little nip to calm your nerves?"

"I'm sure," he answered, and he thought, *Surer than I've been in far too long.*

Daniel rolled, and the wretched blanket slid off his broad shoulder. The clock chimed three, and he regretted his decision not to have a drink. Maybe that would have softened the wooden floor a mite. Maybe it would have kept him from jumping at the cat that yowled its passion from a nearby alleyway.

Tonight, without the defense of a soft bed or the haze of alcohol, he couldn't stop remembering. Usually, he could shove back the boy's face, but tonight the memory only circled around, then came back again like a damned buzzard.

It had happened fairly early in the war, when the patriotic strains of Northern bands still stirred the fire in his soul. He'd been eighteen then, and mad as hell when the rebs had fired on Fort Sumter. To his mother and John, the war seemed so far off, so remote from a Wisconsin farm, but to Daniel it sounded like the future calling him. A future filled with heroism: the defense of the great Union, freedom for the slaves. About the only book outside the Bible he'd read at the time had been *Uncle Tom's Cabin*. No, that slavery business wasn't right at all, and he intended to wear a blue uniform and try and set things right.

He'd been a child then, he realized, a big child playing man, like so many volunteers. But for his size, he could move as quietly as a deer, a skill he'd learned through his love of hunting as a boy. When the lieutenant wanted somebody to sneak through the woods and kill a sentry, Daniel had been proud to do his part.

He'd been damned good at it too. He knew to stay downwind from the horses, so they wouldn't scent him. He could slip in, knife a dozing Johnny Reb, and be back to his unit before the fellow reached the Pearly Gates. The other soldiers took to calling Daniel St. Peter, for the men he sent that way. Like a fool, he'd been proud of that name.

Until it all went wrong. He'd been sent ahead to give warning of the enemy's approach, when he nearly ran into the rebel picket. Like Daniel, the other boy had been alone. But unlike him, the rebel lurched with panic and tripped over his big feet, trying to make for the cover of a fallen tree. Daniel would have preferred to use his knife, but the rifle was his only chance. Lifting it, he shot the reb midfall.

The boy jerked sideways, stifling a cry of pain as blood erupted from his shoulder. His weapon dropped beyond his reach, in the lee of a fallen pine. Daniel stared, and the unarmed reb stared back, wild-eyed. He had hazel eyes, Daniel recalled, sweaty, dark blond hair. He'd been so young, maybe sixteen, and scared to die.

"Please, please, no . . ." the boy moaned. Despite the heat, his teeth were chattering.

Shoot again, and fast, Daniel's mind screamed, but his

hands would not obey. For the first time since the killing started, Daniel realized it could just as easily be him. As agony and terror contorted the boy's face, Daniel knew the damage his stealthy blade had done those past few months.

St. Peter, he decided, was a poor nickname for the devil's tool. He lowered the rifle from his shoulder and wondered how he would ever lift it again.

Stupidly, he didn't even turn at the tramp of footsteps through the leaves, but he recognized Lieutenant Perkins's shout.

"Jesus, boy. Don't be an idiot. Kill him, and then run. They'll have heard that shot for sure."

Daniel shook his head. "No, you go on ahead."

Lieutenant Perkins, only a few years older, gave him a hard shove. "I'm not leaving you here, boy. Now, bayonet him and let's go!"

"He'll bleed to death if we just leave him," Daniel said, ignoring the order.

Perkins swung around the stock of his rifle and cracked Daniel on the jaw. Taken by surprise, the younger man fell hard. He scrabbled to his feet, mad enough to fight.

Perkins met him with the tip of his own bayonet. "I said, run him through. You don't do this, you'll never be worth a damn again."

Drawing a deep breath, Daniel turned back toward the reb. He felt Perkins's weapon prod him, cut right through his jacket. He stared down at the rebel. The boy looked him in the eye.

And nodded just before he closed his eyes for the last time.

Daniel made his first cut count, deep and steady, to the heart. And then he turned and ran away with Perkins, his steel dripping blood.

Daniel grabbed at the blanket and thought about the steel he'd seen that night, the steel in Hannah's pale blue eyes. He would never forget the image of her holding that gun on her ex-husband, ordering him to leave without his shoes or pants. Most women would have been too humiliated to do anything. What she'd once told his aunt Lucinda had proved true: *I'm stronger than you'd guess.* Yet there was something soft in her as well, though perhaps more carefully hidden. He'd seen it when she spoke of horses and when she'd lectured him about his daughter.

Somewhere in the small house, a door creaked. Daniel reached for the gun but otherwise lay still. He listened to the progress of soft footfalls on the wooden floor. Every muscle in his body tensed taut as a bowstring and quivered in anticipation of release.

"Daniel?" The syllables were quiet yet unmistakable. If he lived a hundred years, he knew he'd always recognize her voice.

"You all right?" he asked.

The padding feet grew nearer, and he saw her dim shape settle in a nearby sofa. "I couldn't sleep. I kept hearing Malcolm's voice, saying all those horrid things," said Hannah. "And I knew you were still here. Faye told me before she went to bed. I doubted you'd get much rest, so I thought I'd go ahead and thank you for giving up a good night's sleep."

He raised his aching body and joined her on the sagging couch. "I started off on this, but it's worse than the floor. You don't need to thank me for the night's sleep though. It's Saturday, after all. I would have probably spent it in some heathenish pursuit."

She chuckled quietly. "You're not so very evil, Daniel Aldman. You tried to warn me about Malcolm. Then you came and rescued me."

"*Almost* rescued you. You'd already taken matters into your own hands."

"But you came. Even though I'd given you and everyone

in your family ample reason to turn your backs on me. John would have let Malcolm take me, and gladly.''

"I'm not my brother." He reached out and found her hand. Very gently, he massaged the fingertips. Surprise warmed him when she didn't pull away.

"Thank you," she said, and gave his hand a little squeeze. It sent electric shivers up his spine. "Thank you for coming after me. I never thought that anyone would care again."

Nervous as a schoolboy, he laced those delicate fingers inside his own, callused and thick. He raised her hand to his lips and softly kissed it.

She made a sound low in her throat. He would have sworn it was a murmur of pleasure.

"You deserve someone to care for you, always. You deserve someone to make up for what Malcolm did to you."

He felt her lean close then, so the light cotton of her nightgown brushed against his arm. That's all there was, he realized, just that thin fabric between him and those slender curves. Nothing else at all. The thought made his pulse quicken as he reached to touch her face. To turn her head, to guide it to the right position for another kiss.

This time, no one interrupted to warn of an impending fire. This time, they would not have noticed if they burned.

Their mouths joined, and he allowed his tongue to tease her lips, to part them, to explore the warmth and sweetness of her. Mindful of her experience tonight with Malcolm, he kept his kisses long and gentle and almost painfully slow. While one hand cupped her cheek, the other still laced with her fingers, meshing to the rhythm of their bodies' fervent hopes.

His lips brushed aside her loose hair, then traveled to her elegant white neck. He kissed along its length, from the tender earlobe all the way to an exquisite shoulder. A shoulder bared, he realized, as the nightgown's fabric had slipped over its curve. Her breath came quickly as his hands wandered, one to hold her narrow waist, the fingers of the other to brush that spot where cotton angled above the fullness of a breast.

His index finger traced the tip, then circled. Her breath came louder now.

Daniel tested the neckline of her gown, then slipped it downward farther. She moaned softly as his moist kisses reached her breast. His mouth enveloped flesh and tasted. His tongue flicked across the nipple, while a hand reached to cup her other breast.

He sucked gently, sweetly, and beneath his mouth and hands he felt her body melt, all resistance ebbing into that ageless understanding that lay between the sexes. His own want pushed hard against the fabric of his pants, and he wished desperately to free it. But some instinct told him he must move slowly, very slowly, so as not to frighten her. He stroked her thigh through the cotton, then fumbled with a button on her gown.

With a gasp she pulled away. "I'm not what Malcolm said. I'm no slut."

"Of course you're not. He said that only to excuse himself." He filled his mouth with the delicious sweetness of her firm white breast.

She pressed one palm strongly against his shoulder, insistently enough that he pulled away. "No," she sighed. "This isn't right. I'm leaving Monday if the steamer runs. I'd try tomorrow if it weren't the Sabbath."

"I don't want you to leave."

"We're not children, Daniel. We both know this can't work. Malcolm knows I'm here now, and even if he didn't, your family hates me. People would hear things. There'd be talk."

"Talk," he muttered angrily. "I don't care what people say."

"You would." Her voice was gentle. "At first you'd hear

a few jokes, half whispered and only loud enough for you to catch your name. Then someone would get angry. Maybe because your horse stepped on his foot. He'd say something ugly about me, and you'd hit him. On and on it would go, until your little girl came home crying because the other children called her whore's whelp and her aunt Lucinda wouldn't see her anymore. And finally, you'd end up hating me.''

He reached for her again. Though she let him pull her closer, her body grew rigid. Daniel whispered, ''You might act proud sometimes, but you don't really think you're worth much, do you?''

Her tears soaked through his shirt. Their warm dampness felt as soothing as a balm. ''I don't think I'm worth *that*,'' Hannah told him, ''because I know what gossip does.''

''And I know what *this* does.'' He kissed her once again, but briefly. ''The question is, which one will you give in to?''

CHAPTER TWELVE

Hannah knew she should turn and flee into her room, but something held her. Her mind darted, hummingbird swift, back to another parting long ago.

Robert's kisses had not been so expert, nor his caresses quite so arousing. Still, their breath came faster as they sparked inside the confines of his father's buggy.

She'd pulled away and straightened her buttons, which had gone somewhat askew. "No, Robert, we can't," she told him.

"But we're betrothed, and tomorrow I'll be leaving." His blue eyes brimmed with desire, and his hands stroked the fabric of her sleeve. "Don't you love me, Hannah?"

As she wound her hair into the chignon it had escaped, she remembered all her father's warnings. "You know I do," she told him, though she was far from certain of these strange new feelings, "but we have to be strong. Imagine the disgrace if a child came of this before we're wed. You might not be near enough to set things right. Not in time, at least."

He groaned in frustration. "I—I think if we were careful . . ." But he, too, sounded unsure now.

Hannah kissed him chastely. "Just remember, I'll be waiting. I'll be here for you when you come home."

Except he hadn't. God, how she wished she had succumbed, so at least she could have had that to remember!

After Malcolm married her, sometimes she lay guilty in their marriage bed. She closed her eyes while Malcolm took her and pretended her sweet Robert had come home.

Would she spend her life regretting her chastity tonight? Would she imagine, years from now, all she and Daniel hadn't done? This time there was no question of a child or a ruined reputation; the former was an empty dream, the latter lost already.

Still, she hesitated, wondering if Daniel saw her only as an easy conquest, another fallen woman for a strange Saturday spree.

His lips, when they met hers once more, dissolved her indecision, made her body ache with need and her heart long to draw close to his, if only for a little while. If she could but take one thing with her from Peshtigo, why could it not be a memory of passion?

He fingered her hair as gently as if he stroked a newborn kitten, then ran his hands through the long waves. After a moment, as if he sensed her musings and echoed each one, his kisses fell upon her like spring rain.

All her conscious thought narrowed to the trail his mouth blazed to her neck, her chest, her breasts. His hands, as they slid along her sides and hips, drew from her a long, sighed "Daniel."

His palms continued moving down along her body, continued until they molded the contour of her slender legs, until they found the cotton nightgown's hem. Then, reaching beneath it, he stroked her, unimpeded by the cloth. Soon he touched her where no man save one had ever touched before. But how different now, with this man! How gentle, how unselfish.

Her neck arched backward as his fingertips caressed moist heat. Tiny dots of light swarmed in her vision, then slowly merged into one white-hot sphere so intense, she could not long contain it. She cried out softly as long-forgotten muscles deep within her clenched and then dissolved in ecstasy.

"Hannah, stay with me," he whispered. "Promise me you won't leave Peshtigo."

She kissed him softly, wishing that he hadn't asked the only thing she could not give him. She'd thought he understood.

"Please, don't ruin this," she told him, recovering her voice. "We have now. This moment. Can't that be enough?"

Too abruptly, he moved away from her. "You'd do this and still go?" In the darkness, his voice iced over.

Guilt sparked in her, fueled by Malcolm's accusation. "I thought only that maybe we need each other . . . if only just this once. We *do* need, Daniel. Both of us."

She forced herself to reach out for him. But when her hand touched his shoulder, she might as well have been touching cold steel.

"This isn't like that, Hannah. It isn't about one single night before you go. You make me feel in here." He grabbed her hand and laid it on his chest. "And I haven't—not since Mary. Damnation, woman. Can't you see I care for you? I have almost from the first time we met. If I were just looking to scratch an itch of that sort, I'd go buy myself an hour with Rosalind or someone like her."

Tears burned in Hannah's eyes. She might offer only now, but he spoke as though tonight alone meant nothing. How could he know the chasm she had spanned, the old ghosts she'd resurrected, to offer even that? Damn him for denying her whatever comfort they could have taken from each other. Damn him for ruining what could have been a precious memory.

She took a deep breath before speaking. "If one night together would mean no more than a whore's time, then to hell with you, Daniel Aldman! I don't need you at all!"

Tears streaming down her cheeks, Hannah fled to her room and slammed the door on their desire.

By the time Daniel woke, Faye was up already. She stood cradling a cup of coffee and staring out a filmy window toward the west.

"Mornin'," she told him.

He wondered how she knew he was conscious. After spending the night tossing on the hard floor, he barely felt alive, much less awake. For too many hours he'd regretted pulling back from Hannah, refusing an offer any sane man would have taken and enjoyed. What in hell was wrong with him? Had he suddenly turned into his brother, or had he known, as if by instinct, that he couldn't bear to have her only once?

Now his words had cost him even that chance. Though he hadn't meant to, he'd insulted her. She probably wouldn't let him within ten feet of her again.

Still cursing himself mentally, Daniel ran his fingers through his hair and joined Faye by the window.

"God almighty," he swore as he caught sight of the smoke. The cloud loomed huge and dark, except for its amber underbelly, which flickered with reflected light.

She nudged him with a sharp elbow. "Don't take the Lord's name in vain. It's Sunday, and with all that fire, we wouldn't want to get Him riled. Looks worse'n ever, don't it?"

She handed him her coffee. "Here. You look like you need this more than me."

Gratefully, he took it. "Thanks. Is Hannah up?"

"Sure she's up. She's not a lazybones like you. It's after ten o'clock."

A door creaked, and Hannah appeared, her eyes hard and remote. She'd pinned her hair in place and put on her gray dress, the same one she'd been wearing at the dock the day they met. It flattered her figure, even if the color reminded him of smoke.

"I thought I heard voices," Hannah said to Faye while her gaze avoided Daniel's. "Would you like some help with breakfast? It's the least I can do after all the trouble I've caused."

"I'll say this, you're a worker," Faye told her. "If Rosalind had a quarter your ambition, she woulda turned out fine. Come on and help me, then. Maybe some bacon fumes will even float old Hank outta the sack."

She retreated to the kitchen, but Hannah lingered for a moment, her attention drawn by the window.

Daniel didn't dare to look at her. Instead, he, too, stared at the orange glow, and fear flickered in his gut. Though the fires had hounded them for weeks, this one made him want to find Amelia and hold her close. But first he had to talk to Hannah. This might be his last chance.

"I'm pretty sore this morning," he offered lamely.

"Good." Her voice was flat.

"Been kicking myself all night."

"You should have called me. I would have put on boots and helped."

"I'm sorry, Hannah. Real sorry. I just thought—I thought when you—when you let things go on, that meant you'd changed your mind. I can see now, that was just wishful thinking. What I said to you—" He shook his head. "I never meant it like what you wanted was the same as an hour with some harlot."

She turned toward the kitchen. "I told Faye I'd help her cook."

Still, she didn't walk away. Daniel wondered if that counted for something.

"I don't like the look of this sky," he continued, wanting to fill the awkward space with words. "I ought to go help John out on the farm or maybe join up with another fire detail. But I can't leave my aunt and Amelia on their own either. Wish I could split myself three ways."

"Eat some breakfast first," said Hannah. "Whichever you decide, you need some food."

The fact that she spoke to him at all was something, he supposed. He just hoped the food would be warmer than her invitation.

In a little while they sat down to eat in silence. The griddle cakes and bacon did rouse Hank, though he appeared to suffer from last night's overindulgence. He put his hand to his forehead at the slightest clatter of fork to plate and added the occasional moan for emphasis.

Daniel finished his meal. "Thank you, ladies, for the fine breakfast."

Again his eyes strayed toward a window. Although all were shut, he imagined the odor of smoke even thicker than before.

"Just remember, the river's to the east." He pointed the direction. "If all else fails, get down to the river."

Hannah stood and followed him toward the door. "The river," she echoed. "Is there any other place?"

He sensed fear in her voice. "None better."

She nodded understanding. "Be careful, Daniel."

He turned toward her and took her hand. "I know I have no right to ask this, but please be here when I come back. Please don't go without giving me the chance to say good-bye."

Releasing her, he opened the door. There stood his brother, John, his right hand poised to knock. John's gaze traveled past him and his rumpled clothing to take in Hannah.

Daniel sucked in a startled breath and coughed on the thick air. His brother's raised hand transformed into a fist.

"I half expected to find you somewhere passed-out drunk." John's voice shook with anger. "But *this*, this disappoints me beyond measure. When I saw Chance tied in the back, I hoped there might be some other explanation."

"There *is* an explanation, John, if you aren't too pigheaded to hear it. First of all, we haven't been—"

"Leave this false woman, Daniel. She's unworthy of you."

"Just because you came into town for church doesn't give you the right to preach. Hannah and I did nothing to warrant such a fuss. We've talked, John. We both know she did wrong to lie to you, but she has reasons. If you heard them, you might be able to forgive her."

Hannah stepped forward. "I *am* sorry, John."

"So you seduce my brother to atone for what you did?"

"I haven't seduced anyone. The Barlows have been here every minute."

"And we all know what a respectable house they run," John answered sarcastically. "But I didn't come to listen to more lies. I came to fetch my brother."

"Were there fires near the farm?" Daniel asked, his anger for a moment blunted by concern.

"No, or I would never have left. I should go back, though, but I'd feel better if you stayed with Aunt Lucinda a few more days, until the worst is over."

"I was on my way there now. Do you think we'd all be better off out on the farm?"

John shook his head. "God knows which is safer. My way home may be impassable, and at least Aunt Lucinda's house is fairly close to the water."

Daniel saw the sense in that. "Even so, I hate to leave you shorthanded at the farm. If you have any flare-ups, we'll lose the house for sure."

"If God wills it, we would lose it anyway. But I'll do my

best if our aunt and your daughter are protected. Providing you can find the time to see to them." He glared once more at Hannah.

"You needn't worry, Mr. Aldman," Hannah told him. "I'll be leaving town as soon as possible."

"Don't even speak to me, you vile—" John started to say, until Daniel clapped him on the shoulder.

"Don't say something we're both going to regret. You have every right to be angry with Hannah. You don't have to forgive her. But she doesn't deserve name-calling, and if you decide to raise a hand to her again, you'll have to go through me."

John looked away from him, the way he always did when he was disappointed. Ever since their father died, his older brother had been looking away. When Daniel announced he'd joined the Union Army, when he'd married Mary, daughter of poor Belgian immigrants, when he'd slid into rough friends and wild sprees in the wake of Mary's death. John had spent so much time looking down on Daniel's life that he hadn't bothered to live one of his own.

"I'm heading home now. When all this is over, maybe you should pack your things."

Daniel nodded, surprised at the sudden tightness of his throat. Though he didn't appreciate John's attempts to tell him what to do, he still hated to disappoint his brother. He remembered what Hannah had told him about his family hating her and how, if he lost them, he would come to hate her too. He vowed it wouldn't be so. He could *make* them understand.

Hannah spoke again. "I'm leaving when it's safe. I don't want to come between you two."

When John looked at her, Daniel thought he saw a portion of longing mixed with rancor. "You have already, Hannah, and that's another reason I can't forgive you."

* * *

Peering past the curtains, Hannah watched the brothers leave together, deep in conversation. When she had left the porch, she eavesdropped until their stiff hostility dissolved. After convincing herself they wouldn't come to blows, she withdrew into her room and hoped. The brothers might have their differences, but they still loved each other. Why destroy that for a woman who'd leave Peshtigo the moment it was safe?

She sighed and wished again she hadn't lied to John. Then her thoughts turned to his brother. She remembered Daniel's fingers meshing gently with her own. Her lips tingled with the memory of his kisses, and of kissing him. Daniel's attraction to her hadn't faltered when he'd learned she was divorced. Had her deception been unnecessary after all?

She sighed, disgusted at herself for indulging in a schoolgirl's fantasy. Just as Malcolm would never dream of marrying a mistress, Daniel Aldman would never marry her. What man would want a divorced woman, much less one with her past?

Faye interrupted her thoughts. "I could use your help getting this mending over to the boardinghouse."

"On a Sunday morning?"

"My stomach don't mind eatin' on the Sabbath, and as I recall from just a bit ago, yours don't either. Have to work enough to feed that old sponge I married. Now, you're a payin' boarder, so you don't hafta come. I just thought a little walkin' might do you some good."

Hannah retrieved a stack of folded clothing from the foot of her bed. She decided Malcolm had probably put some distance between himself and Peshtigo, at least for then. She wasn't about to cloister herself to avoid him, so she agreed.

As they left the small house, Hannah caught Daniel's apprehensive mood. There had been clouds of thick smoke all along, but the huge bank to the west looked darker, the orangy reflection more intense. Somehow, today seemed different, the air still and oppressive, the village too quiet. Perhaps with all the smoke, even nature held its breath.

At the same moment, two very different noises broke the silence. The first was a clattering of hooves and wheels as a teamster whipped his horses through the street. The second, even closer, was a shrill, familiar voice. "Miss Mercy!" cried Amelia from across the way.

Hannah turned in time to see her break away from a slightly taller, dark-haired girl and take off running— running directly into the laden wagon's path.

Without thinking, Hannah flung aside the mending and dove toward Daniel's child. The force of their impact rolled them both. Hannah looked up in time to see a pair of coal black horses pulling up too late and wagon wheels rolling only inches past her head. Instinctively, she clutched Amelia closer.

She heard a woman's frantic screaming in the distance, Faye's angry shout at the wagon's driver closer by. But the sounds that filled her ears were the pounding of her heart and the weeping of the child crushed against her body.

"Are you hurt?" Hannah asked her breathlessly.

Amelia pulled away to rub her head and wailed. Hannah heard footsteps coming nearer. Faye stooped down beside her. Beyond her, Aunt Lucinda was running as fast as her thick legs could carry her.

"Amelia! Dear Amelia! I told you not to run off after church!" Lucinda's voice bubbled with anxious fury. Despite her tone, she grabbed the child and hugged her fiercely.

Amelia stopped crying abruptly and wrapped her arms around her great-aunt's neck. "Mercy—Mercy saved me!"

"Yes, she surely did," said Faye. Then she withdrew to roundly curse the wide-eyed driver.

Lucinda's mouth pursed and her eyes narrowed as she looked at Hannah. "I suppose you should be thanked."

"That's not necessary," Hannah told her, standing up and brushing at her skirt. "What *is* necessary is that I apologize. I abused your hospitality when I withheld the truth from you. I am sorry beyond measure."

Lucinda withdrew a kerchief from her pocket and offered it to Hannah. "Your forehead's bleeding. I think the two of you cracked skulls."

Hannah took the cloth and dabbed at the sore spot. A penny-sized red splotch marred the crisp white linen. "My name is Hannah Lee Shelton, and my mother taught me not to lie." She must have banged her head harder than she thought, for pent-up words flowed faster than her blood.

Lucinda's brow furrowed, no doubt with a dozen snide remarks. But she said nothing, instead stroking Amelia's flaxen hair with a trembling hand.

"There's no excuse for what I did," Hannah continued. "I deceived your family, and I hurt you all. But I want you to know it was done in desperation and not because such things come easily to me."

Lucinda nodded. "I liked you. We all did. That's why it hurt so much."

Amelia turned and stared at her with huge blue eyes. "Your name is *Hannah*? That's the lie?"

Hannah nodded and leaned forward to kiss her head. "Yes, an awful lie."

Aunt Lucinda seemed to have recovered from her shock. She set Amelia down but continued staring into Hannah's face. "If you're asking for forgiveness, don't expe—"

Amelia interrupted. "But, Aunt Lucinda, the preacher said in church we should forgive! He says no sin is too big."

"Don't interrupt, child. Let me have a minute with Miss Mer—Miss Shelton. Go back to play with Camille, and if you don't look before you cross that street, I'm going to tan your hide!"

With a pouty look, Amelia followed her great-aunt's instruction.

Before Lucinda could speak, Faye interrupted. "This fine young man"—she gestured to the teamster, a fellow in his late teens whose face still glowed red from the tongue-lashing Faye dished out—"has kindly offered to help me pick up the mending and deliver it to compensate us for his recklessness."

"I'm real sorry, ma'am. My pap told me to get this ware delivered in a hurry, but I'd never want to hurt a soul. I just hope he don't hear, or he'll beat me somethin' awful." The boy wrung his hat in nervous supplication.

Hannah nodded stiffly. "Have a care next time."

"Or we'll have the law on you!" Aunt Lucinda threatened.

He helped Faye into the wagon with her mending, and the two rattled down the street.

"She's a worker," Faye called over her shoulder to Lucinda. "Don't you be too harsh with her."

Lucinda shook her head. "Imagine that woman, driving off with a strange man. What will the ladies say when they see this?"

"I think she's had a difficult life," said Hannah, feeling some allegiance to Faye.

Lucinda shrugged and started walking in the direction of her home. "It's no excuse, for you or her. We've all had troubles, haven't we? I lost my husband years ago, and I never had the comfort of a single child of my own. It nearly broke my heart."

Hannah followed her, but stared down near her feet. "I know. Dear Lord, how I know. It's silly," she said, "but the other women seem to flaunt their babies. And people make such awful comments all the time. 'Just how long *have* you been married?' and 'Any news this month?' Then, after a while, they use the cruelest word. They call you barren, and they tell you you must face it—for your own good, they always say."

"You are *married,* Hannah?" Lucinda's voice iced over.

Hannah shook her head. "Once. He divorced me when his mistress gave him the son I couldn't."

"I see. A divorcée. And I am sure John's letters mentioned he would want a family."

"Yes." Tears blurred Hannah's vision. Why was she continuing to walk with Aunt Lucinda? What in heaven's name did she expect? Saving Amelia's life could hardly buy her absolution for her crimes. But still, she followed, hoping desperately for some sign of acceptance, or at least of understanding.

Lucinda stopped and faced her. "Then why? Why, Hannah? Were you a schemer, trying to steal his property?"

She shook her head. "Of course not. I—I only thought how good I am with animals. I'd help him run his farm. Maybe we would do well, and someday he might love me. Maybe then the children wouldn't matter all so much."

"How could you? How could you rob a good man of his chance at a family?"

She shrugged. "I didn't know John then. I knew only that I couldn't survive on my own. My only offers of employment were"—she felt blood rising to her neck and face—"quite unladylike."

"What about your family? Surely you could turn to them."

"My parents are both dead, and my former husband even managed to spread enough lies to keep my family's farm. As for my other relatives, they were in no hurry to claim a divorced woman."

Lucinda's mouth screwed up in an unreadable expression. "Every other thing you've said has been a lie. Why should I believe you now?"

"Because I have nothing to gain. I want nothing more from you, not even your forgiveness. What the preacher said in church was wrong. There *are* some sins too great."

"Then why talk to me at all?"

Hannah shrugged. "Maybe I need to make some sort of peace before I go."

"John thinks you might be tempting Daniel." The old woman pinned her gaze.

Hannah's heart fluttered. Despite herself, she smiled weakly. "He has it backward. Daniel's tempting me, even though he knows the truth."

"That boy's liked you from the start, if this old head's not full of sawdust. But then again, Daniel might kiss a copperhead if it suited him. You just stay away from him, you hear?"

"I intend to. I won't be here long anyway," said Hannah. She stopped and turned back in the direction of the Barlow house. "I'm glad we could talk."

"You're brave. I'll grant you that. And I thank you for saving Amelia. I'll tell my nephews what you did." Without another word or gesture, Lucinda turned and walked away, toward her own house.

Hannah looked after the old woman and wondered what she'd gained. Not forgiveness, certainly, but something. Acknowledgment? Maybe even a shred of understanding? As Hannah watched her disappear into the distance, she realized she'd doubtless never get another chance to make amends. Whether it occurred because of Amelia's rescue or in honor of the Sabbath, whatever crumb Lucinda offered her would have to be enough.

CHAPTER THIRTEEN

Hannah sat on her bed, trying to mend the dress Malcolm had torn. She sighed. The damage was beyond her mending skills, yet she couldn't spare the dress. With the needle poised in midair, she froze, remembering his threat. *I'm not through with you.*

The shaking started in her hands, then worked its way into her shoulders, and before she knew it, she was weeping silently. If she knew him at all, Malcolm would be back. She'd wounded his precious Shelton pride, pride in a family name that had once commanded great respect in the town his great-grandfather had established.

At one time Malcolm's family owned half the land in the Shelton Creek area. They'd farmed at first, but eventually they built a prosperous mill, and Malcolm's father had opened his own hotel. But Malcolm had been the last male Shelton among a glut of sisters. His father reminded him again and again that their name must, at all costs, be preserved.

Hannah partly blamed the old man for the dissolution

of her marriage. Charles Shelton's ghost whispered demands in Malcolm's ear for sons, and his death had left the Shelton clan an incredible surprise. The grand hotel had been a bust. His other investments had lost money. The proud name was all they had left. It had been enough to marry off all seven sisters, and it had been enough to help Malcolm achieve a captain's post in the Union Army. But in the end it hadn't been enough to satisfy him. In the end he listened too much to that ghost.

She tried to imagine what it must feel like, as the last male Shelton, to be blamed for his wife's murder. Malcolm had dealt well enough with the imagined indignity of being cuckolded, but that was because he'd orchestrated every step. How had it been when she had turned the tables and used the gossip that destroyed her to lash out at him as well? Where she'd been deeply shamed and wounded, Malcolm would work himself into a righteous rage. By turning him away from Peshtigo the previous night, by exposing him to even more humiliation, she had changed his rage from righteous into murderous.

If he caught her again, he'd kill her. She knew it as well as she knew herself. And he would catch her if it took him his whole life and all the money he had left. His pride would demand nothing less.

She peered out a window filmed by ash. God help her to leave here quickly, if the whole town didn't go up in a blaze. It might have been the clouded glass, but the smoke appeared darker than ever. It looked as if, in running from her past, she had fled to hell itself.

The moment John and Daniel walked into Lucinda's kitchen, Amelia excitedly climbed into her father's arms. "Miss Mercy's name is Hannah, and she saved my life today!"

Lucinda helped them sort out her story, and later, when

Amelia went into the yard to play with her new kitten, their aunt told both her nephews more. "I can't tell if the woman was in earnest, but she apologized. She says she doesn't expect us to accept, but she was desperate." Her gaze settled on Daniel.

He nodded. "She told me about it. John didn't want to hear."

John shook his head in disgust. "What does it matter what she says? She admits she lied."

"Worse yet," said Lucinda, "she's a divorced woman. She said her husband left her because she couldn't bear him children."

"Why would she think any man would want a barren woman?" John asked.

Daniel grimaced when he noticed his aunt flinch. Couldn't the clod see he was insulting her as well?

"Your uncle didn't let that drive him from me." Lucinda drew herself up proudly, her back stiff and ramrod straight.

John blushed deeply. Served him right, thought Daniel.

"You're not like Hannah, Aunt Lucinda." John reached out for her, but she pulled away. "You're no liar, and you'd never cheat a soul."

"Perhaps I would have turned out different if my Henry had been so despicable."

Daniel felt hope flare, but he was cautious. "You're not saying you'd forgive Hannah?"

Lucinda shrugged. "No, but she did save Amelia's life. She could have been killed jumping in front of those horses."

"Maybe Hannah feels guilty. So she should," John said.

"She does love that child. Amelia loves her too." Lucinda glanced toward Daniel.

His throat grew tight. "Then, you could patch things up?"

"Aunt Lucinda!" John interrupted. "You can't encourage this—this affair! This is lunacy! The woman is *divorced!* And Daniel is your nephew!''

"And I love you both like the sons I never bore. Of course I'm not suggesting Daniel run off and marry a divorcée. I'm merely thinking that perhaps she's not such an evil creature, just misguided."

John threw up his hands. "Both of you have been beguiled! This woman lied to us. She swindled me. She may still be lying, for all we know."

"Why would she bother?" Daniel asked. "What could she hope to gain?"

"Our sympathy, of course. And eventually you." John glared at Daniel.

He thought about their argument last night, the way she still insisted she was leaving. Daniel shook his head. "You're wrong. If there's one thing in this world I know she doesn't want, it's me."

Cut off by darkness and a wall of smoke, Malcolm Shelton had circled back. He rode slumped over his mount's neck, worn down by exhaustion, rage, and pain. The half-drunk loggers did more than run him out of town. They'd pelted him with anything available, from sticks and stones to a patent medicine bottle that raised a swollen lump along his jaw. He was tempted to try to ride through the smoke. Those shanty boys would kill him if they caught him back in town. But in the end, he felt he had to risk it, or risk choking in hell's antechamber, not far from Peshtigo.

Cautiously, he returned to the cottage where he'd taken Hannah and retrieved his pants and shoes. From there he managed to find a livery stable still open for his horse. The old man working there took pity on him, believing his story about an attack by ruffians, and gave him lodging in his own house for the night.

That bit of charity, *charity* bestowed upon a Shelton,

Malcolm added to Hannah Lee's account. As he tried to sleep, images rattled through his head like freight trains: the hardness in Hannah's face as she held the gun on him, the way she'd sent him bare-assed into the night, the sight of her half-naked body, every delicious curve seeming to cry out for plunder.

He wanted her. The more he thought about her pleas for him to stop and her resistance to his intrusions, the more he knew he had to have her. But not as a lover. That gentle path no longer held his interest. Instead, he wanted her beaten, thrown over, a body to slam into again . . . again . . . again.

And then there would be blood. Blood as thick as that he'd seen in their hometown when she faked her own murder in order to destroy the Shelton name.

He slept late the next day. As he bent over the washbasin, scrubbing the grime from his face, the old man from the livery stable knocked. "Ain't much of a cook, but what I got, I'll gladly share."

Malcolm nodded stiffly, gratefully. He must eat and rest, regain his vanquished strength. And then, Sunday or not, he would find a man to sell him a new gun.

Though the day grew late as she finished myriad chores, Faye killed a hen well past its prime in honor of the Sabbath. She'd done what she could with the scrawny fowl, but the bits of meat served with her dumplings were still stringy. Hannah discreetly shredded hers with a knife so none would get caught in her throat. Still, the creamy gravy and dumplings tasted delicious after days of eating burned-bottom beef dodger and boiled cabbage with potatoes.

"Do you know anyone with a wagon for hire?" Hannah asked.

Still chewing, Hank answered. "Have a friend, name of Ral, who'd probably do."

"I want to leave tomorrow," Hannah said. "I have a little money. I can pay. If the boats aren't running here, he can drive me to Marinette."

"Ain't safe." Hank shook his head. "Even if the road's clear, you could smother with all this smoke."

Faye began clearing the dishes. "Don't go. We'll have rain soon enough. Stay here till then. You're welcome."

She shook her head. "I'm not safe here either. He knows where I am."

"Who? That man that attacked you? He's long gone, Daniel said." Faye placed a reassuring hand on her shoulder.

"He'll come back. Why else do you think Daniel slept here last night?"

Faye and Hank looked at each other and smiled.

"I'd wager he'd sleep on hell's doorstep for the chance to be near you," Faye said. "You sure you want to slip off and leave a man like that?"

Once again Hannah recalled the warmth of Daniel's thick fingers intertwined with hers. She recalled the flow between them as he kissed her on the couch, the spots of light that swarmed, then coalesced, then dissolved into such pleasure.

She was almost glad that it had gone no further. Perhaps he'd been right, after a fashion. What she felt had been too deep to consummate and then abandon.

"I know what I have to do," she told both the Barlows and herself.

Excusing herself, she stepped out onto the porch to check the horizon once more before she packed. The sky had darkened early, thanks to the thick smoke. A warm wind ruffled puffs of sawdust from the street. Compared to yesterday, today felt like midsummer.

The scent of ash left her unsettled. She couldn't wait to breathe air free of the acrid odor.

Why hadn't she left here days before? Surely, she could have taken a stage, or even the railroad if she'd truly wished to leave. But Daniel had brought a steamer ticket, and, at the time, it had seemed good enough. What possible difference could the date of departure mean to a woman who still had no destination?

Discomfort tightened her chest the way it always did when she lied to herself. Had she had a different reason for delaying? She felt as if, with his first kiss in the ruined barn, Daniel Aldman had captured some vital spark within her. Somehow he had stamped her as his own.

Did he already know? Last night he'd wanted her to stay here. The request had gone beyond a virile man's attempt to take what lay beneath the thin barrier of her nightclothes. He had wanted something more substantial, something to endure.

At the thought of putting on the nightgown again, Hannah shuddered with the memory of the secret places he'd caressed so gently, with the memory of his lips, so fiery that even now she sucked in her breath sharply.

Whatever had he done to her? Her face felt flushed, but she was restless. Far too restless to change clothes and bed down for the night.

Tomorrow she would be leaving Peshtigo. Tomorrow she might be leaving her last chance.

The wind blew even harder, from the west, she thought.

Could that sound be more than the wind? Hannah stepped off the porch and crossed the narrow, weedy strip that formed the boundary between the house and street. She felt a strange sensation, like a freezing of the space around her heart as she listened to the growing voice of a distant roar.

A cinder struck her cheek, and she brushed it away quickly. Then another burned her hand, and suddenly, glowing ashes swarmed like stinging wasps. With a muffled cry Hannah raced inside the house.

"There's fire coming! You can hear it, and the wind is blowing cinders all around."

Faye stopped washing dishes and Hank looked up sharply from where he sipped a glass of whiskey at the table.

"Fact'ry boys and the loggers'll get it, like they did the last time," Hank assured her.

Faye went to the front door and looked outside. The wind gave her gray hair a rough tousle. "Maybe I should throw together a few things. Give me a hand, old man."

"With one good arm? We'd be roasted by the time I got through. Don't worry. Those boys'll put it out."

Faye stomped toward him, furious. "You worthless old sot, you'd burn up before you'd lift a finger. You still got one arm left. If I had the other, I'd use it now t'beat your lazy carcass!"

Hank cackled like the late, stringy-fleshed hen. Ignoring him, Faye rushed into her bedroom and began to change her dress.

"What are you doing?" Hannah asked her from the open doorway.

"If we're going to have to run, I might as well save my best dress as an old one. I got a necklace I'll want too, and what little money I have put aside."

"Dammit, woman," called Hank, who hadn't yet moved from his chair. "There's no need t'get breachy over a little bit more smoke."

"It's not the smoke," Hannah said. "It's that awful wind, and worst of all, that noise. Like thunder that rolls and rolls and never quits. Come hear it on the porch."

"Mebbe it *is* thunder. Ever thinka that? We're about to finally get some rain, and you two are yammerin' like a pair of chipmunks." He chuffed a laugh into his whiskey.

"We're going to keep watch, Hank," Faye told him as

she emerged from the bedroom. "And if it looks much worse, we're all heading for the river like Daniel Aldman told us."

The kitten yowled and darted out the door the moment Daniel cracked it open. Her ears laid back, Spice ran wildly, past Aunt Lucinda's small stable and into the alley beyond. Every hair on the kitten's back was raised, as if some great, bristling dog snapped at her heels. Yet no beast chased the kitten, nothing but a swirl of blowing ash.

A thin coating of the gray flakes covered the backyard. Beyond it, just as dismal, rose the dense smoke cloud, flashing eerily. Wind pushed around the soot and thickened the darkness. Above it, Daniel heard a deep voice, a bass howl he didn't recognize.

Amelia, like the kitten, tried to rush out past him. He grabbed her arm and swallowed back his apprehension.

"Spice ran away! Let me go catch her!" The child's voice rang shrill in his ears.

He scooped her up to keep her from squirming from his grasp. Her flannel nightgown felt soft against his arms. "Aren't you supposed to be in bed, young lady?"

She nodded, even while craning her neck to stare in the direction of the kitten's escape. "I was sleeping, but Spice cried to get out of the room. Look, there goes another kitty."

A white streak bolted past. Another cat, for certain, then a third. The hair rose on Daniel's neck and arms. What was it he had once heard about cats? That they sensed coming disaster?

"Fireflies . . ." Amelia squealed. Always she had loved the glimmering creatures, but, of course, they didn't come this time of year. Instead, a shower of glowing cinders rode the rising wind.

Daniel felt his stomach lurch. The wind, the roar, the

cinders, all combined to whet the knife edge of foreboding
that had threatened him all day.

"Go get dressed, Amelia."

"But Aunt Lucinda said to go to sleep." Her voice was
tight with tension, as if she'd guessed already what he knew.

"Just hurry. I'll tell Aunt Lucinda too. Now, go." He set
her down and watched her scurry toward her room. He
fought off an instinctive urge to calm her, to tell her everything would be all right. *Let her fear a little,* he decided.
Haste might save their lives. He roused his aunt, who'd
been reading the Bible in her nightgown.

"Put your clothes on quickly. We need to leave."

She looked up sharply, but her brown eyes were serene.
" 'The Lord is my shepherd; I shall not want.' "

"Please, Aunt Lucinda. Get dressed. Take the Bible if
you like, but hurry. I'll feel better if we're close by the
river."

She shook her head, still with the same eerie look of
peace. "Henry built this house for me. I'll not abandon
it."

He crossed the room in two steps and hauled her from
the chair. She blinked; he had never before touched her
in any but the gentlest manner.

"You get dressed right now, or so help me, I'll put you
over my shoulder and tote you down the street. Imagine
what the ladies would say when they saw *that.*" His voice
rose above the wind outside.

Lucinda nodded and seemed to come back to herself.
"Give an old woman half a minute of privacy, if you're in
such a blamed hurry."

He went to check on his daughter and found her pulling
on her stockings. "What's happening, Papa? Will I still
have school tomorrow?"

"Maybe so," he answered, but he wondered, when
tomorrow came, would there even be a school left
standing?

CHAPTER FOURTEEN

"Come, Hank," Faye begged, her eyes damp with tears. "Come, or we'll all burn!"

The old man took another swig of whiskey and made a wide arc with his stubbled chin. "A fine bunch of fools we'll be, tearin' down the street for nothin'. The boys have put out these fires all along, I tell you."

"We won't be tearin' down the streets alone. I just saw the Johannesons running toward the river with all their little ones in tow. Hurry, please." Faye tugged at his whole arm. "If we can get across the bridge, we'll be safer."

"Now!" Hannah demanded. She finished buttoning her coat. Then, with a sweep of her hand, she slammed Hank's glass from his grasp. It shattered as it struck the wooden floor.

The old man looked in the direction of the golden liquid that saturated the wood grain. Then he shrugged and grabbed the bottle instead. When Hannah tried to strike it too, he stood and held it tightly as far away from her as possible.

Through the window she could hear the rising wind and that deep roar, far more ominous, now louder. Hannah turned away from Hank and grasped the bag that held her best dress and her money.

"Hurry, Faye!" she called over her shoulder. "Leave him, if the fool won't come."

The instant Hannah stepped onto the porch, the hell wind snapped her bag out of her hand. She watched in disbelief as it tumbled down the street and out of sight. She heard a sound like the crackling of rustling leaves, then stared, horrified, at a flaming treetop that struck fifty yards down the narrow street and ignited the sawdust that filled its wagon ruts.

She screamed, but the sound of her voice was impotent against the fury of the wind. The door blew open, striking the back of her shoulder, and she felt Faye's hand slip into her own. Without a word or glance the two left the yard and ran, their legs churning with sheer terror toward whatever refuge the Peshtigo River might hold.

A wild sea of hellfire rolled toward him, driven by a howling wind. Malcolm stared from his hotel window. He felt calm bubbling like a wellspring in his center, the same detached reserve that had saved his life in Gettysburg.

He heard the other hotel guests exclaiming, shrieking prayers and curses, but their fear didn't touch him. Doors slammed as some fled and others hid inside their rooms. With careful deliberateness, Malcolm slipped on his jacket and left for the lobby. The desk clerk was stuffing cash and keys into his pockets.

"Where will *you* go?" Malcolm asked. He wasn't fleeing, helter-skelter, with those other panicked guests. Nor was he about to shiver beneath his bed and wait for the fire to consume him.

The man looked up. He was a smart-looking fellow with

his wire-framed glasses and short-trimmed, thinning hair, the kind of middle-aged hotelier who lent comfort to the guests. His relative calm put Malcolm to mind of his late father.

"Only one place to go—the river," he told Malcolm. "Follow me."

The streets were jammed with people all running in the same direction. They ran bent against the howling wind. Occasionally, horses or knots of cattle stampeded past, just as desperate to escape the flame. The hotelier grabbed Malcolm's arm and pointed down an alleyway. "Head over another block, then turn left," he shouted in Malcolm's ear. "Have to go back for my wife."

Malcolm stared in the direction the man turned. Blazing leaves fell like thick snow from the sky. He'd be killed if he went back, but from the look of him, the man already knew. Was helping Malcolm merely one last service to a hotel guest?

Malcolm nodded and took the alleyway to the next street. Smoke billowed through the channel between the rows of buildings so thick, he could barely see another soul. Still, he ran. He had no choice. He blundered into a woman and knocked her to the ground. He didn't pause to see if she'd been hurt. He couldn't. His carefully composed reserve, like most of Peshtigo, blazed out of control.

For the first time ever, Malcolm Shelton ran for his life.

Daniel ran outside alone to see to the two horses, his own and his aunt's. As he rounded the corner of the house, a blast of wind buffeted him, as hot as if it burst forth from a furnace. He heard both the house and his aunt's small stable creak with the force of it, even above the freight-train roar.

He opened Chance's stall door first and grabbed for the gelding's halter. The chestnut tossed his head, and his hooves danced dangerously close. Daniel hurried him outside and swatted his broad rump.

With a squeal of terror the horse sped off in the direction of the river. Daniel hoped the animal might save himself. In this maelstrom, no beast could be trusted with a rider, and no wagon could be safely guided through the streets.

Another gust nearly lifted Daniel bodily. He ducked against its fury. Ash and cinders stung his face and eyes. He turned back toward the stable. To his horror, the structure leaned and then collapsed.

Beneath the wood and slate debris, a horse's screams rang out. Old Blessing, badly injured, from the sound.

Daniel hesitated. He'd never willingly left an animal in agony, but even finding the aged gelding might take hours, and all that he could offer would be a knife's edge to end his suffering.

Blessing squealed again. His dark eyes tearing, Daniel turned away. If he didn't get his aunt and daughter, they would suffer the same fate. Flaming leaves and branches fell like hellish meteorites, igniting withered grasses, sawdust, and a fence along the street. At least the animal wouldn't have much time to suffer.

Daniel ran into the house. "I've turned the horses loose!" he shouted over the sound. No need to burden either of them with the well-loved Blessing's fate.

Lucinda, white-faced, clutched a quilt and a cloth bag. She stared, fish-eyed with apparent shock. Amelia reached up, and Daniel hoisted her into his arms. With his free hand he led his aunt. She followed meekly as a child.

The wind bellowed at them like a crazed bear. They had to run nearly doubled over or else be thrown down. Around them, others ran as well, all miserably huddled. Some screaming, most silent against the holocaust. The Millers' house blazed like a huge bonfire, and the flames blew to ignite another neighbor's home.

Lucinda was lifted from her feet once. Only Daniel's

firm grip kept her from being swept away. He heard her cry out and wondered if he'd wrenched her shoulder in holding on to her. When he slowed to look at her, he saw the bag she carried had burst into flames, which licked at her skirt. He stopped and forced her to let go of it. It spun into a hedge, which then took up its fire.

Lucinda's skirt, too, sparked and caught. He put Amelia down. "Hold on to my leg!" he yelled. She clutched him tightly, freeing his hands to tear at the burning cloth around his aunt's legs. He freed her of the lower portion of her dress.

Lucinda shrieked, whether in agony from burns or in mortification, he didn't know. Ignoring her cry, he again picked up Amelia and led her farther down the street. If he didn't get them to the water quickly, they would have more to worry over than an old woman's naked legs.

Flames billowed over homes and buildings, fierce and angry. Crowds of people filled the streets, all rushing in the direction of the river. Now and then a singular voice rose up against the gale, and a body blazed, its clothing consumed in a few instants. Once a man fell only steps ahead of Hannah. She was forced to stagger past him and move on.

A red-haired woman burst out of a saloon and rushed at Faye and Hannah, gesturing for both to follow her. Hair streaming wildly, the young woman grabbed at Faye, and Hannah at last recognized Rosalind. But the building she wanted them to hide in already blazed in half a dozen places. Faye shook her head and reached out for her frantic daughter.

Rosalind leapt away and raced back for the burning saloon. Faye cried out in a voice so painful, it needed no words. A cinder erupted, and Rosalind's red locks caught.

Her dress, too, exploded into flames so bright, their light burned Hannah's eyes.

Rosalind fell, and Faye fought her way free from Hannah's grasp. She tore off her threadbare coat with the apparent intention of beating out the fire, but it was already far too late. With a deep wail, Faye turned from her dying daughter.

Hannah took her arm and the two resumed their course.

Smoke choked her, and her eyes refused to stay open against the onslaught of windblown sand and sparks. Hannah tripped over a child's body and sprawled in the street. Nearly blinded by her own tears, she rose and reached for Faye's hand. Grasping it, she forged ahead.

A rock beneath the surface sawdust tore Malcolm's knee as he crawled beneath the thickest smoke. He didn't have the breath to even swear.

Around him, men and women tried to run, but the poisoned atmosphere dropped them one by one. When a strong gust lifted the smoke, he saw a tiny boy wailing at an unmoving smoldering hump. Fear shot through Malcolm as he considered passing by. No one would blame him, no one would know if he simply left the toddler. But he could not. He was still a Shelton, wasn't he?

He struggled toward the boy, every inch costing him another bruise. The cinders fell so thick, he could no longer see the child, but he reached forward, feeling, feeling . . .

Feeling nothing but a tiny corpse, its clothing now alight. Malcolm jerked his hand away, for some reason more affected by this death than by any other.

Dear God. Had Hannah led him into hell itself?

* * *

Another gust of wind cleared the air long enough for Daniel to catch a glimpse of the mayhem by the river. Homes along the riverside shot flames, and the bridge was jammed with panicked men, women, children, and cattle, all desperate to reach the other side. The bridge timbers themselves were beginning to burn, as was the wooden dam's base.

Daniel hesitated, staring at dozens of people who stood frozen with fear along the riverside. A few white faces showed above the darkness of the water, but many more stood stupefied by fear, only feet from safety.

Lucinda moved blindly forward toward the bridge, but Daniel held her back. If people were crowding across the bridge from the east side, that meant fire raged there too. They had no better choice than to jump into the water.

Daniel used his shoulders to shove their way past those who would not move. "In! Into the water!" he bellowed at a woman who clutched two little children. Taking fright, she hauled them farther up the bank.

"We'll drown!" Lucinda screamed.

She might well be right, thought Daniel. He'd swum there as a boy, and he remembered how the bank sloped gently into deeper water. But tonight, cattle milled about, driven by the same instinct that had brought so many people. Logs as well, some in flames, had floated down from the woodenware factory. Either could bump a wader and take him in beyond his depth.

Despite his misgivings, Daniel shook his head. "I won't let us drown!" he shouted.

That was when he realized how limp Amelia felt against him, beneath the coat he'd used to shield her from the motes. Dear God, had his child suffocated from the smoke? With an anguished cry he hauled his aunt into the water.

They waded until Lucinda was chest-deep. Daniel uncovered Amelia's face. Her eyes were closed, and ashes smudged her pale cheek. Sparks and cinders fell like burning snow around them, but Daniel hardly noticed as he splashed the girl with water.

Nothing. He fully dunked her, then brought her to the surface.

Amelia couldn't die! She was all he had of Mary.

With the dunking, some reflex made the child gasp deeply, taking in the fresher air. Her arms jerked spasmodically, and she sputtered. Then she looked up and began to cry. Her blue eyes reflected flame.

"Daniel, you're afire!" Aunt Lucinda screamed.

He felt a burning at his shoulder, which she quickly doused with splashing. The two of them unfolded the quilt his aunt had brought along, and they wet it. The three used it as a sodden shield, a frail defense against the flames that leapt between the banks above their heads.

Buffeted along by the panicked crowd, Hannah found herself in the crush approaching the river bridge. Maybe she should cross it with the others. Surely, the fire on the other side wouldn't be so monstrous, and she feared the dark waters almost as much as flame. Hannah turned to ask Faye what they should do—and choked on her own horror.

It wasn't Faye whose hand she held.

Instead, she peered into the grimy face of a young boy, no older than twelve or thirteen. When she'd fallen over the body in the street, she'd reached out and grasped at the wrong hand. She'd led this boy instead of Faye! Then Faye—Hannah's mind lurched—Faye probably was dead.

As she hesitated, a man wheeled his cart into Hannah's side, knocking her off her feet. She rolled down an embankment toward the river, her ribs flaring agony.

A man, a priest by his dark robes, hauled her up and pushed her into the cool water. Hannah waded deeper, stumbled, and then plunged beneath the surface, suddenly in water well over her head.

CHAPTER FIFTEEN

The mill had caught for certain, and the bridge as well. Daniel moved his family farther from the latter, lest they be killed by its collapse.

"Judgment Day!" Lucinda croaked in his ear. "This sinful world will perish, and we'll all stand before God."

"I'm not ready yet," Daniel said. "I've got amends to make. So let's just plan on living unless the Lord insists."

Above their heads, the quilt steamed and smoldered, so they doused it once again.

Daniel held Amelia close, mindful of the way she shivered. If the fire didn't get her, pneumonia and shock might exact the same cost in the end. He'd give anything to have a place to take her, warm and dry and free from flame.

A gust of wind carried away the roof of the woodenware factory. Blazing buckets and tubs exploded through the opening and then splashed into the river all around them. Daniel heard screams and wondered how many had been struck.

The mill fire guttered noisily, lighting up the scene as

bright as day. Peering across the river's surface, Daniel saw hands fluttering, splashing water to keep both cloth and hair from igniting. Glowing cinders rained continuously, making the air difficult to breathe. Some yards away, he saw arms reaching through the water, splashing more frantically than any others. A woman's face broke through the surface, a woman's face he knew.

"Hold her just a minute." Daniel passed Amelia to his aunt.

Beyond them, the woman floundered and then sank.

"Don't go!" Lucinda screamed at her nephew, but still, she took the child.

Daniel leapt away and swam toward the drowning woman. A flailing arm struck him. He grasped it. Though she struggled, he managed to pull her beyond danger.

Still, she fought, her panic slow to die.

"Hannah!" Daniel screamed.

She paused to look at him, then sobbed, and threw her arms around his neck. "I can't—can't swim! And Hank and Rosalind are dead! And—and I lost Faye, and—"

He splashed water on her to cool her clothes, which were already steaming. "Don't talk! Help us keep from burning!"

Hannah peered around at the hands, each splashing or dousing. If she wished to live, she couldn't spare her horror at the inky water another thought. Instead, she joined the strange fellowship of bathers. If Lucinda noticed, she said nothing. All past squabbles had to be set aside. For then, survival ruled unchallenged.

Daniel took his daughter and heard her coo "Mercy!" in his ear. As he watched a ceiling of flames roll above their heads, he wondered if God had any mercy left for them.

* * *

Hannah didn't know how many hours they spent splashing like pathetic birds trapped in a puddle. No one spoke, yet they worked together to survive: passing Amelia to another embrace when one's arms became too tired, wetting down a spot on another's clothing when it smoked, and always, always showering their small group with river water.

Sharp pain in her ribs flared whenever she lifted arms above her head or took Amelia's weight, yet this barely registered against the bone-numbing exhaustion that soon set in. Beside her, Daniel's eyes glazed over, and Lucinda's face starkly reflected the lurid firelight. Hannah never thought of stopping; indeed, she soon quit thinking altogether. Some primitive part of her brain worked her muscles ceaselessly, distant from despair as well as hope.

She could not think of any future outside their desperate struggle. Nor could she remember any past. Instead, she toiled with the others, hour after hour, mindlessly.

Finally, a hand grasped her arm firmly, made her stop. Released from her trance, Hannah blinked and glanced upward to the sky. The black of night soothed her sore eyes, and she realized the fires were burning down. Along the riverbank she still saw scattered flame, but only a bit of ash fell, like soft gray snowflakes.

They had survived the worst.

She looked to Daniel, who kept Amelia pressed against a shoulder. The child's eyes were closed, her hair and face dark with water-streaked soot. He released Hannah's arm and took his aunt's. Then they waded toward the shore, as others around them began to emerge as well.

Before they reached it, Hannah heard Lucinda's teeth chattering, and her own jaws took up the rhythm. While they'd worked, Hannah hadn't felt the water's chill, but now she shivered with it.

They staggered toward a heap of coals and glowing metal—the twisted bands from the burned buckets. All around, people lay on the hot sand, some writhing and moaning, others still as death. Perhaps they *were* dead, Hannah thought, but she had no strength to care. Amelia's fate concerned her most.

Daniel sank to the warm dirt at his feet and laid his daughter on it.

"Is she—is she breathing?" Hannah asked.

He nodded slowly and then lay down, his arm draped protectively across his child. His eyes blinked once and then closed.

Lucinda fell beside him, her arms tightly curled across her chest. Even in the poor light of the narrow moon, Hannah saw huge blisters on the old woman's bare legs. Swollen flesh wept where some had burst. As gently as she could, Hannah covered her with the remnants of the damp quilt.

"Mercy," Lucinda breathed.

Hannah leaned close and took her hand. When Lucinda didn't speak, she gently prompted, "What is it, Mrs. Pangburn?"

The gray head shook almost imperceptibly. "You can— you can always call me Aunt Lucinda. I forgive . . ."

"Thank you, Aunt Lucinda. Shall I—shall I wake Daniel?"

"Let him sleep, child. I'll be fine. So warm here, nice. Just—I'm just so glad to rest."

Trembling with both fear and exhaustion, Hannah stooped and kissed the woman's forehead. The corners of Lucinda's mouth twitched, and she let out a rattling sigh. She did not draw breath again.

Tears blurred the edges of the scene, but not of Hannah's pain. She felt as if Lucinda had been entrusted to her while Daniel slept. How could she have let the woman die when he had kept her safe all through the fire?

Quiet sobs shot pain through Hannah's injured ribs.

She wept for Aunt Lucinda, and for Faye, who must have died tonight with her whole family. She wept for Peshtigo.

And what of Daniel and his family? Had his brother perished too? Had their home and their animals all been reduced to cinders? A wave of sympathy renewed her tears.

She knew exactly how it felt to lose a family and a home.

His upper body draped across a floating log, Malcolm shivered violently. The left side of his face felt as though a stiff brush scrubbed it raw. Each time the log bobbed in the river, bark scraped his throbbing flesh. He roused enough to shift position slightly and noticed that the night was finally fading.

Through bleary, swollen eyes he took in the log that saved him. Most of it had burned down to the waterline. He hadn't fared much better. Both hands were red and blistered, and half his face sang a stinging lament to a similar condition.

Only luck kept him alive. The log he rode had caught on a snag. If it had rolled instead, he surely would have drowned.

Malcolm stared at the smoking rubble along the shore-line. Could this be Peshtigo? The remains of a tin roof and jutting pipes offered mute testimony. Though he didn't have a good view from this angle, he would wager not an inch of the village remained unscathed. Nothing could survive that fearsome holocaust.

In the distance, through a haze of bluish smoke, he saw evidence he had been wrong. Two men walked along the bank in his direction. He waved weakly and hoped they would spot him. He lacked the voice to even call for help.

So others *had* survived. An old reflex, not yet unlearned, made him worry for the safety of his former wife. As a stranger in this town, would she know where to run? Perhaps someone told her, just as the man at the hotel had pointed out his way. Malcolm tried to picture Hannah leaping into the river, just as he had. Parched laughter rattled through his cracked and scabby lips. Hannah would never go into the water. As a child, she'd nearly drowned in a Shelton Creek swimming hole. Since that episode, she hadn't even learned to swim.

Desolation ebbed through him, almost as painful as his burns. He hoped she had survived. Because he didn't want his wife killed by a random natural act. Oh, no. When Hannah Shelton finally met her Maker, he didn't want it to be an accident at all.

He was surely going to have to give up drinking, Daniel decided. The cannon in his head no longer barked, it howled. He could barely lift his cheek from whatever gritty floor he slept on.

He felt fine hair beneath his fingertips and remembered with a start. Amelia! She lay there beside him, breathing peacefully. This was no saloon. He tried to force his eyes open, but they refused to heed his brain's command. Gingerly, he felt the lids and found them swollen shut.

Fear leapt in his chest, a fear he had never known in battle. How could he care for Amelia, his aunt, and Hannah now that he was blind? Would he, the strongest, have to be the females' charge? He wondered if the sparks and cinders that had burned him hurt them too. Dear Lord, if they all were in this state . . .

He shivered with the chill, but he felt some warmth on his left side. The east, he reckoned. The sun had risen after all.

He turned his attention to the howling he had heard as he was waking. Not of dogs, of men and women, of small children. The moans rose wolflike to the morning after . . . after what? The world's end, as his aunt predicted?

Had last night been Armageddon? Or was it possible such a fire could have been raised by nature's hand?

He would have put his money on the latter, though just then it didn't make much difference. They survived, at least so far, and he would have to see that they remained alive.

"Papa?" Amelia's voice rasped as if she had a cold.

"I'm here. I'm here." He drew her nearer.

"That noise is scaring me. Why are all those people crying?"

"They're sad, and they're afraid. Probably some of them are hurt. Are you all right?"

"My throat's sore," Amelia said. "Papa, what's wrong with your eyes?"

It would be ridiculous to lie, yet he hated to admit it, as if mere words would make his blindness real. "They're very sore. It hurts to open them. Could you be my eyes today? We need to find Aunt Lucinda and Miss Mer—Miss Hannah."

"They're here. Miss Hannah's lying next to Aunt Lucinda. I think they're both asleep."

"Here, take my hand," said Daniel. "Show me where."

He let her lead him a few steps, as if he were the child.

"Watch out. Don't step there. It's too hot." She yanked him to one side. Then he felt the tug as she knelt down. "Aunt Lucinda?"

Amelia let go of his hand. "Aunt Lucinda?" she repeated, her voice rising like a piping bird's.

Daniel squatted down and reached out. His fingers brushed the dampness of the quilt. The flesh of his aunt's face, when he found it, was every bit as cool. Far too cool for a living body.

"Oh, God." He hung his head, and his eyes burned even more intensely. "Oh, God. Not her."

"Aunt Lucinda? Wake up!" Daniel felt the corpse jerk as his daughter shook it.

Moisture forced its way through Daniel's swollen eyelids. "She can't wake up, honey. Aunt Lucinda's gone away."

"No! She's not. You can't see her, but she's here. She's just asleep."

"No, Amelia. She's not breathing. Aunt Lucinda's gone with Mama. Mama will keep her safe for us."

"*You* were s'posed to keep her safe!" his daughter accused. "I want Aunt Lucinda to come back."

"She would if she could. But now she wants us to help each other. Amelia, where is Hannah?"

"Over there." His daughter's voice was sullen.

"Where?" he asked, frustrated.

Amelia didn't answer. When he reached out, he felt her huddled beside the woman who had raised her these last three years. The girl's frail shoulders shook, and her cries came hoarse and quiet. He laid his hand across her back. "Shhh. Shhh. You say good-bye to Aunt Lucinda. It's all right. I know she'd like that. I'll check on Hannah now."

With no other option, he blundered about on hands and knees until he brushed against the gritty cotton of a soiled dress. *Please, God*, he prayed for the first time in three years. *Please don't take her too.*

He felt along an arm, and then a shoulder. She didn't move at all. His breath hitched in his throat. He thought he'd saved them all.

Her neck, when he felt it, was warm beneath his touch. Or was that just the heat of the new sun? No, not only that, for her throat worked as she swallowed, and then she lurched to wakefulness.

"Daniel! Thank God you're alive. Your eyes—" A fit of coughing interrupted her. She groaned and fought it back. "What's wrong with your eyes?"

"Swollen shut for now. I'll need your help if you can do it. But Aunt Lucinda—"

Hannah grasped his hand and squeezed it. "I know. I was sitting with her when she died."

"Did she say anything?"

She hesitated for several moments. "Your aunt said she forgave me." Hannah's voice broke, and she wept softly. Then she added for Daniel's sake, "And she said how much she loved you all, you and John and Amelia. She lived for you, you know."

He felt tears sting his eyes. "Are you—are you hurt too?"

"Maybe some cracked ribs, but I'll be fine. We have to get Amelia out of here. Daniel, there are dead bodies."

"But we can't leave my aunt here."

"We'll cover her with the quilt," Hannah said. "We'll come back. We have to go. We'll need to find fresh water."

"The river?"

"No," she said. "We can't drink here. The water's filled with ash, and fish are floating. There are bodies, too, up against what's left of the bridge. I can lead you, Daniel, if you'll take Amelia's hand. We need to look for help."

"Do you think—do you think John might have survived?" Daniel asked.

She hesitated once again. "I don't know. Last night it seemed the whole world was afire."

CHAPTER SIXTEEN

The survivors gathered in a small valley not far from the river. Miraculously, a series of sandy hillocks had spared the place from flame. Amid a world of ash that crunched beneath their feet, it sheltered not only humans but the last green shrubs and grasses.

A friend of Daniel's told them some had survived there last night. Most of those escaped the serious injuries so common in those who had stayed in the river. He promised Daniel he would collect Aunt Lucinda's body and see to whatever arrangements could be made. Hannah left the Aldmans and showed the young man where Mrs. Pangburn lay.

Bending beside the old woman, she laid her hand upon the quilt. "I'll take care of them now," she whispered.

When she returned to the valley, men from the Peshtigo Company had raised a large tent for the injured, particularly the women. Though smoke had thickened her voice and made her breath shallow, Hannah did not avail herself of the shelter. Too many were in far greater need. Survivors straggled in, some with faces blackened, others with hands and feet charred to the bone. Wagons brought from Marinette delivered a few supplies, then went out to pick up what wounded they could find.

Daniel and his daughter rested on a patch of trampled grass. Hannah wandered restlessly, peering at the small knots of survivors, hoping for a glimpse of Faye or perhaps even Hank. He might have changed his mind and left the house.

Others also walked around, asking, "Have you seen my husband?" or "Do you know what happened to my little girl?" Each face was lit by hope, ofttimes beyond all reason. Children, too, searched forlornly for a missing parent, sometimes both.

Hannah asked for word of John Aldman too, but no one yet knew how the outlying farms had fared. Finally, she caught the attention of a company man who had been out examining the streets. Cinders grayed his thick sideburns, and his suit was torn and filthy.

"Please," she asked. "I'm looking for the Barlows, Faye or Hank. I know where they might be."

Tiredly, he turned toward her. "Don't go up there, miss. There's sights no man alive should see, much less a lady."

"But there's no one else to ask for them, or to see they're buried right."

He shook his head. "You might not know them if you saw them."

"I'd know Faye," said Hannah. "She always wore a silver cross around her neck."

The man regarded her with sad green eyes. After a pause he drew something from his pocket. "I took this from a looter. The ruffian had been stealing from the dead. The men would've hung him if there'd been a rope or half a tree left to string him up. You Mrs. Barlow's kin?"

Hannah lifted the cross and turned it all around. "It's hers." The words squeezed out through a throat closed tight with grief. "I lost her when I fell, and I took a young boy's hand instead. The smoke—too thick."

He patted her hand and closed it around the cross. "She'd be glad you survived."

Hannah nodded. "She wasn't kin. Her family burned up too, at least the daughter."

"You keep the cross, then. All we can do for the dead now is bury them and promise to remember. The rest of our attentions have to focus on the living. I have to go back now. They'll need help gathering the victims."

"Thank you," Hannah told him. "I'll remember."

She watched him turn back toward his sad task. After a while someone brought back the remnants of a cabbage crop. The outer leaves were burned, but the insides, still raw and crisp, made up a poor breakfast. She woke Daniel and Amelia, and shared her find with them.

The girl ate woodenly, staring at the grass.

"Can you see at all?" Hannah asked Daniel.

He shook his head, then covered his eyelids with a hand. "They burn just like hot coals. God, I feel so useless. I need to go find John."

"You can't," Hannah said. "I heard they're taking the injured to Marinette in wagons. You're going to have to go and let a doctor check those eyes. And your shoulder's burned as well."

"No, I'll be all right soon. I have to go find John."

"Don't be a fool, Daniel. If you don't tend to your sight, you might never get it back. Besides, you can't get to the farm. And what about Amelia? Do you really want her to see what's outside this valley?"

"Of course not, but we could find someone to watch her."

"No!" Amelia shrilled. Her voice edged near hysteria. "Don't leave me here, Papa. I want to stay with you."

"But John—I can't leave him all alone."

Hannah took his hand. ''Amelia needs you now, Daniel. I'll find John. I'm not badly hurt. I'll go.''

''You can't. It's too far, and they won't let a woman wander by herself.''

''I'll do it. I'll get someone to help. Then I'll find your brother. I promise you, I will.''

Hannah's voice. Though half conscious, Malcolm recognized it as he was loaded on the wagon. Dear God, don't let her see him! Don't let her guess that he was there.

If she recognized him, would she scream? Did he look so wretched? Or maybe she would cry out accusations. In his present condition, how could he defend himself against her lies? People might believe him an abductor if they didn't know he was only defending his good name. The men who rescued him might well dump him back in the river, or at least remove him from this wagon, bound for help.

Malcolm knew enough of the wounded he'd seen during the war to realize he was badly hurt. He'd be all too easy to kill, or simply to allow to die.

But death wouldn't be the worst fate that could befall him. He cringed as he imagined Hannah weeping, consumed with pity when she saw his ruined face. Yes, there were things worse than dying.

He turned toward the wagon's side, exposing only the burned left half of his face.

Daniel must have been in more pain than he admitted, for he let Hannah help him onto a waiting wagon. Some of those on board moaned, near death. She forced herself to look away from the charred flesh of a man's face. A woman clutched a scorched shawl to hide her nakedness. Her hair and ears had been burned off. Hannah had to avert her gaze. Amelia crawled into her father's arms and buried her face into his shirt.

"Come with us," Daniel said. "You'll be safer in Marinette."

"I can't," Hannah explained. "There are other injured who need the space far more than I. But I'll come meet you later, after I find John."

He shook his head. "Don't go. I've been thinking. With the trees and buildings burnt, there won't be any landmarks. You'll just get yourself lost. Maybe the men who aren't hurt too much will organize some parties and you can ask them to check John."

"I will," she promised. Before climbing down, she kissed him on the cheek.

"Don't forget you said you'd come and meet me, Hannah Shelton," Daniel called. "Don't you dare leave us alone."

"In Marinette," she promised. "In Marinette."

When more wagons came that afternoon, she asked. But each man had his own kin to find, or his own wounds to tend. The wagons available were being used to clear Peshtigo's own streets of corpses. Search parties were already looking, someone told her, though he couldn't say exactly where they'd gone.

"Just let the men tend to the troubles," a rotund woman said. "If you want to be of use, help me with these hurt folks."

For a while Hannah did, though her promise to find John still nagged her. After one o'clock, someone brought her food and coffee. These helped to revive her, but as the day pressed on, she grew no closer to learning Daniel's brother's fate. Feeling stronger, she decided to take matters into her own hands.

Slipping away from the small valley was simple. She was

no one's kin or sweetheart, so no one had a reason to keep an eye on her. For the first time since the evening before, she walked through Peshtigo.

Heaps of rubble smoked, and here and there she saw a roasted horse or dog. A few mounds looked as if they might have been human, but she didn't look too closely. She didn't want to know.

Her mind replayed the rows of neat white houses, all the thriving businesses. She couldn't even make sense of what she saw now. Daniel had been right. Without landmarks, it would be easy to get lost. She glanced toward the river and the half-collapsed bridge to reorient herself.

Wait—upstream, she saw a familiar shape. Could it be a horse? Hopeful, she changed her course. The animal she approached stood trembling, its tail singed to the roots. Its head hung low, the beast still wore a harness and its bridle.

"Easy, girl," Hannah whispered, for she could see it was a mare. Slowly, it responded to the kindness in her voice. The ears pricked forward, and the bay let her come near.

Hannah stroked the coarse brown hair and crooned some soothing nonsense. She felt the mare's thick legs and found no injuries. The horse was merely frightened and in shock, like all of them.

Using the harness, Hannah climbed onto the mare's broad back. Perhaps she should have taken the horse back to the valley, to see if she could find the owner. Later, she decided. For then she'd take the animal's appearance as a sign.

It was time to stop waiting for the men to do her bidding. It was time for her to keep her promise to find John.

Harnesses had never been designed to sit on, and neither had Hannah's dress been made to ride astride. Nevertheless, she made do, with the skirt pulled up alarmingly and the leather chafing at her inner calves. She would have liked to remove the harness, for riding bareback would be more comfortable for both horse and rider. But the harness, at least, gave Hannah something to grip when necessary, and more sense of control. She needed it, she found, for the horse started at puffs of smoke that still rose from piles of charred rubble, or from the ghastly stench of cooking flesh.

Though her sore ribs hurt with every step, Hannah forced herself to ignore their outcry. Soon, however, the unbelievable destruction numbed her senses. Blackened tree hearts poked up amid the former forest like sharp fangs. Mighty hardwoods lay crumpled and hurled across one another, mostly burned.

She followed along the twisted metal remnants of the new railroad for a time to keep her path. At one point she came across what must have been a wagon, burned down to the irons. A heap of ash at one end marked what used to be a horse, perhaps a team. A breeze rose to disperse it, and she caught a glimpse of something ivory, possibly a bone or tooth.

She rode on, forcing herself to focus only on her task. She had to keep her mind off the horrors she was seeing so she could search for John. She wondered if she did this to make up for her own deception to him.

Or did she do this just for Daniel? He had lost so much.

Those were not the only reasons, she decided. She did this for herself as well, so she could be again the kind of person she respected. Not a liar, not a cheat, just a woman helping a family she cared for.

She would find John for them all.

CHAPTER SEVENTEEN

When the first fat drops of rain spattered Hannah, she looked up angrily. "Why not yesterday?" she asked aloud. How many lives would have been saved? How much suffering could have been prevented?

But her anger, all unfocused, dissipated quickly. At least the fires would stop now; perhaps other communities might be spared this region's fate.

Soon the rain hissed down, at first raising puffs of ash, then washing the air free of it. Rivulets of water streamed over Hannah's scalp and ran down her face into her bodice. The previous night, after Lucinda's death, she had removed both coat and dress to dry them in the embers of some pails and barrels. Several men and women nearby did the same, as if they'd been in total privacy. Soon that effort was undone by the rain.

Still, the horse plodded forward, and Hannah continued in what she hoped was the correct direction. Often, she had to dismount to lead the mare around the tangled corpses of half-burned trees, or to try to discern what had once been a landmark. A journey that should have lasted an hour stretched to four, and she worried it would soon grow dark.

Once she found the pile of stones John and Daniel had removed from their plowed fields, Hannah managed to orient herself. Even so, the scene was dismal. Puddles of rainwater lay atop a thick layer of ash. The house, the Aldmans' simple but beautiful white house, had been reduced to a low pile of burned beams and blackened rubble. Nothing in it could have possibly survived. Every inch of field, garden, and pasture was scorched and ruined. Not even one small outbuilding survived.

Bowing her head, she prayed that John had left this nightmare before it had played out. Then she remembered Lucinda's words, *His farm is everything to John,* and shook her dripping head. He had not abandoned it. She knew it in her bones.

After she slid off the mare's back, Hannah tied the reins to the half-melted remnants of a pump. Though she suspected her efforts would be futile, she would keep her promise to Daniel. She would search as best she could for his brother's remains.

She couldn't even find an unburned stick to use to probe the ash. Instead, she used her feet to kick at some of the wreckage of the house. But her ankle boots had not been meant for soaking or today's work. Soon they fell to pieces, and she had to take them off.

With the heavy clouds, the light was failing, and Hannah shivered with the cold. Still, she continued walking through the house's ruin until she drove a nail into her right foot. With a shriek of pain and frustration, she jerked her foot loose and hobbled to a clearer spot. Her cry provoked more coughing, which hurt her side again.

This was lunacy. She might search for days without finding anything, even if she had not been injured. But now her punctured foot hurt even worse than her throbbing ribs, and the rain had chilled her to the bone. She needed to get back to Peshtigo, where she might find at least a tent. Already, she had delayed so long that day was beginning to fade. If she didn't leave then, she might die there.

Tears of defeat trailed down her face. She'd wanted so badly to do this for Daniel, to spare him the anguish of returning there. Her puny efforts had been so impotent.

"Get back while you can," she whispered to herself. The horse lifted its ears as she limped toward the place it had been tied. Exhausted, Hannah paid little heed to the sodden ruins she tramped through.

Until, with a splintered sound, burned wood gave way, and she plunged into a hole. She screamed in terror, arms flailing until one hand found something to grasp. With a jolt that sent a bolt of pain through her injured side, Hannah's body stretched and stopped its fall. Her left foot found purchase on another ladder rung, and she realized where she'd toppled. This had been the well.

Beneath her, something groaned.

"John?" Her voice, high and thin, echoed in the darkness. She scarcely dared to breathe.

"Who?" The voice below sounded even weaker than her own.

"It's Hannah. John, is that you?"

"Hannah . . . Daniel here with you?" John's voice was slurred, but finally recognizable.

Lowering herself carefully, Hannah descended the ladder into the shallow well. With this autumn's drought, the water reached only her lower thigh. In the dim light she could make out John's slumped form, sitting on an overturned bucket.

"I came alone," she told him. "Daniel's in Marinette. How badly are you hurt?"

"Wind picked up a board and sent it sailing last night. Whacked me in the head. Managed to get down here, but

I didn't have the strength to get back up. Why's Daniel in Marinette?''

She hesitated, wondering how she could get him up that ladder. "He's wounded. He needs you."

"How?"

Raindrops, inescapable, dripped onto her head. "A fire. Peshtigo is gone, burned to the ground. Come on. I'll help you up."

"Too tired, Hannah. I don't think I can. You go on. Get help."

She shook her head. "I won't leave you here. It would be too long before someone could come back. Listen, John, I'm hurt too, but I have a horse. We have to help each other get to her."

"Why'd you come here, Hannah? Why'd you really come?" The slur was building in his speech, as if he might soon fall asleep.

She had to rouse him somehow. If he went to sleep, he might never wake. Steeling herself, she lied. "Daniel's dying, John. He wants to see you while he can. You wouldn't want to be too late."

"No, not Daniel!" John jerked toward her, and she grasped his arm. His weight nearly drove her to her knees, but she managed to keep them both upright.

They both groaned as they struggled up the ladder, John ahead of her. She prayed he wouldn't fall, for if he did, he'd take her down, and neither of them would have the strength to try again. This time her prayers were answered. Once outside, John turned and helped her from the pit.

John looked around the ruin of his farm. "God help us. Not an animal alive. I tried so hard, but—"

"*Everyone* tried hard," Hannah interrupted. She pushed back a sodden mass of hair that had flopped into her eyes. "There was no fighting this. All the crews from the factory, all the men of Peshtigo, made no difference at all."

Together they staggered to the mare, who spooked at

their lumbering approach. Thankfully, her reins held. Hannah untied them as John climbed aboard. He reached down and pulled her up behind him.

The mare began the long walk toward Peshtigo. Though the rain tapered off, both John and Hannah were already soaked through. Tiredly, she leaned against his back for warmth. John did not complain.

"You didn't tell me what happened to Amelia and my aunt."

Hannah hesitated, but decided it would be best to tell him the truth. "Amelia is alive. I don't think she's hurt, just shocked. She went with Daniel to Marinette. John, I hope that you aren't angry, but I didn't want you to give up and go to sleep down in that well. You might not have survived if you did that. Daniel isn't dying, but his eyes are swollen shut. There were so many cinders when the mill and factory burned."

To her surprise, John laughed. "Thank God you're such an accomplished liar! Then, he'll be all right?"

Hannah nodded against his back. She coughed, but the effort made her ribs flare with new pain.

John's voice grew somber once again. "You didn't answer me about Aunt Lucinda."

When she could, Hannah spoke. "I'm sorry, John. She died. We spent last night in the river, but she'd been burned too badly."

She could hear the stifled sob inside his chest. "Dear Lord. 'In the way of righteousness is life; and in the pathway thereof there is no death.' I can only hope she didn't suffer. We'll miss her very much."

"She loved you too, all of you. A lot of people died last night. The men were gathering bodies when I left."

They rode on in silence for a long time, until the sky grew dark. Finally, he said, "I still don't know why you came for me. It should be obvious, we have nothing now."

Hannah's eyes fluttered open. She'd been half asleep.

"I did some bad things, but I'm not a monster. I care about your family."

The horse's hooves sloshed through muddy ash. Nearly as exhausted as her riders, the animal stumbled on a hole left by a root.

"Do you love my brother?" John asked quietly.

"I'm not certain," Hannah answered honestly. "I think I could if the situation weren't so . . . difficult. He's a good man."

"He can be." His voice sounded distant, as if he were remembering some other time. "He can be the best man I know."

By the time they arrived in what had been Peshtigo, John's head felt clearer than it had since the fire of the night before. He felt Hannah's breaths rasping against his back and thanked God for her warmth. He might have died down in that well without her. He still marveled that she'd come for him at all. Remembering his wretched insults and the way he'd struck her face, John felt sick with shame. Perhaps he had misjudged her, despite the lies she'd told. Surely, she must love his brother. Otherwise, why would she have ridden across this ashen wasteland to find him?

The horse plodded toward the river, guided only by the thin light of a crescent moon. *Poor beast,* he thought, wishing he had feed to offer, or even strength to rub the mare's tired legs. Neither was in his power now, but at least all three of them would soon find water.

As they topped a sandy rise, men walked up to greet them.

"We saw you coming. Are you hurt?" He recognized the voice. It was Gunderson, the owner of a hardware store.

"John Aldman," he identified himself. "We could use some help."

Strong hands pulled them both off the horse's back. A wave of dizziness made John's knees buckle and bright dots cloud his vision. When it cleared, he saw that two of the men were carrying Hannah to a tent. A thin shaft of fear restored him to alertness. Why hadn't she awakened?

"Hannah," he called after her.

"The ladies will see to her," Gunderson said. "She doesn't look too bad off. Don't have enough tents for the men, but we can find you blankets and a dry spot underneath one of these wagons." He gestured toward them. "Come over to the fire first. The ladies from Oconto sent some grub and coffee. I'll bet we have some left. One of the fellows will take care of your horse."

With a weary nod John took the arm Gunderson offered. Though he considered himself a religious man, he would have nearly sold his soul for the coffee, food, and blankets the man offered.

CHAPTER EIGHTEEN

Daniel lay on a narrow pallet inside the elegant lobby of the Simonton Hotel. He knew that only because he'd heard someone call the place by name, for it sounded like somewhere altogether different. It sounded like a hospital camp. All around him he heard those noises he most associated with the aftermath of battle: soft moaning, barked orders, calls for bandages, and constant reminders that everything needed to attend the wounded was in desperately short supply.

After the bayonet incident, he'd volunteered to become a surgeon's assistant. Though the mounds of sawn limbs and the blood were somehow more gruesome than combat, at least he'd had the satisfaction of knowing what he did was to help.

The smells here, too, brought back the nightmare: death amid the whiskey, given to numb pain. Only this death had a different note to it, an ashen sharpness he would not forget.

He thanked God for Uncle Phineas. After a kind-hearted, half-grown boy had fetched the old man, Phineas took Amelia from the frightful experiences of this temporary hospital. Daniel had been worried for her. Though she seemed unhurt, she'd grown all too quiet. The only things she'd asked for were her lost doll, Sally, and the missing kitten, Spice.

Though Phineas might have had little use for most of his kinfolk, every woman in Wisconsin, and any mule who'd ever drawn breath, Daniel trusted him to take good care of Amelia. And God help anyone who tried to stand in his way! During the short time he was there, Phineas had browbeat the overworked doctor into checking Daniel right away.

"Oh, I expect he'll be all right," Dr. Heinrich told the old farmer after a quick examination. "The burns look superficial. We'll try some salve a couple of times tonight and check him in the morning. But I think a few days' rest will set him right."

As if he could rest. "What time is it?" he asked aloud in the direction of the feet he heard shuffling nearby.

He recognized the woman's sigh. She'd been helping Dr. Heinrich since he'd been brought there, hours before. "You've been asking me all day," she snapped. Her voice sounded young and tired. "I have more to do than check my watch. It's after ten o'clock and high time you were asleep. Didn't you hear the doctor say to rest?"

He snorted, impatient with his discomfort and the endless hours of waiting. As irritating as he found her, he couldn't blame the woman for getting fed up with his question. He'd probably asked the time on at least a dozen occasions already. He couldn't help it though. How could he relax, not knowing if his brother was alive? How could he abandon his worries over Hannah and how Aunt Lucinda's body had been handled? How could he stop wondering about his daughter or what any of them would do now to survive?

Not far away, a woman screamed shrilly. "We're on fire! We're on fire! Throw more water on us!" She'd been screaming it all day, just as he had asked the time. Daniel had heard the doctor and nurse whispering that her four children had all died. Though the woman had survived, her hands were nothing but charred bone.

Was he like that poor woman, obsessed with the passage of time, worried for a brother he would never see again? He thought about the farm and tried to imagine flames burning around all the plowed acreage, ignoring fields and house. Perhaps John slept there tonight, exhausted and filthy, yet safe in his own bed. Maybe Hannah had persuaded a rescue team to search for him, but instead they'd found him, safe and sound, and all enjoyed a drink to his good fortune.

Perhaps, Daniel tried hard to believe, it was all still there: his brother, the farm, and his old life to return to. He stared the image down in his mind's eye, then let the focus soften into an exhausted sleep.

Sometime after dawn, Gunderson shook John's shoulder. "I think you'd better come. The ladies couldn't wake your wife. They think we better get her to Marinette."

John brushed dried grass from his hair and shook his head. Wife? What wife? Where? He sat up and banged his head on the wagon's underside. With that jolt, yesterday rushed back, and he realized the man squatting down beside him had meant Hannah.

"What's wrong?" he asked as his hand rubbed at the sore spot. He grimaced as he accidentally brushed the bump he'd received in the huge fire.

"I haven't seen her, but my wife says she's pale as milk and her breathing's rough. You better come with me."

John nodded. "She's not my wife. She's my brother's—" On short notice, he couldn't imagine how to term Daniel and Hannah's relationship. He settled for "She's my brother's lady friend. He's laid up in Marinette as well. Can I help you hitch the horses?"

Several had sickened during the night, so Gunderson and John ended up taking Hannah, a young mother with a badly wheezing infant, and an old man who, like John, had come in from an outlying farm last evening. Much of his body had blistered where his clothes had been burned off.

John's heart sank when he saw Hannah Shelton. Her breath rattled in her chest, not unlike the sick baby. He could feel heat rising from her body even before he laid his hand to her pale cheek. How had she managed to find him and crawl out of that well last evening?

A guilty thought crept through his consciousness. If she died, that would at least keep her from his brother. Finally, the woman who had stolen all his hopes would forever be out of his life.

The idea withered as quickly as it came. Though he still harbored some anger, he couldn't really wish her dead. Not after she'd rescued Amelia from the speeding wagon. Not after she'd saved his life. Not after he remembered Mary's death.

He'd never really cared for the young woman Daniel loved. Her English was broken and her ways strange to his family. His brother could do better, he had reckoned. He pictured her pretty face, the sprightly way she'd moved even when she'd been carrying his niece. Though they'd never spoken very much, he did recall her ready laughter. Musical, it flowed like the moonlit river of her golden hair.

He saw her still, sometimes, in Amelia. Amelia, whom he treasured as if she were his own. Amelia, to whom he showed the love he had so long withheld from Daniel's wife.

Too long. Too late now to make amends for all of that.

John found some cool water and a cloth to take with them.

" 'And be ye kind one to another,' " he whispered as he wet the scrap of blanket. As Gunderson drove, he washed Hannah's hot face. For himself far more than her, John finished the verse. " '. . . forgiving one another, even as God for Christ's sake hath forgiven you.' "

Daniel cared for her, John reminded himself, and so did Amelia. His disapproval of the woman would exact too high a cost. John swore to himself he would tell his brother he would support him in any relationship that might develop with Hannah Shelton.

That is, he would if he could now keep her alive.

Hannah's head banged against something hard. She tried to look to see what it had been. But her eyes seemed stuck together, and the feeling of movement, jolting and bumpy, nauseated her.

Instead of opening her eyes, she grasped at the cloth that served her as a blanket. Horse blanket, most likely, from the smell. Still, it protected her against the chill and kept her from shivering so violently.

"Just a few more miles, Hannah." A voice—her father's? —loomed near and above her.

That couldn't be her father, could it? Wasn't Father dead? An image of his unconscious form assailed her. Blood was dripping from his ear. That's right. The horse had kicked him. Father couldn't be here now.

Then, had that voice been Malcolm's? It seemed even less likely. Malcolm despised illness, and she was sick now, wasn't she? He would have found some aunt to tend her, or hired a girl from town.

More blood dripped through her memory, the blood that she had sloshed across the wooden floor.

No, Malcolm would never care for her again. Then who? She forced herself to look.

"There's the girl." John Aldman put a fresh cloth on her forehead. "It won't be long now. You have a fever of some sort, but there's a doctor in Marinette. Daniel's there too."

Hannah tried to process the events of the last few days, but they were swept up like playing cards caught in a tornado. Try as she might to grab at one, it spun off in the wind.

Her eyelids sank as slowly as a cat's beside the fire, and she let the last cards flip away.

A voice rumbled into Hannah's consciousness, a woman's voice hoarse with exhaustion. "Daniel Aldman? I'm sorry, but he's gone."

Hannah tried to force herself fully awake, to bellow out denial, but she had no strength to do so. She felt as if the stranger's words had robbed her of her will.

Daniel. Gone. How could he have died?

Hannah moaned miserably. Her head pulsed painfully, and tears squeezed through her lashes.

Daniel. Gone. Had he, too, taken ill? Had they survived the fire only to succumb to the aftereffects of smoke or river water?

Dear God, why hadn't she ever told him how he made her feel? Why hadn't she promised what he'd wanted that night at the Barlows?

As with Robert, her strength had once more cursed her. She had forever lost her chance to love this man.

The doctor, a sharp-nosed, tired-looking man, took John Aldman by the arm and pulled him out into the hall. "We'll keep her here, alone. She's probably contagious.

Fever like hers could sweep through these burn victims in no time."

John glanced anxiously toward the half-closed hotel room door. "What will you do for her?"

The middle-aged physician ran a hand through thinning brown hair and sighed. "What we can. Tepid sponge baths, and perhaps she'll take a willow bark tea. The rest is up to her."

"Will she live, then?"

The doctor peered at him through a smudged pair of spectacles. "Does she want to?"

"What?"

"So many have lost children, husbands, parents. She's very ill. If she doesn't wish to live . . ." An attractive young blond woman who'd been helping Dr. Heinrich waved for his attention down the hall. "Please, excuse me, Mr. Aldman."

The blond woman stared at John for several moments, until she saw him looking back. Then she hurried after Dr. Heinrich.

John watched them both recede into another nightmare, another person's need. Cautiously, he opened the door to Hannah's room. Now she lay alone, thrashing uncomfortably in a hotel bed. No one here had time to tend a woman who might well be contagious.

"Don't take my farm, Malcolm," she muttered. "You've taken everything. Please don't take my father's farm."

He went to the washbasin and dipped a white cloth into cool water. After wringing it, he laid it on her brow. She tried to push his hand away, though her eyes never opened.

"Lie still, Hannah," he said quietly. "Rest easy until I can come back."

John borrowed a horse and rode out to his uncle's farm. He was relieved to see how well it had fared. The same rough log house glared stubbornly across fields now barren after harvest. The same dairy cattle and black mules grazed untroubled on brownish grass refreshed by yesterday's rains. A nearby barn stood like a monument to everyday farm life.

One of the mules looked up and brayed a greeting at John's borrowed mount. A minute later Uncle Phineas burst out of the house, doing something John had never seen before. The old man was laughing. He called into the house, "I told you he's like me! That John's too stubborn to burn up!"

Squealing, Amelia pushed past the gray-bearded bachelor and raced toward her uncle. John slid from the bay gelding and lifted her up into his arms in a fierce embrace.

"Uncle John!" she cried. A few moments later, Phineas clapped him on the back so hard, he nearly choked.

"God bless you, boy, you made it!" the old man shouted. "Here, let me take your horse, and you go see your brother."

Eagerly, John relinquished the reins and carried Amelia inside the cabin. Daniel was standing, peering through swollen eyelids that leaked tears. Without a word he crushed his brother in his arms.

"You're squashing me!" cried Amelia. John put down the child, and his brother hugged him even harder.

"Daniel, your eyes. Can you—"

"A little," Daniel answered. "They're getting better by the hour. Where's Hannah? Is she with you?"

So quickly, the mood of their reunion changed. "She's at the big hotel in town, where you were. She's pretty sick. I think you'd better come."

"Sick? What happened?"

"She came alone to find me yesterday," John said. "It was raining hard, and she fell into the well, where I had hidden. I'd taken a good hit to the head. I was just sitting there, sort of dazed. Hannah made me climb out to where she had a horse. If she hadn't come, I'd be there still."

"So how did she get sick?"

"I don't know. Exhaustion, rain. It poured all the way to town. By the time we made it back to what was Peshtigo, she was burning hot. She didn't even wake up when they pulled her off the horse. Doc Heinrich called it fever. He asked me if she'd want to live. I don't know how to answer that. I thought that you—"

"What are you saying, John?"

"I'm saying that I won't stand in your way. Maybe Hannah hurt me, but like you said, I think she had her reasons. And maybe"—he glanced toward Amelia—"maybe I've learned some hard lessons about being quick to judge. I've been so quick to spout Scripture, I've forgotten the Good Book's warnings on that very subject. Daniel, I believe Hannah Shelton saved my life. That ought to be enough to buy her one more chance."

Daniel grinned and again reached out to hug his brother. John quickly stepped aside. "My ribs can't take another one," he said. "You save some of that for Hannah, but don't be too long."

"You sound tired, John. Stay here with Amelia. I'll get Uncle Phineas to drive me into town."

John nodded and slid tiredly into a rocking chair. Before him, gray ashes lay inside the hearth, remnants of a tamer sort of fire.

A broad-hipped woman blocked Daniel's way into the room. "I'm sorry," she began to tell him.

"I have to see her," Daniel interrupted. Through the haze clouding his eyesight she looked like a woman cast in iron. Certainly, she might weigh as much.

"She's delirious. She won't even know you're here.

We're taking care of her. I'm Mrs. Brannon. You ask for me, and I'll let you know how she's doing."

"She'll want to see me," he insisted.

Still, the woman remained wedged in the doorway. "Do you want to catch it too?"

"Catch what?"

She shrugged. "Take your pick. This could be a lot of things. None of them very good."

"How bad off is she?"

"I'd be guessing." The woman gave a jowly frown.

"Guess."

"My sister was like this last winter. She died late in the night. Some don't though. You might try praying. It couldn't hurt."

"You're a real comfort," Daniel told her wryly, "but I'm going in. I'll take care of her."

"You still need doctoring yourself."

"I'm fine, fine enough to move you if I have to. Neither of us would like it much."

With a grunt of annoyance the iron woman moved her bulk. "If you catch this and die, don't complain to me."

The two exchanged a twisted smile, an unspoken sign of truce, and Daniel moved into the room.

And immediately wished he had not come. It was the smell that did it, that peculiar smell of sickness, death. During the war he'd known it well, but since then, only once. With his wife. He began to sweat, and through his swollen eyes he saw another time, another fever.

To the slender form wrapped in a white blanket, he whispered softly, "Mary . . ."

The stout woman had been right. His back rested against the door he had just pushed closed. He did not belong there. Tending the sick was work for women. His daughter was his job, that and helping John to get the farm rebuilt. What if he, too, took fever? What if he, too, died? Panic slammed his heart against his chest wall.

Filled with desperation to escape to open air, he reached for the knob. He couldn't even breathe within this miasma of memory.

"Daniel . . ." Hannah muttered. "Daniel, I'm so sorry. I never let you know."

He froze, all his size and strength useless against a few mumbled words.

"I couldn't tell you. How much you meant. How much you made me feel." Her voice was little more than whisper, but he heard every word.

The words thawed him, melted away his indecision. In an instant he knelt beside her. "Hannah." He said her name like a benediction, as much to reassure himself as her.

She opened her eyes, her clear blue eyes, to gaze at him. Rivulets of sweat rolled down her face to mingle with her tears. He felt heat rolling off her pale face in waves just like the river fire.

"John lived," she told him simply. "We didn't make it, but John lived. He'll take care of Amelia now. And we'll see Lucinda soon."

"Hannah? I'm alive. You're alive. Here, you have to drink now. Cool water will taste good." He lifted her up with one strong arm and raised a glass to her parched lips.

She pushed the glass away. "Mother's here. She's singing to me now. I can't quite make out the words. Do you hear her too?"

"She wants you to get better." Again Daniel tried to make her take some water. This time she sipped at it, then coughed, her lungs rattling with congestion.

He forced her to swallow more, then washed her face with some of the cool water. He thought he saw her smile, though he suspected the gesture was for whatever specters she now saw.

"I'm going to stay with you," he told her. "I'm going to stay till you get better."

Her eyes slid closed again. "Mary says that I should stay, then. Mary says I belong here."

The stout woman, Mrs. Brannon, brought a tray with food and coffee. She lit a lamp against the dusk and offered to spell him for a while. He declined and thanked her. Then he returned to the straight chair where he'd sat most of the day, in a room that felt crowded with old ghosts.

Mary says that I should stay, then. He shuddered at the memory of those words.

Mary was a common name. Maybe Hannah knew someone named Mary. Another Mary who had died.

Or perhaps his own memories had evoked her. Maybe Mary *had* told Hannah to stay there. That would mean that she approved, that somewhere, somehow, she guessed what Hannah had come to mean to him.

And what he meant to Hannah. If her delirium did not speak louder than her heart.

He took her hand, a hand that felt impossibly warm. "You have to live," he told her. "I can't lose you now."

Hours later another tap at the door jarred him from uneasy thoughts. When he answered, his heart leapt to his throat. Mary, in the hallway, held a flickering candle in her hand. Her soft blond hair hung loose behind her, past her shoulders like a girl's.

"My mother sent me to see if you'd like anything. I hope I didn't wake you." The voice was wrong, no accent. Not Mary's, but he recognized it anyway.

Daniel swallowed, embarrassed by this trick of light, of memory, and his still-dim vision. Thank God he'd realized his mistake before he'd blurted out his surprise!

"N—no," he stammered. "We—we're fine. But I want to apologize. I know your voice. You're the woman I kept asking for the time."

She laughed, an odd sound in this grim place. "I'll

admit, I thought of prying the crystal off my watch so you could feel the hands. But it's all right. My name's Bess, Bess Brannon. If you need anything, I'll be downstairs all night."

"Thank you. For everything you and your mother are doing," Daniel said.

"What else could any Christian do?" she asked. "I feel fortunate my family wasn't lost. But might I ask you something, if it's not too personal?"

He nodded his assent, and she continued.

"Is this woman your wife?"

Daniel glanced back toward Hannah and took a deep breath. "Not yet," he answered simply. "Not yet."

Daniel woke with a jolt. He hadn't meant to fall asleep, slumped against the chair's unyielding edges. He'd been asleep when he lost Mary. He could not forget the shock of seeing her, of knowing that the stillness of her body went far deeper than sleep. Though he knew better, he'd often wondered if, awake, he could have stopped her passing.

Grayish light filtered through the curtains, and he could tell his eyesight had greatly improved. The contours of Hannah's pallid face were sharper; the loose hair consisted of dark strands, not just a blur. She lay so still. Like Mary.

A rushing noise, like the firestorm, filled his ears.

Somehow, just beyond it rose a sigh. Hannah's sigh, soft and female. She rolled toward him in her sleep.

Again her eyes opened, as if she'd sensed his gaze.

"I thought I heard someone say you were dead," she told him.

Huge fingers trembling visibly, he took her hand in his. Heat no longer rolled in waves off her flesh. "I'm fine," he assured her.

Accented by dark smudges just beneath them, the pale

blue of her eyes stood out like the sky over Lake Michigan on a day sharpened by the sun. He leaned forward and kissed her forehead gently, then offered her some water.

This time she drank eagerly. When she finished, she said, "I was so frightened."

He nodded. "That makes two of us."

Hannah slept throughout much of the day. Daniel, too, dozed, his back tortured by the unrelenting chair.

Early in the afternoon, John arrived. A good night's sleep, a bath, and a set of Phineas's worn but clean clothing had left him looking far less ragged than on the previous day.

With Hannah resting peacefully, Daniel stepped into the hall and embraced his brother once again.

"Is she—" John began to ask.

"Better than last night for certain, but she's very weak."

"And you? Your eyes?"

Daniel nodded. "I can even see the freckles on your forehead. How's Amelia?"

John grinned. "Uncle Phineas has a litter of kittens in the hayloft. Your daughter will be fine."

Daniel nodded. "She talk much about Aunt Lucinda?"

"Not yet. She cried for her doll instead."

"Will you watch her for another day? I don't want to leave here till I can be certain about Hannah."

John nodded. "Amelia will be happy you're taking care of her. I imagine you know why."

Daniel nodded, chuckling. "That little girl's a worse matchmaker than Lucinda ever was. Lord, John, I'm going to miss that old woman."

"So am I. I'm about to go check on her burial arrangements. We'll have a service soon as I can manage. There'll be lots of services around these parts the next few days.

I'll let you know when I find out the details." John's gaze avoided his. Daniel was grateful, knowing both of them would be embarrassed by tears now.

"Thank you," he said simply. "We'll have to start rebuilding soon. Winter comes on early."

"You're willing?"

"What else would we do? Hopefully, the money and valuables we buried will be a help."

John nodded. "There's enough to make a start. We're better off than most."

Daniel glanced back toward the doorway. "It sounds ridiculous when you consider all our losses, but right now I feel like a damned lucky man."

Hannah heard a light tap at the door, then someone speaking to Daniel. She recognized the voice of the stout woman who'd been helping Dr. Heinrich. "I thought, since you haven't keeled over like I warned, you could help clean up your wife."

Wife? Was that what Daniel told them, or had the woman just assumed? Either way, he said nothing to correct her error. Through slitted eyelids Hannah watched him carry in a steaming basin and some clean white cloths.

She was so tired, she didn't make a sound. Earlier, Daniel had given her spoonfuls of broth, as if she'd been a baby. The effort of sitting up had exhausted her last reserves of strength.

He set the basin on the washstand and gazed at the clean water. She smiled to herself, imagining him thinking he could stand a wash himself.

She watched as he removed his shirt. Opposite him, in the mirror, the muscles of his chest rippled as he washed his upper body. The burned area on his shoulder looked less angry than she expected. Her interest quickened as he leaned forward to touch the singed hairs of his upper chest.

Behind him, she chuckled. "Preening like an old tom turkey."

He turned to look at her. "I thought you were asleep."

She shrugged. "I'll bet that bath was meant for me. If you'll give me a wet cloth and turn your back, I think I can manage to wash."

Hannah sat up quickly. Too quickly. With a groan she sank back on the pillow.

"Here," Daniel offered. "Let me get someone to help you."

She shook her head. "They have so many to take care of."

He gazed at her intently. "Then I will. There's no need to be prudish. I came to make sure you're taken care of. Here. Lean forward, and I'll help you with the dress."

She looked uncertain, but after a moment did as he asked.

Daniel fumbled with what seemed to be dozens of fussy little buttons. Before he'd finished unbuttoning half of them, it became apparent his efforts were in vain. The seams of the soot-stained dress were tearing with the strain of his attempt.

"Sorry. There's not going to be much left."

"I've found Wisconsin—very hard on clothes." The filthy cloth slipped over her head. She panted with the effort and closed her eyes as she lay back.

Gingerly, he began to wash her bare arms with a clean cloth. Strange, how exposed she felt. Here she was, still in her petticoat, but she might as well have been naked for the way her heart was pounding.

She was all too conscious of his still-bare chest, of the intimacy of this moment.

"That feels nice," she whispered. The thin strap of the petticoat slipped down her shoulder. Very slowly, he allowed the cloth to round its curve. In the wake of the warm water, her skin prickled with gooseflesh.

Slowly, deliberately, Daniel leaned forward and kissed that shoulder, then the pulsing throat. She stared up into his dark eyes. Her body felt heavy and languid, yet she could not have slept for all the world. The tingling of her neck and shoulder, where he'd kissed them, was far too intense.

With an almost imperceptible shrug, Hannah let the second strap fall too. Again he cleaned, then kissed that shoulder, her throat, and last, her parted lips. His free hand slid along the smooth curve of her waist, then lingered near the ties that held her petticoat. Lingered, then pulled gently to loose them.

He pulled down the fabric, unlaced her corset until her chest was as bare as his. Then, remembering his task, he washed her, his hands traveling so slowly that Hannah wanted to speed them with her own. He helped her to sit up, and cleaned her back as well. When she leaned forward, she felt each cooling droplet as it ran between her breasts.

He took a soft, dry cloth and toweled her back with it. "I mustn't let you chill. It's important that I warm you."

She was trembling now, but not with cold. She lay back and let him dry her front. Then he laid aside the cloth and stared down at the hollow of her throat.

"I see I've missed a spot." He moved closer to kiss away the beads of water. His kisses traveled, soft and wet along her neck. She wanted to cry out, in joy or fear she wasn't certain, but he took her mouth then with his lips.

A shudder rippled through her as she felt his hands slide upward from her waist to test the fullness of both breasts. His thumbs played with the nipples until his mouth moved slowly downward to join in the caresses.

Stop! Why didn't she push him instead of caressing the straining muscles of his back? Why didn't she tell him to move away? Her lips parted, but only a long sigh escaped.

She tried to gather her resolve, but all she could remember was how it felt when she had thought he was dead, how much she had regretted not making love to him before.

She thought of how he'd sat with her so long. She thought of all the gentleness of his attentions. It had been so long since anyone had cared for her, and perhaps no one ever would again. Would it be so wrong to take whatever comfort he was offering for then?

One of his hands caressed her ankle, and he looked up into her eyes. "It seems a shame to wash only the top half."

She shifted her hips as he tugged off the petticoat and her remaining underthings.

"The water's cool by now," she told him.

He smiled. "Don't worry. I can warm you."

Hannah closed her eyes and with her flesh traced the progress of the damp cloth along her feet and legs. She tensed as the refreshing water moved higher, higher, until it raised gooseflesh along the sensitive skin at the insides of her thighs. The coolness glided across her belly. With maddening strokes he dried her, then rolled her over and turned his attention to the backs of her legs, then her buttocks.

She felt so comfortable, so reassured. So tired but pleasantly relaxed. She felt so . . .

Daniel couldn't believe it when he heard the faint rattles of her snores. He ran a palm regretfully along the indentation of her spine, then sighed.

Of course she was exhausted. She'd been so near death last night. Seducing her in this state would have been taking advantage, and he was almost grateful she had put a stop to it.

Almost. He admired her slender curves for a full minute

before covering her with sheets and blanket. Then he looked down at the ruins of her clothing. All of it was stained with soot and muddy river water, and half the dress's seams had come undone.

He buttoned his own shirt and finger-combed his wavy hair.

She was going to need some clothes. He wondered if Bess had by then complicated the matter by informing her mother that he and Hannah were not man and wife.

He need not have wondered long. Mrs. Brannon's fat face rippled like a squall line when he met her in the lobby.

"Bess says you misled me. I'm not sure you know it, but my cousin, Mr. Horatio Simonton, owns this place. He wouldn't think much of an unmarried couple spending the night in the same room. Why didn't you correct me when I brought you the washbasin?"

Daniel frowned. He had no patience for such technicalities. "Didn't seem worth your attention. You have a lot of sick and dying folks. I thought I'd help by taking care of Hannah."

"How? By giving the poor thing something to live for? The buttons on your shirt are still askew, Mr. Aldman. I'd suggest you leave before I have someone remove you."

He stared at her in utter disbelief. Now probably wouldn't be the best time to mention that he'd ruined Hannah's clothes.

How could this insufferable woman be worried about niceties when so many lay near death? He wanted to give her the rough side of his tongue, but some part of him knew Mrs. Brannon was half right. He'd nearly led Hannah down the garden path in her weakened condition. It would be best if he left for now. Hannah would never forgive him if he made matters worse by stirring up a ruckus.

Striding out of the makeshift hospital, Daniel promised

himself that he would be back soon. So what if the old battle-ax was death on unwed couples behind closed doors together?

As long as this town still had a minister, he knew a cure for that.

CHAPTER NINETEEN

Hannah noticed the feeling of the crisp sheets against her nude limbs first. Then her stomach growled insistently. She rolled over on her back, eager to see Daniel and ask if he might get her some real food this time.

But the chair where he had sat was vacant, and that shock brought back all the rest. The bathing, the kissing, the forbidden touches. She felt a flush warm her face, but in spite of it, she smiled, remembering.

Remembering . . . exactly what? Every detail remained with her until— She shook her head, confused. Had she made love and then forgotten? Recalling the heat Daniel's touch inspired, she doubted such a thing was possible. But fevers sometimes did strange things to memory. Still, she felt it more likely that in her weakened state she had drifted off to sleep.

If that were true, had Daniel stopped himself? The thought of the powerfully built man ravishing her helpless body made her feel violated, angry. Could he have done such an awful thing?

Tears blurred her vision as her eyes focused on the empty chair. Had he just taken her and left? Had that been all he'd wanted all along?

No, she told herself. He hadn't made love to her before, even though she had been willing. He must have just stepped out to find some food or attend some personal need. He'd be back. He'd have to.

He'd be back for her.

Hours later, tears rolled down her face. Hannah's hands shook as she brushed aside their moisture. Daniel hadn't come, and the more she thought about it, the surer she was that he wouldn't. He had never said he loved her. He had never promised marriage.

And why would he? He didn't have to, after all. She'd helped him disrobe her. She'd done everything but hire a brass band to communicate her desire to bed him.

"Why buy the cow when you can get the milk for free?" Her father told her that once as a warning about youthful ardor. Did all men live by that crude maxim?

The woman's nothing but a slut.

Had she become what Malcolm called her? Was there any difference between her and Rosalind's ilk?

She shook her head, recalling how Daniel saved her from deep water at the river, how they'd passed that fiery night together side by side. Maybe the disaster had only magnified a passing fancy, focused into hot passion what was never meant to be.

Had both of them been merely caught up in the struggle to survive? Had Daniel truly thought he loved her, in the wake of losing farm and home and aunt?

Fury boiled in her veins. This hadn't been some innocent mistake! Otherwise, he'd be there to apologize and make some excuse in the hope of letting her down easy. If he hadn't taken advantage of her illness, then why would he have fled?

Hope flared at a tapping on the door. Clutching blankets to her chest, Hannah called, "Come in." Her recriminations would have faded; she would have laughed at all her silly fears.

If only it were Daniel at the door.

Bess Brannon turned the knob and pushed, a tray of food balanced on one narrow hip. Her mother, righteously indignant, had no doubt sent her there to puzzle out the Aldman mystery. Had the huge, handsome man used this woman's illness to some immoral advantage, or had he been doing only what he claimed?

The dark-haired woman's tear-streaked face and the pile of her torn clothes beside the bed seemed to answer all.

"Oh, merciful Lord!" cried Bess. She hurried inside and kicked shut the door behind her. "Did he— He seemed like such a *nice* man."

The brunette straightened her spine and used a corner of the sheet to dry her face. "He took care of me." Her voice quavered, and Bess guessed it was herself the woman most wished to convince.

Bess gnawed her lower lip. At only twenty, she hadn't dealt with anything like this before. How did one handle such an unspeakable event without further damaging the woman's reputation?

The blonde put down her tray and stared at the discarded dress. "I'll bring you some of my clothes. I think we're close enough in size. No one has to know. And don't worry, my mother threw him out of this hotel the moment he came down the stairs. She'll have the law on him if he comes back."

Despite her tears, the woman had a lovely face, with

large blue eyes and delicately chiseled features. "Your mother?" she asked, holding the blanket even tighter.

"Of course. When Mr. Aldman told me last night that the two of you weren't yet married, I thought he was sweet to risk his life to stay with you. Dr. Heinrich feared you'd be contagious. But Mother says I'm too naive. She said he just took that basin and went along with her when she assumed you were his wife." Bess shifted her feet, and guilt welled up inside her. "I hope you'll forgive me. Last night I should have realized that his staying wasn't proper. But there are so many people hurt and dying all around. I didn't even think what he'd be up to."

The dark-haired beauty patted the bed for her to sit. When Bess obliged, she squeezed her hand. "I'm Hannah Shelton. I want to thank you for offering the clothing. The fire took everything I had. Don't feel bad about Daniel. I was upset only because I didn't know why he had left."

"But what about—" Bess began to ask. Her gaze dropped to the floor.

"Between a dousing in the river and that downpour the other day, the only thing holding that dress together was the mud. When I took it off, it came to pieces. Daniel left so I could wash. That's all. This was innocent, I promise." She forced a weary smile, and Bess heard her stomach growl.

"Oh. I almost forgot. I've brought some stew and milk. My name is Bess Brannon. Let me help you eat."

As she ate, Hannah concentrated on the wholesome flavors of stewed tomatoes, beef, and vegetables, and the scent of the warm steam beneath her nose. She thought about the fresh-baked bread with gobs of pale butter smeared across it. She tried to concentrate on these and Bess's presence so she wouldn't think of Daniel Aldman anymore. So she wouldn't remember Bess saying "Mr.

Aldman told me last night the two of you weren't yet married." *Yet.*

Still, she found her own words the hardest to forget. *This was innocent, I promise.*

She wished with all her heart she could believe it.

After leaving Hannah, Bess went to face that duty she most despised, bandaging the wounds of the burn victims. One of the women, a widow in her midthirties, handed her a tray and fresh strips made from clean torn sheets.

"Here's a pair of scissors too," Mrs. Tanner added. "Better keep 'em handy when you do that eastern gentleman."

Bess smiled. Captain Hollas, he had said his name was. His face and hands oozed with painful burns, but instead of enduring them with the stoicism of a former officer, the man did nothing but complain.

"Don't worry, Mrs. Tanner," Bess said as she took the tray. "I'll keep them leveled at all times near his tongue. He wouldn't want to lose *that*."

A grin showed off Gen Tanner's smile. "If you decide you need to take it, just be sure to call your ma and me so we can hold him down."

"I know you're busy, Reverend, and I appreciate you doing this. It will take just a few minutes," Daniel said over his shoulder. He wiped his feet to keep from tracking morning dew into the fancy lobby.

No one challenged the two men as they went to Hannah's room. Either Mrs. Brannon hadn't seen him, or she recognized the man of God as an honorable way to rectify the "problem."

When he tapped, he was relieved to hear Hannah's voice invite him in.

He stepped inside, the minister behind him.

"Daniel?" Hannah said. She sat before the mirror with her hair down. She still held the brush she'd been using. "We need to talk in private."

"I'm sure you've heard by now how I was asked to leave," Daniel said. "I've brought the reverend here to set things right."

For a woman who had been sick, the color rose to her face in an instant. She stood, wearing a green dress Daniel hadn't seen before. "T-to set things right? That's all you think of me? Get out, Daniel Aldman. Get out and don't come back! I'm strong enough to help take care of some of the injured now, so I won't need your 'tender care.' Now *go!*"

Daniel spared the minister a sheepish glance. "I suppose that means we won't be needing you. Thanks anyway."

The minister nodded and, with a grateful sigh, excused himself. Daniel didn't budge. Instead, he pushed the door closed.

"Now tell me," he asked, "what was *that* about?"

"It was about what happened yesterday, and I told you to get out."

"What happened yesterday? You fell asleep. That's what happened. Not the most flattering thing, I suppose, but sick as you were, I understood."

Hannah's blue eyes narrowed. "I fell asleep . . . and *you* . . ."

"Went downstairs to try to find you some new clothes. What did you *think* I—" The truth dawned and he took a few steps nearer. "You didn't think I'd take advantage of you in that condition?"

Hannah's blush deepened until he saw rose splotches on her chest. "I awoke unclothed, and you were gone. I—I didn't know what to believe."

"Next time, *I* believe I'll remember to button my shirt straight around Mrs. Brannon." He chuckled at the thought.

"This isn't funny, Daniel. Do you know what they think of me?"

"Do you care?" he asked.

"You don't understand at all what it's like to be a woman. Our reputations mean so much."

"If I didn't understand how you felt, why do you think I'd bring a minister along?"

"That's why? That's the only reason?"

Daniel squared his shoulders as if he were facing down a drunken brawler. "Of course it's not the only reason. I *want* to marry you. I think that's always what I've wanted since we met. But, it seemed the right thing to hurry it along now. I'm not all that much for formalities, but—"

"Don't you see? By bringing in the minister, you confirmed what those women suspected."

"Maybe I shouldn't marry you." He felt his temper rising, blasting past his better judgment. "For a woman with a somewhat tattered reputation, you seem to cherish it an awful lot. Tell me, does what a few old hens think mean more to you than love?"

"What love, Daniel? What love?" She leaned forward, such longing in her eyes that it took his breath away.

Daniel wanted to take her in his arms, to tell her what she wished to hear, to tell her, then to wed her on this very day. He couldn't stand a long engagement. He wanted to make Hannah his right then and there. He reached for her small waist, and she took a step backward.

"No," she told him, her chin held high as ever. "There must be words this time, Daniel. And 'here's the minister' won't do."

That blasted pride of hers again. Here he was, trying to do right, and she was back to playing debutante.

"I love you, Hannah," he growled. Anything to get this over with.

She whirled around, grabbed a teacup from the table,

and hurled it in his direction. It shattered against the door, splattering him with cool brown dregs.

"Either mean it or don't say it," she demanded.

Well, a man had his pride too, and he'd be damned if he'd stay here and swallow his till he could find a way to suit her. Turning on his heel, he spoke over his shoulder.

"A man's words don't have to come in pretty packages to be God's honest truth."

He slammed the door on his way out in case she chose to throw the saucer too.

"Would you like to help change bandages?" Bess asked her the next day. "I can always use another pair of hands. Mother's cousin said you could stay here awhile if we need your help. I talked him into it. I'm afraid Mother still suspects you're a bad influence."

"I'll try to live up to your faith," Hannah said. "Thank you for the dresses. They fit beautifully."

Bess cast a critical eye on her, then smiled. "I think you might fill out the top part better than I did, but I won't hold that against you if you'll help with the captain."

"The captain?"

"He's a treat. Complains constantly about how rough we are, the food, the bed. He acts like visiting royalty instead of a victim here on charity."

Hannah smiled. "He sounds like someone I once knew. Don't worry. I can handle that type."

Bess led Hannah toward the room where several burned men had been crowded. She felt sorry for the others, having to listen to that Hollas fellow.

"I saw your friend come back," Bess said lightly. "With the minister in tow."

"He had the nerve to think I'd marry him because *he* fancied the idea."

Bess turned. "And you said no?"

"Of course. He never even asked."

"Do you think he will?"

"It's hard to say. I insulted him. I even threw a cup."

"He's a very handsome man," Bess said.

"There's more to it than that."

"Of course. You have to find out if you love him. Do you?"

Hannah sighed, considering. "I'm glad the teacup missed him."

Bess smiled. "That's sounds like love to me."

"That's what I'm afraid of." The two women laughed, and Hannah wondered how she could have missed that simple truth. The maelstrom of emotions Daniel stirred in her all boiled down to love. Funny she should realize it only after she'd rejected his strange declaration.

A loud crash from the dining room distracted their attention. Several children, some recovering and others with sick parents, had knocked down a stack of plates.

"You little beasts!" Mrs. Brannon shouted.

"Oh, dear," Bess said as she turned toward the disaster. "Perhaps the captain can wait awhile more."

A pair of exasperated older women put Hannah and Bess in charge of the children while they cleaned up the broken plates.

"Take them outside for a while, and we'll be glad to do the bandages today," one offered.

Happy to get outdoors, Hannah agreed. One of the beleaguered ladies eagerly offered her a shawl against the autumn chill.

"Now, this is how an October day *should* look," Bess declared. Sunshine sparkled through half-bare branches and on thick piles of fallen leaves.

Three boys and two girls followed as they strolled toward the courthouse lawn. Hannah carried the youngest, a three-year-old boy. She held him carefully so she wouldn't press against his bandaged arm. Despite that, he squirmed until he could get down and run.

"I'd never guess he was hurt," Hannah said.

"And lost his family too. Some loggers found him wandering and brought him into town. He says he's Charlie, but we can't get a last name out of him, so we're not certain whose he is. Or was."

Hannah looked after the laughing boy, his sandy hair flapping as he ran. The child leapt into a pile of leaves where the older children played. "What will happen to him?"

"An orphan's home is being set up in the social hall just outside of town. It's possible some of the children were only separated. Maybe their parents will come back."

Hannah thought about the firestorm blasting through the streets of Peshtigo and shuddered. It seemed unlikely many had survived. "That fire was a glimpse into hell, Bess. Hell. Can they even guess how many died?"

"Hundreds, I've heard. Maybe even more. We were frightened here too. For a while it looked like all of Marinette would burn. Mother and I waited on a boat until it was over, while Father stayed to help."

Standing near a huge oak, Hannah surveyed the other children, who ranged from Amelia's age to about eleven. "Are they orphans too?"

Bess gestured toward a spindly girl with coal-black hair. "That one, for certain. Sadie Colton, and the boy with the burned ears. The others have at least one parent sick or hurt."

"Who will care for them?"

Bess shrugged. "Some of the ladies from the church are organizing volunteers. But with so many injured and homeless, we need a lot of help."

Hannah's eyes came to rest on the smallest boy once

more. He was squealing with laughter as one of the girls showered him with leaves.

"I'd like to work in the orphanage, I think. They're going to need a lot of gentling."

Bess smiled at her. "You'd be good at that. Say, is that someone you know?"

John Aldman waved at her from aboard a mule. He swung down from the animal and led it closer.

"I'm glad to see you looking well, Miss Shelton."

Hannah nodded and smiled. "I think we've been through enough that you can call me Hannah. You're looking better too. May I introduce my friend, Bess Brannon?"

John removed his borrowed hat.

"Bess, this is Daniel Aldman's brother, John."

"I think I saw you," Bess said, "when you brought Hannah to the hotel."

"I *do* remember you," John said.

Charlie fell and started wailing.

"I'll be right back," Hannah said. She went to the boy, picked him up, and dried his tears. When she looked up, John and Bess appeared to be chatting like old friends.

A smile tugged at the corners of her mouth. She almost hated to interrupt to see what he had wanted. A furious leaf battle with the children delayed her a few minutes more. By the time she returned to the conversation, she was breathing hard, exhausted from the play.

"You *are* feeling better," John said.

"Not enough for this. They've worn me out," she said.

Bess picked several leaves out of her hair.

"I never got the chance to thank you for what you did." John looked at Bess. "Hannah saved my life."

"I wouldn't go that far," Hannah said. She felt heat creeping up her neck and silently cursed her blushing.

"I would," John said. "Thank you, Hannah, and I'm so sorry—"

"Not half as sorry as I am," Hannah said before he could say more. There was no need for Bess to learn all that had transpired.

"I'm sure Daniel told you we're staying with Uncle Phineas." When she nodded, he continued. "We're going to have to leave Amelia with him for a while and work on rebuilding. We'll try to get a small house ready before the snows get heavy. What I'm trying to say is we'll be gone for several weeks. Do you have a place to stay now?"

Bess answered for her. "I'll see to that. We need all the hands we can get, and Hannah's volunteered to help with the children."

"She'll do well. Hannah . . . Daniel talked to me about the two of you. I want you to know that I approve completely."

Hannah folded her arms. "I might, too, if your brother ever thought to ask."

John laughed. "I can see he has his work cut out for him if he can get past that pride of his. I'd better be going. I need to make arrangements for some lumber."

"Good-bye," Hannah said.

John turned to Bess. "Miss Brannon, I thoroughly enjoyed our conversation."

"So did I," Bess said, her gaze dropping shyly to the leaves.

"I'd be pleased to speak with you again when I come back."

She nodded, and John mounted the mule, then waved good-bye.

Hannah stared after him for a long time. A dull ache began to build behind her eyes. What good was John's forgiveness if Daniel wouldn't come back? What good was his approval if no love remained to bless?

* * *

Malcolm erupted into fury when Mrs. Brannon explained he would be moved. "Am I a sack of potatoes to be carted from one warehouse to the next? I, madam, am a veteran of the Union Army—an *officer*, I remind you, who was wounded during battle."

The stout woman glared down at him, her chin doubling with the motion. "You, Mr. Hollas, are *now* a veteran of the Peshtigo fire, whose wounds mean nothing more than any other person's. Mr. Horatio Simonton, my own cousin, has authorized me to make decisions concerning the housing of the victims. Some must be moved to other hospitals being set up. Since *you* complain most vigorously about the crowding and accommodations here, it seemed fairest to move you first. Fairest for *everyone* involved."

The iron set of Mrs. Brannon's face convinced him the war would have been won sooner with more people like her as officers. With as much dignity as he could muster, Malcolm Shelton submitted to his fate.

CHAPTER TWENTY

Once, Hannah would have found it far too painful to face daily reminders of the children she could never have. But as days passed without word from Daniel, she walled off the portion of her heart that still dreamed of a future with him. Instead, she found it easier to focus on those orphaned by the fire.

Now, as she tended the children, she felt almost grateful for their need. When, within a week, she was strong enough to move into the orphanage, they kept her busy dawn till dusk. And sometimes even longer. Nightmares skittered throughout the wooden structure in the darkness, leaping from bed to bed. Only rarely did darkness pass undisturbed by screaming or a child's tears.

Three-year-old Charlie, so cheerful in the daytime, often crawled in bed with her at night. Hannah held his hand until both fell asleep.

She had never felt so needed in her life, so absolutely certain she was where she should be. She had no time to bemoan the unfairness of her circumstances; here fate had dealt everyone an awful hand.

Two other women helped with the twenty-odd children living there. At least once a week Bess Brannon came and visited or spelled her for an afternoon.

"I've seen John Aldman," she confessed near the beginning of December. "He's been by twice. Once to ask about you, and another time to visit me. I like him, Hannah, very much."

"He's a kind and decent man," Hannah said, but inside, her heart ached. If John could come, why hadn't Daniel? Had she wounded his pride so badly that he was never coming back?

But Bess hadn't finished talking about John. "My mother says it would be foolish to fall for someone who's just lost everything. Father scowls a lot and mumbles about farmers whenever I bring up his name. But I don't think money's so important."

"John will be all right. He's a man with plans, and a good head on his shoulders too." Hannah wondered why she couldn't just *ask* about Daniel Aldman instead of prattling on about his older brother.

"Mother would like me to marry someone as rich as her cousin, Mr. Simonton. He's a very good man, I suppose, but you should see him. Twice my mother's size," Bess said.

"I have some other news," she continued. "You know how cold the hall here is at night. It's simply not a proper place for children during winter, and the social club is ready to get back their hall. The Presbyterians are putting up a bigger orphanage behind their church, staffed by their members. It's been decided they'll move the children there within the week."

"That's not far," Hannah said. "And surely, they'll need all the help they're offered. I'd like to go there with the children."

"I've already asked," Bess said. "They have enough volunteers for now. But don't worry about a place. We still need you here, Hannah. There's someone who would like to talk to you about it this afternoon. Oh, and I almost forgot. I've brought you another dress for winter, and a cloak."

"You can't keep doing that, Bess." Hannah put her hand on her friend's arm.

"I not only can, I want to. Father's done very well in lumber. He can afford to buy me more, and that blue dress is definitely your color. Why don't you try it on?"

"Right now? But I was about to start the soup."

Bess shook her head. "I'll help the other ladies. Remember, you have somewhere to go, and you'll want to look your best."

"Where?"

Bess grinned. "I'm doing my best to look mysterious. Tell me, is it working?"

Malcolm Shelton rode through Peshtigo one last time, looking for some sign he could not guess. Already, he could make out streets amid the new construction, and everywhere around him, hammers banged, saws hissed, and the smell of freshly milled wood filled the air. Men worked together like a host of ants restoring a kicked nest. Where in all this industry would he find evidence his former wife had perished?

He buttoned the coat he had received from among the offerings sent to help disaster victims. Though the gray wool was rather worn, it served him well against the growing chill. Still, it galled him to accept so much charity. His care, these clothes—he'd complained bitterly about each new addition. When he was well enough, he wired instructions for his wife to send more money, but even so, he had to ration carefully to have enough for what he really needed.

As his hired horse clopped through the streets, no one he passed looked on his scarred face with curiosity or fear; each had already seen too many healing burns. A few expressions registered grim pity, but he scowled so fiercely in return, their gazes turned away.

He could expect those sorts of reactions all his life, thanks to Hannah Lee Shelton. She had stripped him of his reputation, a huge chunk of his fortune, and now even half his face with one rash act. Was it too much to ask to see the powder of charred bones, to know for certain they were hers?

Her name had not appeared in the *Eagle* with those of the known dead, but many remained unidentified, as they would be for all time. If only there were someone who had known her and what happened, someone who could complete a deposition saying Hannah had been here.

He nearly raged aloud. Without a body or some evidence that she'd survived beyond Shelton Creek, his reputation would be no better than before. Worse, because of his long absence and return without a trace of his good looks.

Then Malcolm saw something that fed the starved flame of his hope. Daniel Aldman's huge form, riding a black mule. Cautiously, he followed the man along the same route he'd just taken—back toward Marinette. He kept his distance and tried to formulate a plan.

He couldn't hope Daniel Aldman would tell him anything out of the goodness of his heart. As Malcolm thought back to their last encounter, his scarred hand reached unconsciously for the gun he'd lost the night of the great fire. Aldman and his friends had been only too glad to watch Hannah's last humiliation and to jeer him out of town. Or so they had supposed. He'd like to kill the man, if only for witnessing his shame.

If he still had the gun, using it might prove too great a

temptation. Then he would never know for certain about Hannah. Another thought glittered almost out of reach. Suppose . . . suppose his former wife had survived? If Aldman lived, he might have helped her. The huge brute seemed to have some feelings for the woman.

Maybe following Daniel Aldman would be a good idea. Before he returned to Pennsylvania, tail tucked between his legs, shouldn't he take every opportunity to find her?

He brushed away a few wet snowflakes that landed on his face.

After all, despite his wounds, he'd been more fortunate than some. Malcolm Shelton had some money. Aside from the passage home, he had enough left for necessities: food, lodging—and another gun.

Hannah drove Bess's coupe carefully toward Robertson's, the restaurant her friend had described. Judging from the number of rigs and saddle horses outside, there would be a crowd. Feeling foolish, she stopped the horses near a hitching post and decided the light flurries weren't serious at all.

Her gaze settled on the steps leading inside the establishment, and she wondered who was meeting her. Was it some benefactor kind enough to offer her a job, as Bess had hinted? Or could it be— Hannah closed her eyes a moment and tried to picture Daniel Aldman awaiting her in such a place, dressed in a fancy suit.

As if the man would really bother with such formalities on account of his brother's cast-off bride! The idea made her anger simmer once again, until an odd thought struck her. What in heaven's name was she doing, waiting for Daniel to come back with hat in hand? She may have decided that she wished he'd try again, but she'd done absolutely nothing to communicate her wants.

Hannah was so struck by her own foolishness that she

sat for a long time in the carriage, wondering if she should drive right then to Peshtigo. After watching a few fat snowflakes settle, she picked up the reins to flick them across the horses' backs. Then fear froze her.

What would Daniel think of her if she were to suddenly appear without a single word of warning? Hadn't he already told her his intentions by avoiding her so long? How could she risk him turning her away, not even knowing where she would go once the orphans had been moved?

Shivering with the cold, she shook her head. It was time to go inside to see what contact Bess had made for her. It was time to plot some modest future. Whatever opportunity she was offered was no doubt more than she deserved. She should be grateful. After all, wasn't a chance at freedom, a chance to support herself honorably, all that she had prayed for?

Hannah climbed out of the coupe and secured the horses. She felt foolish going in alone, an unescorted woman. Shaking her head to clear her doubts, she strode toward the door with confidence. If Bess Brannon had arranged things, there was nothing at all to fear.

Nothing but the dreams she'd set aside.

His breath caught in his throat, he was so excited to see her. After their last meeting, it seemed impossible that she would be somewhere as mundane as a restaurant—living, breathing, walking toward the door.

She looked in perfect health. Malcolm's scarred mouth twisted itself into a frown. After all she'd wrought, it seemed unfair she hadn't suffered as he had. Then again . . . he allowed his mind to wander to the punishments he planned. How much more delicious they would be on her unblemished flesh.

He needed to put distance between the two of them lest

his enthusiasm smother sensibility. He must have time to think.

Malcolm reined the horse sharply toward the telegraph office. In his mind he composed a message to his dear, dull wife of a setback in his health and yet one more delay.

It took a few moments for Hannah's eyes to adjust to the dimness of the restaurant. As she hesitated in the doorway, the delicious smells of roast lamb, herbed chicken, and fresh rolls vied for her attention. The moment she saw Daniel, though, her thoughts of eating fled.

He looked so uncomfortable sitting at a table in his store-bought suit that she nearly laughed aloud. But her mirth was snuffed out the moment she saw his face. Everything he felt lay exposed in his expression: hope, embarrassment, and worry, all quickly overwhelmed by joy.

"Hannah!" He stood, and the relief in his voice was so palpable that the head of every diner turned as she walked toward him.

It was good to see *him* blush as well. She wished to comfort him, to unsay all she'd said in anger on that last time they'd met. But most of all, she needed to touch him, to reassure herself that he still cared.

She couldn't reach out though. Not yet. Not when fear had turned her feet to lead. It took enormous effort to force herself to cross the distance to his table. She stopped just out of range of his embrace. She would listen to what he said before she decided whether to close the gap between them.

"I took an awful risk inviting you here," Daniel said.

"A risk?"

He gestured toward the elegant place settings. "There's a lot of fancy china in this place you could throw."

She grimaced, remembering the teacup.

He stepped closer. Reaching toward her arm, he stopped himself, as if recalling where they were. "Please, sit down."

"I would, but Bess led me to believe there's a wealthy man waiting here to offer me a job," Hannah told him flatly. She shouldn't tease him, not when she didn't even offer a smile to blunt her words.

He leaned closer. "There's a lot of men around here wealthier than me. Maybe all of 'em, right now."

He pulled out a chair for her, and she settled into it. A well-trained waiter swooped in, and Daniel fumbled through the order for two glasses of wine.

After it arrived, he said, "I missed you. Hoped I wouldn't, what with working on the house and tending to Amelia. But I still did, all the same."

"Then why didn't you come back?" she asked. "Why couldn't you just tell me?"

"It's a hard thing for a man to have his proposal thrown back in his face. A hard thing to try again."

"So you're still calling that a proposal? And you're still blaming me?" Hannah pushed her chair back from the table and began to stand. How could she have thought he'd changed so much?

"I'm trying, Hannah. Please let me."

She hesitated, sat again, and reached for her glass of wine. Her hand quivered with—what? Was she so afraid to hope? Her clumsy fingers bumped the stem, spilling the red liquid on the pristine tablecloth.

She moaned, embarrassed beyond speaking.

"I'm almost glad you did that," Daniel told her. "I was sure I'd do it first."

She stood and started toward the door. Before she reached it, Daniel's hand was on her arm.

"Would you take me for a drive?" she asked.

"I had a dinner planned," Daniel answered. "They'll change the cloth in just a moment."

She turned toward him and tried to focus a plea into her question. "Could you really eat now?"

He shook his head, and she nodded, somehow gratified that this was no easier for him.

He paid the proprietor and followed her outside. Nodding toward the restaurant, he said, "They'll talk about us, you should know."

She wiped a snowflake from her cheek. "If you don't wish to come, then I suppose you've bought that suit for nothing."

"Can't think of anyplace I'd rather be."

Daniel helped her into Bess's gig and untethered the team of two bay horses. As he climbed in the seat beside her, he said, "We'll leave my uncle's mule here. We can collect him after a while."

Without another word he gently chucked the reins. Frisky with the cold, the horses lifted hooves high as they trotted along a road leading toward Marinette's wooded outskirts.

Hannah had a dozen things to say to him, yet she couldn't seem to find her voice. Daniel, too, appeared to suffer from the same affliction, for he said nothing until they were outside town. On a desolate stretch of road he slowed the horses to a walk.

"I had a lot of fine things saved up to tell you," Daniel said. He favored her with a lopsided grin. "I even practiced them on John."

Smiling felt awkward, but she managed to do so. "I'm sure he's using them on Bess Brannon by now."

"Wouldn't doubt it a bit," Daniel said. "He's sweet on her for certain."

"I think she likes him too. If he can get past Mrs. Brannon—"

"If he can get past that one, he's a braver man than I. You should have seen that woman, accusing me of"—his smile faded—"well, what I almost did. I'm sorry for that,

Hannah. It wasn't proper, and I never should have touched you that way after you'd been so sick. It was just that . . ."

His brown eyes looked as fretful as a hound's. Hannah took her warm hands from her pockets and put them around his cold ones on the reins.

"Just that what?"

He sighed. "It was just that I was so scared you'd die on me, like Mary. When I realized you'd live, I couldn't hold back like a gentleman."

"We've both had some trouble controlling ourselves, Daniel. That's not why I was upset." Hannah's heart pounded as she moved nearer to the truth. "What truly hurt me was that you assumed a woman of my background would be grateful for any chance to marry, no matter what the circumstances."

He drew the reins tight, and the horses stood, puffing plumes of steaming air. "I thought you came out here to marry. How was I supposed to guess you'd worry so much about what a few old biddies thought? You didn't even know those ladies."

"This isn't about what they thought. It's about how *I* felt, Daniel."

He shook his head, clearly frustrated by the conversation. "The particulars didn't seem to bother you when you came to Peshtigo to marry John."

She turned away from him. Was he the brute she'd first imagined him to be? "How could you imagine that you know what bothered me? Did you dry my tears each night? Were you there in Pennsylvania to help me choose between whoredom and the next best thing?"

His big hand settled on her shoulder, gentle as a moth alighting.

She wanted to swat it like a fly. "Take me back to the restaurant. You can drive that borrowed mule right out of town and straight to hell."

"We're not going anywhere until I have my say." His voice was unyielding as stone.

"Haven't you already said enough? I sometimes wonder if you even think about your words, about how they might hurt me."

"Oh, I think about my words all right," Daniel said. "I think about how they turn on me every time I talk to you. Lord, Hannah. You're in my mind every minute, but when I try to tell you, nothing comes out the way I planned."

Though her shoulders stiffened with disgust, she let him turn her face toward his, then kiss away the cold tears on her cheek.

"I was wrong, Hannah." His voice shook with emotion. "Wrong because even though you're the most beautiful thing I've ever seen, I didn't say it. And wrong because I never told you how you've ruined Saturday night sprees. Whiskey, other women—nothing's been the same since I met you. I never told you how you make me want to be a better man, even a better father to Amelia. Those are words that need a voice, but I kept them all inside because I was afraid they'd all get tangled. That and saying them made me take too hard a look at the man I'd been. I thought you'd marry me and we'd have no need of a bunch of fancy words."

With one cool hand he cupped her cheek. "I love you, Hannah Shelton, and I'd be honored if you would marry me. In October, when Mrs. Brannon said those things about us, I was almost glad. I thought that would give me the excuse I needed to take care of things. I know now I should have stopped to ask you first."

His handsome face grew blurred as her eyes teared.

"What's the matter?" he asked. "Did I say something wrong again?"

She shook her head and freed a last tear, which rolled onto his fingers. "I—I've been so afraid. I never imagined anyone who knew my past would love me. I didn't think it possible. Oh, Daniel, I love you too. From the beginning, you listened to me. You never turned away, no matter what."

"Then, does that mean you'll say yes?"

"Why?" She brushed away the chilling moisture from her face. "Did you hide the minister behind the seat somewhere?"

"Hannah."

"Daniel, do you realize what you're getting? I can never give you children."

"You once reminded me, I already have a daughter. A daughter who loves you as much as I do. Marry me."

She leaned into his embrace. "Yes, I'd like that. I'd like that more than anything."

He kissed her fervently, but this time her fire matched his own. Reaching behind her, she felt him unpin her hair. The dark waves tumbled to her waist, and he ran his fingers through the silken mass.

More kisses fell upon her mouth and then her neck. She shuddered with anticipation as his large hands reached beneath her cloak. First he spanned her slender waist with his long fingers. Then he moved slowly higher, until he cupped her breasts.

Despite the cold, Hannah felt her body tingling, eager for his touch. She shrugged the cloak off and moaned as his kisses fell upon her upper chest. His fingertips reached inside her bodice and stroked her tenderly.

A cold wind shook the carriage, and she shivered with it. Daniel, to her disappointment, pulled away.

"Let's wait. I don't want you sick again."

Speechless with desire, she pulled the cloak about her and nodded in agreement.

"John and I are almost finished with the cabin. We'll build another in the spring, one just for you and me and, of course, Amelia."

She snuggled against him. "Right now I care only about the fireplaces. Make them big and warm."

He kissed her once more briefly. "Don't worry. The next time I see you shudder, *I* mean to be the cause."

They returned to Robertson's and shared a sumptuous steak dinner and desserts. After the meal ended, Daniel fished in his jacket for a ring.

"John and I buried our valuables when the fires looked like they might get out of hand. This ring was my mother's. She gave it to John. But he wanted me to have it, to put it on your finger."

Tears rolled down her face as he slipped it on her finger. After what she'd done, John had managed to forgive her. She felt sure that was more than she deserved.

She leaned forward and kissed Daniel. "Thank you. It's so beautiful. And I'll thank John as well."

She looked down at the ring, its golden gleam kaleidoscopic with her tears. At its center, a ruby sparkled like a single drop of blood.

"Will you come with me to tell Bess?" Hannah asked. "There's someone at the orphanage I want you to meet."

Daniel paid the bill and walked with her outside. He tied his uncle's mule behind the carriage.

"If the Brannons see that creature following their coupe, they'll be mortified," Hannah teased.

"Would you rather I rode after you?" Daniel asked.

"No. I'm feeling reckless. Come with me."

As they rode, Hannah told Daniel about the orphans' coming move. "Bess made it sound like the church home is staffed already."

"You sound disappointed," Daniel said, his voice gentle. "But you couldn't very well stay there and be my wife. Remember, Amelia needs a mother too."

"I know that," Hannah said. "But it will still be hard to leave them. Especially Charlie."

"Is that who you want me to meet?"

She nodded. "He crawls into my bed almost every night."

Daniel grinned. "Are you trying to make me jealous? Lucky kid."

"Don't be silly. He's three, and no one even knows his last name. You should hear him talk. He's a smart little thing, and so cuddly at night."

"It's going to make you sad to leave him, isn't it?"

Hannah hesitated. "I know I shouldn't have let myself get attached, but it's hard to live with children and not grow to love them. Charlie especially. As happy as I am about our marriage, I'm really going to miss that little boy."

Daniel squeezed her hand. "Then don't."

"Don't what?"

"Don't miss him. He needs parents, and a little brother will give Amelia someone to boss around—other than me, that is."

Hannah blinked at him. "But—but you haven't even met him, Daniel."

"You love him. That's enough."

"Are you sure? A wife is one thing, but this will be like adding a whole family."

Daniel smiled sheepishly. "I may decide things quick, but I mean what I say. As soon as we get married, we'll see about adopting him. But let's not wait too long. I don't want this little fellow getting used to sleeping in my spot."

He stopped the team as she kissed him. "Thank you, Daniel. This has been the best day of my life."

"And you said you couldn't give me children. You're just faster than most women."

By the time they reached the social hall, the light was

growing dim. Even so, they saw a buckboard pulled in front.

Hannah felt a lump forming in her throat. She climbed down from the carriage without waiting for Daniel's assistance. With quick steps she rushed into the social hall. Had the Presbyterians come to take the children so soon?

Bess was talking with a small man with a reddish beard. She smiled and nodded, then went into another room. Before Hannah could even formulate a question, Bess returned with Charlie in her arms.

The moment the little boy saw the stranger, he squirmed to get away. Bess put him down, and he ran and leapt into the man's arms, shouting, "Papa home!"

The bearded man was weeping, kissing his son, and murmuring, "Thank the Lord!"

Hannah wept too, if only for selfish reasons. She would lose Charlie for certain, despite Daniel's generous offer. Daniel put a hand on her shoulder and whispered in her ear, "Go kiss him good-bye. Try not to cry, for his sake."

Hannah dried her eyes with the handkerchief he offered and walked nearer to the man. He, too, wiped tears away.

"Thank you, both of you," he said to Bess and Hannah, "for taking care of him. We got separated, all of us. His mama and I made it, but we lost all five of the boys—" He began to weep again but fought to regain control. "We found the other four, but not Charlie. I thought he burned for sure, but Jessie wouldn't let me give up. She's in Oconto, in a hospital they made. I've been checking every hospital and orphanage from Green Bay north. His mama burned up her hands and feet real bad, but maybe now— maybe now my wife can smile again."

At the mention of his mother, Charlie wriggled and looked around. "Mama! Go see Mama!"

"We will, son. We'll go see her as soon as we can get to her. Thank the Lord!" The man extended his right hand

and shook Bess's, Hannah's, and then Daniel's. "I'm Josh Hankins. May God bless you all."

He kissed the boy again. Charlie spotted Hannah for the first time and reached out toward her.

"Ha-nah!" he said.

Holding back her tears, Hannah hugged and kissed him. "Save some for your mama. You be good."

"Good. Be good." Charlie gurgled a devilish laugh.

"He doesn't have much, but there's an extra set of clean clothes. I expect you'll need them," Hannah said. She collected the boy's clothing and gave them to his father.

Eager to return to his wife, Josh Hankins took his son and walked out of their lives.

CHAPTER TWENTY-ONE

Bess pressed a cool cloth to her eyes, but she was far too late to ease their swollen redness. Only Father could have done that, if he had the spine. Instead, as always, he sided with her mother, even though she suspected he really sympathized.

In the weeks since Daniel and Hannah had become engaged, she'd spent more time than ever in the company of John Aldman. Her father watched warily last Sunday, when John escorted her to church, but beneath his gray mustache he frowned and held his tongue. A veteran of two older daughters, Bess's father had seen gentleman friends come and go. He tended not to take such things too seriously, for his other girls had settled into suitable marriages.

Her mother, on the other hand, had panicked, as if she sensed the growing depth of Bess's and John's feelings. "A farmer, of all things," she complained. "Just imagine, a life of plowing right beside him, your whole social sphere reduced to church, and children without end. And without help. Not a cook or a nanny or even someone to keep the house."

Bess liked to imagine exactly that. Helping John to build a farm and family. Working together, through the years. John had told her his plan to breed draft horses, and it, like everything about him, filled her with admiration.

It couldn't be long now until he proposed marriage. Even Hannah said he spoke of nothing but "his Bess."

But now, only a few days before Christmas, her mother presented her a train ticket. To Chicago.

"Go visit my sister Nora for a spell," Mother commanded.

Bess had been shocked. She'd never heard of Nora before this.

"If you want to see what happens when a woman marries beneath her station, go see her. *She* eloped. Tomorrow, Bess. I've already written. She'll be expecting you."

"For a visit or a cautionary tale?" Bess asked. "I can't possibly go. I promised John."

"You're going," Mother insisted. In the chair across from her, her father looked away as if embarrassed. He never cared much for what he termed "female antics."

"You don't understand. I love John. Staying with some sad case you've never bothered to acknowledge won't change that."

"Alfred," Mrs. Brannon said. Her husband pushed aside his dessert plate. A servant whisked it and the women's away, then retreated politely into the distant kitchen.

"Bess, your mother is doing this for your own good. You'll have to go. Particularly if you wish me to continue funding your 'private charity.' "

Hannah. Bess stared at her feet. Her father, unbeknownst to Mother, had financed her gifts to her friend. And there were others as well. Bess had always had a penchant for families in distress, old people, and lost puppies. Mr. Brannon rarely turned down her requests. But the implication of his words was crystal clear. All of that would change if she didn't heed her mother's ridiculous request.

Feeling as ineffectual as a child, Bess ran from the room crying. Why couldn't she think of anything else she might do?

And how would she find John to tell him? The Aldman brothers were hours away, at their farm now, and wouldn't come to see them until Christmas. By Christmas she'd be safely shipped away.

After locking her door, Bess knelt by her bed and slipped out her gift to John from beneath her mattress. Something store-bought wouldn't do for him at all. She looked down at the needlepoint, with their two names stitched in a clever rose petal design. She knew instinctively he'd cherish it, but not for its perfection. She spotted several minor flaws. He'd love it because she'd made it with her hands.

She'd meant to have it framed, but now there wasn't time. Brushing away tears, she promised herself they'd have more time later. A lifetime, to be precise. But for now she'd have to find some way to get to Hannah, to tell her what was happening and deliver John's gift.

Before it was too late.

Malcolm smiled to himself and blessed the wisdom of the drunkard. As he'd passed time in a saloon, the old man had reminisced about a long-forgotten place, a cabin he had used when he made wood shingles by hand. Oh, he missed the old spot, with its hard bunks and the endless silent meals of beans and bread and bacon. Sure, he imagined it would still be standing, but that section had been logged out long ago. The trees there would be too young for the taking for another fifteen years or so. After Malcolm bought drinks, the old man babbled about a swift creek and mumbled crude directions. He'd been happy to rekindle a few fond memories.

When Malcolm pulled on the door, it creaked open. Inside, something clattered and rustled in debris. Weak December sunlight streamed through several places in the rotted roof. But the chimney and the fireplace looked sound, and that was most important.

When he brought Hannah, he would need a warm place to hole up.

Hannah's silver needle flashed like a dragonfly darting along the water's surface: stitching, looping, knotting. In the needle's wake, soft cream-colored cloth merged with the lace that Bess had given her as an early Christmas gift.

She felt uncomfortable with all the presents; Hannah was a woman used to making her own way. But she began to realize Bess needed to give them, to help her newfound friend.

Hannah began to suspect Bess had two types of companions: those in keeping with her father's station as a local lumber baron and those humbler sorts, the ones she truly cherished. The brunette was honored to be among the latter group.

The dragonfly bit, and Hannah dropped the needle quickly to keep her blood from spotting the lace neckline. As she sucked the tiny wound, she thought back to that other white dress, the one she'd sewn for Robert and worn to marry Malcolm.

She wondered how he fared back on the horse farm. With a small smile she imagined how surprised he'd be that she survived. Surely, even the citizens of Shelton Creek had heard by then of the region's devastating fires. But she had done more than survive; she'd prospered. After all those lean months, she was living in Mr. Simonton's fine hotel, sewing silk and lace, and looking forward to marrying a handsome, generous man.

Very generous. She recalled Daniel's offer to adopt a

child just because she'd grown attached. She still felt a tender, bruised spot when she thought of Charlie, and she chided herself for selfish thoughts. The boy needed his own parents, and even more clearly, his poor parents needed him. The future she looked forward to would be enough for her.

In a way, the fire helped guarantee it. If Malcolm thought her dead, he'd have no reason to come for her again. If he'd even consider such a thing after his last humiliation.

She looked up at a knock. Did Mrs. Tanner need help again so soon? She'd helped feed those still sick and injured just an hour before.

Bess's eyes teared as Hannah opened the door.

"What's wrong?" Hannah asked.

Bess came in and told her the whole story. "And I just *knew* John would propose this Christmas. They're spoiling everything!"

"Do you suppose they knew already? John might have asked your father. It sounds like something he would do."

"I don't know. I thought he was at the farm with Daniel, finishing the building."

Hannah shrugged. "I haven't seen him, but I'd be glad to give him this. It's beautiful, Bess. I know he'll love it."

"Thank you. Tell him it's a token, a token I'll come back."

"Of course you will. And you'll convince your parents this is not some passing fancy. Or at least your father. I don't know if your mother can be convinced."

"Me neither." Bess examined the dress Hannah had been sewing. "This will be so beautiful. I hope I'm back in time to see you wearing it."

Hannah put her arms around the blonde. The wedding was only a week past Christmas, so her return seemed unlikely at best. "Even if you can't, you should know how important you've been to me. If it weren't for you, I'd be living in one of those makeshift shelters for refugees, alone. Instead, I feel like a queen. Thank you, Bess, for everything. Every day I ask myself what I've done to deserve you."

"Don't you know, Hannah? You're my friend. I've learned so much from you. Even after you lost everything, you still held your head high. You might have been sick, but the moment you were able, you wanted to help others. I want to be as strong as you are."

"God forbid that you should ever have to be," Hannah said.

"Besides, you introduced me to John Aldman."

"It's a wonder your mother hasn't shot me yet. She doesn't speak to me, you know."

Bess smiled. "Most people would be grateful."

Hannah squeezed her hand. "You will always be welcome in my home. And someday I believe we'll be family, when you marry John."

Bess's green eyes sparkled. "Then he said something to you? Was he going to propose? I have to know."

Hannah laughed. Sometimes she almost forgot that Bess was only twenty. The eight-year gap in their ages made a difference. She wondered if it bothered Bess that John was twelve years older, but she didn't mention it.

"He didn't say a thing to me. He probably guessed you'd twist my arm to tell you. Before you leave, Bess, there's something I'd like you to have."

"Oh, Hannah. You don't need to spend what little—"

"Don't fret so about money. You've already learned the most important gifts don't have a price." She went to a small desk and pulled an envelope out of the drawer. "Please don't open it till Christmas. It's a gift of trust. And thank you again for the beautiful material. When I wear it, I'll be sure to think of you."

"When you wear that, you'd better think of Daniel Aldman."

* * *

The wedding was to be a small affair, with only family and a dozen or so friends. Most were Daniel's, but Hannah had added a few of the ladies she met tending orphans and the wounded. By that morning it didn't look like Bess Brannon would be among the guests.

Amelia fingered the lace of Hannah's wedding gown. "You look so beautiful," she said. "When can I get a dress like this?"

Hannah admired her reflection in the looking glass. For the small, informal wedding, the dress was fairly simple. Yet its lines accentuated Hannah's slender curves, and the material flowed beautifully whenever she moved. Carefully, she set the veil atop her head. Behind her shoulders it fell like an autumn mist.

"Someday this dress *will* be yours," she promised, "for your wedding day. Besides, if you looked any nicer, no one would even notice me."

Amelia twirled, flaring her pretty scarlet skirts. "I'll just keep this dress. I don't want to have to get married. Uncle Phineas says I'd have to kiss a *boy*."

She wrinkled her nose to underscore the distaste in her voice.

Hannah kissed the top of her blond head. "That's the best part, honey, when you're kissing a boy as sweet as your papa."

Thick clumped flakes fell straight down on the streets of Marinette, adding to the several inches that came down the night before. Malcolm saddled his horse, relieved that weather and circumstance were finally aligning in his favor.

No more delays, he swore under his breath. Today would be the day he finally paid back Hannah. He swore to himself he would pay her back in spades.

* * *

Bess thanked her lucky stars the train had been on time. On the newly restored line, almost anything could happen, especially since snow was falling once again. She checked the station clock and decided she'd send someone for the baggage later. If she wished to be on time for Hannah's wedding, she would have to rush.

She took half a moment to check her blond upsweep in the reflection of the ticket-taker's window. The wrinkled old man inside mistook her gesture and returned a broad wink. Blushing, Bess nodded and turned her head toward the street. Since no one knew she was coming, she'd have to hire a ride.

The trip to Aunt Nora's, which had started out so badly, turned out a delight. Though her mother's sister resented being thrown up as a caution, she didn't take it out on Bess. Instead, the plump, gray-haired woman welcomed her niece into her white frame two-story and a raucous family Christmas.

Raucous, because of her six children, who ranged from eight through thirty. The older girls had come to visit with their own spouses and assorted toddlers. If Bess hadn't worked with the orphans, she might have been unprepared for the noise level. Nora's "unsuitable" husband, Uncle Geoffrey, fussed over the babies and wrestled the children as if he quite enjoyed them all. That flummoxed Bess most of all, for her own father's dignity always kept him at arm's length from his daughters.

The house, decorated for the holiday, was not the well-staffed mansion of a lumber baron, but Bess loved it at once. Big and welcoming, it smelled of baking pies and cookies, a roast ham, and the scent of love. Geoffrey, a moderately successful builder, might not be "well bred," but he was hardly the illiterate Bess's mother had described. And after the fire that burned a huge chunk of Chicago the same day Peshtigo went up, his future seemed more promising than ever.

All in all, her aunt and uncle's happiness inspired Bess. Instead of fading, as her mother hoped, her feelings for John grew with the separation.

Aunt Nora happily conspired to send her home without notifying Mrs. Brannon, so Bess could see her beau.

"I wish you all the best. You'll have it if you watch where your heart goes, then follow it along. If you follow only money, you'll end up a wretched failure. Your mother has helped raise a sensible young woman. It's time for her to trust you now, to choose what's best for your own future." Aunt Nora folded her into thick arms.

Her thoughts returned to Hannah, and the letter she had given her for Christmas. A gift of trust, she'd called it, and it certainly had been.

Dear Bess, the letter began in lovely, flowing script. *You have been so much to me, I cannot keep from you my story any longer. Your mother may have been right; I am hardly the companion she would choose for her young daughter. I leave it to you to decide, and I promise to respect your wishes.*

The words that followed shocked and touched Bess as Hannah explained exactly how she'd come to be in Peshtigo. But nothing in that letter diminished Bess's friendship one iota; instead, it deepened her impression of the wellspring of strength Hannah possessed. But Bess knew that for Hannah, writing down the words must have taken incredible courage. She wanted more than anything to reach her friend before her wedding, to let Hannah know her trust had been well placed.

Snow fell thick as goose down, and she hoped the wedding celebration wouldn't be cut short. She needed time to talk with the groom's brother.

"Captain Hollas," Bess called up to the familiar face. The burns had set like wax from a half-melted candle, pink and almost shiny. He was riding a huge black horse at a ground-covering trot. The scarred man turned to glare at her, and then his gaze snapped forward. He rode past without uttering a word.

"Old grouch," Bess muttered. "It wasn't as if I was expecting a thank-you."

Dismissing the rude man from her mind, she hired a waiting wagon and rode eagerly toward the church where Hannah and Daniel would be married. Her thoughts, however, centered on sitting beside John in a pew.

Gen Tanner hurried through the snow to church. Her daughter had hidden in the attic of their home to try to avoid watching her two younger brothers. Gen understood her boys could be a handful, but why did Sarah have to choose today to be so obstinate? She had promised Hannah Shelton she'd come early to help her with her veil and buttons, and the delay had put her there not long before the first guests should arrive.

She hoped Sarah would keep the boys from disturbing the punch and cakes she'd set out for visitors. After the couple spoke their vows, the small party planned to move to her home down the street. Normally, someone from the bride's family would have held the small reception, but since both bride and groom were fire refugees, allowances were certainly in order. Besides, thought Gen, no one had gathered in her parlor since her husband's death two years earlier. Perhaps a wedding party would be just the thing to banish those sad memories.

The thirty-five-year-old removed her wrap and shook it in the doorway. For the occasion, she'd arranged her coal-black hair into an attractive set of loops. She hoped a little moisture wouldn't make them slump.

As she hurried toward the minister's office, where Hannah would be dressing, she noticed a man standing nearby, deep in shadow. A gasp betrayed her surprise.

"I apologize. I didn't mean to startle you."

She shook her head. "No harm done, Captain Hollas. I just didn't see you when I first came in. Are you a friend of Hannah's or the groom's?"

She couldn't read the twist of his scarred mouth. "The bride's. A very old friend. I was wondering if you'd assist me. I'd like to surprise her. Could you ask her to come out?"

Gen's smile was empty but polite. She'd helped tend Captain Hollas at the Simonton Hotel, and nothing about him impressed her to his generosity.

"I'm sure she's very busy. The guests will be here soon."

His own smile was disturbing. "Then you'd better hurry. I'd hate her to miss this."

Reverend Fuller claimed that even the most evil temperaments hid some spark of good. In Hollas's case, any kindness offered might qualify for a miracle of God.

Gen Tanner stuck her head into the minister's study. "You didn't need my help at all. You look like an angel."

"Is the groom here yet?" Hannah asked her.

"Not yet. It's just us girls, except you have a visitor," the woman said.

"Bess? Is it Bess Brannon?" Hannah leapt toward the door. If Bess had come back, that would make this day complete.

"I'm—I'm not supposed to say. I believe it's a surprise." Oddly enough, Gen Tanner's face registered more unease than excitement.

Hannah brushed the thought aside and stepped out past her. And screamed as though her lungs would burst.

Malcolm knew he would forever savor the shock and fear on Hannah's face. Her pale blue eyes flared wide, and

TOUCHED BY FIRE

her mouth flew open in a terrified cry. He grabbed her quickly, before her shock subsided and she began to fight.

For a few moments he had feared that the woman with the dark hair wouldn't tell her he was there. How fortunate that he had convinced her, for he would have shot her if she'd given him more trouble. Then Hannah would have had time to prepare. Now the loop-haired ninny stood with her jaw gaping, unable to comprehend his choke hold on the bride.

With scarred hands Malcolm withdrew the needle from his pocket that would make her his. He lifted it to her upper arm, where the lace of her sleeve had torn.

Hannah kicked backward like the stubborn mule she was. Only providence kept her from ruining his knee. Just as she'd nearly ruined his whole life. He spun her around and slung her toward the pews, then swore when she fell and struck one with her head.

Behind him, the door to the minister's office slammed shut, and he heard the sound of a chair pulled up against it. He drew his Colt and fired three shots through the wood.

Something heavy thudded against the door, and he heard the thin sound of a child's scream. Malcolm's pulse raced. Not a child! He'd kill Hannah if she'd made him harm a child.

Turning back to his ex-wife, he was gratified to see she hadn't moved. He pocketed the hypodermic syringe, a new device he'd discovered after his war injury. With it he could dose her quickly with enough morphine to make her sleep. But now her unconsciousness made it unnecessary.

Her veil obscured his vision as he hoisted her over his shoulder. Tearing it off, he tossed it to the floor.

Today she wouldn't need it.

As he ran to where his horses had been hidden, Malcolm felt pleased to find his mind in fighting form. He felt no panic, only eagerness to move on to the next step in his plan.

At the nearby Pendleton Hotel, Daniel Aldman fumbled with his tie.

"Here, let me do that," John said. His brother's smile looked amused. "I think you're even worse off than the first time."

"I'm not nervous," Daniel said. "I just don't hold much with these fancy clothes. Far as I'm concerned, some prissy English fella is sniggering up his sleeve for inventing the uncomfortable things."

"Uh-huh. Probably sitting around in homespun snorting corn liquor while he does."

"You're laughing at me, aren't you?"

"Not a chance. I don't want to give you cause to bring it up if I get Bess to marry me."

A woodpecker-quick rapping interrupted. Daniel opened the door.

"Amelia, what on earth? Hannah will have a fit if she sees what you've done to that dress! Hey, wait. What's wrong?"

"Ha-Ha-Hannah!" She screamed the name again and again, tears streaming down her reddened face. She'd torn her frilly dress, and when Daniel lifted her, he saw a fine mist of red droplets on her face.

"My God. This is blood. Are you hurt, Amelia?"

The girl shook her head, and Daniel felt panic rising like bile in his throat.

"Hannah's hurt?" he asked. When she nodded, Daniel passed her to his brother. "Keep her here, John. Make sure she's not injured."

He sprinted out the door and downstairs, his mind unable to hurdle one horrible thought.

Malcolm must have come back. And after last time, he'd be mad enough to kill.

As Daniel ran, he forced himself to imagine other explanations. Broken glass, an accident—but none explained his daughter's terror. Despite the falling snow, sweat poured down his back by the time he raced into the church's front door.

And stopped dead. Hannah's veil lay draped over a pew.

The first few guests came in, the women Hannah knew. He ignored them even though he could hear them whispering speculation about his wild hair, his untucked shirt.

John clattered in behind them, still holding Amelia in his arms. Her sobbing had stopped, and she clung to her uncle's neck, crying, "Hannah! I want Hannah!"

Daniel picked up the fallen veil and saw another spattering of blood. "My God," he said. "The bastard's killed her."

He turned to the nearby office door, recognized the bullet holes for what they were. Behind him, he heard a woman's gasp.

He tried to open the door and found it blocked. That didn't stop him. He threw a shoulder into it, determined to smash it into kindling if need be.

The door gave, but there was weight behind it. *Hannah's weight,* Daniel thought. He pushed more gently, and in the door's wake saw a smeary trail of blood. And now a hand, a single pallid hand stained scarlet.

"Oh, God!" he swore, shoving himself inside the door. And turning slowly to face what he knew would be a dead body . . .

But not Hannah's. Instead, Gen Tanner lay sprawled helplessly behind the door. She wasn't dead either. The blood-soaked fabric of her violet-colored dress rose and sank in time with shallow breathing. She'd been shot twice, in the shoulder and the midsection. Gut-shot, as they'd called it in the war. Daniel wouldn't put much on her chances.

"Get a doctor!" his voice boomed. "This woman has been shot!"

John forced his way into the room without Amelia. Staring down at Mrs. Tanner, he gave voice to Daniel's question. "Where is Hannah, Daniel? What in heaven's name has happened here?"

CHAPTER
TWENTY-TWO

The motion of the horse made Hannah's head bob painfully. With each jolt her skull pounded, forcing her awake. Though thick haze obscured her vision, she could make out the horse's black mane and the gray trunks of bare trees as they spun by. Cold numbed her hands and feet, made it hard to tell where she stopped and the animal began. Melting snowflakes stung like bees against her unprotected neck and face.

She felt so dizzy, wanted so badly to fall off the horse if only to stop the sickening motion. But something held her tightly in the saddle. That something was an arm around her waist.

Abruptly, she remembered. Malcolm, his flesh ruined by the slick scars of heavy burns. He'd come—come to—her wedding? Her gaze flicked to the yards of creamy silk that flowed behind her. Dear God in heaven! He was abducting her! Taking command of one limp arm, she swung back an elbow, but the blow bounced ineffectively off his shoulder.

Malcolm reined in the huge horse. "So you're awake now," Malcolm said. "I'm glad. We can't have you dying prematurely."

Hannah flung herself away from him and, to her shock, met no resistance. With a grunt she landed facedown in the packed, ice-crusted snow. The freezing moisture penetrated the thin fabric of her dress and set her shivering. She wanted to get up, to run, to scream for help, but nothing worked as she expected. Legs, arms, and vocal cords all refused her need.

In front of her, Malcolm's boots stood, glistening with snowflakes that settled on black leather. "You hit your head quite hard. You won't be running anywhere so soon. Now, get up and stop this foolishness, or do you wish to freeze to death?"

As he dragged her to her feet, she looked around. Besides the horse, she saw nothing but thick snowfall, a narrow track, and endless gray tree trunks.

"I *said*, do you wish to freeze?" His hand fisted in the neckline she had sewn with such care. With one hard jerk he tore it to her waist.

She stood frozen like a fawn when the wolf's eye falls upon it.

"Answer me!" he shouted as if he didn't fear he would be overheard. He glared at her, his face marred by contempt and slick scar tissue. "Look at you, in a wedding dress. Did you imagine, after you ruined me, I would allow this?"

Violently, he tore the dress from her. The skirts tangled in her legs, and she fell again as he pulled them out from under her. This time the cold combined with terror to afflict her with palsied, painful tremors. Grabbing her by the arm, he wrenched her to her feet once more and slapped her, then again, until the thick haze overwhelmed her.

* * *

Amelia clung to her father, shivering and weeping silent tears. In a pew near the church altar, Daniel sat with her and stroked her hair.

His initial reaction had been to run outside, to see if there was any trace of Hannah. John brought both their coats, and the two of them ran up and down the streets like madmen, stopping strangers and asking questions as they ran.

Few people were out, and no one had seen anything save the confusion after Mrs. Tanner was discovered. The snow was falling harder, hard enough to rapidly fill tracks.

Defeated, John and Daniel returned to the church, where Amelia wept in Bess Brannon's embrace. Quietly, Daniel took his daughter and tried to comfort her.

He had to focus on his child's pain to keep from falling into the chasm of his own.

Someone had brought the doctor, and the sheriff was there as well. A round-bellied man with wire-framed glasses and a tendency to whisper, Sheriff Skinner leaned forward to ask another question.

"And how do you know, Mr. Aldman, that this Malcolm Shelton is the man we're looking for?"

Daniel kissed his daughter's head. "He came to Peshtigo before the fire and threatened Hannah."

"Why? What was their relationship?"

"He was married to her at one time."

To his credit, Skinner didn't raise an eyebrow. His voice hissed like the rustle of dry leaves. "And he was angry? Jealous? Displeased that she had left?"

"All three, I suppose." Daniel had no intention of telling this man Hannah Shelton faked her death.

"Do you have any idea where he might have gone?"

Daniel shook his head. "Not unless he's taking her back home to Pennsylvania."

Skinner nodded. "I have men checking the train station, but I can't see him taking a woman there against her will. It would be—ah—against her will, wouldn't it, Mr. Aldman?"

Daniel clenched his teeth. "What the hell are you trying to say, that they're in league? Hannah's scared to death of Shelton."

The sheriff lifted a hand in apology. "No offense intended, of course. I had to ask, however unlikely. If she would have gone willingly, he wouldn't need to shoot the other woman."

"How *is* Mrs. Tanner?" Daniel asked.

"The doctor's in there with her. He hasn't told us yet. But I've seen my share of saloon shootings. I wouldn't say it's promising. I've sent a man to fetch her parents. She's a widow, I believe. Very well thought of in this town."

Numbly, Daniel asked, "Does she have children?"

Skinner held up three fingers, then wiped his spectacles with a handkerchief. "May I ask your daughter a few questions?"

"Amelia?" Daniel asked gently.

Her voice tore at him like raw pain. "It was a monster, Papa! A monster with a shiny, awful face! I saw a monster grabbing Hannah!"

A prickly, itchy warmth brought strength to Hannah's limbs, strength enough to clutch the woolen blanket tighter against her bare skin. Somewhere nearby, a fire crackled. Judging from the smell, the smoke had first backed up. But she didn't care about the acrid odor, only the blessed warmth and the pain that each small movement brought her.

Her head throbbed viciously at the back where she had struck it. Other hurts, too, vied for her attention: her arm where he had grabbed her, her wrist where she tried to catch herself when she pitched off the horse. Her cheeks felt swollen, and she imagined angry red handprints from Malcolm's blows.

But warmth flowed through her now, thank God. That must mean she was safe. Daniel must have found her and brought her back to the hotel. She hoped he'd beaten Malcolm to a bloody pulp, or, at the very least, had him arrested. She needed Daniel to hold her and let her sob out her fury at their spoiled wedding day.

Fingertips stroked her sore cheek, and she fluttered toward full consciousness. Daniel. She had to talk to Daniel now.

When she opened her eyes, ghostly shadows danced around the room. Only firelight kept it from total darkness. The figure crouching over her was silhouetted by the golden flickers, but even so, she knew it couldn't be Daniel.

"Hannah, I have dreamed of this so long."

The voice made her jerk as though she'd been doused in ice water. A jolt of alarm shot through her body, and she snapped upright, or tried to. A rough hand on her shoulder shoved her backward, and in her weakened state, she was no match for Malcolm's strength. He pinioned her with a knee on her chest until she exhausted herself struggling. When she grew still, he spoke again.

"You almost disappoint me. There's so little fight left now."

The pressure on her chest made breathing difficult, words nearly impossible. She struggled with the one most urgent. "Why?"

Malcolm chuckled. "Business, at first. I meant only to take you back, and perhaps to punish you a bit for your deceit. But I was careless last time; I somehow let you get the upper hand. As always, you used it to devastating effect. How could I allow that, Hannah?"

Across the small room, a thick log settled deeper in the

fire. A shower of sparks flew out past the hearth, only to fade out on the dusty floor.

"I fixed this shack myself, so I would have a place to bring you. We couldn't begin our journey until you'd been prepared."

His last sentence brought a whimper, though she'd been trying to disguise her terror. Something about his voice made her fear his "preparations" more than murder.

"Did you ever give a thought to me when the fire struck in October? Did you even wonder if I'd managed to survive?" The pressure of his knee grew greater, but Hannah's silence seemed to infuriate him. "Well, did you? Answer me."

He moved off her chest and shook her until her sore head banged against the filthy floor.

"Stop," she told him. "Can't—talk with you on top of me."

Appeased for the moment, he released her. "Now, answer!"

"I—I thought you'd gone back to Shelton Creek," she whispered.

"How could I, after what you'd done to me?"

"You sound just like you did when we were married, Malcolm." Contempt colored her voice, a defense against her rising panic. She struggled to sit up. "You're whining, blaming me. Men who fancy themselves important should accept responsibility."

"For this?" he bellowed, gesturing toward his ruined face. "Would I have been in Peshtigo, Wisconsin, in that hellfire, had it not been for you? This *is* your fault, Hannah! You're the one who ruined me this way!"

"I had a hand in it, and for my part I *am* sorry. I never meant you to end up like this, Malcolm. Please believe me."

"I'd sooner take the counsel of a serpent."

"Fine. But while you're listening to my 'slithering,' listen to this too. Your choices set all this in motion. *Yours.* The lies you told about me, the campaign back home to steal my farm and destroy me. Your attack in Peshtigo. And last of all, your pride. The pride that wouldn't allow me victory in even one small skirmish. You could have gone home to your new wife, Malcolm. You could have rebuilt your business. *My* business, on my land. You are still a Shelton, and even if they whisper, people will eventually ignore a few suspicions. Especially when no body turns up.''

"If you don't cooperate, one will." He ran a finger along the curve of her throat.

A deep emptiness yawned before her, and Hannah closed her eyes. If she returned with him, could her abduction be ignored? Would Malcolm, with his scarred flesh, play the victim and send her to jail for fraud? He still had friends in power, and Hannah yet remembered what they'd done to her last time.

Fearing Malcolm's touch, too aware of her nude body tucked beneath the blanket, she lied quickly. "I'll cooperate. I'll go back home with you and face the courts."

At least she'd have some chance there. Maybe somehow Daniel or Bess Brannon could be contacted for help.

"Judge Clarke will punish your deceit, but I have a more personal affront to settle." Knotting his fingers in her hair, he smashed his mouth against hers.

A shock of revulsion swept through her, so strong she felt that she might vomit. Desperate to push him off her, she pummeled his neck and chest with the heels of her hands.

He laughed, and she could see the firelight glinting off his teeth. "That's my Hannah. This is just the way I wanted you."

Then he curled his fist and landed a heavy blow near her right eye. Her vision grayed, but terror kept her conscious. Her nails ripped as he tore away the blanket.

"No," she cried. "Please don't!"

* * *

"I'm going out again," Daniel said.

John took him by the arm. "You can't. It's far too dark to track them, and the weather's worse than ever."

Daniel went to the window for what must have been the hundredth time and swept aside a heavy velvet curtain. "She's out there in that, waiting for me to come and get her."

John gestured toward the second hotel room, the one Bess had rented. "And your daughter's right in there. Do you want her to wake up tonight and find you gone?"

Both men turned toward a soft tap at the door. Daniel crossed the room in two steps and let Bess inside.

"She cried herself to sleep," Bess told them. She smoothed her blond hair with a hand. "I thought she'd never let go. You look exhausted too. Both of you. Why don't you try to get some sleep?"

Daniel shook his head. "I'm going to see if I can get a lantern."

"To do what?" Bess asked. "If you couldn't make out tracks by daylight, what chance would you have now? We've been through this already. He didn't go to the train station, and the snow's too bad for him to get too far. Most likely, he'll be close by. I'm sure Sheriff Skinner is doing everything he can."

"Is he out there right now?" Daniel demanded, pointing to the window. "My God, how could they just disappear without a trace?"

"Let's think about this Shelton," John said. "You said he wanted to take her back to their hometown. Where is it? Maybe someone there would know his whereabouts."

Daniel shook his head. "She never said the town's name."

"Shelton Creek. She wrote me in a letter. It was Shelton Creek," Bess volunteered.

"Am I the only one who didn't know all this?" John asked.

Daniel shook his head. "By the time she told me, you'd already washed your hands of Hannah. I didn't see as telling would do anything but hurt you more."

John's eyes flicked to Bess, and Daniel guessed he was uncomfortable discussing his earlier relationship with Hannah.

John sighed and stared at Daniel. "And this divorce— this complication with her former husband—it didn't bother you?"

"All it did was make me want to keep her safe." Daniel strode back to the window and stared out into the snowy night. "A hell of a job I did with that."

Bess crossed the room and put her hand on his shoulder. "You couldn't have known he would come back. Even Hannah thought she was safe."

If Daniel heard her, he gave no indication. "What if he's already killed her?"

"If that was his aim, he would have shot her at the church, like Mrs. Tanner," John said. "He wanted her alive."

Daniel raised his fist to his forehead, but he couldn't block the memory of Hannah on that cottage bed, her dress slashed open by Malcolm.

He knew why Malcolm wanted Hannah. The knowledge detonated in his brain, so appalling that he began to shake with rage.

"I'm going to kill that bastard," he swore, "if it's the last thing that I do."

"No," Bess argued. "You can't kill him, Daniel. There's a little girl in the next room who needs her papa. Not in jail, or dead of a bullet. She needs you with her. Hannah knew that, didn't she?"

"*Doesn't*—doesn't she. Don't talk about her like she's dead. You don't understand. Shelton will—there are things men do to women, to hurt them." He remembered hauling another Union soldier off a woman in Missouri. The man had sneered and told him "spoils of war." That had been one of the few occasions he had ever lost his temper. He nearly beat the man to death.

Bess lowered her voice. "I know about rape, Daniel. I'm not a little girl."

Another knock interrupted. John opened the door, and Mrs. Brannon burst in.

"Bess, what in heaven's name are you doing here? I had to hear it from a neighbor that you were back in town, and now"—she gave a haughty sniff—"to find you in a hotel room with these two—"

"Mother, I was at the church this afternoon. You heard about what happened?"

"You—" The stout woman hugged her daughter and changed her tone completely. "You poor dear. You're upset, then. I know the Shelton woman was a friend."

"*Is*," Bess corrected her mother with an eye toward Daniel. "We don't believe she's dead."

Mrs. Brannon peered up at him. "No, no. Of course not. And I am sorry, sir, about your wedding. A terrible tragedy. Nothing like this has ever happened in Marinette before."

"I was caring for Mr. Aldman's daughter in the next room until she fell asleep. Mother . . . I'd also like you to say hello to John Aldman. You've met before, at church."

He took her hand. "Your daughter has been a great help to us," John said politely, "and I'm pleased you've come. Bess tells me so much about you. Your approval means so much to her."

Mrs. Brannon jerked her hand away. "My approval might be more forthcoming had I not found her in a hotel with two men after dark. You might be more sensitive as to a young lady's reputation."

"I apologize. The circumstances—" John began to explain.

Daniel interrupted. "Ma'am, my bride has been abducted, a woman's been shot, and my little girl only just stopped crying. Right now I can't stop thinking about what that madman might be doing to my Hannah. Your daughter offered help because we needed it. Do you honestly think—can you honestly imagine that we've had the time or inclination to get everything we do approved by you, the minister, and a half dozen stuffy old ladies from the garden club?"

Mrs. Brannon lowered her head like a bull. "Bess, we're leaving now."

She started toward the door, but Bess held her ground. "I'm staying in the next room with Amelia, Mother. She needs someone to care for her and keep her calm. These men can't do that right now. I have to be here. It's what Hannah would want."

"No matter how I try to put you in good company, you always find some charity case to befriend. Did you learn nothing from your visit to my sister's?"

"Yes, I did. I learned to watch where my heart goes and follow it along. Tonight my heart is here. In this place." Bess took John's hand. "And with this man."

"Your father is waiting in the lobby," Mrs. Brannon said. "If you don't come down right now—"

"Will you shut me out of your life the way you did Aunt Nora? That would hurt me, Mother. It would hurt me very much, but I couldn't let it stop me. So think about it before you lay down an ultimatum you don't want to keep."

For a moment Mrs. Brannon glared. Daniel admired Bess's resolve. The older woman had a formidable will.

Silence stretched, taut as a drumhead. Finally, Mrs. Brannon punched through with her words. "All right. I suppose the staff here could be persuaded to bring a cot into the child's room. I'll be staying there with you, to help."

"*You'll* be sleeping on a cot?" Bess asked.

Mrs. Brannon shook her head. "Certainly not. You will. I shall share the child's bed. I'll return shortly with a few things."

"Thank you." Bess hugged her mother. "We'll need all the help we can get."

CHAPTER TWENTY-THREE

In the morning Malcolm tended the horses, then brought in a pot of snow to melt for water. At least ten inches had fallen since the previous afternoon, yet the sky was clear and brilliant blue. As he opened the cabin door to go inside, sunlight fell across Hannah, and he winced.

She didn't even look like the same woman. Purplish bruises marred her delicate face, and the right eye had swollen grotesquely. Where one forearm lay outside the blanket, he saw his fingerprints, as if in ink, against her wrist. If he removed the blanket, he knew he would see more painful-looking marks, even places where his teeth had broken skin. But instead of filling him with satisfaction, as he'd imagined, her beaten body only caused him shame.

Had any Shelton ever served a woman so? She must be the very soul of evil to drive him to this extreme. Because of her, he'd shot a woman and possibly a child. Because of her, he'd beaten and he'd raped.

Her words came back to haunt him. *Men who fancy themselves important should accept responsibility*. Could he be responsible for this? He shook his head. She had a serpent's tongue, but for now it would be silent. For now he'd shoved her proud words down her throat.

After melting water near the rebuilt fire, he placed some in a cup beside her. Certainly, he was capable of kindness, now that she lay still. The injection he had given would help to ease her pain. The morphine would also keep her quiet, so he could plan what he must do.

While he recovered in Marinette, he'd thought about his plans a great deal, and they had seemed so simple. After the abduction he would take her to a hidden place until the authorities stopped looking. The supply of morphine he had stolen would help keep his former wife in line. In a few days or a week they would ride southward to Green Bay and board a train for home.

If only he hadn't lost his head and shot the other woman. He hadn't planned to, but events had moved far faster than his reason. He had known her from the hotel hospital, and he had feared that between her testimony and Daniel Aldman's knowledge, he'd face trouble back home. Questions at the very least would certainly await him when he arrived with Hannah.

Questions her bruised face would help to answer.

He could be forgiven some things. A woman of Hannah's reputation, and one who'd been his wife, could never have him charged with rape. But the other shooting would undo him if he were linked with Hannah's disappearance from Marinette.

Malcolm groaned. Perhaps the slut never told Aldman where she'd lived in Pennsylvania. Perhaps no one would track him down. But the hope was thin, for the entire village bore his name.

His best chance would be to return without his former wife. He could concoct a story about tracking her to Peshtigo, trying to save her from the fire. It would be in the newspaper, and if he played it right, his scars might elicit sufficient sympathy to shield him from the harshest questions.

He began to boil coffee using some of the snow water. God, how he hated compromise. He'd come to this godforsaken state to bring Hannah back and avenge his wounded pride. Though he'd certainly made her pay for her attack, he would never completely set to rest the gossip.

He would have to live with it, he realized. The best thing he could do was kill her and move on.

Nausea gave her focus. *Think about the queasiness,* Hannah told herself. *Think of it swirling in your stomach, churning toward your throat. Concentrate on not vomiting. Then you won't remember all the things he did.*

Useless. They came anyway, dark flashes. Broken pieces of a pain so sharp and jagged, the edges cut like shards of glass. She dared not try to grasp a piece and turn it, examine any thought.

Tears leaked out beneath her swollen eyelids. She couldn't help assigning the most razorlike a name. It had been rape, a word she'd heard discussed only in whispers, an act more filthy than divorce.

She'd thought she would die. She'd fought so hard to make him kill her. But in the end she wasn't strong enough, and, God help her, she'd survived.

She tried to move her arm to wipe away a tear. Hurts flared, no longer quite as dull. Whatever he'd shot her full of must be wearing off.

Hannah tried to catalog her wounds as she lay still, but the task was hopeless. She had become all ache, with some spots only more or less insistent.

Her mouth felt dry as tinder, and she thought longingly of snow. There must be snow outside this building. Snow to quench her thirst.

"There's water right beside you."

His voice. Had he read her mind? She started, all her instincts warning her to run, but her body was far too battered. Finding the right eye swollen shut, she forced open her left. She had to see Malcolm, to locate the threat and edge away.

Her gaze fell on the water. As much as she wanted to die, her body urged her hand to take the cup.

It might be anything, she thought. *It might be poison.* Not caring, she tried to lift it to her mouth. Her battered hands refused to grasp it, so she used them together clumsily, as if she were a child wearing mittens. She drank quickly, desperate to moisten her parched mouth.

"Not too fast, or you'll be sick," he warned. "Morphine does that, first few times."

She wanted to ask why. Why would he beat her senseless, then give a drug used to ease soldiers' pain? But she couldn't talk to him, couldn't risk that anything she said might anger him and bring a repeat of last night.

"Who was the child?" he asked.

Hannah lowered the cup and stared at Malcolm. He was sitting cross-legged by the fireplace, sipping coffee. Child? Most of yesterday flashed on and off like fireflies in her memory. What did Malcolm mean? What was he expecting her to say?

"At the church, who was the child?" he repeated.

The lightning flashes coalesced into an image of Amelia, and Hannah abruptly found her voice. "You didn't hurt her, did you? You didn't hurt that little girl!"

"I didn't even know that she was there, but when I fired—I never set out to hurt a child, Hannah. Did *you,* when you spread that blood around your room?"

He was blaming her again, blaming her for something he'd done to Amelia.

She raised both hands to her face and sobbed aloud. Even if she managed to escape Malcolm, how could she face Daniel knowing she'd caused his child to be killed?

* * *

After a few hours of troubled sleep, Daniel was awakened by Abel Skinner at the door.

"Mrs. Tanner passed away," he whispered without preamble. Uncomfortably, the man adjusted wire-framed glasses.

Daniel backed up and let him step inside. "Wake up, John," he called.

"I heard," John said. He rubbed his eyes. "Poor woman."

Skinner continued. "Dr. Heinrich says she was conscious for a while. Long enough to say who did it. Fellow by the name of Captain Hollas. Fire victim. He was treated at a couple of Marinette temporary hospitals for burns to the face and hands. Nobody knows where he came from, and none of those Christian ladies tending him liked him in the least. Sounds like an ill-tempered, demanding ass."

"Sounds just like Malcolm Shelton," Daniel said. "Maybe he never got out of Peshtigo in time. I thought we ran him off."

"About six feet tall, black hair, dark eyes. Is that your man?"

Daniel nodded. "He's from Shelton Creek, Pennsylvania."

"I'll wire the law there. If he turns up, they'll have questions. If he turns up with the woman, they'll have proof as well."

"He'll know that, won't he?" Daniel asked. "He'll know he can't go back with her."

"Maybe. But he's not a rational man if he's carried a grudge this far. I've wired every train station within two days' ride. They'll be looking for him and for Miss Shelton."

"He couldn't ride far yesterday, not in that storm. Where could he be hiding?" Daniel asked.

"We've checked the local hotels and boardinghouses. No luck. But there are cabins here and there out in the woods. It's a big area, although since the fire, it's shrunk. We won't need to check the burned lands."

"How many roads and trails are there going out of town to the likely areas?" John asked.

"Maybe half a dozen. But the snow covered any hoofprints."

"Hoofprints. So someone saw a horse?" Daniel splashed his face with cool water from the basin.

"A big black, heading northwest."

"Shall we, John?"

John nodded.

Daniel shook Skinner's hand. "You've had a busy night. Thanks for all you and your men have done."

"We're not finished," the sheriff said. "We'll keep looking until we find her. I'd recommend that you stay here. This man is armed, and he's already killed one woman."

Daniel nodded grimly. "And we're going to find him before he makes it two."

After a hurried breakfast, the brothers went to the livery for their horses. Phineas had bought a pair for Daniel as a wedding gift. The two bay mares had been driven into town for use after the ceremony. Now John and Daniel rented saddles from the livery.

Their uncle met them, and they shared the morning's news.

Phineas pulled a huge pistol out of his belt and offered it to Daniel. "I know you don't hold with guns no more, but even the Bible says there's times to kill. When you find that bastard, give him some of this."

"Where the hell'd you get this hog-leg?" Daniel took it carefully. Though very old, the gun had been recently cleaned and polished.

"Had it since I come here, back in 'forty-seven. Still shoots straight as ever. I use it now and then when a weasel's out to get my chickens. Figure if it can kill one kind of low-down weasel, it'll be good for another."

Daniel clapped a hand on his uncle's shoulder. "Thanks. You've been mighty good to us."

Phineas rubbed his shaggy beard and lowered his gaze. "Don't speak no more about it. You and yours are all the kin I have that I can stand. I know I told you women were just trouble, but your Hannah's a rare one. She don't make a man feel like he's all dirty feet and clumsy hands. Now, you go get her back."

As the morning wore on, harsher pain crept through Hannah's haze. She tried to assess her condition while keeping still as possible. Though every part of her ached, a lump on the back of her head and her right eye felt most swollen. Her wrists and hands were stiff and badly bruised, but she didn't think he'd broken any bones. In several spots, caked blood made her skin stick to the coarse blanket. Through slitted eyelids, she checked the room and found herself alone. Rolling to one side, she used her elbows to push herself to a sitting position.

She must have slept awhile, for she had not heard Malcolm leave the cabin. Daylight as well as cold air penetrated chinks in both the walls and ceiling. Was it possible that he had gone away? Or was he waiting out there to see if she would try to run?

She wondered how long it would be until he returned. Fear stirred her empty stomach once again. She couldn't be here, with him, when night fell. For if his appetites rekindled, how could she defend herself?

Hannah pushed back the maddening thoughts that spiraled in like vultures. Instead, she turned her attention to searching the room for anything she might use as a weapon. It hardly mattered whether she killed Malcolm or provoked him to kill her. She couldn't endure his weight on top of her again, the horror as he violated her.

Unbidden, a memory of Daniel circled in. Daniel, who she'd loved so much. Daniel, who would never have her now.

Her sore hands curled like the legs of a dead insect. She felt as empty as a lifeless husk. If she just lay there, unmoving, would it even matter what he did to her?

With a painful moan she staggered to her feet. Yes, it mattered. Yes. If she were going to die, she must do it as she'd lived. She would go out fighting for a chance.

In the dying firelight she searched. Except for her petticoats and undergarments, Malcolm had stripped the room of everything, even the cup she'd used earlier. Could he have given up and left her here alone?

That didn't seem like Malcolm. Wouldn't he gloat or threaten instead of merely slink off? Even so, she supposed it might be possible. He had seemed affected when he asked about the child. Even after everything he'd done, she didn't doubt his statement that he'd never meant to hurt the girl.

He'd meant only to destroy the woman who could have been her stepmother. Could have been.

Hannah remembered that night in the river with Daniel and Lucinda. Each of them took turns holding Amelia, shielding her from flame. The three had worked as one to save her against such awful odds. How could anyone take her from them now?

Slowly, painfully, she dressed in all that was left of her garments. Beneath the soft heap, she was glad to find her shoes, even if they were impractical. Gathering the blanket, she wrapped it around her shoulders. She was going to need its warmth when she tried to escape.

* * *

Daniel rode just ahead of John, along another trail. Thin trees stood straight as bristles, reaching for the winter sun. Only the break between them marked the narrow trail. Ahead of him lay an unbroken track of white. The only tracks he noticed were the tiny footprints of birds and small rodents, none large enough to pierce the frozen crust.

His head ached from lack of sleep and the glare of the sunlit snow.

"Let's go back and try that other branch," Daniel called behind him to his brother.

Just as tired, John nodded, and they turned their animals. And saw it. The first time, they'd passed by.

Daniel was first to slide off his mare. Heedless of the snow dampening his legs, he knelt and lifted the edge of cream lace that peeked out above the surface of the snow. John was beside him in a moment. Both held their breath as Daniel picked up the ruined wedding gown.

"For the love of God . . ." John muttered.

Daniel couldn't speak at all. Instead, he leapt aboard the mare and urged her to a gallop. If Malcolm had killed Hannah already, only time and a good thaw would lead him to her body. But if there'd been some reason he had taken her, there must be a cabin, or Hannah would have quickly died of cold.

And if they were in that cabin, then he might still have time.

Hannah pulled the loose board that served as the door's handle and raised a hand to shield her vision from the whiteness all around. Tears collected on her lashes as she squinted. She stood, afraid to move until her eyes adjusted to the light.

A strong hand clamped on her upper arm. "Get back inside. You'll catch your death, dear Hannah."

Hannah wedged her body against the doorjamb, too repulsed to move. Malcolm's face came into focus.

"You look terrible. There must be so much pain. I'm going to give you something for it, just like I did last night."

Behind him, she saw his horse was saddled. A second animal carried several packs but not a saddle. Malcolm didn't plan to take her after all. The meaning of his offer crystallized. The shot he gave would truly take away her pain forever.

She shook her head and looked past him for a place to run. "I won't die that easily. Not just to convenience you."

He closed on her, tightening the pressure on her arm. "Why not? Surely, you don't imagine Daniel Aldman will still want you. He might have kept your divorce quiet, but after yesterday, everyone will guess what was done to you. I'm offering a kindness, Hannah, an easy, quiet passing. You must realize there's nothing left for you."

The blanket slid off her shoulders, and she began to shiver. He was right. She thought again of a dead fly, lying beyond pain on a windowsill.

Malcolm let his fingers trace the curve of her bruised neck. "Don't be stubborn—or do we need a repeat of the lessons learned last night?"

His threat shattered her inertia, and with strength born of terror, she slammed her palm into his nose. He cried out in unexpected pain and stumbled backward. At that moment she ran. She clambered aboard his black horse and dug her heels into his sides.

The animal leapt forward, the packhorse trailing of its own accord. In the snow the horse moved slowly, but still fast enough to outdistance a man on foot.

But not a bullet. Hannah heard three blasts before the gelding lurched, then tumbled forward with a grunt.

Before she even realized the horse had been shot, she rolled forward, downward, into a ravine.

Pain flared in a dozen spots, and her vision blurred. Only the cold shock of snow against her flesh prevented her from losing consciousness. Instead, the icy jolt propelled her to her feet at the bottom of the gulch. Remarkably, no trees were growing in it, so Hannah ran along the clear path, heedless of her wounds.

Daniel saw her clad only in a petticoat, in the distance. He drew his uncle's pistol as shots brought down the horse she rode. But he couldn't find Malcolm, even though he heard the gun.

Instead, his eyes were drawn to Hannah, floundering through the heavier snow along the ravine's bottom. He heard her frightened cry, and then another, far more terrifying sound. A crack of ice, not gunfire.

Hannah was on the frozen surface of a creek.

"Don't move!" he shouted, not caring if he gave away his position.

A movement distracted him as a man leapt aboard a gray horse laden with packs.

Daniel raised his gun to fire—and heard a second loud crack, then a splash. He looked where Hannah had been standing—and realized she was gone.

The pack horse's hoofbeats were receding, but he barely noticed. Instead, he urged his own mount closer to where Hannah had disappeared. Leaping off, he slid down the steep bank. He remembered Hannah couldn't swim. In this frigid weather it might not matter if she could.

He saw her face rise from the water, so discolored with bruises, he almost doubted who she was. Her hand clutched the broken edge of ice. Tearing branches from the nearest bush, Daniel slid toward her on his belly. He held them out and called to her, "Hold on!"

Her hands grasped the bare limbs reflexively, and he began to pull. In the distance he heard another shot. His brother. John didn't own a gun, didn't have one with him now. Had Malcolm Shelton shot his brother too?

Hannah's upper body was lying on the snow above the water level. Her blue eyes stared past him, through him, as though cold or shock were leeching life from her.

"Don't let go!" he shouted.

She grabbed tighter, and then the thin branches snapped. Much more quickly than she'd emerged, she slid back toward the opening, and death.

Fire flared in John's forearm where the bullet struck. His instinctive recoil knocked him from his mount, and he rolled into the snow, staining the pristine white with blood. The armed rider had come on him so fast, he hadn't had a moment to react. Even if he had, he wondered what he could have done. He'd been an idiot to come here unarmed.

There were two wounds, top and bottom, and he guessed the lead had passed right through. Though he felt nauseated with the pain, he realized he'd been lucky. Clutching his left arm tightly, he lurched to his feet.

The horse had shied away and refused to allow him to approach, so he stumbled off in the direction he'd seen Daniel ride. God help him if his attacker were still near.

When he saw his brother, John nearly forgot the throbbing pain. Daniel was lying on his belly in the bottom of a ravine, reaching into what looked to be a hole punched through a sheet of ice. Daniel scooted backward, yanking— John's heart jerked at the sight—a drenched body by its dark, matted hair. Awkwardly, Daniel pulled each arm out of the hole. Then, grabbing the wrists, he continued backing toward the ravine's edge until the sodden form lay upon the surface.

John half ran, half slid down the bank to reach his brother. The body Daniel dragged toward him was nearly as white as the drifted snow. It took John's shocked mind several moments to realize this limp mass could be only Hannah Shelton.

Daniel spared him a glance. "I heard a shot. Glad to see you're still alive."

John stared at Hannah's bluish lips when Daniel rolled her over. Against her pale flesh, black and purple bruises stood out starkly. Daniel scooped her into his arms as though her weight were nothing and started running up the hill. "We have to get her warm!"

It took only a few minutes to follow tracks and find the deserted cabin. Inside, a fire's embers still glowed life-giving warmth. Staggering behind them, John picked up the blanket lying in the doorway and brought it to where Daniel had placed Hannah, near the hearth.

"If you've got any of those fancy prayers saved, now's the time," Daniel said as he tucked the blanket's edges around her.

Finishing, he glanced at his brother. "You've been shot."

John nodded and sank to the floor. "Hurts like hell. Bleeding some too. Guess I ought to have a look."

The cabin started spinning.

"Don't you pass out on me." Daniel fished out a clean handkerchief. "You have another one of these? I can make a decent bandage."

His head bobbed in response. He let his brother remove his coat and tend the wound.

"See," Daniel told him as he worked. "The army did me some good after all. This looks pretty clean. Went right between the two bones. Now, if you can keep from fainting, I need you to chaperone."

"What?"

"I'm going to have to get her out of these wet things so I can dry them."

"Daniel, is she—"

"She's still breathing. I was there when she fell through. She was running, if you can believe it. Look at her. Half-dressed and beat to hell, yet she still ran from him."

"What about that man—Malcolm? Will he come back?" John asked.

"I doubt it. The man's not so brave when he's outnumbered. Those kind never are."

Gingerly, Daniel removed her sodden clothing. Every mark that he uncovered thickened the huge lump in his throat. He tucked the blanket tightly around Hannah and kissed her forehead softly. He wanted to cradle her, to hold her forever and protect her from harm.

"Do you think he—" John hesitated, unwilling to even say the word. But Daniel knew what he was asking.

He nodded in reply. The bruises on her thighs left little room for doubt. "I will find that bastard if I have to go from here to Pennsylvania. Any man who would do this to a woman ought to be gelded like a horse—before he's beat to death."

"I thought I saw some dry wood not far outside the door. Why don't you rebuild the fire?" John suggested.

Numbly, Daniel brought the wood, then removed his own coat and rekindled the fire. Afterward, he sat by Hannah, staring at her pale and swollen face.

"She'd warm up quicker if you held her," John suggested. "Go ahead."

Daniel glanced back toward his brother. "This suggestion from Mr. Steady Habits? Are you sure you haven't lost more blood than we thought?"

John frowned. "She needs to get warm, and even more, she'll need to know you're right beside her. Remember how frightened Amelia was? We held her, and then Bess did. She might need holding for a while. Hannah's going

to need it even more. She's going to need to know that
you still love her, no matter what.''

"I'm going to marry her, I swear it."

"I know that. I never doubted it a moment. Why don't
you hold your future wife."

Daniel lay beside her and wrapped thick arms around
the scratchy cocoon of her wool blanket. Thank God he
had her back. All last night he'd been troubled by nightmares of finding her body in the snow, her blood a brilliant
frozen puddle. He never wanted her out of his sight again.

Even now, when he closed his eyes, images assailed him.
Her face as she slid beneath the icy water, her blue eyes
without hope, her flesh colored only by contusions. The
fingerprints against her wrists, the bites along her flank,
the black and purple bruises on her upper thighs. The sad
remnants of her wedding gown, clumped with frozen snow.
With sickening certainty he knew he'd recall those images
until the day he died.

Hannah must be warming, for he felt her begin to stir.
Instinctively, he pulled her closer, but then he felt her
body stiffen. Before he could say a word to calm her, ragged
screams tore from her, and her limbs flailed in panic.
Through her back he felt her heart pounding against his
chest, until she squirmed away.

She sat up and turned toward him, her breath coming
in quick gulps. She held up her hands as if to fend off his
attack. Daniel saw no sign of recognition in her expression,
no softening at all. She looked wild-eyed as a snared beast
leaping toward escape.

"Hannah, it's Daniel. You're safe now." His own heart
thundered in his chest. Had beatings rendered her senseless?

Slowly, her hands drooped, but she made no move
toward him. Instead, she clutched the blanket even tighter.

"You're safe," he told her softly. "I'm here. John's with
me. See him, over there."

Shivering, she dropped her gaze to the floor.

"Malcolm's gone. He escaped when you fell through the ice. But he won't come back to hurt you. We won't let him. The sheriff will arrest him. He'll hang for what he's done." *If I don't kill him first,* thought Daniel. He reached out for her hand.

As she snatched it away, her gaze fell on John's bandaged arm. She stared at him without speaking.

John must have noticed. "He shot me, but I was lucky. The bullet tore straight through."

She rocked back and forth, like a child seeking comfort. "I'm so sorry . . ."

"You're not the one who should be, Hannah. We have to get you to Marinette," Daniel said softly. "We need to have a doctor look at both of you."

She shook her head in answer, then turned back toward the fire. "I won't go. Too cold."

"There's another blanket tied behind my saddle. And maybe some other things on that dead horse. Hannah, you're hurt badly, and you need to get something to eat and drink. It won't take so long." When she did not respond, he added, "Besides, you don't want John's wound to get infected."

"Then take him, and leave me."

Her shoulder grew rigid when he laid his hand on it.

"You'll feel better when you get back."

She shook off his touch. "I don't want to feel better. That's what you don't understand. Just because you pulled me from that water doesn't mean you got to me in time."

She meant the rape, he realized, and another powerful urge to crush the man responsible ripped through him. "You're alive. That's all I care about," he insisted. "Whatever he did doesn't change the way I feel for you."

"It changes everything. I'm tired, Daniel. Tired to my bones. And I won't go back with you. I want this over now."

Daniel's voice grew more insistent. "We're just trying to help you. You're coming back with us."

She turned toward him, tears streaming down her face. "Or what? Will you force me, like he did? Is that how men behave when women won't do what they want?"

"It's not fair for you to compare me to the bastard that hurt you, and you know it. We can't leave without you. You're the reason we came. Amelia's back at the hotel with Bess, crying her heart out over you. I'm not going to go back and tell either of them you want to give up."

Her eyes widened in surprise, and one bruised hand flew to her mouth. "Amelia. Oh, dear God. I thought he had killed her. I thought . . . he said." She began to sob and fell into his arms.

He stroked her damp hair as she shook with weeping. "Amelia's fine," he whispered in her ear.

"Thank God," she repeated again and again. "Thank God he didn't take her too."

CHAPTER
TWENTY-FOUR

The door was twice Daniel's height, with painted columns on either side and a huge B emblazoned in elegant script at the center. Though Hannah was cradled in his arms, Daniel took a moment to glance at John. "*This* is where she lives?"

Before he could answer, Bess threw open the door. Her green eyes teared when she saw Hannah.

"Bring her inside, where it's warm."

"I hope you don't mind we brought her here, Miss Brannon," Daniel said. "We couldn't take her into town this way."

Bess reached out to touch Hannah's hair, then hesitated when Hannah turned away and moaned. Bess's tears overflowed, and Daniel thought she must have gotten a glimpse of Hannah's battered face.

"Of course you brought her here. I told you we would bring Amelia with us. Come upstairs. She can use my sister's room." Bess started up the stairway, paused and shouted, "Daisy!"

A tall black woman glided into the entranceway and nodded to Bess, but her dark eyes were on the two men and the woman being carried.

"We're going to need a doctor. Have Bo take the coupe and fetch him right away. And tell my mother Hannah's here," Bess said, "but she must keep Amelia away now."

They followed the young woman up an ornate stairway with a gleaming banister. She led them to the most beautiful bedroom Daniel had ever set eyes on. White everywhere, it looked as bright as heaven, with fancy touches of lace and satin ribbon.

Bess pulled back fluffy blankets. "Put her down."

Very gently, Daniel followed her instructions and pulled up the covers. Again Hannah turned her face from Bess, from all of them, and toward the wall.

Bess looked at Daniel's face, a question in her damp green eyes. He nodded. She reached out for John's hand and froze.

"John, what happened to your arm? There's blood." Her face drained of its color.

"I'll be all right," John told her. "I just need to sit awhile."

"Malcolm shot him," Daniel said. "Doesn't look like it hit bone, but still, he needs attention."

Bess took his other arm. "It's a good thing I have *two* married sisters. You come with me right now, and I'll take you to Louise's room."

"I don't need—" John protested.

Daniel grinned at the thought of his brother in one of those frilly female bedrooms. "Go on with her," he urged. "Your color's bad, and you've lost some blood. Bess, don't pay any attention to his fussing."

John glared at Daniel but followed Bess without protesting. He'd been very quiet during the ride back, and Daniel figured he was in a lot of pain. Besides, Hannah didn't need a crowd hovering around her. Only him.

He picked up a carved chair so delicate he feared his weight might snap it and placed it beside the bed. Then he fiddled with the blankets, tucking them around her before he sat.

"Hannah, you're safe now," he told her.

"I'm so cold," she mumbled. It was the first thing she'd said since they started back.

"You'll get warm, and the doctor will take care of you. He'll give you something for the pain."

"No. Don't let him touch me, Daniel."

The lump in his throat thickened once again. "He'll be gentle. I'll stay with you if you want, or Bess can."

"You don't understand. I don't want anyone to touch me. I don't want anyone to stare at me. Bess—she looked like she would cry. Am I that awful, Daniel?"

"Bess is worried about you. We all are. She's just relieved that you're alive."

"Don't lie to me. It's more than that. Everything hurts so much, and I could feel the swelling with my fingers."

"I won't lie to you. You're banged up pretty good."

"I fought him, Daniel. I want you to know that. I didn't just lie there and let him—" The cry came from deep inside her, welled up like the blood from a stab wound. It didn't sound like a woman weeping, like anything so much as an animal howl of pain.

He tried again to take her hand, but she yanked it from his grasp.

"I know you fought," he said. "He wouldn't have hurt you so bad if you hadn't put up one hell of a struggle. But, Hannah, even if you'd been too scared to move, Malcolm is the one who did this. That murdering bastard—"

She turned toward him, her eyes filled with horror, and he wished he'd held his tongue.

"He hurt someone else—he *killed* someone?"

Daniel considered lying, but he knew how furious she'd be when she found out. Slowly, carefully, he considered his words. "Shot right through a door. Gen Tanner's dead. I'm—I'm sorry."

Tears leaked down her face as she stared at the ceiling. "All because of me," she whispered. "If I hadn't—"

"No. I'm not going to listen to you blame yourself. This was his doing, not yours. *His* choice. And I'm going to kill the man."

"The hell you are!" she shouted. "You stay away from him. It's just luck he didn't kill John. If he hurt you, too . . ."

"You think I'm going to give him a chance?" He remembered dozing sentries and men calling him St. Peter.

"Please, no, Daniel." Her voice softened, and finally she reached out and took his hand, though hers was so battered, he was afraid to squeeze it in return. "Please. I need you here. I don't want you to go. Promise me you won't."

The fear in her calmed his anger, his need to crush Malcolm like milled grain. He'd never heard her sound so childlike, so lost. How could he deny her anything just then? Yet, he hesitated, his hatred too strong to surrender.

Gingerly, he touched her face. "When I look at you, when I think of what he did—Hannah, he deserves to die."

"I won't lie here in a sickbed and wait for you like some wilted flower. Yes, he does deserve to die, but he killed a woman. Surely, the law will punish him! Not you! Your daughter needs you, Daniel. I don't think you've ever understood how much. And I need you as well. If you go after him, I swear to you, I won't be here when you come back. *If* you manage to come back."

She meant it, Daniel realized. Slowly, his anger still simmering, he nodded. "All right, then, Hannah. I won't kill him. We'll see what the law does."

"Promise me."

"I promise."

With surprising strength, she gripped his hand until she fell asleep.

"Here's Dr. Albright," Mrs. Brannon told Bess in the hall. "Daisy took Amelia out to ride Mr. Apples, so I can help as well."

Her mother would never be content to stay downstairs, away from all the goings-on, as much as Bess wished that she would. "The pony will be a good distraction," Bess said. "Hannah's this way, Dr. Albright. And John Aldman is resting in this room. He's been shot through the arm."

Mrs. Brannon gasped, and the doctor hesitated, as if unsure which patient to attend. Although he had barely finished his medical studies, the fire victims had seasoned him beyond his years. His brown hair was already shot through with early silver, and his lanky form drooped with the effects of overwork.

"John insists you see Hannah first," Bess said.

She noticed her mother's nod of approval. "I'll tend to this young man of yours, Bess. Perhaps there's something I might do to ease his pain."

Bess nodded and followed Dr. Albright into Hannah's room. Daniel sat beside his fiancée, his hand meshed with hers. As the men introduced themselves, Bess slipped outside. She didn't want to be there unless Hannah called for her.

Those bruises, and the thought of Hollas hurting her friend, made Bess weep anew. The brute had ridden past her on his way—

She remembered Hannah turning from her gaze and wondered if she would ever again be the same person. It seemed impossible that only yesterday she had looked forward to a wedding and a better life. Would there even be a wedding now?

Standing in the hallway, Bess heard two sets of soft voices, one from Hannah's room and the other from the room where John lay waiting. Was her mother truly trying to help him, or was she taking the opportunity to ask questions and assess his social standing? Knowing her mother, both held true.

Bess placed her hand on the doorknob to enter, then hesitated. Her stomach fluttered with butterflies as indignant as caged crows. Caught between her worry over Hannah and for John, she gave up and sank helplessly into a hallway chair.

Too nervous to be still for long, she fetched some needlework from her room, then returned to keep her vigil. The clock chimed twice before the men stepped out of Hannah's room.

"Despicable. The man deserves to hang," Dr. Albright muttered.

Daniel nodded, and his pained expression brought fresh tears to Bess's eyes. He should have been a married man today. Instead, he had to face this tragedy.

"With time, she'll recover. There may be fractures— near the eye especially, or in her left hand, but there's not much to do but try to keep her warm and quiet. You saw she wouldn't take the injection, but the pills will ease her pain. They'll just take a bit longer."

Even through the door Bess heard Hannah weeping. Daniel turned that way.

"No, you stay and talk with Dr. Albright. I'll take care of her," Bess offered. Hannah would need a woman now, she thought.

As she closed the bedroom door behind her, Bess forced herself to picture the burn victims she'd tended. The charred hands and the blackened flesh, the crippled feet. She had lost her breakfast that first morning, and several times thereafter. But she'd always managed to retain her composure. Hannah didn't need to see her weep now. Bess had to stay strong for her sake.

"I didn't want anyone to see," Hannah said. "I feel so dirty. So ashamed."

"The doctor had to examine you. You know that. Remember the children, the orphans? Sometimes they squirmed and didn't want anyone to change their bandages. But we were helping them. We had to. It's like that with Dr. Albright."

"I kept telling him I fought. I did. I never let him."

"Oh, Hannah. You've done nothing wrong. Now it's time to rest so you'll feel better."

Almost imperceptibly, her head shook. "I don't want to feel better. I don't want to feel at all. It was Malcolm, Bess. He wanted to kill me—afterward. With too much morphine. He said it would be a kindness. Daniel wouldn't want me anymore. No one would want me once they found out what he'd done."

Malcolm and Hollas. Were they really the same man? Bess shuddered to think of how close he'd been for so long. "What does this Malcolm know about love? Hannah, Daniel's *here*. He'd do anything for you."

She sighed. "Daniel. He deserves more. Dear God, it's all ruined. Everything."

"Let me bathe you, Hannah. That will help you to feel better. I'll get Mother to help if she's finished interrogating John. By that time the pills will help you go to sleep."

"I'd like that, and I need to know if John will be all right."

For the first time in many years, Bess wept against the broad expanse of her mother's bosom. Mrs. Brannon held her as if she were no older than Amelia.

She couldn't push aside the memories of awful bruises,

the bite marks that had even broken skin. And all the time they worked, Hannah insisted grimly, "Scrub harder. I want him off of me."

"I thought—I thought the hospital work might have prepared me. But it frightens me, Mother, to see what he did to her," Bess whispered.

"It should. It should frighten any woman." Mrs. Brannon stroked her hair and sighed. "I'm so glad your young man will be well soon."

Your young man, she'd said. Bess looked into her mother's eyes. Their sternness had gentled to a soft blue-gray. Bess couldn't hide a smile. "You like him?"

"He's not altogether without charm. Very concerned about Miss Shelton, and very brave as well."

Coming from her mother, it was incredibly high praise. "My heart felt like it jumped into my throat when I saw him bleeding that way. I'm so angry with this Hollas fellow, I could gouge his eyes myself. Do you suppose it's unchristian to hope he hangs?"

"Certainly not. The whole town feels that way after Mrs. Tanner's death. And abducting a bride from her own wedding—why, every man in town and half the women would line up to do the honors. I shouldn't be surprised if some of the rougher class threw a hanging party before he ever made it to the jail. If they can catch him, that is."

"They have to," Bess insisted.

"I shouldn't think, with his scars, the beast would have any chance of escaping justice."

"John is going to take Amelia home, but Hannah . . ."

"The poor woman needs time to heal, and of course she must have privacy. It would be unthinkable to put her back in a hotel. A lady simply cannot be seen in her condition. She'll stay here until she's well, and her betrothed may come to call as often as he likes. Provided he keeps his visits to respectable hours."

Bess kissed her mother's cheek. "Thank you. Thank you for everything."

Mrs. Brannon smiled. Bess knew her mother loved the role of magnanimous matron. But she wasn't finished being generous. "And before your young man leaves, I'd like him to speak with your father."

CHAPTER TWENTY-FIVE

Jacob Handley roundly cursed the telegram. So that's what Malcolm had been up to. The stupid bastard had completely lost his mind, and now it would be up to him to spare his friend the consequences.

He had to admit he'd missed Malcolm these last months. They'd often share a few drinks and talk of women, horses, and the law. Jacob's position as county sheriff he owed mostly to Shelton's influence, so he never spared sharing the most interesting details.

The two of them went way back, to boyhood. Together they'd explored the hills, shot copperheads, even discovered their first whore. When he thought of Big Belinda, his lips curved in a smile, and he stroked a thick mustache the ladies still found handsome enough.

He and Malcolm shared the same opinion of women. Marry one to keep your home and breed your children. But don't let that make you disappoint the others. He and Shelton might be respected civic leaders, even deacons in their church, but that needn't curtail a bit of harmless fun.

Usually harmless, Jacob admitted to himself as he thought of Hannah. She had never understood the rules. Unlike his poor, deluded Belle, she'd confronted Malcolm's excursions with a wall of solid ice. Who could blame the man for tiring of that treatment?

Of course Malcolm had been ruthless in the way he'd handled Hannah. But a man couldn't very well be expected to hand over his business to a woman after all the years and sweat he had invested.

After the divorce, Jacob felt sorry for the lonely woman. He chuckled to himself. The fact that she was the most beautiful thing in Shelton Creek hadn't hurt either. But the ungrateful slut had slapped him—and then she disappeared.

At first Jacob listened to the local gossips. Maybe Malcolm *had* killed her. He sure as hell had temper enough for it. Jacob might have let some evidence slip past him for the sake of friendship, but no proof appeared in his investigation. Nothing but the blood and broken glass.

Finally, he concluded Hannah must have set up the whole thing. Malcolm's indignation, even in private, was too real. And when Jacob thought of it, he couldn't piece together even the thinnest motivation for the man to kill his former wife. She lived in poverty, disgraced beyond redemption, without a single friend to stand beside her, while Malcolm suffered the attentions of townswomen eager to console him after the divorce. Hell, he'd even snagged a rich one for a second wife.

No, he hadn't killed her, but his business had turned sour. And then the fury had built and built, until he barely could contain it.

So he'd gone after her, thought Jacob. And from the looks of this telegram, he'd found her. He shook his head and grimaced.

"By God," he told his glass of whiskey, "I hope this time you finished it."

* * *

In front of Daniel, his horse's breath steamed in the frigid winter air. For the last three weeks he'd spent many hours in the saddle, riding from his uncle's farm to visit Hannah. Each time he saw her, the bruises on her face continued their metamorphosis. Though she still looked battered, she moved more easily.

When she chose to move at all. She spent long hours in a chair inside that room, doing needlework with Bess while gazing out the window. Watching, always watching, terrified, she told him, that Malcolm would come back.

Another snowfall had kept him away for several days, but the last time he'd seen her, Daniel tried to discuss a new date for their marriage.

"I'll think about it when he's caught." Hannah refused to say more on the subject.

Daniel hated the fear he saw in her face as well as the fear in his own heart. Would she ever move beyond this? Would either of them heal?

The letter in his pocket wouldn't help. Though he hated to let her read it, he knew he'd have to. The sheriff had to know if his men were seeking the wrong suspect.

Mrs. Brannon welcomed him warmly, and Bess inquired about his brother.

"I haven't seen him since last time I came. I imagine he's trying to keep warm and keep Amelia out of mischief."

Bess took him to the doorway of the parlor. "I promised Mother I'd help her with the weekly menus," she said as she retreated toward a gold-painted corridor.

Daniel waved, then turned his attention to the parlor, where he was shocked to find Hannah absorbed in a game of chess with Mr. Brannon. Daniel stood in the doorway, too intrigued to interrupt.

As if in defiance of her fading bruises, Hannah peered intently at the board. Her opponent adjusted his waistcoat around a thickening middle and tapped his pipe against the table. Almost nervously, or as if he were trying to distract her. Daniel didn't know the game, but even he could see she had captured most of Mr. Brannon's pieces.

An almost feline smile curved Hannah's lips as she picked up a piece carved like a small castle. "I believe that would be checkma—"

Mr. Brannon leapt to his feet. "Oh, dear. You have a guest, Miss Shelton. I'm afraid our game is at an end."

"But—"

"Entertaining guests is a woman's province, and besides, I'm beginning to regret teaching you this game." He extended a welcoming hand to Daniel. "And I thank you, sir, for the timely interruption."

"You mean *rescue*," Hannah said.

Daniel laughed, as much with relief at Hannah's smile as anything. It was the first time he'd seen her smile since the abduction.

He hated to be the one to wipe it from her face.

"I believe I'll leave you two for the sanctuary of my study," Mr. Brannon told them. "It's the last refuge for a man bested by females."

"He's really very pleasant," Hannah told Daniel as they sat on the divan. "He and Bess convinced Mrs. Brannon to allow me out of bed. Rest is one thing, but I can't just lie there reading and doing needlepoint, waiting to be 'presentable.' It gives me too much time to think and stare out that damned window."

"You sound like Hannah." Daniel grinned at her. "It's good to have you back."

She leaned toward him, then hesitated, as if some painful memory had risen up between them.

"It's all right," he reminded her, repeating the litany she never seemed to tire of hearing. "You're safe, and it's all right now."

She settled into his embrace, her soft exhalation like a breath of spring upon his neck.

"I love you so much," she said.

He stroked her hair and accidentally knocked a pin askew. He moved as if to fix it, but instead loosed all her tresses.

"Do you have any idea how long it took to do that with this hand?" Hannah displayed her left one, still discolored with the bruises that had now faded to green-gold.

"It looks prettier this way." After a last lingering caress, he fished the letter from his pocket. "I have some bad news here."

She sat up straighter, a wary expression on her face. "Tell me. I'm a grown woman, not a child, and despite what some may think, there *is* a difference."

Daniel nodded. Though he agreed with her, that didn't make this any easier to say. "Sheriff Skinner received this letter from some fella back in your hometown. Calls himself the Sells County sheriff. He says he saw Malcolm on and around the day—the day he took you. Says he can produce a deposition from Shelton's wife as well."

Beneath the mask of bruising, her face grew icy pale. But he wasn't yet finished, though he wished to God he could stop now.

"He suggests . . ."

"He suggests what, Daniel? Tell me now."

"He thinks you're on a campaign to destroy Mr. Shelton. Either that or you're hysterical. Maybe confused about what you saw."

"Confused? As if I wouldn't know a man I married?"

"Skinner wondered, with the head wounds, if maybe—"

"Sheriff Skinner was swayed by that pack of lies?" She stared at him, her eyes round with sudden wonder. "And you? You think it's possible that I'm—that I'm mistaken?"

For just a moment he supposed he had, but he'd be

damned if he'd admit it. Besides, Malcolm as attacker made much more sense than some so-called stranger, this mysterious Captain Hollas.

"You're not wrong," he said. "I met Malcolm back before the fire. I couldn't see his face this time, but I remember how he wanted you. He tried then to—to do just what he did. But the witnesses . . ."

She took the letter and examined it, then laughed without a trace of humor. "Jacob Handley. Malcolm's old friend, Jake! They're a pair. A couple of adulterous whoremongers."

"I'll try to convince Sheriff Skinner—"

"Why? Malcolm has more connections than Jesus Christ in Shelton Creek. He's going to get away with this. He's going to get away with *murder*!"

"There has to be something we can do."

"Not *we*. You have a daughter, Daniel, and a farm that needs you."

A jolt of fear leapt through him. "You haven't changed your mind about our marriage?"

"If there's one thing on this earth I'm sure of, it's your love for me. When I think of what you did, how you've stood by me, I feel . . . so fortunate. Another man would have walked away, or at the very least made me feel he was offering to honor our marriage agreement only out of a sense of duty."

He held his peace, dreading what he sensed was coming next.

Hannah shook her head. "I should marry you this minute. But when I think of it, when I think of all that we could have together, I start shaking, worrying, looking out those windows. Thinking he can steal it all away, anytime he wants. There's nothing I can have that he can't take."

"I won't let him. Hannah, I'll protect you from now on." God knows, he would have to find a way. Every time he slept, he had nightmares about pulling her out of that icy creek with her face so bruised, he barely recognized it. He woke up screaming sometimes at images of Malcolm pummeling and—worse yet—raping her. He'd rather die than let her go through that again.

Hannah stood, walked over to the chess set, and picked up a crowned player. "The queen," she explained. "The most powerful piece on the board. Yet if she sits in what she thinks is safety, she'll be taken. Just as I was."

She slid the piece across the board and picked up one of the few remaining black pieces. "Only by attacking can she win the game."

"Hannah? You're talking about some rich man's parlor amusement like it's your life."

"It is. Don't you understand? I tried to hide. I sat and waited for him to come for me, to take everything that mattered. And now they're going to let him get away with it. Even if he never comes within five hundred miles again, I'll spend the rest of my life cringing at every footfall, jumping at each shadow. Pitiful."

She leaned over and swept the pieces to the floor, a gesture so unlike her, he leapt to his feet. A piece rolled across the parquet and came to rest against his boot.

"I *won't* be pitiful. When I think about a wedding, I think of pain and death and—and that man inside me! I think of Malcolm offering a quick and easy death, as if he really wanted to spare me the grief and shame. I don't want to end up wishing I'd accepted his offer. I don't want to settle for whatever crumbs he left me of my life."

Bess stood in the doorway, hands halfway to her mouth. Mr. Brannon came up behind her and discreetly ushered her away.

"Let them be," he whispered, and slid shut the paneled door.

Daniel stood, and, feeling helpless, ran his fingers through his hair. "I should have been there sooner. Maybe I could have—"

She moved into his arms and interrupted with a kiss. Soft and warm, it bound them, then was over far too quickly. "No," she said. "Don't ever think it was your fault. I know you want to care for me. John once told me you're good with wounded things, and he was right. But some things need tending. Others have to pull back and heal all on their own. It's time for me to do that. I can't marry you until I'm whole."

"Hannah, right now we need each other more than ever."

She stepped away from him. "You're wrong. Right now we need to be apart. Otherwise, there won't be any later."

CHAPTER TWENTY-SIX

"Daniel! Dan Aldman!"

Daniel turned in his saddle to face Petey. He wasn't in the mood for socializing, but he hadn't seen his old friend in weeks. He dismounted and shook Petey's hand.

The shanty boy grinned at him, his front teeth chipped from an old saloon brawl. "Come on inside the Blue Spruce. I'll pay you back one of those drinks I owe ya. Looks like you could use one anyway."

Daniel shrugged. Why not? He sorely needed to forget his problems for at least a little while. After tying his horse to a hitching post, he went inside with Petey. The saloon was already populated by the usual assortment of rough-looking men. In one corner, a pair of garishly dressed women laughed too loudly at a grinning logger's tale.

"I'm flush today. Won me a pocket full o' rocks at draw poker last night." The logger scratched his beard, which from the ratty look might be full of crawlies, and shouted out an order for two whiskeys.

"Make mine beer," Daniel amended. "Draw poker,

huh? I'da guessed croquet for a fella with your distinguished manners.''

Petey guffawed and clapped him on the back. "Woulda
done that, too, but the fields was all snowed over. You still
doctorin' that mangy dog I brung you?''

"Sure am. He's healing pretty well.'' If Hannah wouldn't
accept his efforts, at least the mongrel wagged a tail. Petey
had found him singed and starving, lost among the woods,
one last survivor of October's holocaust. "I call him Sam.''

The logger nodded his approval.

Their drinks arrived on a bar stained with earlier over-
flows.

"I heard that Malcolm fella come back for your woman.
They say he beat her half to death. They ever catch the
son of a whore, he'll never live to trial. A bunch of us,
we're gonna see to that ourselves.''

Another logger, Pug Barton, seated himself beside them
without invitation. The huge man was nearly as tall as
Daniel, but far heavier. His nose had been flattened years
before, supposedly by another shanty boy's caulked boot.
He was ugly as sin, with about half the personality.

"I hear he had at her.'' His voice was loud, a challenge.
He threw back a whiskey in two gulps, then licked the
moisture from his lips.

"Private conversation, Pug,'' said Petey. "Do ya mind?''

He acted like he hadn't heard. "Women. They're always
hollerin' about a man's too rough. Hell, Daniel, you were
in the army. You had one of them housewife kits to mend
your drawers. Ever try to thread the needle while it's wig-
glin'? Can't be done.''

Daniel put down his beer. "Didn't know you were such
a seamstress. Hard to figure, with that outfit of yours.''

Pug leaned closer, emitting the odors of old sweat and
rotting teeth. "Ain't no such thing as rape, is what I'm
sayin'. Any man believes it is bein' played a fool.''

Most times, Daniel realized, he could have tossed off a

quick remark to shut up Pug. But today wasn't most times. He felt a flush of anger heat his face. Before he made a conscious decision to strike, his fists were flying.

Pug, for all his size, moved as quickly as if he'd planned this all along. Savage glee lit his tiny eyes as he hit Daniel in the jaw. Recovering from the glancing blow, Daniel caught sight of a gleam reflecting the poor lamplight. A blade's gleam, he realized. His opponent held a knife. But Pug had thrown back one drink too many. His first slash went wild. Daniel grasped his wrist and slung him headfirst into the bar.

He thought he heard wood crack. In one quick motion Daniel scooped up the dropped pig-sticker and slid it to the bartender for safekeeping. With a groan of misery Pug started crawling off. Petey lifted his backside with a boot as he made for the door.

Daniel took his seat once more. "I can't abide any man that doesn't talk right about women," he remarked.

Petey lifted his drink in a toast. "Here's to fancy manners, then. Good thing my mama taught me right."

"Pardon me."

Daniel turned as his brother stepped inside and nearly tripped on the departing Pug. John joined him in the bar and offered him a handkerchief.

"Your mouth is bleeding."

Daniel wiped it. "Hadn't noticed. Must be getting colder out."

"Why do you say that?"

"I figured hell froze over, to see you inside a place like this."

John shook his head at the barkeep's inquiry, then said, "I brought Amelia to Phineas's house. She misses you. Uncle Phineas said you were with Hannah, but I saw your horse tied here instead."

Daniel reclaimed his beer and sipped it. "She thought I should leave."

"So you're feeling sorry for yourself again and thought you'd drown it here?"

"Aw, hell, John," Petey said. "I offered the man a drink. What's the harm in that?"

"Ask that fellow crawling out the door."

"He had it comin'. If Dan here hadn't done it, I'da took him down myself. Talkin' that way about Daniel's woman . . ."

Daniel shook his head. "It's all right, Petey. Thanks for the beer. I need to speak to John now."

Petey's gaze roamed the room, then settled on one of the women, whose breasts threatened to escape a daring bodice any moment. She jerked her head at him by way of invitation.

"I reckon she'll be a sight more grateful to hear of my good fortune anyway," Petey told the men.

He crossed the room to join the dark-haired adventuress. She smiled and leaned forward, her bosom apparently defying the laws of gravity.

"Hannah won't set a wedding date," said Daniel. "Says she won't marry me until she's whole. What the hell does that mean? Have I lost her, John?"

John sighed. "You're asking *me* to explain a woman? Maybe you *were* right. Hell really has frozen over. I couldn't answer you on that. Maybe what happened frightened her so much, she needs time."

"I think that's part of it. And she's damned angry too." Daniel explained the contents of Sheriff Handley's letter.

"So she's afraid, mad, and insulted all at once. If you were her, would you want to talk marriage?"

"Why not? Maybe I'm hurt, too, by all of this. Maybe I think about it every day, dream it every night. Sometimes I dream I get there sooner. Sometimes I dream she's dead, or that bullet pierced your heart and not your arm. I need her right now. I need to keep her safe and close, and she's pulling away."

"So you came here to get drunk and whip some ignorant logger?"

Daniel shrugged, too miserable to argue. "Something like that. But you didn't give me time to attend to the drunk part. I'm only halfway through my first."

"Don't give up on Hannah. Not now. Not yet."

"She was talking crazy, all this stuff about a game and attacking. She said she was tired of being frightened. Pitiful, she called it."

"Pride," John said. " 'When pride cometh, then cometh shame.' "

"Don't you have anything to do with your winters other than memorize the Bible?"

"It's cheaper than whiskey, and it's never given me a bloody lip. Come on, Daniel. Let's go. Your little girl is waiting for her papa. She wants to show you where her tooth is coming loose."

Daniel pushed away the beer mug, still half full, and followed John to where the horses had been tied.

"I'll be there in a bit," John said once they had mounted.

"Going to see Bess?"

John smiled. "Bess's father."

"I thought you looked mighty slicked up for a call on Phineas. Are you going to ask him?"

John nodded. "I feel a fool, walking into that fine house and asking to take his youngest daughter to a little cabin."

"You won't be living in a little cabin long. Can you make him believe that too?"

"I could wait and prove it, but Bess and I—we're in a hurry. All I can do is show him my plans. The rest is up to him."

Daniel clapped him on the shoulder. "You go talk to him, then. And leave the rest to Bess. She'll make his life a misery if he says no. The woman is in love."

"That makes two of us." John laughed and turned his mount toward the Brannon mansion.

* * *

"Today's my day for visitors named Aldman," Alfred Brannon remarked cordially. He shook John's hand and gestured toward a chair near the fire. When John sat, he lowered his bulk into its mate.

John glanced around the room, once more taking in the parlor's elegant furnishings, the portrait of Mr. Brannon, some years younger, the ornate marble chess set on a beautifully carved table. Was it right even to try to take Bess from all this?

"I've been expecting this, Mr. Aldman," Brannon said after a long pause. "I do have other daughters."

"I understand that, sir. But I'm not in the same position as their suitors, I'm afraid. Bess is used to having things, and most everything I had was lost. Before I ask you for her hand, I'd—I'd appreciate it if you'd hear me out." Inside his suit, John felt himself sweating. The wool itched something fierce, but he wouldn't allow himself to fidget.

Brannon lit his pipe, puffed twice, and then nodded.

"Daniel and I have plans for the farm. We've even written out some papers. Nothing fancy, mind you. Just our ideas and some things we've done already. Before—before that business with the wedding, Hannah helped us too. She's got a stake in this, and she knows a lot about raising horses. I'd like your opinions on those plans. You're a man who understands business, and as I see it, if you don't think we have a chance, I have no business asking to wed a woman as deserving as your Bess."

John tried to steady his hands, and his nerves, to pass over the envelope he withdrew from his breast pocket, but even so, it shook. Mr. Brannon took the envelope and unfolded the papers from inside it.

Puffs of smoke rose from the right side of his mouth as he examined the plans.

John wondered if he'd spelled the words right. He bit

his tongue, resisting the impulse to explain or add. Stammering couldn't help his case, couldn't do anything but make him look as foolish as he felt. He glanced once at the paneled door and wondered if Bess was on the other side, listening, holding her breath with him.

The clock on the mantel ticked dutifully, keeping careful count of the longest minutes of his life.

Mr. Brannon refolded the papers carefully, then returned them and their envelope to John. "I may not be a man disposed to dandling children on his knees, but I consider my daughters' welfare a sacred trust, Mr. Aldman."

John tried without success to read the man's expression. He hesitated, a lump rising in his throat.

The older man smiled. "I am relieved to see you are as concerned with Bess's future as I am."

"I love her very much. I don't want her to be disappointed."

"Your plans look sound. Farming hay and grains as cash crops until you can build a self-sustaining herd. Gradually shifting to reliance on the animals. You've investigated markets as well as sources for the bloodstock, and you've even begun financial negotiations with some reputable lenders. You're an enterprising fellow, Mr. Aldman. You remind me of myself some years back. I was no more born to wealth than you were."

"My brother's as much to praise—or blame—as I am, and Hannah made some excellent suggestions."

"So you're not too proud to listen to a woman. Good. You've no doubt guessed from watching Mrs. Brannon run an emergency hospital that she could run the country if need be. She's the best counselor I have. Miss Shelton has a fine head on her shoulders, I've discovered. She'll be an excellent asset to your family business should she continue with her plans to marry Daniel. My daughters weren't raised to sit in drawing rooms playing the piano either.

Oh, Mrs. Brannon takes Bess to all the proper functions, but the girl's not happy unless she's useful. In my view, she'd be completely wasted on the tea and gossip set."

"In that case," John began, "may I ask—"

Mr. Brannon raised a palm. "Not just yet. For one, I still have mudsill manners, for everything I've earned. Would you have a drink, Mr. Aldman? Some coffee, or some cake?"

"N-no, but thank you." What he really wanted was to escape this clammy suit.

"Then let's get down to terms. I'm giving you one year."

"A year?"

The older man nodded. "A year to make a fair start on your plans. You'll want my help, of course, with the financing."

John felt his body stiffen. "No, sir. I do not. I don't wish to marry your daughter for any other reason than the one I've given. I love her very much. The business will succeed or fail on its own merits. Nothing else."

"My wife was right about you. She said you had moral courage. I didn't understand her at the time. All right, then."

"All right?"

"You may ask my daughter for her hand. That business about the year won't be necessary. I trust Bess's judgment, and my wife's. And with Miss Shelton on their side, I am completely outnumbered by the remarkable women of this household."

Just outside the door, he heard an excited female shriek. Recognizing Bess's voice, John laughed and shook her father's hand.

"I don't imagine you'll suffer overmuch wondering about my daughter's answer," Mr. Brannon chuckled around a mouthful of pipe smoke.

* * *

Instead of going straight home, Daniel found himself storming into Abel Skinner's office with Handley's letter in his hand. Sheriff Skinner looked up from some papers he'd been signing.

"The law has had its chance. I'm not going to let this go," Daniel warned the man. "I can't let Malcolm get away with hurting her and killing that poor woman."

Skinner gestured toward a chair, but Daniel remained on his feet, fists clenched with pent-up rage. From the corner of his eye he saw a muscular deputy edge nearer, one hand poised near his gun.

With a snort of disgust Daniel dropped into the chair. Pounding Skinner might make him feel better, but it wouldn't solve the problem. Besides that, it would buy him a slew more.

"Want to talk about it?" Skinner asked, his voice still keeping to its grating near-whisper.

"Hannah says this Handley fellow is a friend of Malcolm's. They go way back. She's sure. The woman knows who hurt her. Hell, *I* saw him with my own two eyes before the fire. He hurt her then, and threatened to do more. I believe Hannah."

"You have to." Skinner pushed aside his papers. "Want some coffee? We can talk about what we're going to do."

"Then you believe her too?"

Skinner nodded. "She seems sensible enough, and honest. Aldman, I've been sheriff here for twelve years. That's time enough to see a lot of shanty boys and farmers beat up women. Hell, I've seen them kill their own wives on occasion. And you know what? Every one of them denies it. 'She fell down those stairs, or she tripped and broke her neck,' they tell me. The throttle marks and black eyes aren't supposed to matter. A lot of them have friends too, or even mamas who will vouch for their whereabouts, swear what gentle husbands they were. Meanwhile, I look at a yard full of beat-up, scrawny, motherless kids.''

Skinner's eyes hardened with what must have been a particularly ugly memory. He got up and poured both men mugs of coffee from a dented tin pot on his wood stove. Steam rose, rich and tempting, from the dark brown liquid.

"I guess it's no surprise that Shelton has a friend too. But his friend being another sheriff complicates things. You and your brother didn't see Malcolm this last time, so in the end it comes down to his word against Hannah's. We'll have to bring in outside law."

"They won't believe her, will they?"

Skinner shook his head. "Divorced woman's word won't be worth much, especially with his loving wife and local lawman speaking out against her. She have any friends at home to back her up?"

"I don't think so."

The sheriff sipped his coffee. "If we could find some sort of proof a man matching his description left the area, maybe we could get a witness to identify him."

"But you've been looking for that witness all this time."

"True. But maybe if Shelton *thought* I had one, he'd do something stupid. Sounds like a real hothead. Any kind of serious investigation might make him mad enough to come back our way again."

"And then he'd try to kill Hannah."

"Sounds like, if you or I were there, we'd have a clear-cut case of self-defense. Sometimes justice works out that way in the north woods."

Daniel tried the coffee, found it strong and to his liking. "I don't like this waiting for him to make a move."

"You play poker, Aldman?" Skinner asked him.

"On occasion."

"Seems to me this is the only hand we'll get. We'll have

to try to bluff him into thinking we've got better. I'll send off a couple of letters. Then we'll have to wait."

"Will you tell Hannah about this?"

"She's already scared enough. Why don't we talk to Mr. Brannon, make sure a deputy's in place? Meanwhile, I'd suggest you buy yourself a real gun. And wait for him to come. You go after him before then, and I'd have to arrest you. It'd be a damn shame to hang a man for killing someone who deserves to die. You hear me, Daniel Aldman? I said *wait*."

"On two conditions. First, watch out for Hannah. I don't want him near her. And second, let me know when he's seen near this town. I can't stay here right now. Hannah—Hannah's made it difficult. But I want to be the one to kill him. I want to be the one."

CHAPTER
TWENTY-SEVEN

"I went ahead and did just what you asked." A huge chair overwhelmed Jacob Handley's small form, but his voice boomed out its usual unlikely bass.

Malcolm's mind had wandered, distracted by the shapes that seemed to writhe inside the fireplace a few short feet away. Half-remembered images twisted into blood-soaked passion: his and his former wife's. Since he'd been home, he'd spent long hours contemplating flame, reliving the night he hurt Hannah.

"What's that?" he asked his friend. Outside, a frigid wind whipped at the window, as bitter as regret.

"I let that lawyer fellow who's been asking know where he could find her. That way, at least someone else could say she was alive. She won't even have to come back. Lawyer Bloom likes to chat with folks. The word will get out she's been located alive."

"I don't imagine she'd dare show her face here, but I almost wish she would. Dear Hannah . . ." Still gazing into the flickering hearth, Malcolm sipped his brandy and remembered how she'd looked the last time he had seen her. Although her wounds at first had horrified him, he knew he'd finally humbled her. Finally, after everything she'd done.

A smile contorted half of his scarred face, only to falter once Melissa Shelton came in bearing a tray with two thick slices of pie.

"I thought I told you, we don't want to be disturbed," Malcolm snarled at his wife. He didn't need his friend to see her bruises either, to ask questions that were none of his damned business.

"I—I'm sorry. I thought you'd like dessert. It's just—it's—good to have you home." She stared mostly at the floor, but when she looked at him, her blue eyes glimmered with something. Could it be fear, or did she merely pity him his scars?

"I've been home long enough for you to give me an hour's privacy." Malcolm grabbed a plate and managed a stiff nod. He didn't chastise her too severely despite her cowering devotion. She might be stupid as a post and about as energetic in the bedroom, but he didn't want to drive her off, especially since her father's money was seeing the farm through these rough times.

When she left, Jacob took a bite of apple pie. "It's finished, Malcolm. Hannah's beaten. If she comes and makes a fuss, I'll charge her with fraud. I imagine all I'd have to do is threaten it and remind her we're a small county. We don't have separate cells for lady prisoners. God knows what might happen if we leave a little prize like her locked up with the drunks and scoundrels."

Once more Malcolm half smiled with the unscarred flesh on the right side of his face. "I imagine she'd go squalling all the way back to Wisconsin."

"You have her farm. You ruined her name. Hell, you even went after her and paid her back for all the trouble she caused. If she comes back to take care of this business, you stay away from her, you hear? I'm telling you for your own good, she's beaten.''

The apple pie, his favorite, formed a doughy lump in Malcolm's throat. Beaten. Yes, she had been. His lust stirred with the thought of beating her again. Of beating her to death.

The letter Mr. Brannon brought her was the last thing Hannah expected, especially with that postmark, Hampton Falls. She had an aunt there, Hilda Blackard, but the woman had barely spoken to Hannah since her divorce.

Hannah grimaced. There'd been no help from that quarter, even when she had sunken to her lowest point. She suspected the letter was some sort of condemnation for leaving town the way she had.

She sat on her bed and turned up the lamp against the wintry gloom so she could read. This didn't look like Aunt Hilda's script, and for good reason, she discovered. Hilda Blackard had died months before. Her attorney, Adam Bloom, wrote that Hannah was her aunt's sole heir. She'd need to travel to Hampton Falls to claim the proceeds from her estate.

Sole heir? Hannah's trembling fingers dropped the letter, and she bent to pick it up. Aunt Hilda had been widowed back before the war by a successful shopkeeper. She'd borne five babes, none of whom survived past the third year. But even so, Hilda had a living brother with three grown children, none of whom had been disgraced by scandal. Had Aunt Hilda argued with him and changed her will before Hannah's divorce? Or had the old woman pitied Hannah's suffering despite the fact that she had seemed indifferent?

Perhaps Mr. Bloom would tell her. The letter offered instructions that would authorize the estate to pay her traveling expenses. Because her location had been unknown, the house and property had already been auctioned. To her surprise, he hinted the amount raised by the sale was not inconsequential.

Hannah felt the blood drain from her face. That meant she would go home so much sooner than she'd planned. To Hampton Falls, eight miles east of Shelton Creek.

She went to the washstand and splashed cool water on her cheeks. The mirror showed two months had leeched the shocking hues of her bruised face to faded browns and yellows. Still, Mrs. Brannon would doubtless argue that she wasn't ready to be seen in public.

True. She wasn't ready despite her careful planning, despite the necessary distance she had put between herself and the man she dearly loved. But she found her face less troubling than her fears. Fears of prison, pain, and death. Fears of her former husband, Malcolm.

A single tear plopped into the washbasin, and she cursed it. Would she be forever nothing but a pathetic wreck, or would she take this risk?

Now was her best chance. She'd never have a better excuse to travel to Sells County. It was as if God or the Fates pushed for her return.

How ironic, Hannah thought, that she would be going about another will. Despite her poverty, Hilda Blackard's mattered little. The will she truly sought would be the key to her revenge.

Dear Daniel,

Important family business takes me to Hampton Falls, Pennsylvania. I will not delay, dear, for my home is where you are, where all those are who know me as I truly am, yet still welcome me into their homes and lives.

I feel so fortunate to have found you, to have survived that fiery cataclysm by your side. Your ceaseless love has seen me through the unbearable, the unthinkable, this win-

ter. *The gift of time you have allowed me has given me the strength to begin to heal myself.*

I know our separation has been costly. With all my heart, I am sorry you were hurt. I promise you, when we next meet, there will be no more delays. I will marry you if you'll still have me, in whatever place and style you wish. The wedding means less to me than the marriage, and especially your love.

Daniel, I pray you'll understand why I have left this letter. If you were to come with me, so close to Shelton Creek, I fear you would find Malcolm. Of all things I have borne, I could least abide your death or imprisonment on account of that vile man.

I will return as soon as possible. Please, dear, wait for me.

Hannah's hands shook as she reread the letter. May God forgive her for the lies and half-truths, the implication that she, too, would stay as far as possible from Malcolm, that she truly intended to return. She added her love and signature, then blew across the ink until the paper dried.

She had little time left for delay if she were to deliver it as planned. Bess had told her Daniel and his family were visiting Uncle Phineas for the day.

Bess had arranged a light sleigh for her use while her own family attended church services. Hannah had explained a bit about the inheritance to her friend and why it was important that Daniel not learn she was leaving on tomorrow's early train until it was too late for him to come.

"But, Hannah, why don't you leave me the letter? I could have it delivered to his cabin and save you the drive," Bess had suggested.

Hannah shook her head. "I want to do this, Bess. I want to feel wind on my face and have time to think. It's a fine morning, and I love driving a sleigh. Please do this for me."

"Mother will be livid." Bess smiled. "But then, she usually is."

Mrs. Brannon, though she liked John Aldman, hadn't been prepared for Bess's engagement to what she termed a "near pauper." She hadn't spoken to her husband for two weeks after the betrothal was announced.

Hannah bundled up in her heavy coat, scarf, thick gloves, and a blanket for her outing. With the letter tucked in an envelope inside a pocket, she went to the Brannon stable and found Bo harnessing a beautiful white horse.

The slim young man looked at her with disapproval etched on his coffee-brown features. "Miss Brannon said to hitch up Blizzard, but he's mighty frisky. You want me to drive you?"

"No, thank you. I can handle him. I'll be back before dark."

"You sure you don't want some help, miss?"

Hannah checked the harness carefully and smoothed a strap that might have pinched the gelding. "I'll be fine," she promised. She climbed into the sleigh, arranged her scarf and blanket, and began the long glide over the snowy pathway.

The cold air felt sharp inside her lungs, and her eyes stung with all the whiteness, so bright it made the horse's clean hide look yellow-tinged. The Brannon mansion, near Marinette's outskirts, soon receded as she rushed toward Peshtigo. She felt, like the horse, deliciously alive.

A slight chuck of the reins encouraged Blizzard to a gallop. She laughed with the simple joys of speed and winter sunshine. As the horse's hooves kicked up a spray of snow, it seemed possible she would succeed, and that someday she might live to become Daniel's wife. Here, the risks of her journey to Sells County seemed inconsequential. She *must* overcome them, for her cause was just.

*   *   *

What in God's name was that foolish woman doing, Deputy Lemaster asked himself. He couldn't have been more surprised if Hannah sprouted wings. Though he knew she was unaware of the sheriff's new plan and the fact that he was watching, Jean Lemaster still couldn't believe a lone woman would drive a sleigh herself. Particularly a woman as young and attractive as Miss Shelton. Now, besides watching out for her former husband, he'd have to ward her from errant groups of rowdy loggers or whatever scoundrels might roam the woods on a pretty Sunday afternoon.

The former shanty boy scratched his jet-black curls and swore in his father's French. Wishing in vain for a cup of Skinner's coffee, he nudged his blue roan gelding to an easy lope and hung back, far enough to watch her without being seen.

Sensibly, Hannah checked the horse's gait. With the frolics out of his system, Blizzard contented himself with a safe and steady trot.

When Hannah passed through Peshtigo, she could scarcely believe the changes. From the ruin, a small town had emerged. New homes and businesses had sprung up like summer weeds. Smoke spiraled warmly from dozens of fireplaces. Snow blanketed scorched earth with clean, concealing whiteness. In the spring, that melting snow would give rise to new life. She imagined fresh green grasses growing over the ashen waste, creating rich pasturelands for horses and cattle. In some ways the autumn fires may have given area ranchers and dairymen a costly boon.

In another hour she arrived at the Aldmans' farm. The cabin stood larger, lovelier than she had expected. Nearby stood a brand-new barn, still a shell according to Daniel, but enough to get them started in the spring.

A dog she didn't recognize charged out of the barn door and started barking at her horse. Blizzard kicked once at the shaggy, brown-haired creature, then steadfastly ignored its outraged woofs.

Hannah climbed out from the sleigh. The coyote-sized dog turned toward her and growled.

"Hello." Hannah spoke soothingly. "Are you Daniel's friend? So am I."

Slowly, she reached toward it with a hand. The dog wagged its tail and approached her for a pat.

"You're quite a guard dog, aren't you?"

As if in answer, the dog flopped over on its back and wriggled in the snow.

Hannah took a moment to rub his chest before she tied the horse.

Afterward, she walked to the cabin, feeling a little like a thief. As she expected, the door had been left unlocked. She left it open long enough to light a lamp, then closed it.

She looked around at the sparse furnishings. A simple table and several stools sat in the room's center. A pair of deerskins lay not far in front of a fire's glowing coals. Pieces of fabric had been hung to offer some privacy to the two brothers for their "bedrooms." A ladder led into a loft, where Amelia's bed must be. Another skin was draped over the railing.

The Aldmans' possessions were few but neat. The cabin felt welcoming and snug against the freezing winter.

Hannah reached inside her coat to take out Daniel's letter.

With a bang the door flew open. Silhouetted against the bright light was the figure of a huge man, an ax in his right hand. The man limped, just like Malcolm.

Startled, Hannah shrieked and backed up two steps. She

shoved the envelope into the pocket of her skirt to hide
it.

The man limped into the room and shut the door behind
him. The lamplight lit his face.

"Oh, dear God, Daniel, you scared me."

"What are you doing here?" There was no welcome in
his voice.

"I—I wanted to get out, so I had Bess get me a sleigh."

"Why would you come here when you thought I'd be
gone?"

"I started driving, and before I knew it, I was in Peshtigo.
I thought I'd come to see the cabin. What happened to
your leg?" She hated lying, hated even worse the suspicion
in his words.

"Slipped on the ice last evening. Thought I'd stay today
and rest it, but I felt well enough to chop wood behind
the barn. Then I heard Sam barking." Daniel peeled off
his gloves and stuffed them in his pockets, then removed
his jacket and hung it from a peg. "You came to wait for
me, didn't you? You're going to break it off for good."

"No! Oh, Daniel, never!" The cabin felt uncomfortably
warm. She unwound a scarf and slipped off her own coat,
then wondered at her vigorous denials. In a sense, wasn't
that exactly what she was doing?

"You wouldn't even see me last week, and then you
sneak out here all alone. What else, Hannah? What else?"
As she hung her coat beside his, he grasped her wrist and
spun her toward him.

She jerked her arm away and rubbed it. "I have to leave
now." She didn't want him to see the way her eyes had
filled with tears.

"No, Hannah. Please don't. I never meant to frighten
you. It's just—you shouldn't be driving in the snow yourself. I want you to be safe." He reached toward her but
didn't touch her. His huge hand, outstretched, trembled
like a dry leaf in the wind.

She stared at that hand, only inches from her shoulder. So tentative, afraid even to touch her. She slid her fingers through his, kissed each one, then stepped closer. "Nothing you could ever do would frighten me. I—I came to say how very sorry—"

He bowed his head to interrupt her with his own kiss. Soft at first, and gentle, until she closed the narrow gap between them. Hannah felt tension draining from her, from both of them as their kiss deepened. A ripple of pleasure ignited beneath her belly and left her tingling to her lips.

So hard, so hard to pull away, to remember she was leaving in the morning. Leaving, perhaps never to return to him again.

His hands moved to frame her face, caressing. Then, at his swift mischief, she felt her hair slide loose to her waist. His lips brushed her ear, and she shivered with heat rather than the chill of early March.

"I don't ever want you to be sorry, Hannah," Daniel whispered. "God knows you had reason to want some time alone. It's just that after what he did to you, I was so afraid. So afraid you'd never want another man to touch you. When you pushed me away, I didn't listen to your reasons. I kept thinking those were just excuses to be rid of me."

"It *would* save me a lot of time repinning my hair." She toyed with the fringe of brown waves at his neck, then gave one curl a playful tug. This time she sought his mouth for a second taste. Just one more kiss before she told him. One more kiss and she would stop.

Then she felt his hands skim the contour of her waist, felt her body come alive beneath his touch. She knew she shouldn't let him, yet she pretended not to notice as his fingers fumbled with the buttons of her bodice. Instead, she concentrated on the way his tongue flicked between her lips, how easily her mouth opened to accept it. When his kisses faded to her neck, her knees buckled with unexpected weakness.

Daniel scooped her into his arms, then laid her on the hides before the fire. He paused to rekindle the flame and put on another log, then turned to gaze at her.

"I could make you wish you hadn't come here." He sat beside her, moved only inches from her face. "You look so beautiful, your skin all pink with the cold. Yet you feel so warm and sweet. If I kiss you again, I don't know how I'll ever stop myself."

Beautiful. She might call him that as well, with his masculine, broad features, the firelight reflected from his deep brown eyes. If she went through with her plan, she might never see his face again. Might never feel his touch. Could she take that risk? Could she not leave him, too, with this at least?

With a delicate shrug she let the bodice of her dress fall open. He didn't hesitate, but kissed her with increasing passion, leaning closer as she unbuttoned his shirt.

She did what she had wanted for so long and ran her fingers through the thick tangle that grew across his chest. She tugged at the buckle of his belt and smiled at his gasp.

"I think I'd like to see you in the firelight," she whispered.

He slipped off the shirt, then removed his boots and made a pile of his jeans. Nude, he lay beside her, with all his want exposed before her eyes.

Hannah let him help her follow his example until she lay naked beside him, naked only inches from his touch.

She knew what he was thinking, recognized the pulse of anger in his eyes as he gazed over faded bruises and the scars from Malcolm's teeth. She saw sorrow as well, with the memory of her pain.

"Are you certain?" he asked as his fingertips grazed her cheek.

"More certain than I've been of anything." She leaned

forward to kiss him, amazed how starved she felt for the taste of his strong mouth.

He parted her lips without effort, deepening the kiss, then broke off to brush his lips along the hollow just above her collarbone. His hand cupped her breast as gently as he might hold a baby bird.

Shivers sparked inside her as his thumb and forefinger gently squeezed its tip. Then she gasped as his lips found her and enveloped her, surrounding her with warmth and want.

He stopped what he was doing to look into her eyes. "I don't care what the preacher says. From this moment I consider you my wife." His mouth took her once more.

She lay back, her eyes closing, not caring about tomorrow's separation, not caring about anything except that he continue. His fingertips caressed her thighs, then moved to stroke the source of moisture deep between them. She moved against him rhythmically, nearly weeping with a need as sharp as pain.

Grasping his upper arm, she positioned him above her, heard him groan with his desire. But first he looked into her face and kissed her softly. "Do you want this, Hannah? Do you truly want me too?"

She stared into his eyes and saw the love there and the depth of his concern. She knew that he would stop if she but asked. Instead, she grasped him tightly, then pulled him onto her, inside. They both moaned with the long-awaited contact; both cried out each other's names.

She gave herself up to the power of an ageless cadence. Their bodies moved together, driven by all that they had been through, all they dared to hope. Soon there was nothing but their motion, obscuring all else in her mind. No past, no tomorrow, only the movement and the pleasure, the moist warmth . . .

Nothing else. Not Hannah, and not Daniel. Something greater came together as they moved. Something glowing, something blinding, something too intense to be contained by flesh.

She barely recognized her own cry. Barely knew Daniel's as it followed, one split second later. He lowered himself beside her, his hair drenched in sweat, his dark eyes staring at her as if she were his universe.

"Hannah." Her own name, breathed in firelight, sounded like a prayer. "I love you."

She wanted to say how much she loved him too, but sorrow withered the words like flowers touched by frost. She still meant to leave him, to leave without a good-bye. Would he ever understand, much less forgive her, for making love with him today?

"What's wrong?" He must have seen some inkling in her features.

She wanted to explain it, but the truth caught in her throat. Instead, she forced her face into a smiling facade. "What could be wrong, Daniel? Whatever could be wrong?"

Inside, her heart ached that even now she had to lie.

He pulled away from her, looking ill at ease.

Hannah felt sick, imagining he was thinking of the rape, blaming himself for pushing her too soon to intimacy. She opened her mouth to reassure him and then closed it, not knowing what to say.

Outside, the dog began to bark. When Hannah strained her ears, she could hear the distant sounds of hoofbeats.

Daniel groaned. "Dammit. Let me take a look."

He strode naked to the cabin's single window and peeked out past a muslin shade. "John and Amelia. Of all the . . ."

Roused by their approach, Hannah grabbed her clothing and fled behind the nearest cloth divider. Though she couldn't see Daniel, she heard him fumbling, no doubt to do the same.

"Locks," he complained. "When we build our house,

we'll have a bedroom with five locks. Hannah, I want to talk about this later.''

Within a few scant moments the door hinges squealed and Amelia's voice piped like a bird's. "Papa! I got sick, right inside the church too. Is Bess here, or is Hannah? We saw the sleigh outside."

"Hannah's here. She's—she's resting. You know she hasn't been well, so she had to take a little nap after she drove here.''

Hannah smiled at his excuse as she slid into her dress. She gave her hair a practiced twist, but it stubbornly refused to reform in a chignon.

"I want to see her!" Amelia whined.

Ten locks, Hannah decided. They'd need ten locks on their bedroom door. She wanted to see Amelia too, but not just then.

She decided to give up on repinning her hair. Instead, she hastily finger-combed her hair and left it loose.

Perhaps this interruption was all for the best. She wasn't certain she could have lied to Daniel one more time. Glancing toward the bed, she decided to hide the letter now before she lost her chance. After withdrawing it from her skirt's pocket, she slid it inside the bottom of the pillowcase she'd embroidered herself.

Hannah prayed Daniel wouldn't find it until she'd left Marinette. And then she hoped he'd visit Bess before running off half-cocked to do something they would both regret. For all their sakes, she couldn't allow Daniel to avenge her. That task should rightly fall to her alone.

CHAPTER
TWENTY-EIGHT

He had to marry Hannah, and he had to do it soon, Daniel decided. After yesterday, he couldn't bear to be without her. A memory of their bodies, moving, flooded him with fresh desire.

Guilt darkened the image as he remembered afterward, the sadness in her eyes. Did she still think of Malcolm, despite the way that she'd responded? Would she heal in time of all the scars he'd left on her?

Surely, with his patience, with his gentleness, he could make her well. He promised himself again he would keep her safe forever, safe with him.

Sitting at his bed's edge, he sighed tiredly and rubbed the leg he'd bruised falling on the ice. Thank God Amelia had finally fallen asleep. After dinner last night, her stomach started hurting again, and he'd spent most of the night escorting her back and forth to the outhouse. He'd finally grabbed a few hours of shut-eye leaning up against her bed, but he was due at least a few more sprawled out on his own. As far as he could see, the only positive was that his fatherly duties had kept him too busy to think of other things.

Like Hannah, lying beneath him, accepting him into her. He ached with want just remembering her sweet cry, the feel of her quick breaths against his flesh.

Surely, she'd see reason now and set a wedding date.

Daniel sighed and lay back on his pillow. Beneath his head he heard a crinkling sound. Curious, he lifted the pillow and watched an envelope slide out of the case.

Dear God, it was a letter. She'd come to end it after all. Why, then, why had she allowed him to—hell, there was no sense in imagining what the letter said. He might as well open the damned thing and read it.

Daniel's hand trembled as it reached toward the lamp to turn up the narrow flame. That task completed, he opened the envelope carefully, as if his huge fingers might jar the letters from the page.

He opened it, read quickly, and then shook his head in disbelief. She would leave him with just a letter, and then slink off to Pennsylvania? This made no sense at all. What "family business" could possibly entice her to return? From what he understood, Hannah's family had disowned her. Why, then, why would she have done this thing?

I don't want to settle for whatever crumbs he left me of my life. She'd said that right after she'd picked up the chess piece and made some statement about attacking. That day she'd sounded so resolute, so sure of what she was about. Though she'd never again made such remarks, Daniel hadn't been able to forget them. Those words and her determination had convinced him that Malcolm Shelton hadn't broken her at all.

Now those same words, coupled with this letter, convinced him Hannah's message was a lie. She wasn't going back to Pennsylvania to attend to some family matter. Her purpose was far darker. She meant to destroy Malcolm, to kill him so he'd never threaten her again.

   Again and again he reread the single page, as if trying
to absorb the meaning from the slant of her neat script
and the expensive fiber of the Brannon stationery. He
tried, without success, to convince himself he was wrong,
that Hannah would not do this thing.

   She would though. He knew it in his heart. And if she
succeeded, the gentle woman he had come to love would
be utterly destroyed.

   He thought about the young man he had been,
marching off to join a faraway war, his notions of loyalty
and honor filling him like the first puffs of spring warmth
filled white sails. He remembered killing, in all innocence,
killing for his cause, until that last time. Until that bloodied
bayonet.

   Had it destroyed *him*? Afterward, he'd turned to the
surgical corps and helped to save instead of slaughter. At
the war's end he'd returned home, married, and fathered
a daughter. The healing touch he honed amid the piles
of ruined limbs had helped him build a future tending
horses and cattle on the farm. None of those things had
destroyed him, he admitted, but they had forever altered
him.

   He thought of Hannah with his daughter. God, how
Mary would have loved the woman; how grateful she would
be to know how Hannah treasured Amelia. He thought of
Hannah's strength, her kindness, the passion of her kisses,
and more than ever, he wanted to protect the woman that
she was. Though he knew Malcolm had driven her to a
place beyond innocence, committing murder would drive
her, instead, beyond redemption. If her attempt succeeded, she would be jailed or even hung. If it failed and
Malcolm caught her, he would surely finish what he had
so nearly accomplished outside Marinette.

   At the thought of Malcolm, hatred pumped through
Daniel's body thick as blood. He longed to kill the murderer himself with his bare hands. He remembered the

smeared puddle of Gen Tanner's blood on the church floor, the bruises and the bite marks all over Hannah, Amelia's incoherent terror after the shooting and abduction. His fists clenched in rage as he thought of the smug alibi sent by Shelton's sheriff friend.

He realized how much he'd wanted Malcolm to return here, to try for Hannah once again. His daydreams had been filled for weeks with visions of revenge.

Then he remembered Hannah's insistence that he not interfere. He had a daughter to think of, she insisted. Didn't she understand that in all the ways that mattered, she now had a daughter too? Couldn't she see how much Amelia needed her, how much *he* needed her?

Perhaps not. Hannah had been thrown away by a husband, the remnants of her family, even the community in which she'd lived. All for the crime of being barren. Maybe it would take years of loving for her to believe that she had value, that she was far more than some dried-up brood cow.

Damn her for a fool! How could she discard what they had on the chance of getting even? The notion sounded wrong, too unlike Hannah. Even when she'd pulled off the hoax with splattered blood, she'd acted more out of a need for security than vengeance. Then maybe that was it. Maybe she found the idea of looking over her shoulder the rest of her life so repulsive, she'd do anything to avoid it.

I won't be pitiful, she'd told him. Pride too. It was all mixed up with fear and pride.

John would have a Bible verse on that one, he imagined, but he didn't want to hear it just then. As the first rays of dawn paled the cabin's window, all he wanted was a quick word with his brother before he went to stop Hannah from leaving.

He could only pray he'd be in time.

* * *

Bess should have been surprised to see John on a Monday. Under normal circumstances he would have waited until the weekend to return. But nothing had been normal since that morning. She'd seen Hannah off at the train station first thing, the way they'd planned. Within the hour Daniel showed up at her door, demanding to see Hannah. He'd barely listened to her explanation, but stormed away amid a cloud of frustrated oaths.

Now John had arrived, and it was barely past the noon hour. Bess's stomach tightened as her mother announced him. Mrs. Brannon took Amelia to the library to read the child a story so Bess and John could talk in Father's study.

"Do you have any idea what you helped set in motion?" John demanded.

Bess bristled at his tone. "Hannah is a grown woman. She had good reasons for wanting to keep Daniel here while she went to Pennsylvania."

"Malcolm tried to kill her, and you sent her right back to him. Don't you realize she's the only witness who can tie him to Gen Tanner's murder?"

"Calm down. Hannah's not going anywhere near Shelton Creek. She promised. I tried to explain to Daniel, she's inherited her aunt's estate. She wants to get it settled so she can help finance the horse farm here. This has nothing to do with her former husband."

"Use your head, Bess. This story of hers—does it make sense? She's going back to kill him, or maybe this whole inheritance story is something *he* concocted to lure her to the area. How can you be so naive?"

"Don't you dare speak to me as if I'm stupid. Hannah wouldn't lie to me. And she's certain Malcolm's put this past him by now. Why shouldn't he? He got away with murder."

"He hunted her down once and waited months to take

her. Does he sound like a man who puts things past him? Besides, if Sheriff Skinner thought she was safe, why would he post a man here to watch over her?"

"Post a man? What are you talking about?" Bess's heart fluttered in her chest.

"Sheriff Skinner sends his deputies to keep an eye on her. Didn't your father tell you?"

Tears blurred Bess's vision. "No. You men never tell us anything, and then you think we're being silly when we don't understand. Hannah's right. You *do* treat us as if we're feebleminded."

"There's nothing feeble about either of your minds. You're just more emotional, that's all, and more prone to get in trouble."

Bess ground her teeth in frustration. "I'm beginning to think I don't know you at all. If you had confided in me before this happened, I never would have helped her."

"If you had asked me about this scheme the two of you cooked up, she'd still be safe right here. Daniel's going after her, of course. I only hope he reaches her in time."

"I am not apologizing, John. I did what I thought was right with the information I'd been given. Hannah will be fine. She has to be. Maybe both you and Daniel should trust in her more. And in me as well!" she added. Despite her angry words, she'd never been so frightened. Could Hannah have gone to kill the man who'd raped her? It seemed impossible, but so did much about the woman. Even more alarming was the idea that Malcolm might have lured Hannah to a place where he could silence her.

"If anything happens to either of them—"

"Stop!" Bess crossed her arms and took one step forward. "I've listened to your insults long enough. I will *not* be threatened too. How can I contemplate marriage to a man who thinks I'm some sort of hysterical ninny? More prone to trouble, my aunt Nora! I think you should leave before either of us says something unforgivable."

"Too late for that," John snapped. He turned on his heel toward the doorway.

Another thought occurred to her, and she forced herself to take a deep, slow breath. "If you can refrain from insulting me again, there's something else I think you should know."

John turned toward her and glowered. "What else?"

"She said she'd need protection for the journey, in case of rough men at the stations." Bess hesitated, trying to glean a clue of Hannah's motive from the memory of their conversation. She recalled no hint of either fear or lust for vengeance. Frowning, the girl stared at the carpet's ornate border and continued. "She talked me into buying her a little two-shot derringer. When Hannah left here, she was armed."

John slammed the door on his way out.

Skinner felt his mouth pucker in irritation. "You're sure she left Marinette?"

"*Sacre bleu!*" swore Lemaster. "You don't think I can tell when a woman boards a train? I learned she had a ticket for Chicago, but beyond that, who knows where she'll go?"

"Damn." Was Hannah running, or was she going after Malcolm Shelton? Skinner poured Lemaster coffee, then himself. He considered wiring the law in Shelton Creek, then remembered what Daniel Aldman had told him about Handley. Any message he sent would go straight to Malcolm Shelton. Then if Hannah showed up, she would have no chance at all.

"What you gonna do?" His deputy curved both hands around the coffee mug to warm them.

"Nothing," Skinner answered. "Except let Aldman know everything we do. We don't have funds or cause to chase her. She hasn't done anything illegal—yet."

* * *

By the time Daniel packed a bag, made arrangements for Amelia, and returned to Marinette, he'd already lost much of the day. He muttered curses when he learned the train schedules would delay him in Green Bay until morning. Blast Hannah for her deceit! When he caught hold of her, he'd tell her exactly how he felt about her foolhardy intrigues. She belonged with him, where he could keep her safe forever.

A nightmare vision disrupted his fuming. Hannah's pale hand jutting just above the icy water. Hannah, when he'd pulled her from it, blue-lipped and battered nearly beyond recognition. Raped and bleeding and so desperately ashamed. Dear God, how could he live through it again?

Shaken by fear for her, he sat alone aboard the crowded Green Bay line. His expression must have persuaded his fellow passengers to give him a wide berth. Just as well, he decided. Just then, even the bare minimum of civility was far beyond him. Until he held Hannah in his arms, nothing would be right.

It was too late to be visiting. Too late to pound on that enormous door. But John did it nonetheless. He'd left Amelia with his uncle, and afterward he'd ridden until the skies grew black and a waxing silver moon rose.

He shivered against the chill of the spring night. The smells of moist earth and young grasses reminded him he should be on the farm, preparing to sow seed. But he couldn't go back yet, not until he spoke to Bess. Once again he hammered on that great emblazoned door.

Daisy opened it a crack and peered out. The black woman's eyelids were puffed with sleep, and her gray robe hung askew. Recognizing him, she jerked awake.

He wondered if she was remembering the day that he

arrived, shot through the arm. The day that he and Daniel brought Hannah back.

"Mr. Aldman? What are you doing here?" Despite her questions, the tall young woman ushered him into the parlor and lit a lamp.

"I need to talk to Bess now."

"You sure she wants to see you? She's been crying up there all afternoon." Daisy nodded toward the staircase. Then her eyes narrowed in consideration. "Besides, it's late. The missus would flay you with that sharp tongue if she knew you was here now."

"I'm going to talk to Bess. Either you can get her, or I'm going to her room."

Daisy rolled her eyes. "Lord, they'd keep me up all night, then, with all sorts of goings-on. I'll see if Miss Bess will come down now. But don't you upset that girl, or I'll wake Mrs. Brannon in a hurry."

John nodded miserably and took a seat, then waited. From Mr. Brannon's study he heard the ticking of a clock, the clock that had once marked the long seconds before the older man gave his blessing to John's request to marry Bess. Might that same clock tick out the last seconds of their love tonight?

The minutes ticked by slowly. John wondered if he should come back in the morning. Then, at last, he heard Bess's footsteps on the stairs. He stood, awaiting her.

Bess must have been in bed, for her gold tresses streamed wildly against a pale blue dressing gown. Her eyes, too, were swollen, but John suspected it was from tears instead of sleep.

Bess stood in the parlor's doorway, frowning. "Did you come back to tell me how stupid I was? I doubt your words could hurt more than the ones I've used to blame myself. You don't need to tell me anymore."

Her voice hitched, then broke into bitter tears.

John crossed the floor in an instant and encircled her

within his arms. "I'm sorry. I'm afraid for Hannah and my brother, and earlier I spoke without thinking. I know you love them too. Hannah is your best friend. You would never do anything to hurt her, to hurt either of them."

"If something—if something happens, I'll never forgive myself," Bess said.

" 'Your sins are forgiven you for His name's sake,' " John quoted. "God knows, we all do things we regret. I have, and one of them was hurting you. I need you. I love you, Bess."

She leaned into his embrace.

John stroked her fine hair with his fingers. "Losing Hannah would be hard enough, for both of us. I don't think I could bear to lose you too."

"I love you so much. I was so afraid that it was over." Bess arched her neck and met his kiss with a passion that surprised him.

Out of the corner of his eye John saw Daisy's dark face in the doorway. She smiled and nodded. Then he heard her soft footsteps receding toward her own room as she made a gift of privacy.

John and Bess soon put it to good use.

Before she reached Chicago, Hannah turned the ruby of her engagement ring downward, toward her palm. When she switched trains, she carefully but discreetly displayed the plain gold band to any eyes that roved in her direction. A woman traveling alone, she had fielded far too many inquiries on her way to Peshtigo. This time the ring and her absorption in a borrowed copy of *Little Women* kept her conversations to a minimum.

Throughout the journey, only one lout pestered her, and that occurred not far west of Pittsburgh. Exhausted by rushed meals, bad food, and little rest, Hannah resorted to feigned tears inside her handkerchief, and the opening of what promised to be a long, dull tale of her dying mother. The greasy clod excused himself without further ado. It seemed he sought only a woman's laughter, not her tears.

The train disgorged only herself and two gray-haired gentlemen at the small stop of Hampton Falls. Cold drizzle chilled her as she hurried into the cramped station office. Behind a desk, a balding man with a fringe of sandy hair shuffled papers and glared in her direction. A map of fine wrinkles underscored his look of irritation. Hannah glanced behind herself, certain her appearance couldn't be the cause of such hostility.

Neither of the other passengers had followed.

"I'm Miss Shelton. I was to be met, but the train's running a bit late."

"Nothing new in that," he muttered. He took a moment to check the time on an expensive-looking pocket watch. Then he sighed, as if in regret, and pushed aside the sheaf of papers. "You don't remember me, I take it."

She looked more closely. Deep-set hazel eyes sparked a memory. "Roger? Roger Lee?" The years had been hard on her cousin. Though only a half dozen years her elder, Roger looked nearly old enough to be her father.

But at least his identity solved one mystery. The frown, indeed, was meant for her.

He nodded, his scowl untouched by her recognition. "Hannah Lee Shelton, I never believed you'd have the gall to show your face in Sells County again."

"Mr. Bloom asked me to come." She glanced out the window and watched a porter move her bags to the shelter of the station's eaves.

"Mr. Bloom." His voice curdled the two words with contempt.

Hannah now recalled Roger as a child, often petulant and whining, always worried someone else might get more than he did. No wonder he had wrinkled prematurely.

"He wouldn't accept your death without a thorough search," Roger complained.

"How glad the family must have been to learn I was alive." Hannah tried to resist the smile tugging at the corners of her mouth. Poor Roger. For once, perhaps the only time in all his life, he *had* been unjustly slighted. Dour and unlovable though he appeared, Roger had never done a single thing she'd heard of to humiliate the family, or even raise an eyebrow.

"Aunt Hilda's will—perplexed us," he explained.

"It surprised me too. I still have no idea why she left things as she did."

"Some silly spat with Father, we imagine."

The unnamed "we" must include her other cousins and their respective spouses. Lord, how they must hate her. Hannah swallowed past the lump that hurt made in her throat. Roger and his siblings were right to resent the terms of their aunt's will. But they had been so wrong before, so eager to condemn her. Not even Nettie, dear, sweet Nettie, took her side when Malcolm blasted her with his unfounded accusations. None of them would even listen. Could she buy amends by offering to split this inheritance with her uncle's children? Should she? Apparently, Hilda Blackard felt different, for whatever reasons she might have had. Perhaps, if she could learn what they had been, she could make a fair decision.

"I need to speak with Mr. Bloom. Is he still in the same office?" Hannah asked. Outside, the chill rain hissed harder against the walls and windows.

A muscle twitched in Roger's jaw, and he again began riffling through his stack of schedules.

She laid a hand across his precious papers. "If you, Alice, and Nettie want to talk, I'll be in town for a short while. I understand that before you didn't wish to listen, but maybe now—"

Roger stood. A small man, he had to draw himself up

ramrod straight to glower down at her. "The very suggestion that you breathe the same air as my two sisters deeply offends me. You are a convicted adulteress, I remind you, and I cannot imagine how you bewitched Aunt Hilda into rewarding whoredom. As far as the family and I are concerned, the bloody death you so obviously staged was the one you deserved. May the devil take you, Hannah. Find someone else to ask directions. I'm too busy for the likes of you."

She felt so stupid standing there, her eyes welling with tears. Stupid she could still be hurt this way. But still, she couldn't change her feelings, the bitter shame that bubbled up inside her, heedless of the fact she hadn't wrought this awful mess.

"May God forgive you, Roger." Her voice trembled like the crowns of the nearby pine trees in the rain. "You can't know how wrong you are."

She spun on her heel and strode out into the storm, too miserable to even wonder why it mattered that she hide her tears.

Adam Bloom was used to being hated, but he didn't like it any better than most people. Maybe lawyers in the big cities made enough money to soften the blow, but he was just a small-town attorney, a man who knew every family in Hampton Falls and a good many from the surrounding area as well. Most folks he considered friends, and he'd helped more than a few through hard times. Still, in his line of work, a man made enemies.

The Lee family's scorn particularly stung. Alice Lee Hall's children went to school with his boys, and Nettie and her husband lived just down the road. He and Roger had been playmates years ago, although Roger's bellyaching had been grating even then.

It would have been a natural thing to give up on finding

Hannah and dole out the money to Mrs. Blackard's brother and surviving nieces and nephew. It would have been so easy. But it wouldn't have been right. Adam went all the way to Philadelphia as a young man to study the law because he believed in fairness. He still did, though both education and experience informed him fairness didn't always have too much to do with law. Sometimes, though, the two dovetailed, and he felt his job was to see it happened more often than not.

The fair thing to do was let cantankerous old Hilda have her say. She'd done it in his office with her will, and she'd paid his fee without complaining. The old woman had been adamant that Hannah Shelton inherit her estate. Her reasons, she claimed, were personal, but she didn't want her brother, Edwin, or any of his ilk, as she called Roger, Alice, and Nettie, to have a cent of it.

The money had been Mrs. Blackard's, so the fair thing was to carry out her will. Even though it cost him his lease. Bloom crumpled up the eviction notice and tossed it in an uncharacteristic gesture of frustration. Alice's husband, his landlord, had signed it.

Adam resumed packing one last box he'd brought for moving files to his house. He wouldn't do as much business there with his family bustling about him, but perhaps, when this blew over, he would rent another office.

When he heard the door creak open, he hoped a customer would interrupt his packing. Heaven only knew, he could use the business now. Instead, when he looked up, a bedraggled woman stepped inside, dripping with rain and hauling two damp bags.

"Oh, dear. You're Mrs. Shelton." In answer to her nod, he apologized. "I'm so sorry. I completely lost track of the time."

She lifted a shoulder. "The train was late, and waiting there with Roger was too awkward. I thought I remembered your location."

For the moment, thought Adam unhappily. But he remembered his manners and ushered her closer to the stove. "You need to warm up. We'll have to get you out of those wet clothes."

She raised an eyebrow, and he blushed deeply. "I mean only—you're soaked through. I've spent too long finding you to have you catch your death. I was just leaving for home. Why don't you join me, and Mrs. Bloom will help you get more comfortable before we talk."

At the mention of his wife, she nodded. Adam ran out to the livery to have his rig made ready. Glad he'd indulged in a covered runabout, the attorney drove it the short distance to his office, then helped Hannah move her bags into the boot and climb inside.

"Am I doing the right thing to come here?" she asked as he drove.

He glanced at her, noticing the barest smudge of bruising near one of her blue eyes. Despite everything he'd heard about the divorcée, he found her disarmingly pretty, not seductive. The woman didn't strike him as some sort of harlot.

"You're doing what your aunt wanted. What could be more right than that?"

"My cousins are so angry. They don't think I deserve—"

"This doesn't concern who's most deserving. It concerns Mrs. Blackard's wishes. She trusted us to respect them. This is about trust."

"You're right. She trusted us to carry out her wishes, not to wonder whether they were right."

For several minutes the only sound was the rising hiss of rain against the buggy top. The noise swelled until conversation became impossible. Gradually, the onslaught diminished to the slow tapping of isolated drops.

Hannah spoke once more. "We spoke of final wishes,

and that reminded me. I needed to ask you about a different type of situation."

"Please do," Bloom invited.

"When we get to your house, can you tell me everything you know about an irrevocable trust?"

Margaret Bloom proved as kind and charming as her husband. The plump woman adjusted a curling upsweep threaded with a few thin strands of silver and ushered Hannah into a room to change into warm clothes. She refused to let Adam and her new guest talk a word of business until she'd plied them both with hot soup and fragrant tea.

"Miserable cold rain," she declared. "I'd almost rather take the snow."

With her stomach full and her body warm, Hannah tried to stifle several yawns. Mrs. Bloom was quick to notice.

"Adam, let the poor thing rest before your lawyer talk knocks her unconscious."

"Oh, no, please," said Hannah. "There's so much I need to know. I'd sleep much better if we could have our talk."

Mr. Bloom shooed three of his young sons out of his study and promised Margaret he'd stop speaking the moment Mrs. Shelton began to doze. He closed the door behind them and gestured toward a comfortable tan sofa.

Hannah settled into it as the attorney took a chair. "Please call me *Miss* Shelton. I know it's not quite proper, but I'm not married anymore, and the Mrs. just reminds me of his lies."

"Everyone suspected you'd been murdered," Adam told her. He sounded no less curious than the next man. Hannah imagined there'd been unending speculation after her disappearance.

She frowned, uncertain of what she might tell him. "I don't want to get in trouble, Mr. Bloom."

He waved a hand dismissively. "Let's just say I represent you now. Attorney-client privilege. I can't gossip about anything you say, but I can help you forestall any problems that might come of what happened."

She looked down. "I left. And I didn't want anyone to ruin things for my new life. After Malcolm took my farm, I couldn't earn a living in Shelton Creek or anywhere around here."

Adam pulled a file from the box he'd brought home from the office. One of the papers tucked inside detailed the remains of the Blackard estate. "You won't have to worry about that anymore. As you can see, your aunt's money relieves you of that burden."

Hannah felt warmth flush her face. Aunt Hilda hadn't left her wealthy, but "comfortable" might be a fair assessment. She thought of the new start it could buy the Aldmans for their business.

Should she take it, then return to Peshtigo to try to salvage her relationship with Daniel? The thought had its appeal, if she hadn't already gone beyond forgiveness with her breach of trust. She thought of all she'd risked when she had left him. Tears welled in Hannah's eyes at the thought of how she must have wounded him. She imagined rushing back, begging his forgiveness.

But Aunt Hilda's money wasn't why she'd come here. She had taken this chance to recover from what had been done to her and from what she'd done as well. Only one inheritance mattered to her now. Her father's farm, his business, the house that had been meant for her. She swore again that she was going to take them back from Malcolm, even if it killed them both.

*   *   *

"Stay put," Jacob Handley ordered Malcolm. "You heard what your lawyer said. Listen for once in your life, and stay the hell away from her."

Although the whiskey and the house were Shelton's, Jacob poured them both another drink. "They might have their suspicions, but as long as you keep your distance from anything to do with Hannah, you'll never see the inside of a courtroom."

Malcolm nodded and gulped the whiskey quick as water. Talking about his former wife appeared to give him quite a thirst. "But the letter from that lawman in Marinette said there was another witness who identified my likeness. Between that and Hannah's testimony, a judge might choose to indict. This isn't Judge Clarke we're talking about either. It's some Wisconsin court."

"They'd have to extradite you, though, to get you out of Pennsylvania. You really think that's going to happen to you here?"

"It doesn't matter. By that time the legal bills and gossip will ruin me for good. Melissa's father won't bail me out again. As I see it, Hannah's left me no choice now." Malcolm glared into his empty tumbler.

Jacob stood. He'd heard enough of this. "You've had choices all along. You just made some wrong ones. Quit blaming her and live with what you still have left."

Malcolm looked up sharply. "What's that? Poverty, disgrace? The loss of yet another wife?"

"Your life and your freedom. Take them or leave them. You've got to understand. There's only so much I can do and keep my job. If you get caught going after her, you'll swing."

"Then I'd better not get caught."

Drooping with exhaustion, Hannah soon took to the Blooms' hastily arranged guest room. With six growing sons, their house lacked the luxury of space. Two of the boys, however, volunteered to give up their room to "camp out" in the dining room. The gangly youngsters thanked Hannah profusely, assuring her they considered the sleeping shake-up an adventure.

Hannah lay down on the crisp sheets Mrs. Bloom had put on the bed for her. The fuzzy wool blanket tickled just beneath her chin, but it felt so warm and comforting, she didn't rearrange it. She expected to drop into sleep immediately, but instead, she felt eager for the new day to begin.

She was far too close to Shelton Creek, and too close to her farm. More than anything, she longed to gaze over its gentle slopes, to greet the familiar brood mares that now fattened in the winter pastures. Soon they would drop foals, just as the grass grew a tender shade of green and pale tree buds began to swell. When she closed her eyes, she could see the stables and the carriage house and the huge yellow and white two-story where she'd been born. Who knew? Maybe Queen would be there still, waiting patiently to rub against her hand with warm, inviting purrs.

Adam Bloom's words had reassured her. An irrevocable trust, such as her father had used to bequeath her the farm, could never be undone. All she needed was a signed and witnessed copy of the will and an honest court to back her.

An honest court, she thought miserably. When Malcolm, in front of Judge Clarke and his unscrupulous attorney, had torn up the original will, all three men had laughed, as if the idea of Hannah taking possession of the farm had been too ludicrous for serious consideration.

Hannah rolled onto her side, her knees drawn nearly to her chest. Tears squeezed through eyelids locked against the awful vision. That day, the day of her divorce, she'd believed that she would die. Though she knew there was a copy of her father's will, she'd been too demoralized to try to find it at the time. Malcolm's lies had ruined her, and his lies would keep her from the farm, she thought. Even if she managed to retrieve the copy, she could think of nothing to prevent him from shredding that document too.

Humiliated and defeated, she'd slunk quietly away like the wounded animal she'd been.

No more of that, she swore. This time she had her own attorney, a man who wouldn't be cowed or bought by Malcolm's money. Bloom's confession regarding the cause of his eviction convinced her he would help her find a conscientious judge.

All that remained was for her to retrieve the copy. If Malcolm hadn't found it and destroyed it already. And if he didn't catch her in the act of taking it. In either one of those events, all she could do was pray. Pray that two bullets from a derringer would be enough to stop a beast.

Later that night she dreamed of Daniel, tasting, touching, having her in all the ways she wanted. Hannah awakened damp with lust and nearly sick with longing. She'd never known desire could afflict a woman so. It felt like fever sometimes, the chills along her neck, the heat inside her building toward explosion. It felt like that tonight.

During daylight hours she shunted him away, the memory of his face, his voice, his body. But in the darkness, all alone, she knew she'd been imprinted by him somehow, set forever with his stamp.

She didn't even know if he would have her back. She wondered again if this lie might have proved one too many for even Daniel's patience. He'd never understood how desperately she needed to reclaim the lost part of her soul. So she could be healed for him, healed and whole and unafraid.

Daniel deserved more than a hollow husk, the shell she had become. And she would get it for him, for him and herself.

When Daniel Aldman's train pulled into Hampton Falls, afternoon sunlight warmed the air. Daniel slipped off his jacket, collected his lone bag, and headed for the station-master's office. From what he'd seen coming in, the town wasn't much more than a village. The arrival of a woman like his Hannah would be bound to catch somebody's eye.

He started with the bald man in the office shuffling papers. The man's expression made him look like he sucked lemons for sport. He'd hate to gamble with the fellow, for he doubted that wrinkled face twitched twice a year.

"I'm looking for a woman who might have come through here yesterday," Daniel began without preamble. "I'd be obliged if you could help. She's a little thing, like you, and real pretty, about twenty-eight or so. You see her?"

He'd been wrong. The man's expression did change. The scowl deepened his fine furrows. "You the law?" he asked. "Out to bring some trouble?"

Daniel grinned. "Me? Not unless she considers marrying a problem. The lady's my betrothed."

"I didn't see any ladies yesterday. Would you need to buy a ticket somewhere else?"

Daniel stepped closer to the counter. "Who else worked here yesterday? Maybe I could ask them."

"I make it a point to watch all the passengers debark. I told you, I didn't see a lady."

"Her name's Hannah, Hannah Shelton. She came about her aunt." Poker face or not, Daniel would have sworn the man was lying. Something about the tightening of his voice.

To his surprise, the stationmaster laughed. It was an unpleasant sound, like a tubercular cough. "Hannah Shelton? The adulteress? I heard she was dead."

Why would this man hate her? Daniel wondered. He stifled the temptation to knock the fellow through a wall and turned back toward the doorway. "Then you won't mind," he tossed back, "if I poke around a little while for her ghost."

No one had seen Hannah. Though Daniel questioned people at the station, nearby businesses, even the local general store, he could find no one who recalled her. The one lawyer's office he found bore a sign reading CLOSED FOR BUSINESS. He began to fear she'd lied about her destination.

That meant she must have stopped at Shelton Creek. The idea chilled him despite the unseasonably mild weather. If she'd done that, she might have already killed Malcolm. He might find her locked in jail, or, even worse, she could be dead.

No, not that. He refused to think it. His Hannah was alive, and he would find her. He'd go as quickly as he could. A visit to the local livery stable yielded him the rental of an enormous bay gelding with black stockings that rose halfway up his walnut-colored legs. The liveryman promised speed and strength, and though Daniel had never been hard on his mounts, he planned to make use of both qualities that afternoon.

Adam Bloom didn't like the idea of lending her a horse.

"I'll pay you a fair price for her use," Hannah promised. She stroked the mare's gold neck and swept the long, black forelock from her eye. The horse nudged her, demanding another pat.

"That's not the point. Women can't just go cavorting around the countryside. Tell me where you need to go, and I'll drive you there."

"You don't have time to escort me all over Sells County, tracking down my uncle and my cousins. I heard you telling

Mrs. Bloom at breakfast how it would take you half the day to set up your office things, and my business already took your morning and past lunch. Besides, I don't need your buggy for this trip. I ride as well as any man, and I don't want to fool with wheels stuck in the mud. Just let me use the mare—what did you call her?''

"Tillie. She's a favorite with the boys, as gentle as a lamb.''

"We'll get along just fine. I'll take good care of her.''

Bloom sighed and nodded. Women were his weakness. Margaret had him wrapped around her little finger, and he thanked God he didn't have to deal with females in court.

He thought of one last argument that might dissuade her. "Mrs. Bloom doesn't ride, so there's no sidesaddle on the place.''

"Good,'' Hannah answered. "I can't abide the things. This skirt of mine's wide enough.''

"But the ladies will—''

"Gossip? Let them. It's about time I gave them something new to talk about.''

Malcolm was exercising his favorite stallion. Normally, the chore would be left to Joseph Went, his manager, or a favored stable boy, but his best boy had slipped and broken an arm on February's glassy ice. Besides, Malcolm enjoyed Honor, his old scapegoat. He considered the Arabian his first partner in crime.

When he glanced up, he noticed a strange boy loitering not far from the gate. The young fellow's eyes lingered on the muscular black horse Shelton was straining to control. On a fine day after a long winter, Honor felt like lightning under saddle. He should have opted for a lunge line instead of riding.

The stallion bucked as he dismounted. Despite landing

on his bad leg, Malcolm retained his footing without a stumble. He turned Honor loose and laughed as the horse bucked and plunged about the paddock wildly.

"He's a beauty, mister," the boy remarked. He was so taken with the horse, he hadn't even glanced at Malcolm's face.

Shelton smiled in recognition of the quick gleam in the lad's brown eye. The dark hair reminded him of himself at that age. What would it be? Maybe twelve. If only Hannah had given him a son like this, how different both their lives would be. He tried to imagine it, the two of them together with a boy who looked like him. Hannah gentle as she'd been when they had married. And his fantasies would never have turned dark. Bringing pain would not be his only avenue to pleasure.

God, he hated her for all the joys she'd stolen. Yet somehow, the presence of this child eased the ache a bit.

"I'm getting too old to fool with Honor's spring shenanigans. Would you like to have a go?"

Malcolm watched a grin spread across the lightly freckled face. It faltered for a moment when the boy saw the burn scars, but enthusiasm triumphed.

"Would I ever!" he all but shouted back. He hopped onto the gate and shimmied over. "Oh, almost forgot. I'm Jack Lee, and I've got a message for you from my pa."

Dutifully, he handed a crumpled note to Malcolm. Jack Lee? He'd be Roger's son, and that was Hannah's cousin. Malcolm's heart thumped faster. What would Roger want from him? The Lees had steadfastly ignored him after the divorce.

"Should I go catch the horse, sir?" Jack's voice rose hopefully.

Malcolm ignored him in favor of the paper in his hands. A slow smile spread across the unscarred portion of his face. Hannah had at last arrived, and that fool Bloom had her staying in his home. Roger thought he might want to know.

Malcolm nearly laughed aloud. Roger, selfish Roger, hadn't wanted Hannah to return. Shelton had heard about the Lees' odd problems with their dead aunt's will.

Unfortunately, Adam Bloom wasn't the sort of lawyer who understood how easily, how profitably, old papers could be torn. Now Roger was hoping Malcolm might make his problem go away.

By the time he looked up, Honor was snorting into Jack's outstretched hand. The boy smiled at him almost shyly. "They say I've got a way with horses."

"Do you?" Malcolm asked him. He limped closer and took the stallion's reins. "Why don't you climb aboard and see?"

Hannah hadn't meant to visit any members of her family. Roger's denunciation had convinced her of their hatred, and Adam Bloom's explanation of her aunt's will convinced her that she owed him nothing. But Hannah hadn't counted on Nettie's shriek of recognition as she rode down Bloom's street, past a respectable buff-colored house with deep brown trim.

"Hannah! Hannah Lee! Oh, my goodness! It's enough to put me in a faint!" The petite woman bobbed her head as if looking for a place to swoon. If the years had been unkind to Roger, they'd left Nettie nearly untouched. She still moved like a sparrow, and she remained so thin, even a tight-laced corset might fall down to her knees.

Hannah lifted the mare's reins and turned Tillie toward the woman. Unsure of her reception, she said nothing.

Nettie put down a sack of flower bulbs and peeled off gardening gloves. "What's the matter? Don't you recognize me? I haven't changed *that* much."

Laughing, Hannah slid down from the horse and took

her reins. "You haven't changed at all. It's just that—I saw Roger."

Nettie made the same rude hiss she had when they were children. "Roger! Don't mind that cad. He's just mad about the money. He has an awful lot of debts. Couldn't be satisfied unless he and his wife had all the finest, but a stationmaster's salary won't cover the cost. So what do you suppose he did? Borrowed, borrowed, borrowed— nearly sold his soul for all those fancies. He talked Father into pestering Aunt Hilda, and worst of all, he tried some scheme to separate her from her savings. Made her so mad, she disinherited us all. As far as I'm concerned, Roger ought to be in jail."

Hannah impulsively stepped forward to hug her cousin. "Is that why Aunt Hilda did it? Oh, Nettie, I thought you'd hate me too."

"Hate you?" Nettie's voice shrilled in her ear as she squeezed back. "Of course not. I was sorry back when all that situation happened with your husband. It seemed to me no one listened to your side. It's like that for us women."

"It would have helped me if *you'd* listened. I always thought you were my friend."

Nettie pulled back and lowered her blue eyes. "I—I'm sorry if I hurt you. It's just that I had a reputation to maintain, and it happened during my confinement. I had twin girls, you know, Rose and Anabelle. They're inside now with Christopher's mother. She's come to live with us."

Hannah couldn't imagine where on that thin body Nettie could have carried twins. She tried to smile tolerantly at her cousin's excuses. There was no use arguing about slights from the past.

"Nettie, it isn't fair that Hilda punished you and Alice over Roger. Maybe I should—"

"Hush. I won't hear a word of it, though it's kind of

you to offer. I can't speak for my sister, but if that old crone wanted to disinherit me, I don't give a lump of coal. Christopher and I do fine."

This time Hannah's smile was genuine. Nettie hadn't changed a bit.

Her cousin's head bobbed upward, her eyes bright with enthusiasm. "I'll tell you what. I'll prove to you I'm not like those other women. I'll invite you in my home right now, in front of my mother-in-law and all the children. You come inside and have some tea with me. We'll talk. You can tell me anything you want. I won't care who finds out."

Perhaps it was because she had been too long without acceptance from any family members. Perhaps the thought of the risk she faced compelled her. Hannah chose to ignore Nettie's disloyalty and instead chance her acceptance.

"Before I go inside," Hannah said, "I want you to know something. Malcolm lied. He didn't want me, but he needed the farm. If you can't accept that, I'd better not stay."

Nettie stared at her a moment before her eyes widened. Their lower rims glistened with fresh moisture. Then she nodded so rapidly, her beaver tail chignon bobbed against her neck. "I do believe you, Hannah. Maybe I can help you too."

Daniel wasn't sure about his next step. If he asked around for Hannah in Shelton Creek, could he endanger her? He rode down the main street, lined with shops, a blacksmith, and two livery stables. He could tell right away he'd come to a town that considered itself civilized. He saw two schools, three churches, but no saloons or bawdy houses in evidence. He'd bet his bottom dollar they were here, tucked away somewhere along a back alley or a disreputable thoroughfare along the outskirts. Men's appetites didn't change that much from place to place.

Right then he would have liked a drink to clear his head. But, as before, thoughts of Hannah pushed back the temptation. How could he find out about her without stirring up more trouble? The more he concentrated on the problem, the better he liked the thought of a saloon. At least there he could hear the talk of local events and glean a little information without raising suspicion.

He dismounted near a general store with the neatest boardwalk he'd ever seen. The wood, free of scars from loggers' caulked heels, was also clean of tobacco. A well-polished spittoon stood self-righteously just outside the door. Hannah hailed from a pretty fancy place, he decided.

A man with slicked black hair and what Daniel thought of as a dandy's suit stepped outside the building. In his arms he carried a small box filled with bottles of varying sizes.

"Excuse me," Daniel said. "I was wondering if you knew a place a man could buy a drink."

The young gentleman shared an oily smile. "If you're in need of refreshment, let me offer you, instead, my tonic. I've been selling this for three years, and let me assure you, it's a fine cure for the temptations of drink and cheap company. At only two dollars a bottle, it's a bargain."

Daniel couldn't resist playing along with the fellow. He'd seen grown men get pie-eyed on remedies like this. He pulled out a bottle of the tonic and twisted off the lid. "So what's in this stuff?"

"The finest ingredients, secret extracts discovered in Siam. The recipe, I believe, was smuggled from the land of pyramids and elephants."

"That's an awful lot of far-off places," Daniel remarked. "How do I know this works on Americans?"

"Why, I give it to my own dear mother," the young man answered. "She says it's done wonders for her health."

Daniel sniffed. "Smells like alcohol to me. Seems like the saloon might be cheaper. How about those directions?"

"Are you insinuating my sainted mother is a drunkard?" The smaller man stiffened.

Daniel had to frown to keep from grinning. "Naw. She probably takes it from you just to be polite, and pours the stuff out the back window as soon as you go out. But some of those *other* folks that buy it, they just might be drunks."

The smaller man stormed off, and Daniel had to ask another fellow for directions to the drinking house.

"I might hire that boy, Jack Lee, to help exercise the horses," Malcolm told his wife as he changed his clothes. Usually, he didn't share the details of his business with Melissa, but he considered the boy such a find that he felt nearly exuberant. Besides, that evening, thanks to Roger's help, Malcolm planned to end his problems.

"Can we afford it?" Melissa asked timidly.

"What's the matter? Don't you believe I can provide?" He turned a hard gaze on her, and she shied from it. She'd been difficult when he insisted that she swear that he had been home when he wasn't. She was an honest woman, and he'd had to slap her hard to make her see the sense of his request.

He never used to lay a finger on his women, but after Hannah, he'd discovered the act had a kind of sickening appeal, like tearing off a scab or dispatching a diseased foal. He'd taken Melissa after he'd returned, and in its way he found that struggle far more satisfying than her usual limp submission.

Even the whispered threat of force now made her muscles stiffen and sudden tears spring to her eyes. She wouldn't tell, of course. What woman could complain of a husband using rape to take what, in all fairness, belonged to him already? She'd be laughed out of town despite her father's money. No, Melissa had been easily defeated. When the authorities asked for his whereabouts that evening, she would dutifully provide him with an alibi.

An alibi for murder.

CHAPTER
TWENTY-NINE

Hannah tied the mare in a thickly wooded copse nearly one half mile from the farm. She had grown up running through these tree-lined hills and pastures. She remembered every draw and outcrop, every creek that gurgled with the late winter's runoff. She hiked through shrubs and grasses whose moisture soaked the bottom of her dress, whose soil changed the deep green, trailing fabric to a muddy brown. More than once a thorny arm of bramble snagged a coat sleeve and tore the filthy skirt. No matter. If her gambit failed, even the attire of queens would never save her; if she instead succeeded, she could buy or sew another dress.

As she picked her way close to the house, she breathed a prayer that the copy of her father's will still lay hidden in the place where she had stored it. Her father had insisted that she have it and that she tuck it away, in case anything happened to his lawyer, Alan Ryan.

Something *had* happened to Mr. Ryan, all right, not long after her father's death. He had passed away after a brief illness and left his records to a successor, Borden. The unscrupulous little worm had easily joined Malcolm, Judge Clarke, and Jacob Handley and their unholy alliance. With his fall went her last chance, she'd thought.

"We'll slide this inside here." Her father lifted a false bottom out of a bottom drawer in her oak dresser. She'd never realized it was there before. "And you needn't mention it to anyone, not even Malcolm. Chances are you'll never need it anyway," he said.

She'd thought it was strange, the way he particularly mentioned Malcolm. Though he never said another word to confirm it, she had the oddest feeling he didn't trust her spouse. At the time, she'd shrugged away the intuition and forgot about the hidden copy. She had other things to think of soon enough.

Far grimmer things, like the horse's kick that took her father's life. Honor had been her father's joy, but the stud colt had been high strung from the start. After the accident Hannah, in her grief, wanted to destroy the horse, but Malcolm had persuaded her that her father would not have wished it. Malcolm, the very man who'd come across the gruesome scene.

She'd decided to keep Honor, knowing in that case Malcolm had been right. Any horseman knew the dangers: a snapped neck or a crushed pelvis, a hard kick or a crippling fall. All were risks assumed when dealing with animals that outweighed them five or more times over. Her father understood, and he never would have wanted his moment of uncharacteristic carelessness to cost a fine young animal his life.

Tonight she would reclaim Honor—and all the rest as well. Slipping among the trunks of a stand of pine trees, she caught her first glimpse of the house. The second-story balcony, the white scrollwork against yellow, brought tears to her eyes. *Home,* her heart cried. *Home!*

She settled back amid dry needles, determined to bide

her time in silence. She hoped, she prayed, that Malcolm and his new wife would go out. On this night every week, some of Shelton Creek's biggest hypocrites steadfastly attended a deacons' meeting, and their wives met too, to gossip over shortcomings, real or imagined, of the congregation's members. When Malcolm left with her replacement, Hannah planned to go inside and take the hidden will.

If he didn't leave, the task would be far riskier. She still intended to slip into the house. Within a month of Hannah's father's death, Malcolm had insisted he and Hannah move into the master bedroom. They'd used her parents' furnishings and left the dresser, with its precious hidden document, in one of the smaller bedrooms down the hall. She prayed it remained inside the bedroom with the second-story balcony, the one she'd so loved as a girl.

That upstairs door had never been kept locked. Once, before her Robert left for war, she'd climbed down from that balcony to meet him for a walk. She smiled at the memory of their stolen kiss, so many years ago. Afterward, she climbed the porch railing and onto the porch roof before hoisting herself back to the balcony and the safety of her bed.

She only hoped she might be so limber now.

Melissa was brushing her straight gold-streaked hair into an elegant upsweep. She'd put on one of her more attractive dresses, the tight-waisted burgundy affair that he'd once liked so much. Only twenty-five, she still had a girlish look about her he'd found so fetching. Now Malcolm felt only irritation as he watched her prepare to leave the house.

"We aren't going tonight," he said.

She turned toward him with a frown. "But you've dressed to go out."

"You're wrong." His voice took on the edge of command he'd used so effectively during the war. "I'm not feeling well. I'll be in bed this evening. You'll say you were right beside me, attending to my fever."

The stupid girl was shaking, actually quivering with fear. She opened those thin, passionless lips as if to protest, then dropped her gaze to her hem. After a slight hesitation she swallowed audibly, then found her voice. "All true. I—I'm not feeling well myself."

Feeling magnanimous, he kissed her on the cheek before he left.

As Hannah waited, she leaned against rough bark and thought of Nettie's offer to set the gossips straight. She'd done right, she decided, by begging her cousin to do no such thing. The women would believe exactly what they wished, and Nettie's reputation would only suffer if she tried to interfere. Instead, all Hannah asked was friendship. If she succeeded in displacing Malcolm, she would certainly need that.

The sun sank behind the hill just to the west, leaving her in quickly cooling shadow. She buttoned her coat against the growing chill. From within the house a lamp's light painted a long rectangle of warmth upon brown winter grass. She thought she saw a cat's shape humped along the sill. More than anything, that presence made Hannah long to stand up straight, brush off her skirts, and stride back to her house as she had done a thousand times before. As she would do again, God willing.

As if in answer to her prayer, she saw the side door swing open. Someone, she couldn't make out who, exited and disappeared in the direction of the carriage house. Some twenty minutes later, a closed rig clattered from the yard.

Two hundred yards west of Hannah Shelton, another watcher stood hidden by the woods. Though Daniel Aldman didn't know the area, he'd found what he needed to know by asking where he might purchase a sound mount. Malcolm Shelton might be a scarred-faced bastard, several men agreed, but he still owned some damned fine horses. They'd rambled on with a dozen tales about the famous Shelton clan, including the ones that concerned his missing former wife.

"He killed her, pure and simple," a farmer claimed.

A man who'd introduced himself as a harness maker gave his flabby jowls a shake. "I met her once myself. Pretty as a picture, but sharper than a Philadelphia lawyer. She got the best of him, I wager."

What seemed to be Sells County's favorite argument ensued. Daniel left before it came to blows. Maybe men weren't more civilized here after all, he thought. But at least he'd gotten good directions.

Now he watched the house, but he hadn't yet formed a plan to take him further. Apparently, Hannah hadn't shown herself around town, or he had a feeling every wag in the county would be trumpeting the news. Was she even here at all?

The dim lights of the first stars seemed to swirl inside his head. Had Hannah run somewhere else? Maybe all of this had been some clever fabrication. Certainly, she'd already proven adept at setting up deceptions. Could she have done it a second time in order to escape her past?

More important, could she have run from *him*?

A coach left the carriage house, driven by a span of chestnut horses. Daniel couldn't see the driver in the poor light, but he swore he could *feel* Malcolm Shelton's presence.

The same man who hurt Hannah. The same man who shot down an innocent widow woman not three paces from his six-year-old daughter.

If Hannah was in Sells County, had Malcolm already found her? Or could she be hiding somewhere, seeking to kill him?

Quickly, Daniel calculated the distance to his livery horse and started sprinting through the undergrowth. He'd have to hurry if he wanted their two paths to converge.

Hannah had nearly reached the door before she realized her mistake. The rectangle of light remained on the dried grass. Either someone was still at home, or the lamp had been left burning.

The latter seemed unlikely. She could easily recite Malcolm's legion flaws, but carelessness was not among them. Particularly not with oil lamps.

"Check the downstairs lamps." She still remembered his sharp elbow at her side when she'd nearly fallen asleep. Even if she assured him half a dozen times she'd checked already, Malcolm would insist until she walked down the steps and looked. Rarely could he be persuaded his own feet might serve the same purpose.

Hannah sucked in a raw breath, thinking of it. Though her childhood memories were all tied up inside this house, other recollections drifted through its rooms as well. Painful as her mother's sudden death, her father's. Painful as the day she'd been forced out of these walls.

Her pulse roared in her ears, reminding her of the roaring of the great wildfire. Fear threatened to consume her, a blaze fueled by her inertia.

Something slithered across her chest and landed with a tiny chink beside her foot. Squatting down, she retrieved

Faye Barlow's battered necklace. That old woman had
endured so much: a self-pitying husband, a fallen daughter,
poverty. Yet she had continued, working with the energy
of half a dozen women to survive.

Hannah's struggle was about survival too. She squeezed
the cross until its four points pressed pink marks into her
palm. Then she dropped it in a pocket, determined as
Faye Barlow to go on.

Walking stealthily along the lower floor, she peered
inside windows like a Peeping Tom. She saw nothing but
the cat, a sleekly silvered tabby who washed himself serenely
on a medallion-backed sofa in the parlor. Her mother
would have had a fit to see an animal ensconced on her
best piece of furniture.

Hannah decided she would climb the porch again, right
then, before she lost her nerve. Maybe Malcolm had grown
careless and left the kitchen peg lamp lit. People changed.
She'd watched him harden into cruelty and violence over
just a few short years.

Nervously, she fingered the outline of the gun inside
her pocket and whispered one last prayer. God help her
if anyone could see her, she thought as she pulled herself
onto the porch rail.

Her skirt snagged on the scrolled wood beneath the
porch roof. Perched upon the overhang, Hannah yanked
it hard, expecting cloth to tear. Instead the painted wooden
gingerbread snapped off and clattered to the porch below.
Hannah sat stock-still for several minutes, listening for
the sounds of her discovery—or perhaps the gunshot that
would end her life.

Thankfully, the evening remained quiet, the only noises
those of a light breeze troubling the pine tree crowns
across the road.

She crawled toward the balcony and grasped the railing
to pull herself aloft. The old wood shifted, and she reached
out for a sturdier handhold.

* * *

The road agent shot out of the brush on a big bay, grasping the far horse's bridle before Malcolm could react. After only a moment's hesitation, Shelton reached inside his coat for his revolver.

The robber had been swifter. "Stop right there," he warned. The clicking of his pistol convinced Malcolm to comply.

While he glared at his assailant, the huge man made a gesture with the barrel of his gun.

"Take the gun out, easy, with your left hand. Then toss it that way, far."

"I'm not carrying much money," Malcolm said. Who could have imagined, a highwayman here in Sells County? His good friend, Sheriff Handley, would hear about this!

"I'm not a patient man," the large man warned.

Malcolm tossed the gun, wishing instead that he had been an instant faster. He didn't have time for petty theft of all things.

"Now out. I'll have a word with you."

A word? Was that the latest euphemism? Malcolm climbed down slowly, not wanting to give the man an excuse to pull his trigger.

"I told you," Malcolm repeated, "I don't have much cash."

As he stepped down, a huge fist clipped his chin. With an explosion of pain, he spun, then hit the ground. He began to fear much more than robbery.

"You—you're welcome, of course, to what I have," Malcolm explained. "The rig too—you can take it. It's quite valuable."

The man hauled him to his feet as if his six-foot height were weightless.

The rising full moon lit the face of Daniel Aldman. At

first, so far from Wisconsin, Malcolm hadn't recognized
the man.

"I don't give a damn about your money. *That* was for
my daughter. You scared her half to death."

Aldman's fist slammed into his stomach, doubling him
over with a violent retching sound. Bereft of the larger
man's support, Shelton collapsed into a throbbing heap.

"That was for Mrs. Tanner and the three children you
left without a mother. I'd do more, for Hannah, except I
made a promise. I'll break it, though, if I don't find her
soon. Where is she?"

Malcolm groaned and swallowed bile, too miserable to
speak. Aldman would kill him, he was certain. He tried to
make his brain work out some sort of plan.

Daniel hauled him to his feet again, and that was when he
realized, the fool had put away his gun. Could he somehow
reach it? Almost before he completed the thought, Aldman
pushed him backward and punched him in the eye.

"Aw, hell," Daniel told him, looking down at his limp
form. "I wasn't going to do that, but I thought it would
be fair to give you one for John. You shot my brother,
Shelton."

"None of it—my fault," Malcolm muttered. "Only
wanted *her*." He tasted blood, hot and metallic, running
down into his mouth.

"And you got her, didn't you? Destroyed her wedding
day, hurt her . . ." He glanced skyward and swore, evidently
struggling for control. "An animal wouldn't behave the
way you did. God knows, I ought to kill you where you sit.
But I won't if you'll just tell me where she is."

"Hannah? How would I know?"

He stomped on Shelton's left hand, ground the boot
against it until Malcolm howled. "Hannah told me you've
got President Grant beat for connections around here.
You know all right."

"Get off! I'll tell you. Just get off my hand."

Daniel removed his boot and stepped back. Malcolm swore a silent oath that he would kill the man. He'd murder both Hannah and her lover.

"She's—she's at the home of her attorney, Adam Bloom. It's in Hampton Falls, off Big Cedar Road. Ask anybody there for the directions."

"And I imagine you were going to pay a social call."

"I was going to a church meeting, for your information." He doubted Aldman would know his church lay in the opposite direction.

"If ever there was a man in need of preachin', you'd be him." Daniel reached for his right hand. "Don't worry. I'm through with you, unless I don't find Hannah. Then, somehow, somewhere, I'm sending you to see St. Peter. See how you like imagining someone after you."

Malcolm let Aldman help him to his carriage. His wounds throbbed relentlessly, but he brightened at the thought of the rifle lying on the carriage floorboards. He'd been taken by surprise, but he wasn't finished yet. After he blew a hole in Daniel, his own injuries would excuse him of the crime.

Self-defense would be so much simpler than explaining Hannah's murder.

Malcolm wasn't prepared when the sharp crack of the rifle spooked his team. The horses wheeled toward home, their terror curbed only by the reins in his right hand.

Hannah peered into the window at her old bedroom. Moonlight filtered in, partly eclipsed by her own head. She barely made out the bulk of her four-poster. Someone had pushed it up against a different wall. Shivering with anticipation, she pushed open the door. The hinges squealed softly, like hungry newborn pups. She drew the derringer and entered, then shut the door to stem the draft.

Her gaze roved the dimness, and she felt panic tightening her chest. *Find it!* her mind demanded. Find it—
then get out! She felt along the small room's borders,
found a chest in shadow, knelt . . . and bit her lower lip.
Dear God, this wasn't it. Malcolm must have moved it, sold
it, maybe even burned all her possessions when she left.

No, that couldn't be right. The four-poster looked the
same, as had her mother's favorite sofa. The dresser was
well made and had been in good condition. Somewhere,
he would have it still. But where? The idea of sneaking
through the whole house searching made her chest feel
cold and hollow. She couldn't do it, could she? Could she
take the chance of being caught?

Her breath hissed out quietly between clamped teeth.
She'd seen someone leave the house. Logically, that someone must have been Malcolm. If there hadn't been a second person, she had to guess it was his wife who had stayed
behind.

She didn't quite believe it. He'd never let her stay home,
even after Father died. "Socializing with the wives is cru-
cial," he'd instructed. He probably sensed the biddies, like
their husbands, would gossip about anyone not present.
She couldn't imagine he'd become more flexible when
dealing with the second Mrs. Shelton.

The woman *had* to be gone. The house stood empty but
for the unfamiliar cat. Hannah convinced herself it must
be true.

She leaned her head into the hallway. Across it, another
door stood open, the one her ailing grandmother inhab-
ited when Hannah had been very small. Despite the old
woman's death in Hannah's fifth year, she still thought of
it as Grandma's room. She still associated it with powdery
white flesh, weak cries, and the heavy smell of decay. She'd
never liked that room, had avoided it throughout her childhood. From a dusty corner of her memory, Grandma's
creaking voice invited her, "Come in, child. Come in."

She hurried across the hall and felt her way inside. The moonlight from the windows in the front room did little to guide her. This room's windows were only darker squares in colorless, dim walls.

Hannah stubbed her toe on a bedpost and gasped with quiet pain. She felt like kicking Malcolm's wife for moving all the beds. Instead, she sank down to the mattress and began to rub her foot.

A light shone in her eyes, nearly blinding her. She heard the unmistakable metallic click of a revolver.

With a shriek Hannah rolled off the other side and fumbled for the derringer. Would the pathetic little gun be any match for Malcolm's real weapon?

But it wasn't Malcolm's voice she heard. "Come—come out. Please. I won't fire unless you make me."

The voice belonged to someone female, and just as frightened as she was. Hannah, quivering behind the bed, felt sick. Malcolm might be good with guns, but she sincerely doubted his wife's skill. With a little luck she could shoot the other woman first.

In theory. In practice, either one or both might die. Besides, in all of Hannah's imaginings, it had been Malcolm whom she killed. She didn't even know this woman, had nothing against her.

Carefully, she replaced the derringer inside her pocket. "I won't make you shoot," she called. "I'm coming out right now."

Raising both hands, she emerged from behind the bed. The other woman, a white apron tied around her, stepped inside the room. In one hand she held a lamp. The other clutched an old revolver. The barrel shook so hard, Hannah feared it might accidentally discharge. The blonde set down the lamp on the nightstand nearest to Hannah.

The younger woman's face was puffy, and her eyes were damp with tears. "You're *her,* aren't you?" she asked Hannah.

Hannah nodded, guessing the woman's meaning. "I am Hannah Shelton. There's something I needed in this house. I'm sorry if I frightened you. I thought everyone was gone."

"You never should have come. He hates you."

"I know. He'll kill me if he finds me. Or you could. He'd like that." Hannah sat down on the bed, hoping she could get the woman to relax enough to avoid an accidental shot.

Melissa sat across from her on the old bedspread. Lowering the gun, she used her other hand to swipe away a tear. "I don't care what he'd like. I used to think—I thought once I could love him past you, love him into letting go of what you did. He has so much hate, it's just consumed him. Sometimes, he calls out your name when—when he hurts me."

Despite her own problems, Hannah's heart broke for this woman. "You have to get away from him. He's a murderer."

"I know," Melissa whispered. "He said once he had killed to get this farm, and he'd kill again to keep it."

Had killed? Suddenly, the pieces spun together in her mind. How Malcolm found her father, how he'd insisted on keeping Honor even when Hannah had wanted the animal destroyed. Suddenly, so many things made sense. "Oh, my God. He killed him," Hannah sobbed. "He killed Father for this farm."

"Your father?" Tentatively, the woman reached out for Hannah, stroked her hand.

Hannah choked back her own emotions to stare Melissa in the eye. "In January he killed a woman in Wisconsin, and he tried to kill me. Malcolm raped me. Would you like to see the scars from his teeth? Handley said you gave an alibi."

Tears flowed freely down Melissa's face as well. "I had

to. He—he hurt me too, the same way. I couldn't live through that again.''

"He'll hang if the two of us speak out against him. Then we wouldn't have to be afraid again.''

"He's my husband.''

"He was mine too, until he tired of me. He accused me of adultery so he could keep my farm. Come with me, Melissa. We can make this right.''

Melissa shook her head. "I'm too afraid. He'd kill me. I just can't.''

Hannah pitied her.

Downstairs, a door banged shut.

"He's home.'' Melissa's eyes gleamed fear-bright as she stood, facing the door. "I'll keep him downstairs if I can. Can you get out of here?''

Hannah nodded. "Melissa, please, remember, you're braver than you think.''

Tucking the revolver into a pocket, she adjusted her apron to disguise the bulge. Then Melissa hurried toward the stairway without another word.

Hannah thought about her gun. Maybe she could creep downstairs and kill the bastard now, if she surprised him. Remembering her father, she longed to do just that. But other memories rose up even stronger. Daniel Aldman, telling her, "From this moment, I consider you my wife.'' Amelia, twirling in her scarlet dress before the ruined wedding, wrinkling her nose at the thought of kissing boys. She'd forced Daniel to promise he wouldn't hunt down Malcolm so he could be a part of their two lives. Would it be fair to trade their love and hopes for a chance to gain revenge? She shook her head and turned toward her old dresser, the same one where the will had long ago been hidden.

She would take only a minute before she left her stolen home.

* * *

Rifle tucked beneath an arm, Malcolm collapsed heavily into a kitchen chair. "Melissa!" he bellowed.

She scurried down the stairs.

He noticed she'd been crying but said nothing. She cried a lot of late. Maybe it was one of those woman things he'd never understood. He couldn't be bothered to keep up with her monthlies.

"What happened?" she all but shrieked on seeing him.

"A damned road agent," Malcolm told her. "At least I shot the bastard, but I'm plenty hurt. I think he cracked some of my fingers."

"Should I go down the road and ask Mr. Went to fetch the doctor?"

"Hell, no. I've had enough of his kind to last me my whole life. Just get me some whiskey and clean up this eye. I'll need cold water from the springhouse if I'm to soak this hand."

She rushed into his study, and he heard a crash. "For God's sake," he roared, "do you have to break the tumblers? What's wrong with you tonight?"

She appeared with one whole glass and a whiskey bottle. "I—I'm so sorry. I'm just worried about you. First, leaving the way you did, and then, coming back this way. I'll clean up the mess later. Let me go get your cold water. You can soak your hand while I tend to that eye."

She took a piece of crockery out of the cabinet and left the house.

Something thumped above his head. Painfully, he pushed himself onto his feet and walked into the parlor. Melissa's cat sprawled across the sofa. He resisted the impulse to curse it and looked up.

If the cat hadn't made that sound, who had? Could Mouse Melissa have dared to take a lover? Righteous fury boiled in his blood. If it were true, he'd kill them both! He rechecked to see the rifle was loaded and stalked carefully upstairs.

Hannah heard the deep rumble of his voice floating upward through the floorboards. After his first shout for his wife, she distinguished nothing except an angry tone. She had to hurry before he came upstairs! With all the courage she could muster, she turned her back toward the open doorway and knelt before the dresser.

She held her breath as she pulled out the drawer on the lower right. It caught, and she yanked harder. The stubborn drawer pulled free. Tossing aside an unfamiliar quilt, she clawed for the false bottom, prized it up.

Please, she prayed, *let it still be here.*

She heard paper rustle beneath her fingertips before she felt it. With a great sigh she pulled it free. A glance assured her it was the precious copy, duly signed.

"Thank you," she whispered—to God, to her father, to Melissa, who had spared her life and allowed her a few moments more to search. After replacing the false bottom and the quilt, Hannah rolled the paper and slipped it into her skirt pocket, beside the derringer. Slowly, she tried to shut the drawer. It stuck again, and she pushed it somewhat harder than she should have, for it suddenly slammed shut. A vase atop the dresser fell with the concussion and toppled to the floor.

Moments later, just above the whoosh of her pulse roaring, Hannah heard a creak. Her blood ran cold as she remembered. The second step gave only beneath the weight of a grown man.

His rifle raised, Malcolm moved in wraithlike silence down the hallway toward the master bedroom. He cursed the doorways along the way that he must check, for a gut feeling insisted the intruder was in the master bedroom. Melissa, with all her cowering and weeping, must have invited another man into their bed.

Who could it be? he wondered. Joseph Went? His farm manager, a quiet, modest blond man, had been close at hand during Malcolm's long absence. But Went seemed so devoted to his wife and growing brood. . . . Maybe Jacob. Handley considered everything that wore a skirt fair game. Malcolm's vision darkened with fury at the possibility of his friend's treachery. The ungrateful bastard! Had he no loyalty?

The fingers of his injured left hand brushed a hallway table, and Malcolm yelped in unexpected pain. Below, the door banged shut. He heard Melissa's voice float up the stairs.

"Malcolm?" She sounded tense and scared. The bitch.

Another possibility made him swallow hard. Could it be Hannah? Hannah—here? He blinked, considering. Aldman had been looking for her, thought *he* knew where she was.

Would she dare come here for him?

A bolt of fear leapt through his chest. If Hannah had come, she'd come to kill him. What other reason could there be? Was she hidden up here, waiting behind a door, a knife or gun clutched in her hand?

He felt his heart slam against his chest. Maybe she would shoot him if she had the chance. He no longer believed she wouldn't dare, or that she couldn't do it. Something in him almost hoped that she would try. A lurid fantasy edged past his terror. He could catch her, ravage her once more before he slit her throat and bled her like a hog.

With the rifle barrel leading, he approached the doorway of the bedroom on his left. Melissa had left a lamp burning on the nightstand. What had she been doing in this room? Cautiously, he stepped around the bed and found nothing amiss. His sore stomach ached as he bent to peek beneath the bed. He nearly screamed at the sight of a gun barrel aiming toward him.

Then he realized there was no one holding it.

Kneeling, he swore and nearly laughed at his mistake. His "gun barrel" was an old cane, fuzzy with thick dust. Nothing here to fear except the ghost of Hannah's dead grandmother.

Straightening, he pushed open the door across the hall. He had once lived in this room with Hannah. He remembered how he'd suffered with her father's suspicions. Merritt Lee had once accused him of some silly fling that Malcolm had with the Widow Toole. In this room Shelton had made his plans to become the master of this household. Despite his nervousness, he almost smiled with the memory.

"Malcolm!" Melissa's voice again, this time laced with panic.

After a perfunctory check of that room, he shouted down to her. "Get up here." If she had any part in this, he wanted her beside him so she could pay the price.

"Why?" Her query fluttered nervously near the bottom of the stairs.

"I said, come here."

Her steps were slow, as if with dread.

When she appeared, her face gleamed pale as her white apron. "Is—is there something wrong? Your water's downstairs. You should let me wash your face."

"Take the lamp and walk ahead of me into our room."

"What? Why would you—"

"Just do it!"

She trembled but complied. He followed.

"What is it?" she asked as he looked under the bed, inside the wardrobe, behind the brocade curtains.

"I heard something up here." Malcolm began to feel slightly foolish in his failure. "You haven't dragged home another one of your damned cats?"

"I have only the one."

"Something must have fallen, maybe in the attic after all." He watched carefully for signs of her relief, a noisy exhalation, a drooping of her shoulders. He saw nothing but her ever-present fear.

"You scared me. I thought—"

"Don't bother. Thinking's never been your greatest strength. Come downstairs and make me some coffee. I have to soak this hand. It's swelling like a goddamned udder."

Hannah said every prayer she could think of as she lay trembling beneath the bed of her old room. Half didn't make sense: prayers of grace, thanksgiving, and blessings for the dead. The other half were desperate pleas, offers of all sorts of wild pledges in return for her deliverance. She hoped, if she survived, she could remember what she'd promised God.

When she heard Malcolm's and Melissa's voices below, she crawled out from beneath the four-poster and brushed the dust off her. Her nose twitched, but she willed away a sneeze. The balcony door gave the same quiet squeal it had when she'd entered. Ignoring it, she pushed her way outside.

A full moon shone not far above the treetops, painting the whole farm with pale light. Incredibly, Hannah realized, the place seemed wrong now, steeped in memories of blood and deep betrayal. She swore a silent oath she would restore it as her father would have wanted.

She swung one leg over the railing and began to lower herself to the porch roof. And then disaster struck.

With an earsplitting crack, the railing of the balcony gave way. Hannah slid helplessly down the porch roof and tumbled off its edge.

* * *

She must have blacked out for a moment when she fell, flat on her back. Something hard and round jabbed at her cheek. Opening her eyes, she tried to brush aside the cold intrusion. Her hand jerked away, as if burnt, when her eyes focused on the rifle barrel pointing in her face. Somewhere nearby she heard weeping. It sounded like Melissa.

She had fallen in the rectangle of light. Malcolm stood above her, brandishing the gun.

All deals are off, she told God silently.

Something dark, perhaps blood, streaked the left side of Malcolm's face.

"That Aldman you were going to marry," he explained as if in answer to her unvoiced question. "He attacked."

His use of the past tense sent a wave of nausea rippling through her. Daniel must have come to look for her.

"The idiot waylaid me on the road to Hampton Falls," he continued, "but he didn't count on this." He lifted the weapon's tip in victory. "I shot the bastard off his horse."

"You're lying!"

The scarred man shrugged. "Believe what you like. Maybe he'll be waiting for you at hell's gate."

Daniel wouldn't go near Malcolm, Hannah told herself. He'd promised. Oh, God, why hadn't he stayed in Peshtigo the way she'd planned? Tears of rage slid down her face, rage at Malcolm, and, perversely, even more for the man whom she had loved. Why had he followed her?

"You murdered my father." She pushed herself into a sitting position. Father, Daniel, both the men she had loved. In her mind even Robert's ghost shouted accusations. Hadn't Malcolm brought the news of that death too?

He ignored her charge. "Get up, Hannah. We're going inside to my study. Melissa, go upstairs. My first wife and I will need some privacy."

Dear God, he meant to rape her once again. How could he, with his own wife in the house?

"I can't," Hannah lied. "I think my hip is broken."

Her right hand slid down it, down the pocket with the gun. A derringer against that long, steel rifle. She knew already that she didn't have a chance.

No matter. She'd rather provoke Malcolm into firing, rather die, like Daniel, than be touched again by her ex-husband.

The rifle barrel slammed into her right shoulder, knocking her back to the ground. Heedless of the pain, her hand plunged downward toward the weapon.

A shot tore through the night. She blinked in disbelief as Malcolm thudded sideways to the ground. Beside him, arms highlighted by that pane of light, stood Melissa. A revolver smoked in her outstretched, trembling hands. Hannah glanced down. Gore seeped from a hole in Malcolm's temple, which rested in a puddle of dark blood. His staring eyes were wide and round, as if with surprise.

"I—I couldn't—couldn't let him. Not again." Each word seemed caught in Melissa's throat, nearly strangled by her sobs.

Remoteness settled over Hannah like a shroud. Barely feeling her own body, she rose and went to Melissa, then put her own hands on the younger woman's shoulders.

"Let me take the gun," Hannah whispered.

She relinquished it without protest. "I killed him. *I* killed him."

"No." Hannah shook her head. "He shot himself. When he learned I was taking back the farm, he couldn't stand it. You tried to stop him, but it was already too late."

"Too late," Melissa echoed. "Too late from the time I married him."

"Do you understand?" Hannah put the revolver into Malcolm's right hand. His fingers still felt warm, and even then she found his touch unnerving. She removed the rifle that lay beside him on the ground. "He committed suicide. Let me put this away. I remember where he kept it."

Hannah took the rifle back inside. When she returned, Melissa had knelt beside the body. She rocked slowly on her knees and moaned.

"He *did* kill himself . . ." Melissa wiped her hands on her apron over and over, as if to remove what she had done. "He started it the same day he went after you."

"I have to leave." Hannah pulled her by the arm onto her feet. "I have to find Daniel. Don't stay here. Can you go to a neighbor's to get help?"

Melissa nodded, but her damp eyes looked blank.

"Remember," Hannah told her. "This was suicide. And, Melissa?"

The blond woman's gaze snapped toward her.

"Thank you." Hannah embraced the younger woman. "I'm so sorry for my part in this."

Melissa shook her head. "We shouldn't be sorry. We should hope he burns in hell."

CHAPTER THIRTY

I killed Daniel, Hannah realized. I killed him by coming here. She'd known how much the earlier attack had cost him. He'd promised to always keep her safe, said that in his eyes they were wed. What else could he do but follow her, to make certain Malcolm wouldn't hurt her?

But he'd promised, promised her. Again her anger flared, bright as Peshtigo had been that awful night. He had given her his word.

Stupid. She was stupid to let fury wrap itself around her fear. If she should be angry with anyone, it should be herself.

For every star, she wished once that she'd never lied to Daniel, that she'd had the courage to break her bond with him before she'd left. Or maybe if she'd stayed with him in Peshtigo, Malcolm never would have come back. Maybe after a while her fears would have begun to fade and the farm would have been forgotten. Just then she felt so confused, so empty despite the victory represented by the paper tucked inside her pocket.

Tears of regret nearly blinded her as she rode Tillie back toward Hampton Falls. Even in bright moonlight she could see little beyond dark shapes of trees beside the road. Unless Malcolm had left Daniel lying close, she could ride right past him without seeing.

Over and over she called out his name, until the air rang with her fear. Until someone called out from a farmhouse to ask her what was wrong.

The mare resisted Hannah's efforts to turn her nose away from home and the evening's ration of coarse grains. But Hannah mastered her, and the horse trotted toward the white frame house.

"You need help?" a stout woman asked her from the porch. Two little children stared, partly hidden by their mother's broad rear end.

"I'm looking for my husband," Hannah told her, surprised she'd called him that. "Someone told me he'd been shot."

"Let me get Mr. Woodson," said the woman. "He's already in bed."

Maybe she should have gone straight to the Blooms for help, Hannah thought. By then they would be worried sick about her disappearance. But the Blooms were miles away. She had to get to Daniel *now*.

After a few minutes a spindly-legged man in his thirties appeared, still tucking in a faded shirt. "Wife tells me you've got trouble. She says she heard a shot a while back, toward Hampton Falls. Let me get a gun. If there's road agents or hooligans about, we'll want to be prepared."

"Thank you," Hannah told them.

The woman brought a lantern and offered it to her. In a few moments her spouse returned with his hunting rifle.

"We have a hired boy. Should I send him for the sheriff?" the woman asked.

Hannah shook her head. Handley was the last person she wanted to see. Besides, he'd soon be busy at the Shelton farm. "Send him with us, if you would," she said. "We have to find my Daniel quickly." She turned toward the man. "I'm going to ride ahead while you saddle your horse."

"Be better if you didn't," he suggested. "You don't need to see your man that way."

But she'd already seen her share of blood that evening. She'd already turned her horse's nose toward home—and, hopefully, toward Daniel.

"Daniel!" Hannah cried again and again until her throat ached and her voice grew hoarse. With each call she hesitated, straining her ears to hear something, anything beyond the brisk clop of the mare's hooves and the squeaking of the horse's leather saddle.

She stared into the night, her gaze lingering on places silvered with bright moonlight. But close beside them lay deep shadows, reminding her of the dark puddle beside Malcolm's head. Would there be another next to Daniel once she found him?

A sob caught in her throat, and she had to struggle not to give in to it, not to let it rise and grow into an endless scream. She had to stop calling Daniel's name, unable to risk losing control.

"Hannah!"

She jerked toward the sound and held her breath, afraid she might have dreamed it.

"Hannah?"

Daniel's voice—she'd recognize it anywhere.

She stared off to her right, where the sound had seemed to come from, and finally spotted what looked like a tree stump in the moonlight. When she drew closer, she could make out the still form of a fallen horse.

Daniel lay beside it, his leg pinned by its bulk. The only blood she saw darkened the dead horse's ribs.

Hannah slid from Tillie and ran toward him, carrying the lantern.

"Malcolm said he'd shot you! What in God's name are you doing here?" she cried out, unable to keep the anger from her voice. Her hands trembled, making the lamplight flutter like moth wings.

"If the damned fool can't tell the difference between shooting down a horse and a man, that's it. I'm going to have to kill him. I've been lying here forever. I can't seem to get free." Daniel's voice rumbled with impatience.

"Is your leg broken?" Hannah asked him. Thankfully, she saw no other signs of injury.

He shook his head. "I don't think so. It's just caught. Can you give me a hand?"

"I'll try, and there's help coming. A farmer and his hired boy." She went back to loop Tillie's reins around a sturdy branch.

"What the hell were you doing anywhere near Malcolm?" Daniel's words accused her. "Did he hurt you again?"

"Malcolm's dead. He's finished hurting people."

Daniel glared at her. "Damn your lies. You killed him, didn't you? I came to stop you, Hannah."

"I didn't kill him, Daniel. But I would have. He said he'd shot you." She wrapped her arms around him, but he didn't respond.

"Horse first, hugs later," Daniel grumbled. "I guess this means I'll lose my deposit over at the livery."

Hannah's back and injured shoulder throbbed as she threw her weight against the horse's bulk. She groaned. "I can't. I hurt myself falling off my house's roof. Listen, here comes Mr. Woodson."

"Sounds like you and I have some things to talk about." His tone gave her cause to dread that talk.

Hannah called out to the riders. Mr. Woodson and a half-grown black boy arrived quickly. A few hard shoves freed Daniel from the lifeless horse.

Gingerly, he rubbed his right leg and tested it. "It's kind of sore," he said, "but I'm very much obliged."

He shook the man and boy's hands, and they introduced themselves.

"We were glad to come," said Woodson, "when your wife stopped by the house."

Daniel glanced at Hannah, and she shrugged, vaguely embarrassed. He then took her in his arms.

"You want the sheriff, mister?" asked the farmer.

"No, I don't. I just want to get back to the hotel. *Mrs.* Aldman and I have a few things to sort out." The squeeze he gave her arm wasn't reassuring.

"What about the carcass and your saddle?"

"The horse was hired. I'd better let the liveryman know where to find him. I don't think he's going anywhere before tomorrow. Poor fellow."

Both Hannah and Daniel thanked Mr. Woodson and his hired boy again. They assured the pair they could make it back to Hampton Falls together on the borrowed mare.

When Woodson and the boy left, Hannah climbed onto the horse's back behind Daniel. She sat stiffly, trying not to touch him as the mare walked toward her home. "You should have stayed in Peshtigo," Hannah told him. "You could have gotten yourself killed."

"*Me?* Hannah, after what I told you Sunday, after what we did, how could you imagine I'd let you come here alone? Why couldn't you trust me? Your time for lying's past. It's been past since you agreed to marry me."

"Most of what I wrote was true. Everything about you. I *do* love you, Daniel, but I had to do this. And I did have family business, an inheritance from an aunt in Hampton Falls."

"But you didn't keep away from Malcolm. You lied about that, and he's dead now. How am I supposed to believe anything you tell me?"

"I'm not lying, Daniel. I didn't come to kill him. I wanted

only what was mine. I wanted only to get the copy of my father's will.''

"Did you?" Daniel challenged.

"I found it. Now I'll get the farm."

"Was it worth it?" Bitterness edged his every word.

Hannah paused, considering. Somewhere, an owl hooted through the moonlight.

"I don't know."

"You're staying here, aren't you?" Hurt and disappointment strained his voice.

"Malcolm killed my father for that farm. I'll be damned if I let his family claim it. Stay with me?" Hannah's words were part question, part plea.

"I've got a daughter and a life in Peshtigo. You know what I have here? A woman who can't trust me with the truth, who doesn't think I've earned it. I'm going back tomorrow morning at eleven, with or without you."

"I was only trying to *protect* you. I knew if you came this close to Malcolm, you'd go after him."

"You always have good reasons, don't you? Now, tell me what really happened. Tell me everything."

When the knock came, Hannah couldn't fathom the sunlight against the curtains. After all her tears, could it be possible she'd slept? Morning felt like a betrayal, a forced reminder Daniel would soon leave. She started to get up to grab her robe and groaned at her sore back and shoulder.

The knock came louder this time. "Are you all right?"

She recognized the voice of her attorney. "Coming, Mr. Bloom. Just give me half a minute."

She hoped, by then, his wife had forgiven her for worrying them all. Her lies had angered more than Daniel. As she pulled on the robe and ran a quick brush through her hair, she tried to convince herself she'd gotten exactly what she came for. She could reclaim the farm.

Adam Bloom paced the narrow confines of the hall. "We need to talk," he said the moment the door cracked open. "We need to talk right now."

"If it's about yesterday, I'm sorry I was gone so long."

"Yesterday is over. It's much more serious than that." He turned and walked into his study.

Hannah followed, her heart thumping with anticipation. Would he tell her about Malcolm? Had he learned about the death?

In his office he slipped into a chair without inviting her to sit. "Malcolm Shelton and his wife are dead."

"*What?*" Her shock was genuine. Melissa?

Adam nodded. "She shot him, then herself. She left a note. She asked forgiveness, said he'd struck her and she killed him. She couldn't live with that."

Hannah felt her vision gray; then she slid down until she sat on the floor. She felt as if her spine had been ripped out.

Melissa, dead. More blood soaking into the winter turf of the Lee farm. Her father's, Malcolm's, even hers, after a fashion. A memory of the stolen steer's blood flitted across her mind.

"I need to know you weren't involved."

Hannah stared at Adam, barely comprehending. Was he accusing her? He didn't move to help her from the floor.

After a long pause she found her voice. "I went to get the will. Melissa let me. I didn't hurt either of them, Adam. I swear it."

Bloom sighed and left his chair. He reached down and pulled her to her feet. "I had to ask. I know I'm your attorney, but I couldn't defend anything like that."

"Am I—" A hard knot, like an acorn, formed inside her throat. "Am I a suspect?"

Bloom shook his head. "I don't think so. From what I heard, she had a lot of bruises. And old bite marks too. What kind of animal would do a thing like that? Poor woman. She got her licks in, though, last night."

Hannah's arms locked around him, and she sobbed against his chest. "Melissa . . ." The frail young woman hadn't been strong enough to live with the lie Hannah suggested.

Yet another of her lies.

"I've been so wrong," she muttered. "So very wrong. What time is it?"

He drew a silver watch out of his pocket. "Half past ten."

"Dear God, I have to speak with Daniel. I can't just let him leave!"

Bloom hesitated a bare moment. "I'll saddle Tillie while you get ready. Just don't keep us worrying this time."

By the time Adam prepared the mare, Hannah ran outside to fetch her. With neither a mounting block nor leg up, she fairly flew into the saddle. The soreness of her back vanished from her consciousness. Her waist-long hair flapped behind her as the mare leapt to a gallop, for Hannah hadn't taken time to trouble about style.

Daniel. How could she have been so wrong with him? Hannah worried over how much time it had taken her to dress. She should have checked the clock again before she left.

Unlike the rainy afternoon of her arrival, people walked and rode the streets. Behind her she heard a man shout. "It's the adulteress, Hannah Shelton!"

She'd been a fool to think she could outlast that name. Now there would be new conjectures. Had she somehow been the cause of both the Sheltons' deaths?

She thought she could survive the ridicule and speculation, but she'd finally realized she could never bear to go back to the farm. Especially not without Daniel beside her,

to love her and support her through each day. Without
him she could no more face the remnants of her life than
Melissa Shelton.

At the depot she slid off the horse and lashed a rein
around a hitching post. The eleven o'clock, for once on
time, was pulling from the station in a cloud of steam.

Hannah shrieked and raced after the train on foot, as
if she had the power to stop those tons of steel. She peered
at window after window as it gained speed and pulled away,
seeking one more glimpse, one last moment of eye contact
to express all that she felt.

That moment was denied her. She never saw his face.
Panting with the chase, she faded to a standstill, then sank,
defeated, to her knees.

She'd lost him now, forever. She would never see him,
never hear his voice again. He would be as dead to her as
Robert. On her left hand, the ruby sparkled like a crystal
spot of blood. Set inside his mother's ring, it would never
symbolize their union. Her nose ran, like her eyes, but
Hannah didn't have the spirit to reach up to wipe them.

How could she have won her farm, yet feel as if the heart
had been torn from her?

"I was wondering how long you'd take to get here."

At the sound of Daniel's voice behind her, Hannah froze.
She didn't move, sure that if she turned, he'd vanish like
some cruel mirage.

His huge hand, settling on her shoulder, convinced her
he was real.

"I couldn't leave without you," he said. "If that farm
means so much, I'll bring Amelia here."

Gently, he helped her to her feet and cleaned her face
with his handkerchief. Then he meshed his hand with hers
and gazed at her so hard, she felt as though he saw the
core of her and judged it.

"I couldn't imagine life without you," Daniel said. He
sealed his words with a long kiss.

Hannah tasted him, reawakening the tremendous hunger of her dreams. She closed her eyes, losing herself in their reunion. Recovering first, she finally pulled away.

"I want to go back to Peshtigo with you. It's home now. The farm—the farm is steeped in blood. I found out yesterday Malcolm bashed my father's head in and then blamed a half-broke horse. I wanted my old home back because of the people I remember: Father, Mother, my grandma—even Malcolm, or the way I *thought* he was. But those people are all gone, and so many of my memories are ruined." Hannah felt tears sliding between them, soaking the fabric of Daniel's woolen coat.

He stroked her hair and whispered, "It's all right now. It's all right."

She squeezed him even tighter. "I found out this morning Melissa Shelton took her life. That's when I finally realized that the farm is just a piece of land. The people on it were the ones who meant so much. And now all the people in my life live near Peshtigo, Wisconsin: you and Amelia, John and Bess, everyone who means so much to me. If you'll still have me, I want to go back as soon as possible. I want Adam Bloom to sell my farm. The only thing I want from it is Honor, Father's horse."

"Come with me. Help me move my bags back to my hotel room. I'm so glad I changed my mind. Then tell me all about your aunt. I need the distraction."

"Why? Is your leg hurting?"

"No, but I'm considering some real boisterous behavior, and this isn't the place."

"Here it is." Daniel grinned. "The finest room the Hotel Hampton has to offer."

The bed, the chamber set, and the small wardrobe had nothing to distinguish them. Nor did the decor, which consisted of a garish still life and a yellowing bedspread.

"This is the finest?" Hannah asked him, smiling. Tiny Hampton Falls had only one such establishment. Even so, Daniel claimed he was the only boarder. The desk, too, had been deserted when they returned his bags upstairs.

"How do you suppose they stay in business?" Hannah asked.

Daniel locked the door. "At this moment, I couldn't care less."

Before they left the station, Hannah sent a message to the Blooms saying she would be delayed. That obligation had been her last coherent thought. Every other fiber of her being had cried its need to be alone with Daniel, to hold him against her body, flesh to flesh and soul to soul.

But as he crossed the room to meet her, a nervous flutter made her muscles tighten. "Maybe we should find one of those ministers you're so fond of dragging into hotel rooms."

His body, pressed against hers, weakened whatever resolve she had forged. "I already claimed you, and you accepted. When that fellow Woodson said you'd called yourself my wife, that's when I knew for sure, no matter how mad I was at you last night."

His dark gaze pinioned her, soothed away her misgivings. In some way far more basic than a spoken wedding vow, Daniel was right. They were bound and had been since last Sunday. There had never been a possibility that they could stay apart.

"I love you, Hannah," Daniel told her. "You belong to me now."

Hannah smiled. "I love you too . . . and this time Amelia's far away."

He touched her mouth with fire, coaxed it open with his lips and his warm tongue. Again and again it plunged in deeply, tasting, testing, ravaging. Wet and fierce, the kiss made Hannah desperately aware of how long she had been empty. She wanted nothing more than to fill her aching void.

His lips brushed her ear with whispered promises of how he would possess her, be possessed by her, before they left this room. She shivered with them, not in fear but with anticipation. Unable to resist their promises, she ran her hands along his neck and the muscles of his shoulders.

Gently but insistently, he pushed her arms down to her sides. "This time I'd like to see you. I don't want you to move."

She stood, still trembling with need as he unlaced the bodice of her dress.

"Why, Hannah Shelton, I don't believe you're wearing any petticoat, or any corset either."

She felt heat rise in her cheeks. "I was in a hurry to find you. Do you mind?"

"I don't think there's another stitch of clothing underneath this dress. I do hope you were careful climbing on that horse." The fabric began to slide down to where it gathered just above her hips. Slow and teasing, his voice made her long to touch him. "I think I like this sweet surprise, except your hair."

He ran his hands through her long locks.

"I thought you liked it down."

"It's more fun when I unpin it." He wound it gently, then let it slide down to her waist. "There, now. That's much better."

She tried to reach for him. Again he gently fended off her advances.

"Not yet." He moved behind her.

Anticipation made the fine hair rise along the back of her neck. She sucked in a sharp breath when his fingertips reached around to make orbits of the hard tips of her breasts. His lips made a moist journey from her neck to shoulder.

She moaned aloud and tried to turn toward him. But

Daniel held her steady, tormenting her with light caresses along her breasts and sides.

He did something to the dress, and it slid along her legs onto the floor. Daniel turned her toward him, surveyed every inch of her, and smiled.

"You're perfect, Hannah. Perfect." He removed her shoes, then scooped her up and took her to the bed. When he put her down, he finally succumbed to her embrace and let her ignite him with another long, moist kiss.

She helped him remove his clothing with much more haste than he'd used for hers. Leaning forward, he surprised her by kissing and sucking her breasts, driving her back until her head fell on a pillow.

She didn't close her eyes. She wanted to see his muscles work as he caressed her, wanted to watch the chiseled body she now claimed for all time.

His hand traveled along her sides and belly, then between her legs to touch, to stroke, until she nearly wept with need. Grasping his hips, she guided him above her, then embraced him with a welcome of her silky thighs.

Their union brought from each a gasp of pleasure as he plunged into her and she rose to meet his thrust. They found their rhythm quickly, found it and exalted in it until both attained release in one joyful cataclysm far beyond any pleasure Hannah had experienced before.

Sweating, panting, they embraced. Daniel kissed her and made promises about their life together. Hannah smiled, murmuring a contentment that had long eluded her.

EPILOGUE

Although their first legal anniversary remained two weeks away, Daniel and Hannah Aldman would that evening celebrate a date they thought more sacred, the anniversary of the day their hearts were joined. Amelia was visiting her uncle John and aunt Bess in their new house, less than a half mile away. Hannah finished putting up her hair, so later Daniel could take it down again.

He appeared behind her in the mirror. With a laugh Hannah smacked his roving hands from her hairpins.

"Let's not start that yet. I'm too hungry," she told him. The delicious smells of roast pork and vegetables rose from the wood stove. Fresh bread cooled nearby, on a shelf.

"Since you finally dragged yourself away from the barn to cook, I think I will eat." Between their two plates he lit a candle and stared into the flame.

Sheepishly, he smiled. "Ever since the big fire, every little candle seems kind of like a miracle to me."

Preparing their plates, Hannah paused to smile back.

"I think about the fire a lot. With all that tragedy, some spark of it drove us toward each other."

"That *was* a miracle," he laughed.

She lit a second candle before she sat down at the table, for tonight she would speak of yet another miracle.

Tonight she would tell Daniel she was going to bear his child.

ROMANCE FROM FERN MICHAELS

DEAR EMILY   (0-8217-4952-8, $5.99)

WISH LIST   (0-8217-5228-6, $6.99)

AND IN HARDCOVER:

VEGAS RICH   (1-57566-057-1, $25.00)